Salisbury Plain

SALISBURY PLAIN

H. C. Branson

E. P. Dutton & Co., Inc.
New York   1965

First Printing April 1965

Second Printing May 1965

Copyright, ©, 1965 by H. C. Branson

All rights reserved. Printed in the U.S.A.

Published simultaneously in Canada by Clarke, Irwin & Company Limited, Toronto and Vancouver

Library of Congress Catalog Card Number: 65-15243

❦ ❦ ❦ ❦ ❦ ❦ ❦ ❦ ❦ ❦ ❦ ❦ ❦ ❦ ❦ ❦ ❦ ❦

And then King Arthur drew him with his host down by the seaside, westward toward Salisbury; and there was a day assigned that they should meet upon a down beside Salisbury . . .

And thus they fought all the long day, and never stinted till the noble knights were laid to the cold earth; and ever they fought till it was near night. Then the king looked about him. Jesu mercy, said the king, where are all my noble knights become? Alas that I should ever see this doleful day, for now I am come to mine end.

Malory, Le Morte Darthur, Book XXI

To my wife, Annah

❦ ❦ ❦ ❦ ❦ ❦ ❦ ❦ ❦ ❦ ❦ ❦ ❦ ❦ ❦ ❦ ❦ ❦ ❦

I

Chapter 1

For the men of my generation life reached its high point early. In our youth we were touched with fire, as one of our number has said. We were indeed, and nothing afterwards was ever quite able to meet the high expectations we had formed in our youth. There were days and weeks of such intensity that they are still present and living in our minds, while year after year has passed by since, unnoticed and forgotten.

Much was demanded of our generation. We went out to meet those demands with enthusiasm and courage, with fortitude and stubborn endurance; we met the extraordinary demands that were made on us, and we grew in stature as we met them. We lived in a vaster world, with unknown and mysterious regions beyond its horizons. Everything in our world was on a more generous scale, larger and more intense: it was a world of heroes, of beautiful women whose mere presence was an enchantment, of bright colors and soft winds, and at the same time a world of harsh and exhausting toil and continual danger. We fought and marched under a brighter sun, against fiercer winds and more numbing cold. In the lesser age that followed, the great qualities we had learned, our courage and endurance, were wasted. There were no more harsh emergencies to be met, but there were no more triumphs. Our arms were hung upon the wall to rust.

This legendary past, this age of heroes, came to an end for some of us with a slow dwindling; for others it ended suddenly, at a specific time and place. For me, as for many of us, it ended with a sudden shock and an explosion of pain, followed by a curtain of darkness. Afterwards it was walled off from the present by a long period of fever and delirium which lies across the horizon like an impenetrable bank of cloud, a period of slow recovery from wounds thought at the time to be mortal. When I emerged finally from this region of shadows, the world I returned to was new and unfamiliar, smaller, diminished in every way.

On the night of Wednesday, September seventeenth, in the second year of the war, we crossed the Blackwater and opened the Tarsus campaign. The Blackwater was our boundary line, and we were crossing over into enemy country. There was a feeling of excitement in the air. It was obvious to all of us, officers and men, staff and line, that this was no ordinary move: the stakes in the game had been raised, and we had embarked on a bold and hazardous undertaking. This suited our mood at the time: we felt that we were not ordinary soldiers, either, and that we were serving under no ordinary general.

We crossed by the light of enormous fires blazing on both banks of the river, fires kept nourished with great logs and tree trunks and miles of fence rails, with balks and timbers and siding from dismantled barns and farmhouses. Heat and light were diffused in great circles, and the scorched leaves and branches of the surrounding trees swung in the updraft. The flames were mirrored in the black eddying surface of the water, glittered on the rifle barrels of the troops crossing the low bridge in broken step, and shone on the bare sweating torsos of the crews maintaining the fires; the light shone in the eyes of the led horses, the artillery teams, and the mule teams of the baggage train, and the canvas tops of the wagons were a glowing orange-red as they bumped and swayed across the uneven surface. The fires burned with a continuous loud crackling; from time to time there was a roar of sound as some part of the structure collapsed, sending a shower of sparks up towards the black starlit sky.

We were crossing in three columns, our left brigade three miles upstream from the center column, our right brigade about the same distance farther down. The entire command was crossing, in light marching order, leaving everything behind that would slow us down. The cavalry brigade had gone over as soon as the bridges were down, and was now extended in a wide semicircle around our front and flanks.

Early in the evening I was sent over to the right for a report on the downstream crossing. On my way back I found the last half mile of the road solidly filled with wagons, then with artillery, the entire column moving jerkily forward, with frequent halts, towards the glare of the fires and the bridge. I had to pick my way carefully, for the Ohio regiment which was to cross last and form the rear guard had fallen out by the side of the road, and a large number of the men were sensibly taking advantage of the opportunity to get a little sleep while they could.

As soon as I was clear of the congestion around the mouth of the bridge, I looked around for the general. I found him fifty yards back of the bridge, elevated by the slope of the ground above the jostling and confusion of the crossing. He sat his horse and surveyed the scene with detached interest, completely alone at the moment, horse and rider perfectly still, the general bearded, gauntleted, imposing in the firelight, a big man with an easy, accustomed air of command.

I rode up with my report on the lower crossing, raising my voice over the clatter and shouting coming up from the bridge. The general listened: the first brigade crossing was going smoothly; the infantry and the artillery were all across when I left, at nine-thirty, and the baggage train was coming up to the bridge. Gavin—General Gavin Ross—estimated that the crossing would be completed in about an hour. Colonel Keith, with the 17th Wisconsin, was to form the rear guard.

At the end, the general said with grave courtesy, "That seems to be quite satisfactory. Thank you very much, Captain." As I started to turn away, he added less formally, "We've had a long day, John. The staff won't be crossing for an hour or more. You might as well get some rest."

17

This was a grateful sound in my ears. I had been up for eighteen hours, and in the saddle most of the time. I had ridden at least fifty miles, and I was ready to drop with fatigue. At least I thought I was: in the next few days I was to learn considerably more about fatigue. I dismounted and turned my horse over to an orderly, found a level spot and a convenient tree to lean against, and sat back and closed my eyes.

I had entered the service the previous year as a lieutenant on the staff of a volunteer regiment raised by one of my father's friends. When Colonel Henderson was wounded and forced to leave the service, I was transferred to the brigade staff, and served there under a series of incompetent or unlucky generals, under whom at least I learned my trade. I was an experienced and, I think, a competent staff officer when I was finally rescued from this morass by a letter from my uncle, James Lake, offering me a place on the staff of Major General Arthur Canham Pack.

James was my father's younger brother, and the object of my boundless admiration since the year he bought me my first pony and taught me to ride. He was serving as General Pack's chief of staff in a command that later on would have been called an army corps. At the time of my transfer it was made up of three very large infantry brigades, six batteries, and a small cavalry brigade: about twelve thousand five hundred men in all. It was operating in an area some distance away from the armies on either side of it, in one of the many local, nearly independent theaters of war.

General Pack, I found, was spoken of with respect by the officers who had known him at West Point and in Mexico, but, as it happened, none of them knew him very well. The one thing they all remembered was that he had married a countess, who was said to be a very beautiful woman. This impressed them, and it impressed me. Although it was another four months before I actually saw her, she seems to have been with us—we were aware of her, at least—from the beginning.

When I opened my eyes the general had dismounted and James, my uncle, was standing beside him, the firelight shining on his dark hair and mustache, his face lean and dark from the exposure of the summer's campaign, a tall, straight-backed man with a presence of his own: people remembered him. At the end of a long day he was still fresh and cheerful.

James had just come in from the line of outposts in front of our expanding bridgehead. The outposts were where they should be, and he was pleased by the competence and good sense of some of the volunteer officers in charge. I noticed, with something between exasperation and envy, that both men seemed perfectly impervious to fatigue. I was twelve years younger than James and twenty years younger than the general, but I found my head drooping forward and my eyes closing. Not that I was continuously asleep for any length of time: I was aware of the great fires and the black, oily surface of the river, and the noise and shouting from the bridge, and the nearby voices, but there were intermittences in my awareness of them.

They were talking about our opponent, General McGraw.

"I've known Barney for twenty years," the general was saying. "We were in the same class. We served together in Mexico, first under Taylor, then under Scott. Afterwards we were in California together for a year. I know Barney well. In some ways he's a fine soldier. He knows how to handle men, and he's got all the courage in the world. The one thing he hasn't got is imagination. Barney never did an unorthodox thing in his life. He goes by the book and he expects everyone else to do the same. From where we are now there are only two moves in the book. To seize a commanding position on the river road, Wauchope's Point, say. Or to establish ourselves at Jellicoe Gap and hold the east road. I think it's going to take Barney a full day, and more likely thirty-six hours, to realize that we aren't going to make either of the correct moves."

"In that case he shouldn't give us too much trouble," James remarked.

This remark appeared to startle the general. "Don't get any

such idea in your head, Colonel," he said emphatically. "He's going to give us a great deal of trouble. Don't underestimate General McGraw, James. We can outmaneuver him, but after that we have to fight him. He's a brave, stubborn man, and his men are seasoned fighters, as you know well. I think we're going to surprise Barney. I think we're going to catch him at a disadvantage and I think we're going to beat him, but I don't think any part of it is going to be easy."

While the general was talking I remembered the one time I had seen Barney McGraw. Early in August I had been sent down under a flag of truce. We had captured a number of partisans who had been firing on us, and we wanted to know if they were regularly enrolled Confederate troops, and, if so, why they weren't in uniform.

General McGraw's headquarters at the time were in the parlor of a farmhouse a couple of miles out from Jenkins' Ferry. The general was sitting at a table in his shirt sleeves, a solid, thickset man with a heavy brown beard, normally a genial man, I was told, but with authority in his manner. He had an adjutant, or secretary, at another table beside him, and a number of staff officers were standing nearby. We were all being very punctilious, formal, and unsmiling. General Mc-Graw seemed to find this tiresome.

He glanced over the dispatch I handed him, then tossed it over to the adjutant. To me he said, "Those are probably some of Horton's men, Captain. You can tell General Pack that I agree with him in principle about the uniforms. The men should certainly be recognizable as soldiers. I'll talk to Major Horton when he comes in, and tomorrow I'll send a man in with definite answers to both your questions." He turned his head. "Ben, will you make out a note to that effect for the captain to take back."

With business out of the way, he allowed himself to smile. "Well, young man, how is my old friend, Arthur? And how is his beautiful countess?"

"I haven't the honor of Mrs. Pack's acquaintance, General," I replied. "General Pack himself is in excellent health."

My intention was nothing more than a formal and correct

statement, but I had perhaps stressed the excellence of the general's health, and said more than I meant to.

General McGraw burst into a laugh. "And wearing out whole relays of you young fellows, just trying to keep up with him? Never mind, Captain. He always did. Your name, sir, if you please?"

"Lake, sir. John Lake."

"Any relation to the colonel?"

"Yes, sir. James is my uncle."

The general smiled broadly. "Quite a few of my young men seem to know your uncle, sir. When you get back, would you mind asking him why he shot Tom Benning's horse?"

This referred to an incident earlier in the summer. James had been captured briefly while making a reconnaissance with a small cavalry escort. He had escaped while they were passing through a narrow, hedge-grown lane, by shooting the horse of the officer at the head of the column and bursting through the hedge in the momentary confusion. He had slipped off his horse and sent the beast galloping ahead, with the entire rebel patrol in pursuit and made his way back on foot.

"I think I can tell you the answer, sir," I said. "At least I can tell you what James said when somebody else asked him that question."

General McGraw encouraged me to go on with a smile and a nod. The young officers around him, I noticed, had stopped talking.

"James said she was a beautiful little mare, and it cut him to the heart to shoot her. Then he said it would have been about as effective either way, whether he shot the horse or the rider. And that on the whole, whenever he had any choice in the matter, he would rather shoot a horse than a man."

There was a sudden silence all around me. Barney McGraw was startled, then sobered.

"Well, young man, I guess we all feel pretty much the same way," he said finally. "The trouble is, we don't often have much choice." He turned to address his adjutant. "Ben, do you have that note for the captain?"

The dispatch was handed to me and I was escorted back to

our lines. I saw a great deal of McGraw's men after that, but that was the only time I saw Barney McGraw in person.

Other members of the staff came up to join James and the general. I listened to them for a time then lost track of what they were saying and dozed off again. Then someone was standing between me and the light. I raised my eyes, and saw that it was James.

"Hard day, Johnny?" he asked.

"Pretty long one," I replied. "It began at three-thirty this morning, and it's not over yet."

"No. As you say, it isn't over yet." There was a mildly sardonic note in James' voice. "It won't be over until about Saturday. Late Saturday. It's going to be quite a long day. Might as well get up, Johnny. We'll be starting in a few minutes."

The last of the wagons was just coming up to the bridge. We watched it jolt its way over the rough planking and shortly afterwards we crossed, ourselves. We crossed on foot, leading our horses over the low insubstantial bridge, the black water rippling against the pontoons, the current visibly strong and the water deep. No fresh fuel was being added to the fires. The heat was still intense, but the bright sheets of flame had died away, and there was only a glowing red mass of coals which was slowly darkening. The 11th Ohio, with a section of guns, was behind us. As soon as they were across, the bridge would be taken up by the engineers on the north bank and started back to department headquarters. We were not exactly burning our bridges behind us, but within an hour after we had finished our crossing the bridges were gone.

We marched another four miles after we crossed the bridge, away from the river and up to the rim of the Blackwater Valley. We halted for the night at a crossroads marked by four log cabins and a frame store, all crumbling and long since deserted.

Here we were on the edge of the barrens, a rugged upland tract produced by a geological upheaval of some kind in the remote past, a tract which extended for thirty miles along the line of the Blackwater and approximately the same distance to the south. It was a sterile, dreary region, covered with low scrub and stunted oaks, a region of steep ridges and gullied-out ravines, sparsely inhabited and almost roadless. The few inhabitants, sullen and illiterate, were said to be Union sympathizers, but this was a mistake: they merely hated outsiders, and up to this time the outsiders had come from the south. Both sides had avoided the region, except for occasional cavalry patrols, simply because there was nothing there.

Some of the more fortunate men, those in the leading regiments, were able to get as much as five hours of sleep, but most of us had to get along with an hour or two. It was still black night when the drums rolled and the day began. It was still dark, and twenty minutes before sunrise, with only a dim band of gray along the eastern horizon, when the day's march got under way.

The day's march, a long, exhausting fourteen hours of it, was unopposed by the enemy. In the center column we scarcely heard a shot all day; the outer columns had little more opposition than we had, and even the cavalry, far out on the flanks, ran into nothing more than small cavalry patrols.

The lack of opposition was more than compensated for by the difficulties of the terrain. Time after time we made our way laboriously up the steep side of a ridge, the guns and wagons double-teamed, with men hauling on ropes and at the wheels; when we had reached the top of the ridge, we had a fresh problem in front of us, that of getting down the other side without breaking our necks in making the precipitous descent; and when we reached the bottom safely, with only a broken limb or two, or a crippled mule, or a broken wheel, there ahead of us was another ridge to climb.

At times there were soft spots, where the ridges ran in our direction, and the road, or wagon track, wound along the crest and sides of the ridge. These lasted for a mile or two, then the cross-grained, cantankerous going began again.

There was very little shade. The trees were stunted oaks, four to six inches in diameter, with ragged outlines and meager foliage, growing thirty feet apart. The poverty of the soil was still more apparent in the few farms we passed: an acre or two of clearing on a hillside, with a field of stunted corn, a patch of sickly vegetables, and another of tobacco. The farmhouses were small, ill-constructed log cabins, with a lean-to shed attached for a mule or a bony cow. The scrawny pigs were allowed to run loose.

We never saw any of the men. Only gaunt women and children in faded calico, who watched us go by with a hollow-eyed, expressionless stare. I always had the impression that the men were lying just out of sight in the brush, with rifles loaded and primed, waiting for some unwary straggler to come along. This impression was helped out by the fact that two or three of us were fired on as we crossed over from one column to the other. Nobody was hit, but it made the going a little uncomfortable.

All of us, men, horses, and mules, were thoroughly exhausted when we finally halted for the night. Nevertheless the general and the staff were well pleased with the first day. We had broken the back of the march; we were over the worst of the terrain, and if the opposition remained light, another day would bring us out of the barrens. In the meantime, McGraw had lost track of us.

The following day's march began again at first light, with the sun still below the horizon, and for most of the morning was simply more of the same, with half the infantry on the end of a rope, hauling guns and wagons up to the top of one ridge after another, then braking them as they slid down the far side. Towards the latter part of the morning the ridges became less precipitous, the ravines became valleys, and the crude wagon tracks turned into roads.

At about the same time, though, we began to run into cavalry patrols, and an hour later into roadblocks. These were nothing very serious: a few trees felled across the road with a couple of twelve-pounders behind them, and a line of infantry to support the guns. As the day wore on we became quite expert in prying out these roadblocks, and were rarely held up for more than half an hour.

I spent most of the afternoon on the left with General Jones, who was in command of our third brigade. The cavalry had reported an enemy force of undetermined size out in that direction, which might be in a position to intercept our left column sometime during the afternoon. General Pack went over to see about it and to talk to Jonesy, and left me with him when he returned to the center column.

Fifteen years of Indian fighting on the plains had dried Jonesy out. He was a lean, weather-beaten man in his middle forties, with pale gray eyes in a dark face, and a long drooping mustache. He had high cheekbones and straight black hair, and the legend in the camps was that he was part Indian. The resemblance was there, and the story was plausible, but in fact he was of pure Welsh extraction on both sides. He was listed as Gideon T. Jones, but in all the time I knew him I never heard his first name pronounced by anybody, not even once.

About the middle of the afternoon we came to a place where the road bent around to the left, climbed up to a shallow gap in the hills, then swung around to the right again, resuming its former direction. From the top of the rise we looked down on an open valley, two or three miles across, an irregular oval, with a small stream running down the center and curving off to the southeast. The valley was cleared and cultivated, and laid out in neat rectangular fields, with a solidly built stone farmhouse and outbuildings down at the lower end. A narrow road branched off just beyond the gap and angled down to the southeast, past the farmhouse and out of sight.

The opening up of the view and the evidence of civilization and relative prosperity were refreshing after the constriction and sterility of the past two days, but when I noticed that Jonesy and our burly, bearded inspector general, Jack Maitland, had pulled off the road and were looking out over the valley with field glasses, I was fairly sure that it wasn't the amenities of the view they were looking at. As I came up I was aware of something vaguely unusual about the sparse woods of the opposite ridge: a sparkle, a glitter, along the crest of the ridge.

Jonesy handed me his glasses as I drew up beside him. "Here, Johnny, you got good eyes," he said. "Are those fellows on horseback cavalry, or is it the staff of an infantry column?"

The horsemen were easy to make out through the glasses, most of them bearded, and one of them with the swirling braid of a general officer on his sleeve. The glitter appeared to come from the rifle barrels of marching infantry, but the men were hard to see. At one point in the line the glitter came from the polished brass of a pair of Napoleons.

"A general—not McGraw—two guns, and infantry. I can't see the men, but I can see the sun on the rifle barrels," I said, as I handed back the glasses.

Colonel Maitland agreed with me. "That's about it. General and his staff. Brigade staff. Two guns up front for close work. Probably more behind the infantry. No telling how much infantry. Should be a brigade, at least."

"Ross's got some cavalry out there. They can find out for us. Might as well earn their keep," Jonesy said.

As a matter of fact, we could see them earning their keep. A brisk little skirmish was going on in a field below the farmhouse, three or four miles away. We could hear the distant spattering of small-arms fire, and could see a small body of rebel cavalry advancing across the field. They held their ground briefly as our cavalry came out to meet them, then fell back with our men in pursuit, and both sides disappeared into the woods beyond the field.

We lost sight of the rebel infantry as well, as we left our vantage point and moved down to rejoin our marching column. The road was straight and level along the side of the valley, and for an hour the march was easy. Then the valley came to an end, and with it the pleasant open prospect and the good road. We were shut in again, and winding around among steep hills and slanting up cross-grained ridges, up one side and down the other. There were no more roadblocks during these last two hours, but the sound of cavalry fighting was constantly in our ears.

Late in the day, with the sun low and red in the west, we saw the enemy again. We had reached the top of a barren ridge, and for a quarter of a mile the road ran along the crest of the ridge before descending again. We were in the shadow of a higher ridge on our right; there was a lower ridge on our left, barren except for waist-high scrub, and beyond that, two and a half miles away, another ridge on the same level as the one we were marching on.

A rebel infantry column was marching along the crest of the farther ridge on a course parallel to our own. There was a shimmer, a glitter of red as the rays of the low sun glanced off the rifle barrels slanting over the shoulders of the infantry-men. They were slogging along with weary determination in a loose column of fours, with officers on tired horses in the company intervals.

We marched along on this parallel course in plain view of each other for something like ten minutes, at a distance only barely outside the range of our rifled guns. On both sides the men in the ranks were aware of the other column, but were too tired to raise a shout, or to do anything more than cast an indifferent glance across the way. One young officer, magnificently bearded, on a coal-black horse, looked over at us, swung his hat around his head and shouted something which reached our ears only as a faint halloo. Two or three of us raised our hands in acknowledgment, but no one even attempted to call back.

Darkness set in shortly after this, and the brigade halted for the night. In the east the sky was red and glowing from the light of the rebel campfires. I still had a three-mile ride in front of me, and it was after nine o'clock when I reached the center column and headquarters, and reported to General Pack.

❦ *ii*

Headquarters for the night were in an abandoned log cabin on a hillside facing south. A dozen horses were tethered outside and the orderlies in charge of them were sitting on the ground in the moonlight, smoking, and talking in low voices. Inside, the only person in the room with the general was Bob

Kelso, one of the three of us serving as the general's aides. Bob was a shock-haired farm boy with big ears, amiable and intelligent, with a reputation among us for managing intractable horses. He was sitting on a bench that ran along the wall of the cabin, with his legs stretched out in front of him and his head on his chest, sound asleep.

The general was sitting behind a crude plank table, writing a letter to his wife. He looked up as I came in. "Good evening, John," he said. "You have a report from General Jones? Put it on the table. I'll look at it presently. Sit down, please."

I took a place on the bench beside Bob Kelso, and tried not to go to sleep. The general went back to his letter, his rumpled fair hair and bearded face lighted by the three candles on the table in front of him. He wrote steadily, reaching out to dip his pen in the inkwell without raising his eyes from the page. When he came to the end, he read over what he had written, picked up his pen and made a correction or two, then folded the letter carefully and put it to one side.

He picked up Jonesy's report and glanced over it, then turned his head. "General Jones reports a rebel column on the road east of the Hunsicker farm. He gives no estimate of the size of the force. Have you any idea how big it was, John?"

I stood up with all my bones creaking. "Yes, sir. We thought it was at least a brigade. A brigadier general and his staff were with the column. There may have been more of them in front or behind. There was no way of telling."

The general thought this over, then started at the beginning, with questions about the earlier part of the afternoon. I stood with my knees sagging, and laboriously focused my mind on each question, and answered it as well as I could, until the general finally dismissed me with a courteous, "Thank you very much, Captain."

I sat down gratefully, leaned back, and closed my eyes. For half a minute I was sitting on a hard bench with my back against the rough wall of a log cabin, then my mind was drifting gently, and I was cushioned and comfortable, and blissfully at ease. Once I awakened briefly, when Bob Kelso stumbled against me on his way out. I opened my eyes long enough to see that there were at least a dozen men in the room, tired men in dusty blue, who seemed to have been there for a long time. They were talking about somebody named Martin Helper. I remembered the name, but I went back to sleep before I found out who he was or why they were talking about him.

When I awakened again, with the knotty roughness of the wall digging into my shoulder blade, nearly all of them had gone. A shaft of moonlight was coming in the doorway, and someone had put three fresh tall candles on the table. My uncle was sitting across the table from General Pack, and Jake Leslie—Colonel Leslie, our adjutant general—was at the table with them.

Colonel Leslie was fifty-two years old, probably the oldest man in the command, bald and clean-shaven, with a wrinkled, leathery face and deep-set eyes of an astonishingly bright, clear blue. He was probably the oldest, and was certainly the most learned man with us. He had been General Pack's instructor in mathematics at West Point; he knew fifteen languages, including such unlikely ones as Gaelic and Hungarian; and he had been in every country I had ever heard of.

He was sitting at the end of the table, tired, with pouches under his eyes, bending over a map the general had pushed in front of him.

"My God, the names!" he was saying. "Look at them! Tarsus, Antioch, Jericho, Sardis, Tyre. Not to speak of Athens and Corinth, and Rome and Sparta. Every time I look at a map I wonder where we're making this campaign, and who's in command. Alexander? Seleucus? Old Antigonus One-Eye? Good Lord, here's another! Laodicea. How on earth would they pronounce that around here?"

My uncle laughed. "That's pronounced Laddassee, Jake. Like Tennessee. I've been there. Four log cabins at a crossroads, like most of the others. For that matter, if you'll look a little further, you'll find Milan and Lodi, and Moscow and Borodino. Oh, yes, and Waterloo. So maybe it's Napoleon."

General Pack smiled. "I should hope not. I'm happy to say Waterloo is at least three counties away, and not in our district at all."

He turned to Colonel Leslie. "Tarsus is quite a pleasant little town, Jacob. It was my headquarters when we were proposing to run a railroad through here, seven or eight years ago. My wife was quite fond of the town. As a matter of fact, I have asked her to come down and visit us later in the month. I thought she might like to see it again."

Colonel Leslie and my uncle were silent. The general leaned back, and the chair creaked under his weight. He looked from one man to the other, then said mildly, "You gentlemen seem to disapprove. Would you mind telling me why?"

Jake Leslie twisted his weather-beaten face into a wry smile. "Pure superstition, Arthur. I have a dread of counting chickens before they're hatched. Of presuming. Of hybris, if you like. We aren't in the town yet, and we have to beat McGraw first. Wouldn't it be a little more prudent, more reverent, so to speak, to wait until we get there, and then send for her?"

The general was indulgent. "I think I burned my pinch of incense, Jacob. The invitation was entirely contingent. I told her that the campaign was going well so far, and was about to come to a head. That if it turned out well—and we would know in a day or two—I would like her to come down for a visit. What about you, James? Are your objections on an otherworldly basis, too?"

"Only partly, sir." James smiled briefly. "Not entirely. What occurred to me was that we not only have to fight a battle to get into the town, but, in addition, we may very well have to fight to stay there. It occurs to me too, that it might cause some division in the command. Some of our more chivalrous officers might be more concerned with Mrs. Pack's safety than with their immediate duties. Also that there will be casualties if there is much fighting. Men killed and wounded every day. Quite possibly some of us. In that case her visit might not be very pleasant."

For a moment the general's habitual composure was upset,

and there was a note of displeasure in his voice. "I would be grateful if you would give me a little more credit, James. I would hardly invite her to visit us under the circumstances you mention."

I was displeased, myself. I had been hearing about the general's wife, the Countess, from all sides, and I was eager to see what she looked like. I was annoyed with Jake and my uncle for raising these nonsensical objections.

The general recovered himself quickly. "What I had in mind, James, was a quiet period of a month or six weeks while Barney sets up a new base of operations. I don't think he can do it in less time than that, and I don't think he can give us much trouble until he has a new base to work from. I expect that Tarsus will be well behind the lines, and at least reasonably quiet. Does that answer your objections?"

James gave in gracefully. "Yes, sir. It does. Objections withdrawn."

The general, barely waiting for James' answer, turned to Colonel Leslie and said in a bantering voice, "Now that I've knocked on wood, Jacob, do you mind my saying that I think we're going to beat Barney tomorrow? After all, that's what we came for. And tomorrow or the next day I expect to have the pleasure of showing you the sights of Tarsus."

Colonel Leslie shrugged his shoulders. He looked tired and old. "If you can show me a house with a bed in it—a bed with clean sheets; clean, freshly ironed sheets—I'll be willing to let the rest of it go. I can't remember the last time I slept between clean sheets, or in a bedroom. Do they still have such things? For that matter, did they ever have them? I'm beginning to doubt it. I suspect it's just something I read about a long time ago. The Blessed Isles, maybe."

"I think we may be able to manage that for you," the general said cheerfully. "Perhaps it should go out in general orders: A bed, with clean sheets, for Colonel Leslie." He leaned forward to look at his watch which was propped up against the inkwell on the table. "Well, gentlemen, we'll be moving out in about five hours. I suggest that we get on with our work."

The general's air of confidence was contagious. If he was as sure of the outcome as all that, there was nothing to worry about. As usual, he knew what he was doing. At the same time there was an uneasy feeling in the back of my head that Jake was right: that the future wasn't to be taken for granted; that a little more deprecation should have gone with the general's pinch of incense.

At the table they were consulting maps and reports, discussing the terrain and the possibilities still open to McGraw, and arranging to bring Major Saint Chamans' reserve artillery and the ammunition train over to the center road.

My uncle pushed his chair back, and came over and stood in front of me. "I hear you and Jonesy practically ran into McGraw's whole army this afternoon," he said.

"We had a pretty good look at part of it, anyway."

"You'll get a better look tomorrow. Jonesy's not the only one. Gavin's got something in front of him, too. And Billy Roth thinks we're surrounded. The general wants me to go over and cheer him up a little. Better get some sleep, Johnny. Tomorrow is going to be a busy day."

After he had gone there was silence in the room. Colonel Leslie was writing by the light of the candles on the table. General Pack had lighted a fresh cigar and was drinking coffee out of a battered tin cup.

It was a perfectly still night, without a breath of air. The night sounds were all around us, the irregular rise and fall of the chorus of insects, the croaking of frogs from a swamp half a mile away, and in the distance a dog barking at the moon. Mingled with these were the sounds of men and horses: near at hand the pawing and snorting of tethered horses and the low, sleepy voices of the couriers on duty; in the distance, on both sides of us, the confused and indistinguishable sounds of large bodies of men and horses, coming from one of our two cavalry regiments on the right, and from the thirty-six hundred men of our big center brigade on the left. At times it was possible to make out individual sounds, the galloping of horses, and distant shouting as the last belated detachments moved into camp.

Perhaps an hour later—the fresh candles had burned down halfway and the moonlight had moved farther into the room —I was awakened by the sound of loud voices. I had been vaguely conscious of a row going on for some time. As I became fully awake I realized that it wasn't a row; it was just Billy Roth with his sonorous stump-orator's voice, and as usual he was griping about something.

General Wilfred A. Roth was the commander of our center brigade. He was a pompous little man, clean-shaven, with a mane of black hair. He had been a prominent Congressman, which was how he happened to be a general. Billy had some good points. He was good at organization and paper work, and his brigade was always well taken care of. He would have been an excellent officer behind a desk in Washington, or Louisville, but he was no soldier and no general, and he was out of place at the head of an infantry brigade on active service.

What brought me up to a sitting position, with my feet on the floor and my eyes wide open, was the sound of my own name, uttered with great bitterness.

"And then young Johnny Lake comes over and takes away my leading regiment, my best regiment. Young Lake doesn't bother to report to me. I doubt that he even reported to Colonel Franklin. No, sir. He simply turns the regiment off onto a side road and gets it started down the road, and only then, sir, afterwards, when the movement is under way he rides up and has the condescension to inform me that he is acting by your orders. That Jonesy wants the regiment."

Billy was standing on the other side of the table, facing the general. His coat was buttoned up to the neck, and he was wearing a sword and a yellow sash to remind himself that he was a general. His face was red and his eyes were bloodshot, and he was tired, like all the rest of us.

It took me a moment to remember the incident. What had happened was that the head of the column was just coming up to the crossroads when I reached it. I hadn't known how long it would take me to find General Roth, and I took it upon myself to turn the column, to avoid countermarching and holding up the advance. That was early in the afternoon. It was a long time ago, and much had happened since then.

General Pack was conciliatory. "Captain Lake meant no disrespect, Wilfred. He simply didn't have time to look for you. General Jones was being held up. The enemy had a strong position in his front, and the quickest way to turn him out of it was to bring over a regiment from your brigade. You were on his flank. As a matter of fact, if you will remember, General Jones did the same thing for you earlier in the day."

Billy wasn't going to be cheated out of his grievance by conciliatory language. He went on as though he hadn't heard the general. "And when the regiment reaches him, what does Jonesy do? Jonesy, or for all I know, your bright young staff officer, taking command in person. He puts in my regiment— my regiment, sir, the 35th Indiana—against the entire force of the enemy, while he looks on and does nothing. And when the 35th has done his fighting for him and carried the position with heavy loss, he sends it back to me in an absolutely crippled condition."

General Pack interrupted him dryly. "Colonel Franklin reports his loss as two men killed and eight wounded."

Billy didn't even hear him. "That regiment isn't in any condition to move out at four o'clock in the morning. It isn't in any condition to move out tomorrow at any time. Neither are any of the other regiments in the brigade, and neither are the other brigades. They're in no better shape than we are.

"We've been marching and fighting for three days," Billy went on persuasively, as though he were addressing a particularly stubborn committee. "We've been fighting continuously. There hasn't been a moment when you couldn't hear gunfire somewhere along the line. We've been marching—if you'll excuse me, sir—over some of the damndest terrain any army ever marched over. Up one hill and down the other, the country so poor nothing but scrub oak will grow, the roads nothing but miserable cart tracks. The men have been marching from before sunrise until after dark. They haven't had a cooked meal or a decent night's sleep in all that time. I tell you, sir, those men are worn out. It's too much. Flesh and blood won't stand for it. "

General Pack had his back to me. All I could see was the outline of his bulky figure against the light from the candles on the table. He had raised his hand to his beard and his voice was thoughtful: I couldn't tell whether he was being sarcastic, or whether he was simply being courteous and hearing the man out.

"What do you suggest, Wilfred?"

Billy had his answer all thought out. "Two things, sir." He raised his hand with one finger pointing upwards. "First, the men need rest. I suggest that we take up a strong defensive position, call in the other two brigades, and remain there long enough to rest the men. A full day at least, and better, two."

He paused, and held up two fingers. "Second—and to my mind this is fully as important—that we reconnoiter the enemy thoroughly, and then, when we know what we're doing, take our measures accordingly. Advance, if possible. If necessary, fall back. As matters stand now, we're going ahead blindly. We're groping in a fog. We don't even know where McGraw is. All we know is that he's around here somewhere with a force at least as large as our own. And if he's been reinforced, or if he's called in Taylor and Ruthven, he could have a force double the size of ours, and we would be running into a trap."

While Billy was speaking, our cavalry commander, Dick Ross, had come in with his spurs jangling, his fierce cavalry mustache bristling, and his forage cap raked over one eye at an unbelievable angle. He was one of the general's three nephews, and one of our particular friends. The general, who had known him all his life, used to say that Dick was a born cavalryman: that he could swagger as soon as he could walk.

He had taken a seat by the door and was quiet for a minute or two while Billy was talking, but this last was too much for him.

"Taylor and Ruthven, hell!" he said in a loud, scornful voice. "Barney isn't taking any chances. He's got Jackson and Bobby Lee with him, too."   '

There was a shout of laughter in the room. Billy turned to glare at Dick, his face an apoplectic dark red.

When the laughter had died away, General Pack said mildly, "I think you're taking an unduly gloomy view, Wilfred. I don't believe our affairs are in quite so alarming a position as all that."

My uncle, to my great surprise, came to Billy's defense. He had taken Jake Leslie's place at the end of the table and had been writing steadily while all this was going on. Now he put his pen down and looked over at Dick.

"All the same that's not so foolish, Dick," he said. "Reinforcements, I mean. This afternoon we ran into a new brigade over on the right. Helper's brigade. Martin Helper. It's a small one, and Gavin thinks he can run over it in the morning without much trouble. But the point is, we don't know where it came from. It could be one of Taylor's."

Billy Roth was gratified and a little smug. "I think that bears me out, gentlemen," he said to the room in general.

Dick shrugged his shoulders. "Taylor's, or one of Barney's we didn't know about. Nobody ever said we had a complete roster of Barney's command." He looked up at Billy Roth. "Incidentally, Billy, one of the things that was bothering you was that we hadn't located McGraw's main force. You don't need to worry about it any longer. We found it this afternoon."

Everybody sat up a little straighter, and there was a moment of silence which I suspect Dick rather enjoyed, then General Pack said easily, "You might tell us about it, Dick. Where is Barney? Over in front of General Jones?"

"Beyond Jonesy," Dick replied. "In front of him and on the other side, out by Hurt's Corners. We ran over some rebel cavalry out that way. A screen they had out on our side. We hit them good and hard and drove them in, and rode right into their main position with them, and for a while it was quite a Donnybrook. We had taken them by surprise, but it was a whole infantry brigade we had ridden into, and when they began to pull themselves together we broke it off and retired."

"Do you know what brigade it was?" the general asked.

"It was Perry's brigade we ran into. Tim thinks there was another brigade across the road. They had about twenty guns. Maybe more."

"Which was it, Dick? One brigade, or two? And what makes you think it was McGraw's main force?"

Any other man in the command would have taken this as a reprimand, but Dick merely considered the question, then replied cheerfully, "Two brigades. If Tim saw a second brigade, it was there. I couldn't see the other side of the road from where I was. Tim could. He was farther along."

"Two brigades at Hurt's Corners." The general looked down at the map to find the location. "What makes you think it was McGraw's main force?"

Dick hesitated. He scowled at the floor, then looked up and said soberly, "I'm convinced that it was Barney's main force. That's my considered opinion, for what it's worth. I can't tell you exactly why. Only when we ran into them they felt heavy. They felt big and solid. It's something you feel. You can't prove it."

He hesitated again, then noticed Billy Roth still standing by the table, still disapproving. "Besides," he said, a cheerful smile spreading over his face, "General Roth seemed a little worried about where Barney was, and I thought maybe I could cheer him up."

Billy looked at him sourly. "I can't see that you've said anything that would cheer anybody up. You've located one of McGraw's brigades, or maybe two. You aren't sure which. You have an idea the rest of his troops are there, too, but you don't know. It's just your opinion."

General Pack broke in quietly. "It's the opinion of an experienced cavalry officer, Wilfred, which has some bearing on the matter."

Billy Roth was stubborn. "Very well, sir. Only what about the brigade over on the west road? What about the reinforcements that couldn't possibly reach McGraw for two or three days and are already there? What is the explanation for that?"

General Pack wasn't arguing with Billy. He was looking at the map again, and had withdrawn his attention entirely.

After a moment, my uncle answered for him. "I suppose you mean Martin Helper's brigade," he said. "The fact is, we don't have any explanation. It could be Taylor's right brigade, or it could be one of McGraw's. We simply don't know."

"You're being pretty lighthearted about it, aren't you?" Billy said bitterly. "McGraw has been reinforced. Maybe heavily reinforced. Nobody knows. The chief of staff doesn't, anyway. And we're to go ahead just the same."

My uncle was beginning to get a little tired of it. "Don't be a damned fool, Billy. We may not know all the details, but we have a good idea of the over-all strength of McGraw's forces, and we think we can handle them. That's all there is to it."

General Pack had enough of the argument too, and when Billy started to splutter and begin all over again, the general simply extinguished him, put him out like a candle. This was a special voice the general had: even, perfectly calm, and only a little louder than usual, but each word weighed a ton, and when he had finished, that was all. There wasn't any answer.

What he said was, "I'm afraid you will have to leave the responsibility for this command to me, Wilfred. There will be no change in your orders. Your men will be under arms at four o'clock, and will move out at five."

There was a dead silence in the room. Billy Roth had been glaring at my uncle with a flushed and angry face. He turned his head as the general began to speak. When the general had finished, Billy swallowed hard, and made the only possible answer.

"Yes sir," he said.

Shortly after this, men began to leave, and presently someone had blown out the candles and everybody had gone, and the only light in the room was the dim red glow from the dying coals in the fireplace and the bright shaft of moonlight slanting through the door. I could hear the sound of horses' hoofs in the distance, growing fainter and dying away, then the night sounds again, insects and the chorus of frogs from the swamp, and dogs barking in the distance, and nearer at hand, horses and men moving restlessly in their sleep.

The same sounds were in my ears and it was still deep night when I was awakened by the sound of a shot somewhere off to our right, followed by a spattering of shots in return. I opened my eyes and saw that someone had lighted the candles again and built the fire up to a crackling yellow blaze. The general and Colin Ross—his nephew and my close friend—were standing in front of the fire with mugs of coffee in their hands, and by the time I had my feet on the floor I could hear a group of horsemen approaching. Another day had begun: Saturday, the twentieth of September.

❦ *iii*

Several hours later, about seven-thirty in the morning, I saw our objective, the town of Tarsus, for the first time. We were still in the hills, riding through the scrub oak along a cart track that followed the crest of a ridge, when we came to the head of a long valley that opened out to the right. At the foot of the valley we could see open farmland and green meadows, sloping down to a clear stream bordered by willows. The stream swung out in our direction then back again, in a long slow curve, and across the river, in the curve, was the town on a low hill, with white pillared houses half hidden in trees, with lawns and flower gardens, with church steeples and the dome of the courthouse showing over the trees.

It was tranquil and perfectly peaceful, a beautiful and comforting scene: I have never forgotten it. It was seven-thirty of a summer morning and there was dew on the grass; three redbrown cows were grazing in the meadow on our side of the river. There was an air of Sunday-morning calm about the town, as though it were waiting for the church bells to ring and for the streets to fill with people on their way to church, people who were scrubbed and clean and in their Sunday clothes, men and women and little children. It looked like the Promised Land.

I pulled up my horse to look at it, and suddenly I was

choking with emotion and my eyes were full of tears. This was undoubtedly a strange response to the sight of a pleasant landscape, but no one is entirely rational after three days and nights without sleep. At seven-thirty in the morning we had already been in the saddle for four hours, and had fought a battle. A small battle, an action, if you like, but for a quarter of an hour it had seemed fierce and bloody enough. I had been under fire for nearly half an hour, with shells crashing around me and bullets whistling past my ears close enough to hit men standing near me. I had seen two men I knew killed; not friends, but men I spoke to, and knew by name.

Afterwards I had seen what our battery of three-inch rifled guns had done to the enemy position. Our guns were beautifully handled, and it was a pleasure to watch them in action, but the results on the other side, the smashed guns, and the smashed men and horses, were not pleasant. By this time I had learned to accept such things as a part of the day's work, but I hadn't learned to like them.

Hence these tears. I suppose it was a combination of all these things, fatigue, and the excitement of being under fire, and a revulsion from the bloody mess of the battlefield, that made me feel choked and swollen at my first sight of the pleasant little town in the bend of the river.

I expressed all this beautifully. I turned to Colin Ross, who had pulled up at the same time, and said with tears in my eyes, "Oh, my God, Colin, look at those damned cows!"

Colin knew what I meant. He probably felt the same way himself. He turned in his saddle and looked out over the valley, then nodded soberly. "Guernseys, aren't they?"

A moment later he remarked, "You know what I wish, Johnny? I wish I were about eight years old and somebody had sent me out for the cows, and I was barefoot and could feel the wet grass under my feet."

A bugle call reached us faintly from the rear and ended our contemplation of the peaceful morning scene.

I laughed. "I guess somebody else will have to get the cows," I said, and we moved on.

Colin was the youngest of the general's three nephews. He was twenty years old, twelve years younger than Gavin, ten years younger than Dick. His brothers and his uncle were immensely proud of him: he was the bright young hope, the pet and baby of the family. A very big baby, incidentally: six feet five, and about as broad as a house. Colin didn't smoke, or drink, or swear, and nobody, not even Dick, told an off-color story in his presence. I was a lttle wary of this puritan streak, and doubtful about getting along with him, but his friendliness, his courtesy, the innate sweetness of his disposition made it impossible not to like him. Within a few days I found myself being careful of my language when we were together simply as a way of returning his courtesy.

He was a year younger than I was, and had a fresh beardless face. I suspect that I was inclined to patronize him by virtue of my superior age and my mustache—at least until the time I saw him cut off and surrounded by eight or more of Horton's irregular cavalry. He had ridden down and shot and sabered half of them before we could even make a move to help him. And when the survivors turned and ran and it was all over, he came trotting back, perfectly cool, as though this were something he did before breakfast every morning.

Colin had joined me on the right about six, after our fight was over. I had been sent over before daybreak, over four miles of narrow road winding through the sparse woods, riding by the light of a low yellow moon. The headquarters tents were pitched in an open field at the left of the road, the canvas reflecting the red glow of the campfires. Men and horses were moving about, silhouetted against the light of the fires, and a small cavalry detachment was just moving off down the road.

General Gavin Ross—Colin's brother—was sitting in a camp chair by the fire in front of his tent with three or four of his staff officers, all of them men I knew. Gavin was a close friend of ours, a big, powerful man with a bristling sandy mustache, ten years out of West Point, an able and very aggressive commander.

He was cheerful and full of talk this morning, which was the way the prospect of battle affected him. I sat and listened, and was grateful for the comfort of a canvas chair and bitter coffee.

"Nothing much to do for a while," Gavin said. "We want to hit them as soon as it's light, but there's no point in getting there much before. We had a good look at their position before dark yesterday, and they were still there an hour ago. Young Bader found a good position for his guns, and we found a road around to the rear. Strong position from the front, so we aren't going to do it that way. Joe Marsh has taken two-thirds of the brigade and gone around. He'll come in on their left flank and rear, while we hit them in front. I thought James might come over this morning. He went over the ground with me yesterday."

"He's over on the left," I said. "The general wants him to stay with Jonesy today."

The moon was nearly down by this time, and the stars were bright overhead. The activity around the campfires was subdued, the men resting while they could. The air was still and tepid, with an occasional faint breath of wind from the southwest.

After a time Gavin turned his head and remarked, "Your uncle's quite a man, Johnny. Best natural soldier I ever saw. He's got a natural feeling for command. For handling troops. He's got an instinctive feeling for what they can do and how far he can push them, and when they've reached their limit. You should have seen him at Shiloh the first day. He had a regiment of perfectly raw troops—fresh from the country, hardly knew their right foot from their left—and by God, so long as James was leading them, they stood and fought like veterans. And James riding up and down on a big black horse and having the time of his life, with every sharpshooter in the Confederate Army taking a shot at him. It was a wonderful thing to see. Did he ever serve abroad?"

"I don't think so. Not that I ever heard of," I replied.

"Jonesy and I were talking about it the other day," Gavin went on. "A lot of our volunteer officers are good men.

They're brave, practically all of them, and some of them are pretty good soldiers. But they're all amateurs. That's where the difference is. James is a professional. So is Saint Chamans." [Saint Shammons was the way Gavin and the rest of us pronounced the name.] "They're both professionals, and damned good ones. They've been in a lot of out-of-the-way places. Jonesy thought they might have served together somewhere. Italy? The Crimea? India? Some place like that?"

At the mention of Robert Saint Chamans, I suddenly remembered a comment Jonesy had made the previous afternoon, and began to laugh. Robert had come up about something, and as he rode off Jonesy had given a wry shake of the head and muttered something about that damn' handkerchief up his sleeve. He had then turned on me and demanded,

"You noticed any of the rest of them lately, Johnny? Sammy Brock, Christie, young Harper? Shiny boots, clean uniforms, shave every day. All of them polite. 'I beg your pardon, sir?' Handkerchief up their sleeve. Even getting a British accent. Artillery used to be a lot of roughnecks in my day. Not ours, though!"

Gavin looked at me in surprise, and I explained, rather elliptically, "Jonesy says he's going to recommend that a handkerchief, worn up the sleeve, be made regulation equipment for the artillery."

Gavin gave a hoot of laughter. "When did he say that?"

"Yesterday afternoon." I repeated Jonesy's entire comment.

This delighted him. "You know, by God, it's true. I was noticing young Freddy Bader just a couple of days ago. I'll tell Robert. He'll make a joke out of it, but he'll be pleased all the same. He's got a lot of respect for Jonesy."

From a distance, over towards the left, there was a flurry of shots that kept up for a minute or two. Gavin listened intently, then relaxed.

"Dick seems to be stirring up some trouble over there," he remarked.

He leaned forward to look at his watch by the light of the campfire, then snapped it shut and stood up.

"Time to start moving," he said, with an air of relief. "It'll be light in half an hour. You stay with me, Johnny. I may have to put you to work."

Gavin's leading regiment was already under way when we reached the crossroads, marching down the road to our left at a good swinging gait. Behind us the sky was still dark in the east, but the moon, low in the southwest, still gave some light, and the dark mass of the regiment was clearly visible as it swung along the pale surface of the road.

The attack went off without a hitch. Everything was beautifully on time. Just as we began to hear the first shots of the day as our skirmishers were driving their pickets in, I happened to glance over to the left and saw that the blackness in the trees was beginning to dissolve, and through the sparse foliage of the stunted oaks the sky in the east was gray. And by the time the other regiments were up, and deploying on either side of the road, it was light enough for the men to see where they were going.

At the same time, men with shovels were leveling off a passage up the steep slope on the left of the road, leading to the clearing on the hilltop that Gavin's battery commander had picked out the night before. As the guns came up they went up the slope with a rush, one after the other, the guns bouncing crazily behind the teams; they galloped up to the position on the hilltop, swung around into position, and began firing. All this without a moment's pause, in a single continuous motion. I felt like applauding.

And finally, within ten minutes of the time our guns opened and firing became general along the line, Colonel Marsh made his attack. We could hear the sound of heavy fighting off to the right, and could see the gunsmoke beyond the strip of woods that obscured our view, and we could see the gunsmoke advancing steadily into and through the woods.

It was all over in half an hour, a wonderfully neat and well-managed little operation. We captured seven hundred men, about a third of them wounded, and buried fifty-three dead.

Colin came over with orders from the general while we were

paroling the prisoners. General Ross was to close in to the left, within supporting distance of the center brigade. Actually, the movement was already under way. Gavin had already started off his guns and his baggage, including the captured equipment, and four of his seven regiments. The others would be ready to follow in half an hour.

Colin and I started back along the lower road, ahead of the three remaining regiments. After the deep bay, where we had stopped to look out over the meadow and the town, the road climbed up into the woods again. The road was simply a wagon track winding along the crest and sides of the broken ridges, which were covered with a thin growth of oaks and waist-high scrub. Gavin had already sent over a courier with the results of the morning's fight, so we were in no pressing hurry. We rode at an easy trot, and slowed down to a walk on the hills. Colin told me that his cousin was coming to join the staff sometime next month.

"Good," I said. "We need some help. Bob Kelso and I were talking about it. With four of us we can get some sleep once in a while. Say every third night."

"I don't think you'll like him," Colin said. "He's a little fellow. A smooth little fellow."

We were walking our horses up a stony hillside dappled with sunlight filtering through the thin foliage of the oaks. The ruts of the wagon track had washed out into small gullies and we fell into single file, Colin going ahead, while I followed behind the laboring haunches of the big gray he was riding. The air was still, and it was beginning to be hot.

When we were abreast again, I said, "Quite a family party you're going to have. The general's wife is coming down, too."

Colin turned his head and looked at me in surprise. "Lucy? My aunt? Is she coming? I haven't heard anything about it."

"They were talking about it last night," I said. "You were out. Or maybe you were asleep. The general asked her to come down to Tarsus for a visit. Jake and my uncle didn't think it was such a good idea, but the general wasn't asking them."

"When is she coming?"

"As soon as we get settled in Tarsus, I suppose. Or as soon as it looks as though things are going to be quiet for a while. It's going to seem strange to have a woman around headquarters. I wonder if I still know how to eat at a table."

"You'll get used to it." Colin grinned at me. "Just the way you got used to wearing shoes every day."

I looked for something to throw at him, then gave it up. After a moment I said, "Is she really a countess? Or is that just what everybody calls her?"

"Oh, no. She really is. Austrian. Countess Alexandra von Reille."

I found this quite marvelous. "Where does the Lucy come in?"

"That's one of her middle names. Maria Luise Christina. She's got three or four more. She met Uncle Arthur in Washington. Her father was the Austrian ambassador. Count Casimir Ernst Adolphus Patrick von Reille. They were Irish, originally, and the eldest son always has a Patrick in his name. Patrick O'Reilly. They emigrated about the time of Cromwell. The first Patrick O'Reilly went into the Austrian Army and fought the Turks, and ended up as a lieutenant general and baron. His son married an heiress, and was a field marshal and count. Lucy's grandfather was an aide-de-camp to the Archduke Charles, and fought against Napoleon. He was a field marshal after Leipzig."

I was still marveling. "How did she happen to marry the general? Wasn't that pretty much unheard of?"

"I don't know. It probably was. But Uncle Arthur was in the army and an officer, and that made him one of the gentry. And he always could be pretty impressive."

We rode on for a few minutes in silence, then going back to the beginning, Colin remarked, "It's going to be nice, having her down here. You'll love her, Johnny. She's really beautiful, and she's perfectly simple and unpretentious and kind to everybody. The Countess doesn't show at all."

Colin thought for a moment, then changed this. "Or maybe that's the way it shows."

"She sounds wonderful," I said. "Even though we will have to wash our faces every day."

"Wait!" Colin pulled up his horse suddenly, and put out his hand to check me.

It was about nine o'clock by this time, warm and perfectly still. As we sat and listened we became aware of a new sound ahead of us, faint but unmistakable, like no other sound on earth: a rustling sound, a whisper, a low vibration in the air, quite steady, that seemed to lie along the horizon: the sound of battle at extreme distance.

Colin looked at me. "Hear it?"

I nodded. "We seem to have caught up with Barney McGraw. Or maybe he has caught up with us. You'd better go back and tell Gavin. I'll go on ahead."

Chapter 2

The sound was just ahead of me when I came out into a clearing, a field sloping down to a small tributary river on the right, the road running across the field and up into the woods on the far side. From somewhere beyond the woods a column of black smoke was rising straight up into the air. One of our Indiana regiments, the 34th, was in reserve on the right of the road, the men resting but still in ranks, the officers on foot, gathered together in small groups. A battery was in reserve on the left of the road, and beyond the battery a squadron of cavalry.

As I crossed the field and started up the ridge, one of the officers of the 34th shouted something at me. I assumed that it was nothing more than a greeting from someone I knew, waved my hand in reply and kept on. A moment later the meaning of the words, which I had heard clearly enough but hadn't bothered to understand, penetrated my mind.

What he had shouted at me was, "Get off the road, you damned fool!"

What made the meaning of his words sink in was the bursting of a shell squarely in the middle of the road, no more than fifty feet in front of me. I took his advice and got off the road.

From the crest of the ridge I could see across to a similar ridge a mile away, sparsely wooded like the one I was on, with light showing through the trees along the sky line. The shallow trough between the two ridges had been partly cleared. There were open fields on either side of the road, and meadows and clumps of trees, and patches of woodland. A small brook bordered with willows meandered down from the left, crossed the road, and reached the river at a point midway between the ridges. There was a haze of smoke along the ground from the firing. Almost in the center, in a clump of trees back from the road, a farmhouse was burning fiercely, with tongues of bright-orange flame leaping up over the tree-tops and a cloud of black smoke billowing upwards.

Behind the screen of willows, long lines of men in gray and butternut were deployed in the fields, and behind them an apparently endless stream of men poured out of the woods and down the road. Rows of guns stood in the field, still harnessed and ready to move forward with the troops, and behind them, higher up the slope, two four-gun batteries were firing over their heads, shelling the road and the woods on our side of the valley. I could see the distant gunners working with sponge and ramrod, loading and firing, and the white puffs of smoke from the muzzles. Occasionally, for half an instant, I could see the menacing shallow curve of the shell before it burst. The guns seemed to be firing noiselessly, the sound lost in the uproar near at hand.

Most of the fighting appeared to be centered around the burning farmhouse, and farther to the right, in the wood on our side of the brook, the South Wood. Two of our batteries were returning the enemy fire, one of them beyond the wood and out of sight, the other a line of six three-inch rifles that had been pushed out on the left of the road. While I was watching, the battery on the right—probably Brock, who had been with Jonesy from the beginning—dropped three shells, one after the other, squarely in the middle of the enemy column marching towards us down the road.

I had ridden over the top of the ridge, and pulled up where an opening in the trees gave me a view of the battlefield. Here I found myself in the midst of the 24th Illinois, which was in line just inside the edge of the woods along the slope.

The major of the 24th rode over towards me, picking his way carefully through the trees.

"Looking for the old man, Johnny?" he called out as he approached.

I nodded, then glancing over at the opposite slope, "Think you're going to need some help, Major?"

"We sure as hell are. In about fifteen minutes old Barney McGraw is going to come tearing up that road like a bat out of hell, and we're going to need all the help we can get."

A shell passed over our heads with an ugly rushing sound, and burst a hundred yards back, near the top of the ridge.

The major turned his head. "You'll have to cut your fuses a little shorter, friend," he said, apparently addressing the explosion.

He turned back. "The general went by a few minutes ago, if you're looking for him. The colonel's over on the left. Jonesy took the right and gave him the left. The old man was looking for Jonesy."

"Where is he?"

"Over on the right somewhere. Probably in back of the woods."

Jonesy wasn't behind the woods, he was in the woods, and the general had gone by the time I got there. The South Wood stood on the level ground in front of the ridge we were on, about halfway down to the river. It was a large, irregular clump of woods, more thickly grown and tangled with underbrush than the comparatively open woods of the ridge. Just now it was the scene of heavy fighting. A bluish haze drifted up through the treetops, and beneath it the wood was exploding with gunfire.

One of Jonesy's aides took me to the place where Jonesy had been, to a little glade in a hollow about fifty feet in, and left me there. The glade was protected from any kind of direct fire but was not a very comfortable place, even so, for it was strewn with ammunition boxes, some of them broken open and empty or half empty but most of them full. A lovely place for a stray shell to hit.

A couple of tired, dirty soldiers from the 17th Missouri were lugging one of the boxes off to the front when I got there. A captain from the same regiment was sitting on the ground with a dazed look on his face, holding his arm, and the colonel of the 10th Iowa, Marcus Pellam—a forty-five-year-old lawyer who had turned into a fine soldier—was sitting on an ammunition box, looking down at a bloody handkerchief wrapped around his wrist.

He looked up as I approached, and seemed to think he ought to apologize for being there.

"Shell fragment through the wrist, John," he explained. "Really nothing much. No excuse for my shirking my duties like this. Only Jonesy insisted." There was a fretful note in his voice. I imagine he was in considerable pain.

"Sorry you're hurt, Colonel," I told him. "Only you know Jonesy. Do you think you'd have any hide left on you if he thought you were shirking anything?"

Colonel Pellam smiled faintly. "No, I guess I wouldn't, John."

I had noticed, without paying much attention to it, that leaves kept drifting down from the trees, and while I was talking to the colonel a large branch, cut through by bullets, came crashing down a few feet away. At the same time the firing in the wood suddenly swelled in volume and was mingled with hoarse shouting, which grew louder and closer on our left front.

I went out to see what was going on, pushing my way forward along a crude trail where the undergrowth had been recently trampled down. As I went forward and the firing grew louder, men from the 10th Iowa began to pass me, individual soldiers, then two or three together, then larger groups, drifting back slowly with frequent glances over the shoulder.

A little farther on the point of the break was clear—or as clear as anything was in this woods fighting. The corner was formed by an enormous oak tree. A fallen tree lay to its right with a line of our men behind it and the line was prolonged to the right—if you could call it a line—by little groups of men, prone, or kneeling, or sighting around trees, taking advantage of whatever cover was available. There was a small, swampy open place in front of the fallen log, and the beams of the late-morning sun slanted down through the smoke at a steep angle.

It was on the left that McGraw's men were coming through with wild whoops, in a line that had become ragged as the men paused to load and fire, then ran forward again. Jonesy had brought up men from the right and was doing the obviously necessary thing, strengthening the shoulder of the break, and extending his men down to the left to take the attacking force in flank.

He was standing on a stump in the angle, the most conspicuous man on the field, wearing a slouch hat over one eye, a black and white checked shirt with a star on one shoulder to make it a uniform, and a revolver belted around his waist in place of a sword. His voice was imperious and angry and had an astonishing carrying power, a rather high tenor voice that rang like a trumpet.

Just now he was trying to get the frightened but resolute captain of a Missouri company to extend his men to the left instead of bunching them up behind the troops already in line.

"On the left, Captain," he called out. "Put them in on the left. Oh, no! Jesus Christ, no! Extend the line to the left!"

The captain turned an anguished and uncomprehending face towards him, and almost at the same time fell dead as a bullet struck him behind the ear. Jonesy leaped down from the stump, strode over to the knot of disorganized men, grabbed a sergeant by the arm, and pushed him over to the left front.

"Look, God damn it! There they are!" he bellowed, holding onto the sergeant with one hand and pointing with the other to the ragged line of men crashing through the undergrowth no more than a hundred feet away. "For Christ's sake, get your men into line and start firing!"

The line had already begun to form, and, as the firing started, it was repeated by the sound of firing from the foot of the pocket. The men who had been pushing forward across the front of the line were now drifting backwards in small sullen groups, and behind them was the re-formed line of the 10th

Iowa, cheerful and aggressive now, the men shouting as they advanced.

Colonel Pellam came forward with them, a tall, bareheaded man holding his injured wrist in his other hand, not giving orders, not directing the attack, but just being there, which was all the men seemed to need.

A minute or two later three companies of the 17th Missouri that Jonesy had sent for came piling in behind the 10th Iowa, and the line was solidly established again.

With the immediate danger past, Jonesy seemed to lose interest. He took off his hat and mopped his face with a red bandanna, and stayed long enough to give a few perfunctory directions to the officers who had come in with the supporting troops, then started briskly to the rear.

I waited for him and went back with him. He affected an air of great astonishment when he caught sight of me. "Hey, boy, you lost or something?" he demanded. "Don't you know they don't let staff officers up this far? Too many bullets flying around. They might get hurt."

This was a standard joke, and I gave him one of the standard answers. "Bullets? Were those bullets? I thought they were bees." I let the joke go. "Too damned many bees, Jonesy. Have you seen the general?"

"Saw him half an hour ago. He's probably somewhere in back. Look, Johnny, you go find him and tell him I'll clear out this woods for him if he'll send me another regiment. If he can't spare one, tell him to keep my left clear and I'll hang onto this position as long as he wants me to."

General Pack, when I finally found him, was in an open grove on the forward side of the ridge, mounted, with Jake Leslie beside him. Both of them had field glasses raised to their eyes and were looking out over the field. There were others behind them, including Billy Roth, who did not look very happy. The grove was not particularly exposed, but it was on a portion of the ridge that McGraw's gunners were shelling methodically, from end to end, and every so often one of the shell bursts would be uncomfortably close.

What General Pack was watching was the massing of Mc-Graw's troops on the other side of the valley for what was obviously going to be a major assault straight up the road against our center. They were still in the process of deploying on both sides of the road, but no more of them were coming over the hill, and, as soon as they were formed, the attack would begin. There was something formidable about this mass that was building up against us, and a fascination in watching it take form, and in waiting for the moment when it would begin to move. It was like watching a force of nature: flood-waters piling up behind a dam, or an avalanche beginning to split off on a mountain side.

Robert Saint Chamans rode up about this time, wearing a beautifully tailored uniform, his boots shining with polish, his blond mustache carefully waxed, a fresh white handkerchief in his sleeve. His voice was nonchalant and his manner was easy, as usual, but his message was crisp and direct.

"General, can you give me a little more room on the right?" he said. "I want to put a battery in there, and I don't want my gunners picked off by sharpshooters in the woods. If I can get a mass of twenty-four guns together, I think I can break up this attack for you."

My message from Jonesy had become perfectly apposite. I rode up to the general and said, "I've just come from Jonesy, sir. He says he can clear out the woods with another regiment."

General Pack turned his head and looked at me without surprise. "Good. Who's over there, John? Colonel Franklin, isn't it?"

"Yes, sir. The 35th Indiana. The 16th Kentucky just beyond."

"I think General Jones had better have both of them at his disposal." The general scribbled a note in his order book and handed it to me. "Give this to Colonel Franklin, John, and get him started. Then go on to Colonel Powell and tell him to be ready to help out if he's called on. Both of them will be under General Jones for the time being."

Colonel Franklin had been expecting the orders I had for

him. In fact, he had gone over to see Jonesy a few minutes earlier and knew exactly what he wanted, so there was no delay at all. Afterwards I went on and gave the general's message to Colonel Powell, and stayed long enough to exchange a few words with the colonel and his son, who was serving as his aide.

It was about eleven-thirty and the sun was nearly straight overhead. There was a marked lull in the fighting, and the field was almost quiet for a minute or two at a time. In one of these moments of silence I noticed, with a feeling of sudden astonishment, that it was a nice day, a pleasant, warm September day. The firing in the wood had died away, and for a few minutes there was no sound of musketry at all, but only the heavy, concussive booming of cannon fire: from close at hand, where Brock continued his slow, careful firing at the enemy batteries, and from the left, where Saint Chamans now had both his three-inch batteries in action. The firing was effective. Several of McGraw's guns had been hit and put out of action, and others had been forced to withdraw. The number of shells coming over was much reduced.

I stayed long enough to watch the beginning of Jonesy's attack, which ended the lull in the fighting, to watch the Indiana regiment swing out into the open beyond the enemy's line of defense, then move into the woods with a rush and a crash of musketry. The troops already in the wood pushed forward at the same time; the fighting was heavy and still growing as I started back.

The sound was with me all the way back to the center, but soon after I reported, it began to diminish in volume, and half an hour after the opening of the attack we held the entire South Wood. As the sound of the firing died away, we could hear the ring of axes. Having taken the position, Jonesy meant to hang on to it.

McGraw's preparations were now complete, but in the meantime the situation had changed. We had been given time to bring our formidable artillery into position, and we now held the South Wood. Consequently the heavy attack straight up the road planned by McGraw, which earlier had appeared so menacing, would now have to face the massive artillery fire of Saint Chamans' line of guns, and would be taken in flank at the same time from the South Wood.

They could undoubtedly see this as well as we could, but General McGraw was an obstinate man, and the movement was begun. We could see a shaking in the willows along the line of the brook, as though the trees themselves were going to march against us, then swarms of armed men emerging from the willows and ranging themselves in long lines. We held our fire until an entire brigade was across and forming on our side of the brook, then with a stunning burst of sound our twenty-four guns opened fire with rapid successive rounds of canister and grape. When the smoke began to clear away, we could see that the shattered remnant of the brigade was being hastily withdrawn.

This brief advance and withdrawal was over by quarter after twelve, and during the next hour and a half there was little further action. The guns kept up an intermittent duel with the batteries across the way, and there were occasional bursts of firing along the skirmish line, but that was all. At this time McGraw began shifting troops over to his right. Some of the more optimistic souls around the general thought that McGraw had had enough, and was beginning to retreat.

The general smiled at them. "Nothing so easy, gentlemen. General McGraw is a stubborn man. He's tried our right, and he's tried our center. Now he's going to see if his luck will be any better on the left, and I think we had better take measures to meet him. He's going to put everything he's got into this one."

McGraw's concentration was partly hidden from us by the fringe of trees along the brook, and completely hidden by the dense patch of woods across the brook and north of the road which we referred to as the North Wood. This was somewhat larger than the corresponding South Wood, which was on our side of the brook and to the right of the road. The North Wood reached down almost as far as the brook in places, and at the nearest point, where our lines curved out around a wooded spur pushing out from the ridge, it was hardly more than sixty yards away. Beyond the North Wood the valley opened out for another half mile of open meadow, then the opposing hillsides curved around to meet in a high ridge which enclosed the head of the valley.

While McGraw was shifting his forces, we were moving over to meet him, extending our line constantly to the left until finally, of the seven regiments originally on the right, only two remained south of the road.

About half-past one Gavin sent in one of his staff officers to report his position and ask for orders. He was just coming up to the crossroads about a mile back. From that point, if he came on directly, he could be up in another twenty minutes. The alternative was to take the other branch of the road, which angled over to the north, and come into the road Jonesy had been on in the morning at a point about half a mile north of our present position. This would bring him in on McGraw's flank and rear, but would add another two miles to the march, with a corresponding delay in the time of his arrival.

The general's reply was positive, and without hesitation: he wanted General Ross on McGraw's flank. Since we were expecting an attack in force, he would be grateful if General Ross would press his march as much as possible. Without exhausting his men, of course.

This was about twenty minutes before McGraw renewed the battle with his attack on our left. During the period between the repulse of the tentative attack on our center and the opening of the attack on the left, there were only two incidents that seemed to be of any importance, either at the time, or later on.

The first of these concerned Billy Roth. Billy was never at his best on horseback. On a horse, his clothes always looked too big for him; his hands were lost in his sleeves, and his big campaign hat seemed about to come down around his ears. He never knew what to do with his sword, and at any gait faster than a walk he bounced around with all the grace of a sack of potatoes.

Billy had been following the general around, not being of any particular use, just being present. At this time—about one o'clock—most of the members of the staffs, Billy's as well as ours, were absent on various errands. Only James and Robert Saint Chamans were with the general, and I had just returned and was waiting for orders. The immediate question was, which regiment to leave in the South Wood, Jonesy's Missouri regiment, or Roth's 35th Indiana, and this depended on the relative shape the two regiments were in.

Without giving the matter any thought, General Pack turned to Billy Roth and said, "Wilfred, you had better go over and talk to General Jones. He may want to keep both of them. At any rate, you can decide the matter between you."

With that, he turned away and went on talking to James and Saint Chamans.

Jonesy was still in the South Wood, and, now that the attack had been broken up, the obvious way to get there was straight across, in front of our lines. It was not a particularly dangerous route; several of us had already been over it. At the same time, they were still throwing shells at us, and there was a certain amount of long-range rifle fire from the sharpshooters along the brook, so that it wasn't exactly a comfortable ride, either. There had been some unpleasantly near misses, and it definitely was a place where a man could get himself killed.

Billy gave the general a white-faced look of appeal, but the general had already turned away, and there was nothing to do but go on. Billy started out well enough. He even kept his horse at a trot, with Billy lumping along on top of the horse at that unhurried gait. Unfortunately, after he had gone a couple of hundred yards, a shell burst in front of him. It wasn't especially close and none of the fragments came anywhere near him, but lamentably, it was enough for Billy, and he turned back.

General Pack looked at him in surprise as he rode up. Billy swallowed hard, and said, "Excuse me, General, but I'm not quite clear as to what you want me to do in case General Jones wants to keep both regiments. Shall I tell him that my orders are that one of them is to be sent in any case?"

This wasn't a bad try: it didn't sound unreasonable. But it wasn't good enough.

General Pack looked at the set, white face and the shaking hands, and said, "Yes, tell him that, General." Then, with reproof in his voice, "I'm surprised at you, Wilfred. General officers aren't expected to take unnecessary chances. Go around the back way, sir. I don't want my officers killed for nothing."

Billy looked quite happy as he rode back over the hill. Robert Saint Chamans watched him go with a delighted smile on his face, and James said mildly, "Sometimes I wonder that you don't send him a little farther back, General. Say as far back as Cincinnati."

The general smiled. "Yes, or back to Washington. Back to his seat in Congress, where he can tell us how to run the war." He shrugged his shoulders. "Who would they send me to replace him? And if you take the brigade, where am I going to get a chief of staff? Not that you can't have the brigade any time you want it."

James shook his head. "That's very kind of you, sir, but I'm quite satisfied where I am. I think I see what you're talking about."

The general was gratified. "Yes, of course you do. There is no point in humiliating the man. It would destroy his usefulness altogether. And I suspect that both of you underestimate General Roth. Actually, Wilfred is a man of parts. He's an excellent administrator. He's even a little of a general so long as there aren't any enemy troops around to upset his thinking. He got the brigade off very well this morning, if you noticed. No, the only trouble with Wilfred is that he's a born coward. Obviously he doesn't belong here, but I could name you a lot of others who don't belong here, either. Some of them with more than one star."

The other incident was also trifling. There had been intermittent firing on the skirmish line all along. This firing was heaviest and most sustained, as you would expect, where the lines approached each other most closely, between the salient and the line of Confederate sharpshooters in the willows along the brook. I had gone down with a message of some kind for Major Beatty of the 11th Michigan, in the salient, and had stopped to talk to the major. While we were talking, there was a sudden whoop of laughter from the men along the firing line.

This was totally unexpected. The situation was fairly tense. In spite of our temporary successes up to this time, we were still largely outnumbered, and expected a heavy attack at any moment. The men were bracing themselves to meet the attack, and on the whole were quiet and rather grim. The major and I looked at each other in astonishment, and went down to see what was going on.

It was a dog, the inevitable dog that appears to disrupt the dignity of public occasions. This one was a big, clumsy puppy, part collie and part hound and the rest miscellaneous farm dog. He was cavorting about the open field between the two lines with his tail in the air, wildly excited by the strange insects that kept buzzing past him, chasing them with clownish exuberance, snapping at the sound of their passage. Men from both sides began to whistle to him and call, Here, doggie! Here, Rover! Here, Fido! He ignored them and went on chasing the fascinating insects, until one of the vicious little things bit him, bowled him over, and left him stunned.

Suddenly all of us were sobered, and sorry about the dog. I wanted to go out and get him—he was closer to our side than theirs, just at the foot of the slope—but knew better than to expose myself to the fire of the sharpshooters along the brook.

Apparently I was not the only one who felt this impulse, for some softhearted fool was over the breastworks and bounding down the slope, someone familiar and very big, someone I knew well. He was bending over the dog—it was Colin, as I might have known—then he was coming back up the slope with the dog in his arms. The firing fell away then stopped entirely, as though everybody was holding his breath, until Colin and the dog tumbled over the breastworks and into our lines.

The dog had not been seriously hurt, for later in the afternoon I saw him following Colin around happily, wagging his tail, and being petted by everyone.

The attack that had been building up in and behind the North Wood came a little before two. The great difficulty in meeting this new attack lay in finding a place for the artillery. The advanced position of the North Wood narrowed the field greatly on our left, and the problem was to find a location far enough back for the guns, far enough out of musket range so the gun crews wouldn't all be killed by the first volley. This was the first half of the problem; the second half was getting the guns there.

Major Saint Chamans had gone over to the left as soon as McGraw's purpose became evident, and found a rather cramped space for twelve guns on the far side of the salient. Afterwards he had taken our chief of engineers with him, and had gone around in back of the ridge to look for a possible route. They found that a road would have to be cut over the ridge, a task that would take at least two hours. This was certainly more time than McGraw was going to give us.

The only possible alternative was to run the guns around the outside, through the sixty-yard bottleneck between the tip of the salient and the brook. This was obviously a risky business, since the rebel sharpshooters were not only hidden by the willows, but were also protected by the banks of the little stream, which were three or four feet high, and formed a natural breastwork.

Once the decision was made, the two batteries of twelve-pounders, Fairbanks and Harper, were pulled out of line, and the two batteries of three-inch rifles were swung around to a forty-five-degree angle, enfilading the brook to that extent. Brock had been sent for, and when he came up with his rifled guns, they were put in line still farther to the right. Three companies of the 17th Missouri were brought over to protect the guns, and they wormed their way almost down to the smoldering ruins of the farmhouse.

The firing along the skirmish line had become heavier while

these preparations were being made, and McGraw's line of battle was beginning to show at the edge of the woods. There was no time to lose, and Saint Chamans began firing while Brock was still getting his guns into line, plastering the line of the brook and shredding the trees with canister and grape.

One of the gunners said to me, "Maybe we can't hit them fellows along the creek, but we sure as hell can spoil their aim." I could see what he meant.

With the first crash of the guns, Fairbanks got under way, his first gun moving out and rounding the point at a full gallop, with the second close on its heels, and the others following. It looked like a Roman chariot race. They rounded the corner at full speed, then slowed down to a trot as soon as they were out of danger, and wheeled into line, one after the other.

As soon as Fairbanks' six guns were in line, Harper began coming around, Gareth Harper leading the way and lining up the guns as they came in. In the meantime, while our guns were engaged in shelling the line of the brook, McGraw had moved a three-gun battery out into the open and was firing at the guns racing around the point. After the first few shots, three of Brock's guns were shifted around to engage them, and succeeded in putting one of McGraw's guns out of action. The others, however, kept on firing and barely missed Harper's third gun, came close enough to kill one of the crew of the fourth, and with a preposterously lucky, or unlucky, shot, made a square hit on the limber chest of the fifth gun and blew up the ninety rounds of ammunition it was carrying.

The result was appalling. There was a great burst of flame and a deafening explosion that hit us like a sledge hammer, together with the tearing sound of shell fragments ripping through the trees, and the cries of the men who had been hit. For a full minute or more the front line was completely hidden in smoke. As the smoke slowly drifted away, we could make out the shattered bodies of men and horses, the disintegrated fragments of the gun carriage, and the gun barrel itself, blown forty feet away, past the dead horses and broken carriage of the number-six gun. At the same time, dim figures began to appear through the smoke, groping their way towards us in small groups, followed by larger groups, and finally by a solid line.

The explosion of the limber chest and the beginning of McGraw's attack were simultaneous, as though the explosion had been a prearranged signal. As the smoke lifted, the rebel line, which had been coming on slowly through the haze, raised a yell like a Comanche war whoop, and broke into a trot. A volley from the 11th Michigan staggered them briefly, then they came on again.

The guns were already in trouble. Fairbanks, on the left, was firing double-shotted rounds of canister as fast as his men could load, and was keeping a semicircle clear in front of him. Harper, with his four remaining guns, was protecting Fairbanks' right and keeping the ground clear in his own front, but his right was open and gravely threatened by the Confederate line, which was beginning to appear out of the smoke.

General Pack watched this situation developing, then beckoned to Jack Maitland, who was the nearest responsible officer, and said to him, "I think we had better get those guns clear, Colonel. You had better take the Illinois regiment in with you, too. Colonel Campbell's regiment, isn't it? Anyway, take both of them in, the 11th Michigan and the Illinois regiment. And don't worry about the gap in the line. We'll take care of it."

Harper was in real trouble by the time Jack Maitland reached the line. He had cleared away the threat to his right by wheeling two of his guns around and firing rounds of double canister, frightfully effective rounds, into the swarm of men who were almost on top of his guns. But while he was freeing his right, he had left open a ninety-degree angle of dead ground between the guns he had wheeled around and the pair still facing forward, and the rebels in the second line were pouring into the angle. They were checked briefly by a blast of canister from the number-two gun, but the men around the edges of the blast came on without pause, and a moment later there was a milling hand-to-hand fight around the guns, with bayonets, sabers, revolvers, clubs and fists.

At this moment Jack Maitland came charging down the hill with the 11th Michigan, while the 24th Illinois moved down to the edge of the woods in support. The charge was brilliantly successful at first, and the two center guns began firing again. They had time for only a round or two before the third line of the attack came washing up over them, pushing the Michigan regiment back almost to the foot of the ridge. Jack Maitland rallied the regiment and held it steady while Colonel Campbell brought the 24th Illinois down, then the two regiments charged forward with a shout and cleared the guns again. This time, though, there was no one to work them: the gunners were either dead or dispersed, and Harper's guns were merely a trophy to be fought over.

In the meantime, James had returned after bringing up the 16th Kentucky, and Jonesy had come over from the right. Jonesy had a hole in his hat and a rent in his checked shirt, and he was grumbling about a horse that had been killed five minutes earlier—a damn' good horse, a damn' expensive horse—until he became absorbed in what was going on in front.

At the moment we seemed to have succeeded in pushing the enemy back: how far back, and for how long, it was impossible to tell. The haze of smoke had become thicker and it was hard to make out exactly what was happening, but we could see that our men had pushed out beyond the guns and were firing into the smoke ahead. Over on the right, around the corner of the salient, Saint Chamans' line of guns was still firing heavily, keeping down McGraw's artillery fire and chewing up the supporting lines.

To escape this fire, McGraw was shifting his attack still farther to our left, showing more and more troops in the fields north of the wood, in support of the line that was already across the brook and menacing our left. Jonesy eyed this mass of troops moving in on us.

"Seems to me we could use our third brigade about this

time," he remarked, raising his voice over the sound of the firing. "Where the hell is Ross, anyway?"

"He should be up almost any time now," the general replied mildly. He reached for his watch and looked at it without anxiety. "Certainly within half an hour."

"I hope to God we can hold out that long."

General Pack snapped his watch shut and put it back in his pocket. "I think we can manage," he said easily.

The line on the left was coming on steadily. I was watching it with something like dismay, when out of the corner of my eye I caught a sudden glittering over on the extreme left of our line. I looked over in that direction and saw a long line of horsemen coming out of the wood and forming in the open, with the sun glittering on their drawn sabers. They came out at a walk and formed in two long double lines, turned somewhat inward to face the flank of the enemy's line of infantry. There was a momentary halt while a cavalry officer—Dick Ross, recognizable even at this distance—rode rapidly down the front of the line. He wheeled his horse around at the center of the line, looked over his men, then with his saber glittering in his hand, stood up in his stirrups and pointed forward. The lines of horsemen began to move, first at a walk, then at a trot, and finally, gaining weight and momentum, at a full gallop.

It was wonderful. I drew in a deep breath and felt my heart swell with admiration, and I was telling myself that it was the most magnificent thing I had ever seen in my life, when I heard Jonesy's voice behind me, rough with anger and incredulity.

"For Christ's sake! What does that damn' fool think he's doing?"

James turned his head. "Oh, my God!" he said with the same air of shocked disbelief. Then, with resignation, "I suppose we'll have to get him out of it somehow."

General Pack agreed. "I'm afraid we will. Will you see about it, James? If you please. Take Persant and Dove. We'll fill in."

He turned away and addressed Jonesy.

"Go over and see Major Saint Chamans, will you please, General? See what you can do over on the right. If you can get a battery, or even a couple of guns, far enough out to rake their line of advance, it will give General McGraw something to think about."

Neither James nor Jonesy waited to see what the results of the cavalry charge were going to be. For a short time it looked as though it were going to be a smashing success. The line of infantry which had looked so overwhelming was stopped dead in its tracks, while the rebel officers tried frantically to change front to meet the mass of calvary sweeping down on their right. They were in the midst of the change, the ranks disorganized, facing neither one way nor the other, when the full weight of the cavalry charge hit them. The entire right brigade, the right half of the line, was crumpled up, and the extreme right of the cavalry, overlapping the line, pressed along the front of the second brigade.

This was the extent of our success. The inner brigade, with more time to maneuver, succeeded in throwing back a line to face the cavalry; and Dick's second line of horsemen, piling in on top of the first, was itself taken in flank by a second line of infantry coming up in support of the first. In addition, though the formation of the first brigade had been broken up by the sheer weight and momentum of the charge, its casualties had not been heavy; with support at hand, the men recovered quickly from their brief demoralization, and continued to fight as individuals.

All this happened very fast. First there was an ordered line of cavalry attacking an ordered line of infantry; then there was a moment of anticipatory disorganization in the infantry, followed by the heavy impact of the line of charging horsemen. After that, there was simply chaos—a boiling melee of slashing swords and gunfire, horsemen and men on foot, dismounted cavalrymen and loose horses, a struggling mass without flanks or front or rear.

A third line came out of the wood, and with this added weight the mass began to push slowly in our direction, and to join the fight directly in front of us around the guns. Just at this moment there was another beautiful sight, the 34th Indiana and the 43rd Ohio moving out in line, with James at one end of the line and Colonel Persant, of the 43rd, at the other, both mounted and holding their horses down to a walk to keep pace with the infantry.

The general was standing perfectly motionless with his hands clasped behind his back, watching the line move out past Fairbank's guns and into the haze, which was now very thick. A moment later I noticed that General Pack was no longer staring intently into the smoke, but was looking at something beyond the area of the fighting and farther to the left. I looked in the same direction, and saw that more troops were coming out of the wood and deploying in the open fields to the north. The general kept his eyes on them for another minute or two, then looked at his watch again.

He snapped the case shut and said to me in his usual calm, untroubled voice, "John, will you kindly go find Colonel Pellam and tell him to bring up his regiment, and to put it in on the left of Colonel Powell? And I think you might as well tell him that he can expect to be heavily attacked soon after he arrives."

"Yes, sir," I said, and waited for him to go on.

He had been about to say something further, but had changed his mind. "Let me know when the regiment is up, John. I'll go over and talk to Colonel Pellam myself."

As a matter of fact, I know perfectly well what he had started to say. The 10th Iowa, Colonel Pellam's regiment, was the last regiment we had in reserve. Not only that, but it had been badly chewed up in the morning's fighting, and had been ordered over the hill and into reserve for just that reason. Ordering up the 10th Iowa was scraping the bottom of the barrel. That was the part of the message the general thought better of, and preferred to deliver in person: that they were going to be heavily attacked, and wouldn't be supported because there was nobody left to support them.

The regiment was over to the left and behind the ridge. There wasn't anything even resembling a road that led in that direction, but the wood was fairly open, and I rode over to the left and up the slope at a trot, with my head on one side or the other of my horse's neck most of the time, ducking low branches. As I reached the crest of the ridge I glanced back, and saw that the tangled melee in the center had sorted itself out into two opposing lines, dimly visible through the smoke. The heavy body of enemy troops which McGraw had deployed north of the wood, the force which General Pack was bracing his lines to meet, was still in the same place, some distance to the rear of the battle. This astonished me, for I would have sworn they had already begun to advance. I pulled up short to see what was happening. For half a moment I had a dreamlike feeling of unreality, as though something had slipped, as though events were moving backwards; and when the troops literally began to move backwards, I sat paralyzed, completely disbelieving what I saw. The line was moving backwards; they had their guns behind them, and were firing them in the wrong direction.

A moment later my mind began to function again, and it was perfectly clear what was happening. I felt like whooping with excitement. I could hear artillery fire from a new direction, the northeast, and could see gunsmoke rising in the woods on the far side of the valley. Then I could see our men coming out of the woods and sweeping down the hillside in beautiful order, the two Wisconsin regiments leading, and Gavin himself riding with them on his big white horse.

It was a beautiful sight. It was marvelous, and it was almost the last thing I saw for some time. The very last thing was a tiny black speck that I saw out of the corner of my eye, a black thing that was coming towards me at a monstrous rate of speed. I knew I ought to do something about it, to duck or move out of the way, but I didn't have time. And the last thing of all was a great sheet of fire and a blinding wave of pain that quite suddenly winked out into blackness.

The fact that the shellburst didn't kill me was one of those minor miracles that are a commonplace on every battlefield. My horse apparently took the main force of the burst, and was almost literally blown to pieces. The clothing on my entire right side, from collar to boot heels, was shredded by fragments of shell, and I had nineteen separate wounds on that side of my body. There was a long gash under my cheekbone, and another in the scalp above my ear where a fragment grazed my skull and with another quarter of an inch would have taken off the top of my head. Strangely enough, out of all this carnage, the most serious and painful wound I had was the broken arm I got in falling from my horse.

The appearance of our third brigade decided the battle. McGraw's original superiority had been whittled down until we were fighting on equal terms, with both sides equally weary after a slugging match that had been going on for eight hours. With the arrival of our third brigade, McGraw was not only outnumbered and called upon to meet fresh troops with his weary men, but was taken off balance as well, as we came in on his right flank and rear. No troops could have been expected to hold up under those conditions, and McGraw's two divisions simply disintegrated and ceased to exist as an organized force.

This was on Saturday afternoon. Saturday, September twentieth. General Pack left Gavin and the first brigade in charge of the battlefield and the prisoners, and marched seven miles into Tarsus with the other two brigades the same evening. He moved out at four o'clock Sunday morning and surprised Taylor on the march, coming up to join McGraw, and ran over him in a sharp little battle that lasted forty-five minutes, capturing more than half his force, and dispersing the rest.

On Monday afternoon he caught up with George Ruthven and defeated him in a running fight that went on until after dark. Jonesy and the cavalry kept up the pursuit on the following day, and reached the river on Wednesday morning, half an hour after Ruthven and what was left of his command had crossed.

This was exactly a week after we had crossed the Blackwater to open the campaign. We had inflicted a crushing defeat on

McGraw and driven both his principal lieutenants out of the district. We held Tarsus and Glamorgan County and the entire district down to the river. We had reached our objectives, accomplished what we set out to do, and finished the campaign.

II

Chapter 1

I remember the month of October that year—October in Tarsus—as a season among the blessed. It was a season of great happiness, when each separate day was a marvelous privilege in itself, with the promise of still more marvelous adventures and still greater happiness just over the horizon, tomorrow, or the day after: a season with enough delight in it to color and perfume a whole lifetime.

All kinds of things converged to give it this intensity. This was in the earlier part of the war, when we were fighting on even terms, with no crushing superiority on either side, and nothing at all inevitable about the outcome: a period of dubious battle, with the outcome depending on ourselves, on the strategy of our generals, and on the fighting qualities of our troops.

What we had, we had earned. We had won a battle and a campaign by hard fightng and long marches and superior generalship. Now we were resting after our labors, and enjoying a well-earned season of tranquillity. We were proud of ourselves, and of the general, and of each other.

The state of morale in the command was tremendous. In a dozen different ways, all of them highly profane, the men were saying, Just give the Old Man a couple more commands like this one, and, by God, the rest of the boys can go home. We'll finish up the job for them. Every line captain was positive that he had the best damned company in the outfit. The men, though they acknowledged the merits of others, were all of them positive, by God, that they belonged to the best damned company, and the best damned regiment in the command.

They were even proud of the staff. They knew that three of us had been wounded, and they had seen us on the field in the midst of the fighting, so for a week or two they forgot the usual gibes at the soft and easy life we were supposed to lead. Even Billy Roth was included in the general good feeling. The men took a perverse pride in exaggerating his lack of military qualities, and ended by excusing him: Hell, nobody ever said he was a soldier, anyway. And when a rumor started that he was to be replaced by James or Jack Maitland—both of them extremely popular with the troops—the men protested. They didn't want any change. They liked it the way it was.

The general feeling of pride in the command was one I fully shared in. I admired the general and the men around him more than I have ever been able to admire anyone since, and even now in remembering them I still find them admirable. Some of them were fine soldiers. All of them were brave, and some of them were outstandingly brave, with a conspicuous shining valor that was reflected in the deference and admiration of the men.

This quality came out in different ways. Under fire, General Pack seemed to grow in stature, to be more than life-size, and to control the battle from on high. Looking at his untroubled serenity, you had the impression that he had the battle in his hands, that everything on the field was according to his will, and that even a repulse, a temporary failure, was simply a part of his design.

His nephew, Dick Ross, was at the opposite extreme. Normally full of careless good humor, with the sound of the first shots you could see anger mounting in him; his eyebrows came together in a scowl, and as the blood mounted to his head his face slowly turned the color of heated bronze. He fought all his battles in a state of anger, a clearheaded, sharp-eyed anger, which mounted as the opposition grew stronger; and in really heavy fighting he led his troops with an unbridled fury that was both formidable and effective.

My uncle's style was at still another extreme: it was a game he was playing, a complex and dangerous game for enormous stakes—pain and death and mutilation were a part of them. He played the game superbly, with confidence and great skill, and like any expert—horseman, cardplayer, diplomat—he appeared to enjoy the challenge to his skill. Danger he found exciting, and he was cheerful and wholly at ease on the battlefield.

I think they all had something of this, in one form or another—Dick's two brothers, and Jonesy, and Robert Saint Chamans, and Jack Maitland, and all the others—whether it appeared as coolness, or exhilaration, or anger.

I suppose the prospect of battle, or the sound of battle ahead of us, affected others much the way it affected me. It was like a plunge into cold water, abominably cold, freezing water. I dreaded the plunge, and the first few minutes were even worse than I had feared; then at some point I forgot myself, and fear was dissolved in activity and excitement until danger itself was almost a pleasure.

As I discovered, as many others had discovered before me, it wasn't whether you were afraid or not that mattered, because fear was taken for granted: it was what you did in the presence of fear, or what fear did to you. If it stimulated you, sharpened your perceptions and your judgment, you were a soldier, no matter how badly your knees were shaking. And if it had the contrary effect, slowed down your mind and your judgment, you weren't, no matter how good your training.

I suppose these were the conclusions I came to after the Willow Run battle, during the week or so that I was lying in bed in the Robertson house in Tarsus. Some of the conclusions, at any rate, because all kinds of strange and wonderful ideas were running through my head.

One of the strangest of them was a sense of gratitude towards the small black object I had seen out of the corner of my eye, which came towards me at a monstrous rate of speed and turned into a sheet of flame. The gratitude was towards the shell and the gunner who had fired it in such a way that I was wounded but not killed, and I was grateful for the wound because it was my entrance fee: I had gone through the ordeal and come out on the other side, and was now a proven member of the brotherhood. It was a good brotherhood: I still feel that it was an honor to belong to it. To be looked up to, to be admired and trusted by twelve thousand brave men is no mean thing at any time and place. I was twenty-one at the time, and at that age there are still heroes in the land. These men were heroes and paladins, and it was a great thing to be made one of them.

I would have given my right eye for the privilege if it had been required of me. Fortunately, my wounds were nowhere near so drastic. I had been heavily bruised, and had a large number of superficial cuts and lacerations; I had a broken arm that was splinted and immobilized; and I had suffered a concussion from one or the other of the shell fragments that grazed my head, and was unconscious for twenty-four hours. I had been hit about three in the afternoon—Saturday afternoon—and it was about three in the afternoon on Sunday when I came to.

It was only a very dim sort of consciousness that I came back to for three or four days. I was lying between clean sheets in a large and comfortable bed. There was a fire in the room, a cheerful wood fire, with leaping flames and glowing coals, giving out a pleasant warmth. It was in a fireplace across the room, where I could see it over the foot of the bed. When I turned my head to look over at the window it went away, but when I turned back it was there again, and I could contemplate it as long as I wanted to.

The fire was not always merely cheerful. It changed its shape and its mood. At times it became bold and exciting, and swelled into a great pyramid of flame with small figures moving around it. At other times, cooled and circumscribed, it became the red disc of a low sun: this was pure desolation, frozen ground and gaunt bare trees against a red winter sun. Or it shrank, and became nothing more than a row of small pointed flames. The scene then became portentous, for some grave cause was being tried: James was there, proud and defiant, facing two majestic figures, one kingly, the other old and wise. At the beginning I was filled with sorrow because I was on the other side, but the roles and the characters shifted around until it was no longer possible to tell who was the judge and who was on trial, and the scene ended in mere confusion and drifted out of sight.

Another kind of confusion occurred when it was a house that was on fire, and it was the courthouse that was burning (a great event of my boyhood), and we were all running to see the fire; but most of us were on horseback, and it was not the courthouse, after all, but a farmhouse that was burning, sending up a great pillar of smoke, and I knew how this one was going to end. Sure enough, a small black object was hurtling towards me, the fire vanished suddenly, and the world went black and empty. After a brief moment—this succession alone was invariable—I heard the sound of distant church bells, and felt a deep and wonderfully comforting sensation of peace; I looked out over green meadows in the early morning and saw cows grazing and felt the dew on the grass; in the distance were the church steeples, the trees and gardens and houses, of a town built on a hill.

The origin of these hallucinations—there were more of them—is plain enough in some cases, and difficult or impossible to locate in others. In my pastoral vision of Tarsus, or the Elysian fields, there was no fire, but with this exception the fire flickered brightly in my bedroom all day and all night. I was astonished and half incredulous on Wednesday, when I came out of my fever, at finding that a chest of drawers stood where the fireplace had been, and that the actual fireplace, in an entirely different part of the room, was clean and empty, and had evidently not been used for months.

From Saturday until Wednesday these feverish visions, each with its aura of emotion, followed each other endlessly through my head. Running along beside them, on a parallel track, were other impressions that came into my mind from outside, dim and confused visions of reality.

When I looked over at the window on Sunday afternoon, I saw that it was a clear summer day. There was a tree outside my window with its leaves rustling gently in a light summer breeze; in the far distance was a hazy line of blue mountains.

Dr. Ferguson was in the room with me, a big man in a frock coat, fifty years old, bearded, and kind. He was looking down at his watch, and he had my wrist in his hand, and his finger was on my pulse.

When I opened my eyes, he was counting. He saw that I had awakened, but he went on counting for another thirty seconds, then let my wrist fall and said, "Well, John, how do you feel?"

This was a hard question. I seemed to hurt all over. Nothing was very clear in my head, and I was weak and sick, yet somewhere, far in the back of my head, I felt wonderful. I thought the question over for quite a long time, and, when I finally had my answer ready, was astonished at the slow, laborious effort it required.

"Pretty good. Pretty bad. Both."

The doctor snapped his watch shut and smiled at me. "You're doing fine, John," he said. "We'll have you out of here in a few days. As good as ever."

After he had gone, I looked over at the window and watched the leaves twisting back and forth on their stems and shimmering in the light breeze, and decided that it was a beautiful tree and that I loved it, then drifted off to sleep again.

Towards evening, Jake Leslie, our learned adjutant, came in to see me, and sat by the head of the bed and quoted Horace. This was pleasant. I was glad to see his leathery wrinkled face and his bald head, and I knew that he was a friend of mine, but it was a little too much trouble to remember exactly who he was and where I had known him.

I slept for a little while after he had gone, and when I opened my eyes again it was dusk, and I could see a rectangle of clear blue sky through my window. Instead of growing darker, the rectangle of sky grew paler, and presently the moon came up. Again, much later, there was a white full moon in the sky; a faint breath of wind stirred the leaves of the tree outside my window, and the night was so bright that I could distinguish the greenness of the leaves. Finally, when I awoke just before dawn, the sky was a pure luminous blue and the morning star was high over the horizon, shining with un-earthly brightness and purity, the most beautiful thing I ever saw in my life, beautiful beyond tears, tranquil and blessed and remote.

Monday and Tuesday were hot September days. I still had a good deal of fever, and dozed all through the day and lay awake with my visions at night. Dr. Ferguson was in and out during both days, and Jake Leslie came in two or three times. Towards evening on Tuesday, my uncle and Colin Ross came in and tried to tell me what had been going on, but gave up when they found that I didn't remember the Barney McGraw they were talking about. I had heard the name, but I kept thinking it was somebody on General Pack's staff, and that made everything they said rather confusing. They gave up after a few minutes. James went out, and Colin simply sat with me for an hour or two. After he had gone I dozed, then lay awake and watched the moon rise, then dozed again, and finally fell into a heavy sleep.

When I awakened, the sun was pouring into the room and it was the middle of the morning. I was soaked in sweat and weaker than a pup, and my whole right side shrieked with pain when I tried to move, but the diffused pain and the fever were gone, my mind was clear again, and on the whole—so long as I didn't try to move—I felt fine.

This was on Wednesday morning. From then on my re-covery was rapid. Later in the day an orderly helped me over to a chair by the window, and I sat up for an hour. The following day I was able to get up by myself, and spent most of the day sitting at the window. By Sunday I was able to get dressed, with some help, and to go downstairs, with my arm in a sling and a rather theatrical bandage around my head.

It took me some time to realize just where I was. For the first few days it didn't matter, and it was only at the end of that time that it occurred to me to be surprised at being in a house instead of in a field hospital, at having a roof over my head instead of canvas. As I became fully conscious, I found there was more to it than that: I was lying between fine linen sheets in a large mahogany bed; I was in a large and handsomely furnished bedroom, with a flowered carpet on the floor, mahogany chests and dressing tables, crisp white curtains at the windows, and a marble fireplace. The water bottle on my night table was a fine crystal decanter, and during the few days that my meals were brought up to me, they were brought up on a silver tray.

Sometime in the afternoon I had the orderly help me over to a chair by the window, and had my first look at the town. My first look, at any rate, since Colin and I had seen it from a distance in the early morning the week before. From the cove in the hills we had seen that the town covered a low hill on the opposite bank of the river, with the river curving around the base of the hill. From that vantage point the most conspicuous landmarks of the town had been the bell tower of the courthouse, and close by, the white columns and red brick of a large Georgian mansion.

This was obviously the house I was in. In a second-floor bedroom on the east side, facing the courthouse square. From my window I could see a broad lawn enclosed by a low iron fence. On the right I could see the main street, and, down a block, the row of two-story brick buildings which housed the stores and offices of the little town. Beyond the low fence a cross street ran past the square and down to the river; across the street, in the middle of the square, the solid red brick and limestone of the courthouse was visible through the trees.

It was a warm September afternoon, and the courthouse square was dappled with sunlight. The street was almost deserted. Halfway down the block a bony gray horse was tethered in front of a store; a ragged Negro was dozing on the box of a decrepit farm wagon which was being pulled at the slowest possible walk by a very tired old horse; a woman in a sunbonnet was crossing the street; and two of our men, in blue uniforms, their caps pushed back, were sitting quietly on a bench facing the street, apparently taking in the sights.

General Pack had established his headquarters in the house I was in, the only very large house in town. It was the seat of the local magnate, Judge Alistair Robertson, who owned most of Glamorgan County. The judge had been a prominent public figure before the war, United States Senator for two terms, and during Pierce's Administration, Minister to the Netherlands. He was said to have been opposed to secession, and to have retired to private life at the outbreak of the war.

We met the Robertson family one by one during the course of the first couple of weeks. I had begun to come downstairs at the beginning of the second week. In the morning, when it was still cool, I had a chair carried out on the lawn, and sat in the sun and read. Later in the morning, as the sun grew too warm, I had the chair carried back to the pillared veranda on the north side of the house, overlooking the long shaded lawn which extended all the way down to the river.

The first time I saw the Judge was the first morning I was out on the lawn. I was around at the side of the house, in the sun, with my stiff right leg out in front of me, resting on a stool. I was feeling good that morning, feeling the placid contentment of the convalescent. I was reading a beautiful, morocco-bound copy of the *Odyssey* that I had found in the house, reading a line or two at a time, then simply basking in the sun for ten minutes before going on to the next line.

This placid mood was broken by the sound of a voice about three feet away from me, a sonorous voice, full of anger and authority.

"Young man, where did you get that book?"

I hadn't heard anyone approach, and I was startled. I looked up and saw a man about sixty, dressed in black, clean-shaven, with thick gray hair and a deeply lined face. He was slight, even a little frail, and not especially tall, but he had more dignity than any six-footer I ever saw.

I answered his question in a low, guilty mumble. "I got it in the house, sir." I sounded like a schoolboy caught stealing jam.

"You're being pretty free with other people's property, aren't you?" He paused, then added bitterly, "Just like a Yankee, to steal a book he can't even read."

He went on without waiting for an answer, towards a small wicket gate on the courthouse side of the grounds. About the time he reached the gate I began to recover from the over-

powering manner and the reprimand, and to resent the statement. At the same time he paused, with his hand on the gate,
then turned around and came back.

This time I was ready for him, but what he said was,
"Young man, I owe you an apology." His manner was still
cold, and I had the impression the apology was meant as much
for himself as for me. "It's not your fault that Mr. Pack has
taken my house. Furthermore, I dislike talk about Yankees,
and patriotic rant in general. And I don't suppose you would
have taken the book if you couldn't read it."

"I was going to tell you that, sir," I said. "Also, that you can
read a book without stealing it."

"Yes. Yes, of course," he agreed. "That was another one of
the foolish, angry things that people go about saying, these
days." He glanced down at the book, and his face softened.
"*Andra moi ennepe, Mousa,* eh? It's a fine book you're reading, young man. I wish you joy of it."

He nodded a little less coldly, and let himself out by the
wicket gate at the side.

Two or three days later I saw his son for the first time,
Colonel Alexander Blair Robertson, usually called Blair. The
general had gone out early that morning, and had taken most
of the staff with him. James was in the general's office, formerly the Judge's study, and was writing a letter. I had
stopped to talk to him, then had gone across the hall to the
library to look for something less exacting than Homer to
read. While I was standing there, confused by the multitude
of books along the inner wall, wondering which of them I
wanted to read and whether I wanted to read at all, I heard
an altercation of some kind on the porch, by the door leading
to the street.

I put my head around the corner to see what was going on,
and saw that the sentry was standing in front of the door with
his musket across his chest, barring the way to a man on
crutches. The man on crutches was in his late twenties,
slender, with dark eyes and a thin face, and bore a strong
family resemblance to the Judge. He was wearing white cotton
trousers and a long dark coat, and he had a stiff leg, evidently

artificial. I hadn't heard what he told the sentry, but only the tone of voice, which was one of suppressed rage.

The sentry, a farm boy from one of the Illinois regiments, sounded harried. "I can't help it, mister. I got my orders," he was saying. "Nobody comes in here without he gets permission."

At the same time, James appeared in the opposite doorway. It was a hot day, and he was wearing a white shirt, open at the neck, with the sleeves rolled up, and he still had a pen in his hand. When he saw what had happened, he went to the door and said pleasantly, "Let him pass, Martin. You're keeping the gentleman out of his own house."

The sentry stood aside with an air of great relief, and the young man swung himself through the doorway on his crutches. He handled them awkwardly, and I could see it coming when he rested the point of one of the crutches on a small rug on the polished hardwood floor, and put his weight on it. The rug slid over the floor, the crutch with it; the artificial leg gave way and buckled inward, and the young man sprawled backwards into an ignominious sitting position.

James stepped forward with concern on his face, and said, "Oh, Lord! I'm sorry, Colonel. Here, let me give you a hand."

Young Robertson glared up at him, his eyes full of fury. "Damn you, sir. I don't need your help."

He had obviously hurt himself in falling, and was not only humiliated but in pain.

James ignored his angry rejection, though he let his hand fall. "Those contraptions are awkward until you get the hang of them," he remarked easily.

There was no response to this, and James went on talking. "A cousin of mine lost his leg in a hunting accident about ten years ago. Caught his foot in a bear trap, and had to wait for help. They found him in an hour or two, but it was twenty below zero, and his foot was frozen. They finally had to amputate above the knee. He's got a stiff leg now, and walks with a cane, but it doesn't get in his way too much. He rides, and gets around, and goes abroad every year or two. He says it's a damned nuisance, but not much more than that."

At the end of this improvised fable young Robertson was still glowering, and still casting about for some handhold by which he could pull himself up.

James tried again. "I came within a quarter of an inch of getting a leg like yours at Shiloh, Colonel. A rifle ball through the lower thigh, under the knee. As it was, it killed my horse and gave me a nasty fall, but the wound didn't amount to much."

The name, Shiloh, caught Robertson's attention. He looked up at James, and, I think, saw him for the first time.

"Shiloh," he repeated. "Were you there?"

"I was," James replied. "It isn't a place you're likely to forget if you were."

Young Robertson agreed with a wry face. "No, you don't forget it."

He looked at James again. "Was the horse you were riding—the one that was killed—a black horse?"

"Black as night. Tonnerre, I called him. Not the easiest-riding horse in the world, but more endurance and more heart than any horse I ever owned. I was sorry to lose him."

"Were you on the left of the hornet's nest around noon? Our left, I mean. Your right."

James laughed. "I was, and a damned uncomfortable place it was to be."

Young Robertson was quite transformed. He was simply sitting on the floor now, no longer struggling to get up. The anger had left his face, and he was smiling.

"I thought I had seen your face before, sir. You're Colonel Lake, of course. We were just opposite you at the time, and not very far away either, if you'll remember. May I tell you, sir, that your conduct was greatly admired on our side of the fence? We knew you were bound to get hit, but we almost hoped you wouldn't, in spite of the fact that you were in our way."

"That's very handsome, Colonel. I thank you. A compliment to be proud of." James was obviously gratified, but he was also as nearly embarrassed as I had ever seen him. He seemed to feel that an explanation, or perhaps an apology, was called for.

"To tell the truth, I wasn't feeling very heroic. I wanted to be a thousand miles away. The trouble was, I had a new regiment with me. They were good boys, and I liked them, but they were perfectly raw, and the only way I could keep them there was to stay out in front where they could see me. I knew we couldn't stay there very long, but I wanted them to stand and fight long enough for their self-respect. Long enough to give them a little something to feel good about. If they broke after that, it wouldn't matter so much. They would remember that they had put up a good fight while they could. You must run into the same problem on your side—"

James broke off ruefully. "Only for God's sake, Colonel Robertson, let me give you a hand. You shame me."

This time Robertson accepted James' hand gratefully and pulled himself to his feet and took the crutches James handed him. They moved down the hall and into the office, and James sat on the corner of the desk, and young Robertson in the chair by the door, with his crutches beside him.

I hobbled in after them, still pretty well covered with bandages. James glanced over at me and remarked that while he approved of me on the whole—I was his nephew, incidentally—he was disappointed that I didn't have sense enough to stay out of the way of shellbursts.

Robertson gave me a crooked smile. "Something we have in common, Captain."

There was some further conversation, easy on both sides, then the purpose of Colonel Robertson's visit finally appeared, when he remarked that he had come over to pick up some of his clothes—if any of them were left.

From this remark and a few inadvertent expressions, I gathered that he had expected to find the house occupied by a crew of thieves and ruffians, and looted from top to bottom. He was astonished at finding the house intact and almost as usual, and both surprised and gratified at finding himself met with consideration. Half an hour after he left, James sent two orderlies down to the Robertson's other house, carrying a trunk full of his clothes—all we could find—between them.

This small act of courtesy, together with Colonel Robertson's recollection of James at Shiloh, had a happy effect on our relations with the Robertson family, and through them, with the community as a whole. Not that we were thought of as friends by any means, but at least we were now generally looked upon as human beings.

Chapter 2

❦ ❦ ❦ ❦ ❦ ❦ ❦ ❦ ❦ ❦ ❦ ❦ ❦ ❦ ❦ ❦ ❦ ❦

On the thirtieth of September we went up to Jenkins' Ferry with a cavalry detachment to meet the general's wife and escort her in to Tarsus. The general was unable to meet her himself, and sent James in his place, as his official representative. Colin went along as a representative of the family, and I went along for the ride. There may have been a trace of malice in the general's choosing James to represent him, because of the vigorous objections James had raised when the visit was first announced. On the other hand malice, or irony, was not the general's usual style.

As a matter of fact, he had only one joke, and a very mild one at that: orders from Washington, especially when he disapproved of them, he referred to as orders from Above, and raised his eyes piously to heaven. Colin was shocked every time he did it. Jake Leslie gave him a quotation from the *Inferno* to go with it: *Vuolsi cosi cola dove si puote cio che si vuole e piu non dimandare*—which translates roughly as, "Thus it is willed there where what is willed is done; ask no further." When the general thought an argument had gone on long enough, he would look over at Jake and say, "Colonel, will you favor me with that line from Dante you were quoting the other day?" Jake would oblige, and the general translated. Then he would smile and say, "I'm afraid that's about the size of it, sir," and that was the end of the argument.

I was still listed as convalescent, and had to get Dr. Ferguson's permission before I could go. Dr. Ferguson told me he thought I would find it a pretty long ride, but I could go if I wanted to. Only, for the love of God, to stay on my horse, and watch out for my arm. It was coming along beautifully and he didn't want to be bothered with it much longer. So if I had to break anything, to do a good job of it and break my damned neck. I said I would try to oblige him one way or the other.

The cavalry escort was more than a guard of honor. Mc-Graw had withdrawn his shattered command east of the mountains, and the left wing, under Ruthven and Taylor, had been driven across the river, so there was no organized body of the enemy left in the district. During the battle, however, a substantial number of men had been cut off from the main body. Gavin's brigade and the cavalry had been occupied for the past week in rounding up these survivors. They had succeeded in breaking up the larger groups and bringing most of the men in as prisoners, but there were still scattered bands of them hiding out in the wooded hills to the north and west.

We left the house before daybreak, riding three abreast along the unpaved main street, past the courthouse and the square, downhill past the darkened houses of the town, and out across the bridge at the foot of the hill. None of us had anything to say at this hour, and we rode together in silence.

It was a wonderfully great pleasure to be out in the open again, and to be going somewhere. I was intensely awake and filled with the unreasoning delight of the convalescent, absorbed in the sight and feeling of the early morning, the soft dawn wind on my cheek, the gentle rustling of the leaves, the muffled beat of the horses' hoofs on the beaten earth of the street which suddenly became loud and hollow as we crossed the planking of the bridge. A cock crowed off to the right and was answered by another in the distance, and a little later the faint sound of a bugle reached us from somewhere ahead.

An hour later we picked up the seventy-five cavalrymen of the 12th Michigan who were to form our escort. By that time the sun was over the horizon, on our right as the road curved around to the north, and it was a clear, warm, late summer morning. The woods were still almost wholly green, with no more than an occasional patch of yellow to indicate the lateness of the season. The country was mostly in meadow and pasture, alternating with fields of stubble and with orchards and frequent patches of woodland. The crooked rail-fences along the roadside and between the fields were still intact: conclusive evidence that no large body of troops had been stationed in the vicinity.

Although this was the main highway leading to the north, the only building we passed for more than an hour was a deserted and broken-down frame structure at a crossroads, which had once been a tavern. Occasionally we could see a thin vertical line of wood smoke, coming from a cabin a mile or more away; and for half an hour the pillars of a large country house were in sight on a hillside in the distance.

James pointed the house out to me when we first caught sight of it.

"Know whose house that is, Johnny?" he asked.

I had no idea.

"That's Peter Taylor's house. He and Judge Robertson are cousins. They own most of the county between them." James laughed. "I can imagine Peter Taylor and Barney McGraw have had some pretty strong words between them by this time. Taylor thought he should have had the command in the first place, but Barney outranked him."

Shortly after this the slope of the road began to increase; signs of cultivation became fewer, then stopped entirely; and the range of wooded hills which had been visible ahead for some time began to close in on the right to meet the range on the left whose flank we had been skirting all morning. At the point where the hills met, the road mounted a steep incline and followed a narrow pass between abrupt wooded slopes for a quarter of a mile, before emerging into the open cultivated fields of the Blackwater Valley on the farther side.

Beyond the pass the hills fell away, and for the last five miles the road wound gently downhill past the woods and farms of the Blackwater Valley to the river. The column took these last five miles at an easy pace, and we trotted across the bridge to the little town of Jenkins' Ferry on the farther bank a few minutes past noon.

Jenkins' Ferry was the terminus of the railway since the railway bridge, a mile and a half upstream, had been burned six months earlier. Neither side had held secure enough control of the territory to consider it worth rebuilding. This had made the town an important supply center. All the existing warehouses had been taken over and new ones had been built; there were blockhouses at both ends of the highway bridge, and others guarding the warehouses. Two regiments of infantry, with a small force of cavalry and some guns, were stationed there as a permanent garrison.

We had barely crossed the bridge and mounted the rise leading into the town, when a couple of staff officers came riding out to meet us. One of them was a rather awkward young lieutenant from the garrison, the other a major on the department commander's staff, a big young man with a bristling red beard.

The major greeted James in a loud cheerful voice. "Hello, Lake. How are you? What's all the cavalry for? You going on a raid?"

"Hello, Tony," James replied. "I hardly recognized you behind your whiskers. We came up to meet Mrs. Pack. Is she here yet? Or is your railroad still running?"

The major grinned at him. "It's still running. We can lay track faster than they can tear it up. We average about three miles a day, and a bridge once a week. Yes, she's here. We got in a couple of hours ago. The general thought he had better come along and hand her over in person. Once you see her you'll understand why. The general sent me over to get you. The lieutenant, here, will take care of your men."

A hundred yards farther on we came to the main street of the little town. The major led us off to the right, while the escort continued straight on towards the railway and the raw new sheds of the depot. The main street was merely a widening of the unpaved country road that came in from the left, with a row of houses on either side, then a row of weatherbeaten wooden stores with hitching racks in front. Halfway down the block the street swerved out to the left around an enormous oak tree, six feet in diameter, with gnarled branches as large as ordinary trees.

To the right of the tree and partly under its branches was the tavern around which the settlement had grown, a low building of red brick with a long porch along its front, only a little above the level of the street. The porch was in deep shade, cool and refreshing after the heat of the sun and the glare of the road. There were horses tethered to the rack in front of the tavern, with orderlies lounging about, and a number of officers in scattered groups along the length of the porch.

We dismounted in the shade of the enormous oak tree and followed the major onto the porch. It took a moment or two for my eyes to become accustomed to the comparative dimness of the light. At first, all I could see was a group of officers standing down at the farther end of the porch. A moment later, I saw that they were standing around a table, and that people were sitting at the table, among them General Crawford, the red-faced, clean-shaven Mexican War veteran who had been brought out of retirement to command the department. Then, as someone moved, I caught a glimpse of apple-green silk and smooth shining bronze: a woman's dress and the back of her head, the hair parted and drawn back smoothly into a knot.

Colin pushed eagerly ahead of us and plowed his way through the crowd of officers on the porch—something he did easily, being as usual, considerably bigger than any other man there—and as he approached the woman at the table he called out,

"Lucy! Aunt Lucy!"

The woman turned her head, and her face lighted up with pleasure. She stood up and held out both her hands. "Why, Colin! Colin, dear! How nice!" She leaned forward and offered him her cheek to kiss.

Colin took her hands and kissed her on the cheek, and straightened up, still holding her hands. He was beaming with pleasure and laughing at the same time, and repeating over and over, "My, it's nice to see you! My, I'm glad you're here!"

His aunt was laughing with him and at him. "It was sweet of you to come to meet me. But, great heavens, such a big young man! And to think, the first time I saw you, you were just this high!" She held her hand about three feet above the floor.

She had a light, clear contralto voice with a lovely silvery note in her laughter, a note like a silver bell, and she spoke with a faint and indefinable trace of accent that was neither French nor German nor British, yet partly all three and wholly charming. I had caught only a glimpse of her before she was hidden by the broad shoulders of her nephew. Now, as Colin moved aside, I saw her for the first time: a woman of thirty in green silk, with a graceful figure and soft hair that appeared to be brown in the shadow and would be almost red in the sunlight; a beautiful woman with dark eyes that were actually gray, with lights that were sometimes blue and sometimes green; a laughing and affectionate woman who was glad to see her nephew.

I had expected to meet a beautiful woman, but in speaking of her I hesitate to use the phrase, for it seems to limit her: actually, this was only one of her attributes, and not even the first one I noticed. What I noticed first of all, with surprise, was the intensity of her presence, and the first thought that came into my mind, inelegantly phrased but perhaps adequate, was a surprised, This is really somebody!

Immediately afterwards, of course, I saw her. I saw her, and felt the warmth and radiance of her character, and at once fell helplessly in love with the beautiful woman, the Countess, the general's wife, and with the kind and loving woman beneath. I fell in love with her as one falls in love when young, once in a lifetime, with an entire and selfless devotion. The boundaries of the world were suddenly enlarged; the atmosphere had suddenly become mysterious, richer, and full of promise.

I had stopped short a few feet away on first seeing her, not daring to intrude further. I was standing there bemused, looking at her face, watching the movement of her lips and eyes, quite unaware of anything else, when Colin put out a big hand and drew me closer.

"Aunt Lucy, this is Johnny Lake," Colin said heartily. "Johnny's my best friend, in spite of the wicked life he leads."

She turned and smiled, and I was enveloped in warmth. "I'm so glad to meet you, Captain." Her face suddenly became grave as she noticed the sling, and the bandage around my neck. "You are wounded, Captain?"

Colin broke in cheerfully. "Johnny was a little careless about getting out of the way of a shell the other day. He'll know better next time."

I suddenly found that I was relaxed and at ease, and wonderfully happy. "About ten days ago, Ma'am," I replied. "I'm nearly over it by this time. The doctor says I'll be ready for duty in another day or two. We've been looking forward to your visit, ma'am. Colin has been telling us about you. He seems to approve of you."

She laughed with delight. "Why, Colin! How sweet of you! I always hoped you approved of me, but I had no way of knowing. Thank you, Captain Lake. That was very kind of you."

Colin was pleased and embarrassed at the same time. His face grew red, and he turned away. At the moment, General Crawford, who had been waiting indulgently for a break in Colin's exuberance, caught his eye.

"Pack come with you, Colin?" he asked in the muffled bellow that was his normal voice.

"No, sir, he didn't," Colin replied. He turned back to his aunt. "Sorry, Aunt Lucy. I should have told you. He sends his apologies. He meant to come, but he got held up at the last minute."

General Crawford broke in again. "Man's a damned fool, with a wife like that, not to come and meet her. What's holding him up? Anything serious?"

"No, sir. Nothing serious. Just Billy Roth."

At this, there was a loud burst of laughter from the general and the others at the table. Colin looked a little startled, then smiled, and explained.

"Some kind of trouble down by Wilson's Landing. Billy wanted reinforcements. The general sent Jack Maitland over to see if there was really anything wrong, and moved a couple of Jonesy's regiments over, to be on the safe side. He thought he'd better stay where he'd be available, just in case Billy was right."

The general smiled, then said, "Sorry he didn't come. I wanted to hear about the dust-up you fellows had with Barney McGraw."

"James can tell you about it, General. He came up with us."

"Lake? James Lake? Where the hell is he? Excuse me, Countess. I don't see him."

He stood up and peered down the veranda. At the far end, near the steps, James and the bearded young major who had met us were talking to the proprietor of the tavern and to a red-striped artillery officer from the garrison.

The general sent a tremendous bellow down the length of the veranda. "Lake! Jamie Lake! Come here! I want to see you!"

James put up his hand in a gesture of acknowledgment, and started down the veranda. General Crawford sat down again, then looked over at Colin's aunt.

"Excuse me, ma'am," he said. "I'm used to talking to five hundred men half a mile away. They never have any trouble hearing me, but the people around me complain about their eardrums, sometimes."

She smiled at him. "You're like the Irish hero, General. The one whose shout was so loud it could be heard for eight days."

There was a burst of laughter from the table, and General Crawford, still laughing, stood up and said, "That beats me, ma'am. I figure that ten minutes is about the best I can do."

James had come up by this time, looking fresh and cheerful. The old general put his hand out across the table with a look of genuine pleasure on his face, and said, "I'm glad to see you, Jamie. How are you?"

"Fine, General. Thanks," James replied. "You're looking well yourself."

"I'm glad to hear it, Jamie," the old man said. "I wish I could say I felt the same way. Still, I've no complaints. Let me introduce you to the lady you've come for." He turned back. "Let me introduce you to Colonel Lake, Countess. The colonel is Arthur's right-hand man." His voice took on a flourish. "The only officer he would trust with anything so precious as yourself."

James laughed pleasantly at the old man, and the general's wife acknowledged the introduction with a smile.

"I am happy to meet you, Colonel Lake. The general speaks of you often in his letters. He tells me he is fortunate to have you on his staff."

James was pleased. "That's very good of him, Mrs. Pack. I think the staff—the entire command, for that matter—feels the same way about him. That we are fortunate to be serving under a general we all admire." He smiled. "Now let me discharge my commission. I am to tell you that the general was greatly disappointed at not being able to meet you himself, and I am to extend to you the greetings and welcome of the entire command. Which I herewith do."

The general's wife returned his smile. "Thank you, Colonel. Thank you very much. How soon do you propose to start back? My maid is lying down, and I have a few things to do, but nothing that will take more than a few minutes."

James looked at his watch. "Can you be ready to leave in about three-quarters of an hour, Mrs. Pack? We have quite a long ride ahead of us, and there is one rather awkward stretch we would like to get through before dark."

General Crawford looked up. "Where's that, James?"

"Jellicoe Gap. The notch in the hills just beyond the Jellicoe farm. It could be difficult after dark."

"Have any trouble on the way up?"

"No, and I don't expect any on the way back. Not any serious trouble. You may not know it, General, but we really did quite a job on Barney McGraw."

"Yes, so I hear. But for God's sake tell us about it, James. I'm sure the Countess would like to hear about what her husband has been doing."

"Indeed I would," she said.

"Talking about your successes is always a pleasure," James admitted cheerfully. "I'll be glad to tell you about it."

More chairs were brought out and placed around the table. James began with the choice of route, the route nobody thought was possible, and the survey that made it possible, and went on from there, describing our movements in considerable detail. Most of the time he was addressing the old general, who listened with close attention, nodded with approval, and once or twice looked as though he were about to applaud.

The general's wife listened with equal absorption, and when James turned to her with an explanation of something obvious to those on the scene, but confusing to an outsider, she followed him closely, and was quick to understand.

This interest on the part of those at the table was natural and to be expected. The revelation of the campaign as something extraordinary, as an outstanding feat of arms, only came to me when I suddenly realized that all conversation behind us had stopped, and that the officers of the garrison had gathered around to listen. This was immensely gratifying, and as I listened to my uncle's casual voice and the details of the campaign, I felt a swelling of pride at having been there, at having borne a part in the heat of the day, and the campaign seemed to become history.

All this time I was intensely aware of the beautiful woman on my right, the Countess Lucy, aware of the faintly perfumed aura around her, of the soft dark hair at the back of her neck, of the outline of her profile, and of the animation of her face as she followed James' account of the battle. And at one point, where James nodded at me and mentioned my name, she turned her head and smiled at me, a warm, personal smile which seemed for a moment to surround me with radiance and to leave a glow behind it.

At the end, the general's wife stood up with a shimmering of green silk. All of us stood up with her, while she excused herself to get ready for the five-hour ride down to Tarsus. The men followed her out of sight with their eyes, then came back to the campaign.

The man on the general's right, one of his staff officers, summed up the matter. "A campaign you can be proud of, sir. A brilliant feat of arms."

James looked dissatisfied. "McGraw made mistakes, and we took advantage of them," he said. "We had first-class troops, and they were well handled all the way down. The operation was carefully thought out—we went to a lot of trouble before-hand—and the execution was good. To tell the truth, we are proud of it. Only brilliant doesn't seem to be the right word."

The officer smiled. "Have it your way, Colonel. I withdraw the word. But I'm still full of admiration. Now what are you going to do?"

"Why, for the time being we'll try to keep Barney off balance with minor operations while we build up our forces. What we want to do, as you know, is to open a major offensive about the middle of November. But that depends, as we all know, on a lot of extraneous factors. What the other armies are doing, and how successful they are, and who gets the rein-forcements—"

I didn't wait to hear the rest of James' reply. I knew what it would be, anyway; we had talked about little else all week. There was still half an hour remaining before we were due to leave, and I was suddenly conscious of the weight of my fatigue. I excused myself, and Colin and one of the officers of the garrison found a place for me to lie down, on a couch in an unused parlor. I stretched myself out on the couch and immediately fell asleep.

As it turned out, it was more than an hour before we started back. I awoke feeling greatly refreshed, and ready to start the day all over again. The cause of the delay was not any excessive concern for my slumbers, but Madame Lucy's maid, Gerda, who had suddenly developed a superstitious dread of the journey, and for half an hour refused to go on. Gerda was small and sturdy, and almost any age at all; she was dressed in a servant's sober black, and was ordinarily so unobtrusive as to be almost invisible. The argument was over by the time I woke up, and Gerda had been persuaded that she was wrong. Or perhaps not. At any rate, when we started back she was in the carriage with a black veil over her head, sitting opposite the general's wife.

The general's wife had brought her own horses and carriage with her, a low-slung traveling carriage with a black lacquered finish, trimmed in silver, drawn by a pair of beautiful matched bays with silver mounted harness. Although it seemed much too urban and elegant for the dusty country road we were on, in fact it was strongly built, light, and comfortable, and she had brought it with her at the general's suggestion. A corporal from the escort was on the coachman's box, a shock-haired young fellow in a dusty blouse with his cap on the back of his head, delighted with the beautiful horses, but a little awe-struck at the honor bestowed on him.

The Countess sat in back with a green silk parasol over her head, and a long, white silk scarf wound around her neck. She and Colin kept up an intermittent conversation, largely about what had happened at home since Colin left, and what various people there were doing. Colin was still beaming with pleasure, his aunt affectionate and sometimes a little amused. Occasionally she turned and said something to me, out of kindness and natural courtesy, and for a time the conversation would be three-sided. I was grateful, but it wasn't really necessary: it was delightful enough just to be riding beside her, and aware of her presence.

The first two hours of the ride were without incident. The road wound uphill at an easy grade, past woodland and orchards and open fields, and past an occasional farmhouse. The country on this side of the divide was moderately prosperous farming country. Most of the cattle were gone and some of the farmhouses deserted, but none of them had been burned, and the fences were still intact.

We were just approaching the Jellicoe farm, near the top of the grade and a quarter of a mile from the notch in the hills through which the road passed over to the other side, when the sharp crack of a rifle shot came from somewhere ahead of us, followed by a ragged spattering of rifle fire. James and Captain Newcome came tearing past us in a tremendous hurry and disappeared around a bend in the road. Colin started to follow them, but went only a little way, then stopped and got off the road to let the column go by. The corporal on the coachman's box swiveled his head round to ask me what to do.

"Better get off the road," I told him. "We'll wait and see what's going on."

The Jellicoe house was on our left, a two-story frame house, the unpainted siding weathered to a silvery gray, set in a grove of maple trees a hundred yards in from the road.

As we turned off into the yard, twelve men from the escort, under a sergeant, turned off with us, while the rest of the escort went past at a gallop. The twelve men who had turned off into the farmyard fanned out in the manner of men going through a familiar routine; one group rode around to the back to search the barns and outbuildings; the other group dismounted in front of the house, and two of the men went up to the door, knocked, and disappeared within.

Meanwhile the sound of firing continued in front, still sporadic, but heavy enough to be alarming under the circumstances. Colin came back presently, dismounted and tied his horse to a hitching rack in the yard, and came over to the carriage.

"They've got a little skirmish going on up ahead," he explained to his aunt. "It may take a few minutes to clear them out of the way." Then, to the corporal, "We might as well get out of the sun, Fred."

The corporal scrambled down from the box and led the horses into the shade of the maple trees in the yard. I dismounted, and went around to join Colin at the side of the carriage.

Once on my feet I discovered—with surprise, as usual—that I was tired. Colin suggested, with some concern, that I ought to rest while I had the chance. I was grateful for the suggestion, and sat on a bench with my back against a tree trunk, while Colin stood by the carriage and talked to his aunt. Occasionally he broke off, and turned his head to listen, as the sound of gunfire up ahead of us increased in volume, or came from a new direction, and presently he went over to talk to the sergeant in charge of the detail that had been searching the house.

A moment later, I heard Madame Lucy's voice, with its delightful trace of accent,

"What do you think of it, Corporal? Are we going to be here long?"

The corporal was honored and a little flustered. "Oh, no, ma'am. Nothing to be worried about, ma'am. We been doing this every day for a week. Ever since the fight."

"Doing what, Corporal?"

"Cleaning out woods like this, ma'am. McGraw's men that got cut off in the fight. They're short of ammunition. That's what they're after. That and horses. We make a big racket and they return our fire, and pretty soon they've shot off all their ammunition. Then we move in on them. Our boys are pretty good at it by this time. We don't hardly ever lose more than a man or two."

Just then there was a sudden flurry of activity in the detail left at the house with us. There was a loud shout from somewhere off to the right:

"Look out! There they are!"

A group of men, Colin among them, came running around the corner of the house and made for the outbuildings at the left and in back, spreading out as they ran. A moment later there was a vicious burst of firing from that direction, quite close at hand. There was more firing off to the right, then a long, beautiful line of cavalry appeared, extending across the entire width of the field in back of the house, coming down the field with drawn sabers at a fast trot. There were a few more shots from somewhere in the center of the field, then about twenty ragged, slouch-hatted rebels stood up out of the tall grass with their hands over their heads and were rounded up by the cavalrymen.

There was some delay after the end of the skirmish. Corporal Flynn, who had climbed up to his coachman's box, climbed down again. The cavalrymen in the yard had dismounted and stood by their horses, bridle in hand. Colin went over to see what was holding us up, and his aunt leaned forward with a smile to say something to her maid. Gerda, whose existence I had almost forgotten, replied with a sniff and a grumpy monosyllable or two, and withdrew again.

The Countess had her parasol over her shoulder, and was cool and undisturbed and entirely at ease, as well as very beautiful. The light beneath the parasol was green and—perhaps only because I was hot and thirsty—suggested water and deep shade, as though it had been reflected from the surface of a forest pool. Or perhaps it went the other way, and the cool green light with its suggestion of water made me realize that I was intolerably thirsty.

Providentially, just at this moment I saw James coming towards us, towards the carriage and the bench I was sitting on, with a dipper full of water in his hand. It was an ordinary tin dipper with a short handle, but it was new and undented; the tin shone like silver and glittered in the sun, and a little water spilled over the side at each step. It was a delectable sight, and I could taste it in advance, and feel its blessed and reviving coolness in my mouth; even the slight metallic taste of the dipper was something to anticipate with pleasure.

It was a pleasure I had to wait for. James went on past me and up to the side of the carriage, and offered the dipper of water to the general's wife.

"It occurred to me that you might be thirsty in all this heat, Mrs. Pack," he said easily. "The water is quite good. They've got a well inside the house."

"Thank you, Colonel. I am thirsty. It was very good of you to think of me."

She took the dipper and drank from it, held it in her hand for a moment, then drank again before she handed it back.

I expected James, as a matter of course, to throw out what was left of the water and go back for more. Instead, he simply stood there, bareheaded, dark-haired and mustached, his face brown from the sun and the wind, with the bright new tin dipper in his hand. He stared at it as though it were something strange, then raised it to his mouth and drank in long draughts until it was empty.

The general's wife looked at him with surprise, or with something more: her lips were parted and her eyes were opened wide. Then I noticed that James was staring at her with the same expression on his face, an expression of great astonishment. This seemed to last for a long time, as though neither of them found it possible to turn away. Actually, I suppose it was a momentary thing, a mere crossing of glances, for, as I got to my feet and started back to get a drink for myself, James turned around and started back with me.

As it happened, I met Colin on the way, with a dipper full of water in one hand, and a dripping canteen swinging from the other. He asked me if I wanted a drink, and handed me the dipper. The water was as life-giving and delectable as it had been in anticipation: it was cold, and had a delightful, faint metallic taste from the dipper.

By this time the men were standing by their horses in the farmyard, and were beginning to get into some kind of order. The corporal had climbed onto the coachman's box again, and Captain Newcome came riding over to ask the general's wife if she was ready to leave. As she nodded, he gestured to his bugler and the high, clear notes of the bugle sounded; the cavalrymen mounted, and we were on our way again.

From here on, the road ran downhill at an easy grade. The heat of the day was past, and after four o'clock we were in shadow most of the way, as the sun passed behind the crest of the hills on our right. In front of us and on our left the ground sloped away to the fields and orchards, meadows and woodland, of the Severn Valley, and in the distance, beginning in the south and marching away to the northeast, was the wall of mountains that we thought of as our boundary. In the late afternoon the shadows grew longer and were filled with purple mist, while in the distance the mountains were still in the sun and glowing with violet and orange. The Countess was enraptured with the scene, and called on Colin and me to share her enthusiasm.

It was dusk when we reached the river road. The general had ridden out to meet us with Jake and Dick Ross and a few others, and we saw them as a group of horsemen waiting for us at the crossroads, not quite recognizable in the failing light. The general dismounted and greeted his wife with a kiss on the cheek, and stood by the side of the carriage for a few minutes. He had a cheerful word for Colin and me, and was even glad to see the horses which had been brought down from home. Before we went on he sent for the officer in command of our escort, Captain Newcome, and thanked him for bringing his wife in safely, and complimented him on his handling of the little fight at the top of the hill.

"James tells me you put your men in as though that was what you did every morning before breakfast. I told James that was what I would have expected. That was why I sent you along. Give my compliments to the squadron, will you please?"

"Yes, sir." The captain was so pleased he couldn't keep his face straight. He was beaming all over.

We dropped the escort off here, since we were now in our own territory. The sun was down by this time, and stars were beginning to appear overhead, but the sky was still pale in the west. After a time, we could see the town ahead of us on its low hill, outlined against this fading light. By the time we rumbled across the wooden flooring of the bridge, full darkness had come on, and yellow lamplight shone from the houses along the street. The lamps were lighted around the courthouse square; beyond the square and visible through the trees, our headquarters, the Robertson house, was lighted from top to bottom, as though for a fiesta. We turned into the driveway, and were home again, bringing the general's wife with us.

Chapter 3

I woke up the next morning with my head full of a diffused sensation of delight, a feeling most familiar as the glow left behind by a pleasant dream whose details have just the moment before faded out of the mind. This time the process was reversed: the sensation persisted, and, as I became fully awake, the reason for it appeared. Yesterday we had met the general's wife and had escorted her in; she was sleeping under the same roof, and I would undoubtedly be seeing her in another hour or two. I remembered her in minute detail, the inflection of her voice, her gestures, the changing expressions of her face, from my first sight of her on the green shaded porch at Jenkins' Ferry until my last sight of her the night before, when she had excused herself an hour or two after dinner, and had gone upstairs to her room.

This was the minute and detailed memory of a young man in love, but this feeling was not peculiar to me. Within a few days it was shared, at least in part, by nearly every man in the command. Our lives were enriched. All our activities took on added meaning and importance because she was there, because she was looking on. We were continuously aware of her, even when we were absent on duty for three or four days at a time: we knew that she was there and we would see her on our return. This was a quality she had in common with the great personages of the stage, whose presence is felt throughout, even when off stage, and persists after their final exit to the very end of the play. As the general's wife, she was one of us;

we were proud of her, and our vanity was pleased because she was a countess. We were proud of her and we wanted her to be proud of us, and we were better soldiers in consequence.

This was the beginning of October, a month of unbroken good fortune, the golden age of the command, and a golden age to many of us who were there. The days went by very fast, yet there seemed to be an interminable succession of them. It was like a period of fine weather when the autumn rains are due. Each day is treasured because it must finally be the last, and to wake up the next day, and morning after morning after that, to a bright sun and a clear sky and still another fine day is a continuing series of miracles.

As a matter of fact, this was true in a literal as well as a figurative sense: the weather was magnificent throughout the entire month of October. It sometimes rained in the night, or for part of a morning or part of an afternoon, but never for a whole day; there was only enough rain, in fact, to keep down the dust on the roads and to keep the pastures green. The warm weather continued well past the middle of the month, and there were days when it might almost have been mid-summer again: the grass was green, the trees were still in full leaf, and the gardens were bright with zinnias and hollyhocks and asters. Towards the end of the month it was cooler, and the trees and the countryside began to show signs of autumn; leaves began to fall and there were splashes of color in the woods.

We were told that this was most unusual: that the weather normally broke about the middle of the month, with high winds and thunderstorms and heavy rains which might last for a week or two, or might continue without a break into the season of frost and winter rains.

During the first few days General Pack went for a drive with his wife every afternoon, riding in the carriage with her, with eight or ten of us accompanying them on horseback. He was showing her our domain, the kingdom we had won from Barney McGraw.

We drove out to visit Gavin, who had his headquarters at a

little place called Argo—half a dozen houses and a mill—at the foot of the range of mountains that formed our eastern boundary. Gavin gave us champagne and showed us around his position, pointing out the main passes in front of us— McKinstry, Jarvie, South Gadsden, and Nine Mile—and rode back with us for dinner.

Another day we rode out in the opposite direction, to Jonesy's headquarters at Jennings' Landing, on the river. Jonesy had our engineering company with him, and his troops, aside from routine patrolling, were largely occupied in rebuilding the wharves which the rebels had burned, and in preparing a strongly fortified depot for the supplies that would be landed here as soon as the river was navigable.

The river was our western boundary. It was our southern boundary as well, from the point where it emerged from the mountain gorges in the southeast, to the indefinite place in the long irregular curve where its direction changed definitely from west to north.

The center brigade, or division, after the reorganization in the middle of the month, was spread out in camps south of town, and General Roth's headquarters were in a small stone farmhouse only a few miles out, so our state visit to the commander of the Second Division was only the beginning of the excursion. Billy joined us here, lumping along beside the carriage with his hat over his ears, and we went on, past the wooded ridge that forms the divide between the Severn Valley and the river, all the way down to the bluffs that form the riverbank.

The bluffs here were a hundred and twenty feet above the water. The river was low and flowed in a number of branching channels divided by sandbanks, with a deeper green water channel just under the bank. The bluffs on the opposite side of the river were a mile and a half away; the bottom lands in between were overgrown with low scrub, with clumps of trees on scattered islands of higher ground. This bottom land had been a favorite hiding place for runaway Negroes. We had our scouts out exploring it with the help of the Negroes, the few of them that were left in the district. It was treacherous, full of quicksands, and dangerous without a guide.

The most conspicuous object on the way back, visible for miles and almost always in view, was a brick mansion with a long row of tall white pillars along the front, set in a grove of trees on the ridge we had passed around on our way down. It was a handsome place; the view from the porch must have been tremendous. But after learning something about its recent history, I no longer felt any very strong desire to live in the house.

Billy Roth was telling the general's wife about the family. Billy had taken off his hat; since we were moving at a walk there was no strain on his horsemanship, and he looked less absurd on horseback than usual. The house belonged to the MacDougals, one of the great baronial families in this part of the state, like the Taylors and the Robertsons. The Mac-Dougals owned all the land to the south of them as far as the river, all the land they could see from their porch.

Young Malcolm MacDougal, the heir to the estate and the only surviving child, had married a second cousin, the daughter of Dr. Frazer MacDougal of Tarsus. He came to suspect his wife of adultery, either with or without reason, and strangled her one night in a fit of jealous rage. The girl's brother challenged him the following day in defense of his dead sister's honor. The duel took place the next morning in the presence of witnesses and with all the proper formalities, and young Malcolm shot his cousin through the heart.

The doctor appeared at the house late that night, quite insane with grief, and announced that he had come to rescue his grandson from this den of murderers. What happened afterwards was never quite clear. Apparently young Malcolm and his father argued with the doctor for an hour or more, over two bottles of whiskey. The argument went on with increasing bitterness until young Malcolm, in a loud, angry voice, called his wife an unprintable name. The doctor stabbed him with a bowie knife. The father was killed when he tried to intervene, and young Malcolm died while trying to load a pistol. The doctor went up to the nursery with the bloody knife still in his hand and forced the terrified nurse to hand over the little boy, who was a year old at the time. He drove all night with the child and reached the railway some time in the morning. He returned a week later, and steadfastly refused to tell what he had done with the little boy, or where he had been. The child was not located for more than a year, when it was finally discovered that he was living with a distant relative of the doctor's wife, in Elmira, New York. No attempt was made to bring him back. The doctor was never prosecuted, but he drank heavily from that time on, and was dead within a year.

This appalling affair had taken place only a few years earlier, a year or two before the outbreak of the war. The only adult survivor of the tragedy, the widow MacDougal, still lived in the house, a grim and bitter old woman.

This account of the MacDougal family was in answer to a question: the general's wife had asked Billy why he had set up his headquarters in the comparatively shabby stone farmhouse on the Tarsus side of the hill, when this large and handsome place was available.

I was riding behind the carriage with Colin, with most of my attention concentrated on Madame Lucy, the general's wife—or more specifically, on the white silk scarf she was wearing over her head, which was all I could see of her most of the time. Even that, and the mere awareness of her presence, was enough to transform the landscape into something more beautiful, beautiful and melancholy just now, than it would have been otherwise. Billy Roth's tale of jealousy and murder, which at another time might have seemed mere senseless violence, now seemed tragic and deeply moving.

Billy described his interview with the widow MacDougal. At the end he laughed,

"I give you my word, Countess, the old woman actually frightened me. A really baleful old woman. I was very happy to get out of her presence. I still get a cold feeling every time I look at the place."

The general's wife shivered. "What a dreadful story!" She

turned to her husband. "Did we know those people, Arthur? Those poor MacDougals?"

"We knew the doctor quite well," the general replied. "He came to dinner several times, and I went hunting with him. A big man, with a big mustache. I don't think we knew the other family."

As we passed around the ridge we had the house on our left, beyond a peach orchard and an overgrown lawn, with an enormous oak tree at the side overtopping the roof of the house. All the windows on this side were shuttered, making the house look blind. The shutters needed paint, the garden and the lawn were overgrown with weeds and tall grass, and the fences were broken down in a dozen places. All these together gave the place a melancholy air of neglect and incipient decay.

On the fourth day we completed our circuit of the compass by going north, to look over the Willow Run battlefield. The road was a miserable one after the first mile or two, a stony, rutted country road leading up into the rough hill country to the north, with its covering of brush and scraggly oaks. The general and his wife were quite mercilessly jolted in their carriage. After crossing the North Branch at the bottom of a steep-sided valley and slanting up the far side, we came to the road we had marched along two weeks earlier, towards the sound of Jonesy's battle.

The passage of our troops was still clearly marked on the road, in the crisscrossing of wheel tracks and the beaten-down underbrush along the sides; but whereas the road had seemed endlessly long before, now it was only a short and pleasant drive to the clearing where our reserves had been stationed and our trains had been parked, and beyond the clearing and over the ridge to the battlefield.

The battlefield was both familiar and unbelievably strange. The road still ran across the cleared valley and up the hill on the far side; the brook and the willows ran down the center of the valley, and the two clumps of woods, the North Wood on the left of the road, the South Wood on the right, were still there. But the entire valley was empty, and filled with a monstrous, incredible silence. Off to the left were the two wide areas of raw earth where more than fifteen hundred men were buried; the farmhouse by the road was a ruined heap of ashes and blackened timbers; and everywhere the ground was littered with debris, broken limbers, wagon wheels, broken muskets, accouterments, and paper; the willows along the brook and the trees along the edges of the two woods were maimed and broken, and the ground was covered with fallen branches.

For a few minutes it was a depressing sight, but as the general pointed out the various parts of the field and described the phases of the battle to his wife, the scene came to life again, and it seemed—to a young man of twenty-one—a glorious thing to have been there, and to have taken part in the battle.

The general distributed accolades all around: he remembered where each of us had been, and what each of us had done, and as he mentioned our names, his wife, who was following his account with close attention, gave each of us a smile and a nod.

Afterwards we rode down into the valley and up the other side, took the right-hand branch at the crossroads, crossed the stream at the bridge where Jonesy's fight had begun, and so came back to the river road, and home again.

This river, incidentally, which the road followed, was not the great boundary river but a tributary, the Severn, our own river, which looped around Tarsus and finally emptied into the main stream about seventeen miles to the southwest.

On the following day General Pack went up to Jenkins' Ferry to confer with General Crawford, taking James and Jake Leslie with him. Gavin happened to have come in that afternoon, and took his uncle's place on our afternoon excursion, riding in the carriage with the Countess, while Colin and Bob Kelso and I formed the mounted escort.

When the general came back the next day he had his wife's riding horses with him, a beautiful little bay named Lassie, and a handsome black with a white star, named Marmion. After that she used the carriage only for visiting the hospital and for errands, and in the afternoons we rode. She was a superb horsewoman, easy and firm on the horse, and graceful even in the awkward sidesaddle. After riding with her a few times, it even began to seem like a reasonable way to ride a horse. She wore the traditional long-skirted black riding habit, with a white stock and a black tricorn, and modified the severity of the black and white with a scarlet carnation pinned to her jacket.

She had a capacity for being pleased with simple things. In view of her worldly background this was rather surprising and very attractive. She loved to ride, to be in the open country and feel the wind on her face, and she loved all the changing details of the countryside. The coloring changed from day to day, as the heavy greens of summer gradually gave way to the lighter russet and scarlet and gold of autumn; from day to day, and from hour to hour, as the mists rose in the late afternoon, and the mountains changed to purple and orange; and when we returned late, the lights of the town were yellow and cheerful in the blue haze of dusk.

This was one of our favorite subjects of conversation. We noted the changes that had taken place since the day before, or in the last couple of hours, and pointed them out to each other. Our topographical engineer, who had been a well-known painter, pointed out dozens of fine distinctions when he rode with us one afternoon. Afterwards we tried to look at the scene with a painter's eye, to see the olive green of a shadow in the woods, or the pale blue of a shadow in a rutted track, and to see the landscape in terms of shape and line and composition.

I was the Countess's usual riding companion during the early part of the month, and rode with her every day. I was still listed as convalescent, and all my afternoons were free. Others went with us when their duties allowed, James and Jake Leslie, and Colin and Saint Chamans and many others, so that at times we practically amounted to a cavalry escort. More often, though, we were alone together; for me these were afternoons of pure delight.

Another favorite subject came up early, my uncle, James.

This pleased me: it was something more we had in common. It began when she asked me if James was in the regular army; ordinarily she recognized officers from the old army at a glance, but James she couldn't place.

I told her that he wasn't. The reply seemed curt, and she seemed to expect me to go on, so I continued, "James was educated for the law, ma'am, though I don't know that you could call him a lawyer, either. He did practice for a while. He was my father's partner for about six months. My father said he had a first-class legal mind. He was sorry to see him go."

"Why did he go, then?"

I laughed. "He said he was afraid of turning into a pillar of the community like my father. He was just restless, really. He was looking for something, and practicing law in a small town wasn't what he was looking for. He went out to California and was out there for a couple of years, and after that he was in Europe. Every so often he would show up at our house. We never expected him, but one morning he would just be there. He would stay for two or three days, or a month, or all winter, then he'd be gone again."

A day or two later, amending or filling in an earlier statement, I happened to mention that James had also been in Algeria and in Egypt.

Madame Lucy said, "He must be very rich, to travel all over the world and not do anything else. May I ask—excuse me, Johnny, would it be proper for me to ask—where all his money came from?"

"From California, mostly." I smiled. "James swears he won it in a poker game."

Madame Lucy looked at me, then burst into a laugh of pure delight. "O, how wonderful!"

I explained. "Mining shares, really. James says there was a blizzard of them floating around. They were like IOU's. You could buy a drink, or get into a poker game, or pay a lawyer with them. Most of them had some sort of speculative value, like lottery tickets, and that was about all. James had a drawer full of them, and so did everybody else. Then somebody discovered the Valparaiso mine, and one of the IOU's in James' drawer was a quarter share in the mine."

"That sounds very impressive," Madame Lucy said politely. Evidently the name meant nothing to her.

"Yes, ma'am," I assured her. "It is impressive."

Afterwards, on later occasions, I told her more about James, more than I would have thought it possible to remember, from my first recollection of him, home from school in the East with an aura of the great world about him, to his latest appearance at our house only a few months before the war. On this occasion he had Robert Saint Chamans with him, and they stayed up talking to my father until six o'clock in the morning three nights in a row, while I tried to stay awake to listen to them.

Dr. Ferguson reported me fit for duty on the nineteenth; my afternoons were no longer free, and others took my place. James rode with her often—too often according to some people, an opinion which annoyed me—together with whoever else happened to be off duty in the afternoon, or happened to be in town.

The one person who never rode with us, or with his wife, was General Pack. I have no real explanation for this. Perhaps he was setting us an example of devotion to duty. Or more likely he felt that the necessity of being available at all times, which would require a route fixed in advance, would hamper the freedom of his wife's excursions. Whatever the cause, there was no displeasure involved, for he was relaxed and cheerful in the evening, and often came in to play a few hands of cards with us, and to drink a glass of hot punch in front of the fire before going to bed.

When the general returned from Jenkins' Ferry, he brought with him, in addition to his wife's riding horses, three of her oldest and most trusted servants: her cook, Mrs. Mott, and a German couple who served as houseman and chambermaid. From this time on the house ran like oiled machinery, with quiet and unobtrusive efficiency. The presence of the servants might have passed without notice except for the drastic change, an improvement out of all recognition, in the quality of our meals. We might ignore the others, but there was no question about Mrs. Mott: we knew she was there.

We dined in state around the immense mahogany table in the Robertson dining room. Thursdays and Sundays were our official reception days, with guests from each of the three divisions in turn, but it was often hard to tell the difference between the weekdays and the state occasions. Throughout October there were sixteen of us on the staff, including the general, and with Madame, seventeen. However, there were always additions and subtractions to be made. Major Stewart, our chief of engineers, spent most of the month over at the Third Division. Our chief commissary, our quartermaster, and our provost marshal seceded, and formed a mess of their own, because the general allowed wine to be served, or because he failed to say grace before meals, or for some such reason. All three of them were rigorous Calvinists, and saw little hope of grace in the rest of us.

Offsetting the secessionists and those of us who were absent on duty were the officers who came in on brigade or regimental business every day. Within a week they had discovered that the best time for such transactions was the latter part of the afternoon, late enough for James or the general to invite them to stay for dinner. In addition, during the relative quiet of October, a number of officers' wives came down to visit their husbands. There was a standing invitation for officers to bring their wives in to dinner, and frequently there were several other women at the table with Madame Lucy.

One of the few I can remember with any clarity was the wife of our judge advocate, Hugo Bliss, who had joined us late in September, after the Willow Run battle. Hugo was a reserved young New England lawyer, who seemed cold and unfriendly during the first few weeks he was with us, and was disliked in consequence. When his wife came down to visit him in the middle of October, we found out what had been wrong with him: he had been married only since the beginning of August, he was deeply in love with his wife, and he had been grieving in exile. His wife was small and plain and made little impression at first, but she was so touchingly in love with her husband, she had so much warmth and kindness in her, and so much plain good sense, that she ended by charming everybody. We were all sorry when she left.

There were perhaps a dozen others. Many of them were pleasant and attractive women, but we saw them only a few times, and they were always in the shadow of the Countess.

We were very elegant at these dinners. The enormous round table was covered with a tablecloth of spotless white damask and glittered with silver and crystal; in the center of the table a silver vase the size of a water bucket held a great mass of red roses. The general sat in an armchair at what thus automatically became the head of the table; his wife sat opposite him in a smaller armchair at the foot of the table. The guests of honor, if there were women among them, sat next to the general; otherwise, with a slight but obviously reasonable departure from custom, they sat on either side of the Countess. That was as far as our protocol went. The rest of us sat in our usual places.

Quite often at the beginning of the month, and again at the end, the general's wife was by herself, the only woman at the table. It never seemed to bother her. She was always perfectly at ease, and the intensity of her presence and personality—the quality that had struck my attention first of all at Jenkins' Ferry—seemed to even the balance. Robert Saint Chamans marveled at this. He said he always came away with the feeling that he had spent a pleasant evening with agreeable men and women, and that it always astonished him to realize that Madame Lucy had been the only woman present.

Another institution that month was afternoon tea. These teas were different in almost every possible way from the state dinners. They were universally spoken of as the Countess's tea parties, but that was *de facto* rather than *de jure;* in theory the hostess was Christina Robertson, the Judge's seventeen-year-old daughter, and Madame Lucy was no more than the principal guest. These afternoon receptions were held in the smaller house down the street where the Robertsons were living now that we had taken over the Judge's house. It was an ivy-covered brick house, without opulence, but comfortable and pleasant. It belonged to one of the Judge's cousins, who was in Virginia with Lee's army, and had taken his family to Richmond.

After seeing Colonel Robertson, with his fine, aristocratic features, I had expected his sister to be a very beautiful young woman. As it happened, by a not infrequent left-handed quirk of fate, the son inherited the features of a beautiful mother, while the daughter resembled her distinguished but not otherwise handsome father. She was dark-haired and slight, and had her father's thrust-out lower lip, his aquiline nose, and his deep-set gray eyes.

The first time I saw her was somewhat earlier, towards the end of September, when I was still swathed in bandages and pretty much confined to the house. One of the living rooms along the north side of the house, looking down towards the river, held a handsome ebony piano. It was evidently much used, for there was music on the rack and stacked at the side, and more music, great quantities of it, in an open cabinet against the wall.

I was sitting just outside this room on a hot September afternoon, with my bad leg on a chair and a book in my hand. I was alternately dozing and looking down the long shady slope of lawn at the river. The only thought I had in my mind, if you could call it a thought, was that I wanted to sit on the riverbank and dangle my feet in the water.

Presently I could hear someone in the room behind me, a woman, judging by the lightness of step and the swishing of skirts. With the French doors wide open, I was practically in the room, and I had only to turn my head to see who it was; but I still had a bandage on my neck, and it hurt to turn my head. For that matter, most of the women I had seen so far chewed tobacco, so there wasn't much incentive.

A little later I heard Jake Leslie come into the room, stop short in surprise, and say, "Oh, how do you do? You're Miss Robertson, aren't you?"

At this, I put my leg down and turned around in my chair

so that I could look into the room. I saw the girl standing by the piano in a faded blue gingham dress, with dark curls on either side of her face, and an absolutely stricken expression, as though she had come to steal the silver and had been caught in the act.

Jake tried to put her at ease. "I hear you're the pianist in the family, Miss. You have a fine collection of music here. Would you feel like playing something? I'd be gratified if you would. I think you'll find the piano is in tune."

The girl's face was scarlet. She shook her head dumbly, then said in a small, strangled voice in which the note of defiance was quite lost, "I don't play for Yankees."

She took a deep shaky breath, and sat down at the piano. "Yes I do, too," she said. "This is what I play for Yankees."

She began to play an arrangement of "Dixie" very loud and fast, with an impetus that carried her halfway through the piece. At that point she began to falter, and the firmness went out of her playing. She missed a few notes, and made a half-hearted attempt to go on, then gave up, buried her face in her hands, and burst into tears.

Poor Jake felt worse than she did. He stood there, with distress all over his leathery face, and made soothing fatherly noises.

She stopped crying after a moment or two, and Jake went on talking. "No, Miss, I just thought it would be a pleasure to hear some music. I haven't heard any for a long time. South German music, maybe. Or North German. It doesn't matter which. I see you have a lot of Bach here, and it all seems to be well used. It's a pleasure to find a young person who plays Bach, these days. Instead of Kalkbrenner and Thalberg and all these wretched bleating Maiden's Prayers, Maiden's Farewells, Maiden's Last Wishes, and all the rest."

The girl was still sitting at the piano with her head bent and her face in her hands. Her shoulders began to shake, and after a moment she said to the keyboard, "You left out the Maiden's Vow at Eve, by Adolf Kleinschmidt, opus three hundred and sixty-one. It's awful. I know a girl who plays it, and everybody thinks she's wonderful. You know, lots of trills and

French pastry in the treble, and a vulgar little tune in the middle that you play mostly with your thumbs, and lots and lots of pedal."

Jake's face was crinkled all over with amusement. "Yes, I know, Miss. Lots of pedal, and the hands not quite together, and deafening applause at the end."

The girl threw back her head with a bright silvery laugh. "Oh, yes! Loud applause and won't you please play us an encore? And the poor girl can't do anything about it because it's the only piece she knows."

She paused, then looked at Jake for the first time, and asked seriously, "Do you really like Bach?"

"Indeed I do, Miss. I once went to Amsterdam for a week for the sole purpose of hearing Franz Meister play the Forty-eight Preludes and Fugues."

"That must have been wonderful," the girl said thoughtfully. She stood up and picked up a sheaf of music—evidently what she had come for—and moved over towards the door.

"I play Bach every day," she said. "I thought nobody else liked it. It would be nice to play for somebody who wanted to listen. I'll ask Daddy."

Evidently she was able to talk her father into receiving Jake, for presently he was going down the street nearly every afternoon for an hour or two. The Judge was extremely fond of his daughter. He felt a particular tenderness towards her, I think, because she was plain, as though he had failed her in that respect, and was trying to make up for this failure by increased affection. I think he was grateful to Jake for his interest in Christina, and for the effect that interest had upon the girl.

Christina acquired another appreciative and respectful listener with the arrival of the Countess, though the acquaintance began in the hospital rather than in the music room. Shortly after her arrival Madame Lucy began the practice of driving out to the hospital every morning, with flowers and delicacies of various kinds for the wounded. The ladies of the town were surprised and gratified to find that she made no distinction between the rebel wounded and our own—though, for that matter, neither did Dr. Ferguson, or the hospital staff.

In any case, she was exempted from the general quarantine we were in as Yankees, and was thought of as the Austrian countess and the ambassador's daughter, rather than as the general's wife. This made it permissible for the women of the Hospital Committee to ride with her in her carriage out to the hospital, which had been set up in the stone seminary building half a mile south of town, and to appear with her at the afternoon teas in the Robertson house.

These grew up quite casually. People stopped in because the Countess was there, and Christina made tea for them. This happened frequently, but not at any set time, nor for any specific list of guests. People stopped in, were given a cup of tea, and stayed for ten minutes or two hours. Christina played the piano, and Madame Lucy turned pages for her. Sometimes she sang, to Christina's accompaniment, though not often. The Judge was almost always there. Quite often his son, the fierce young colonel, came in with his crutches and his wooden leg, and talked to James or Robert Saint Chamans if either of them were there; otherwise he listened to the Countess and his sister and said nothing at all.

Judge Robertson still refused to have anything to do with the general, and was stiffly punctilious in all his formal relations with us. At the same time, he treated us with an easy courtesy in his own house, and I had the impression that he was really pleased to see us—the few of us who were there frequently, anyway. This puzzled me at the time, but I suspect now that the Judge was simply bored. He had been a prominent public figure for thirty years, and was accustomed to travel and conversation and good company. The sense of duty that kept him in Tarsus had deprived him of these pleasures for more than a year.

He was courteous to all of us, and had an obvious pleasure in receiving the Countess—in receiving an accomplished and beautiful woman, as he said, with an old-fashioned bow—but the person he was immediately drawn to was Jake Leslie. Presently Jake was walking down every night, when there was no pressing business on hand—and in October there was hardly ever anything very pressing—to have brandy and water with the Judge. Men of the same generation, both men of learning and wide experience, they sat on the back porch in the dark and swapped quotations from Horace, and talked endlessly about arms and letters and outstanding men, while they smoked cigars and drank the Judge's twenty-year-old cognac.

The only drawback to the magnificent October weather was that the river was still low, and would not be navigable until the seasonal rise began. We had counted on supplying the command by water from the middle of October on. This meant that we had to continue hauling in our supplies by wagon train from the railhead at Jenkins' Ferry. There was no particular difficulty about this in October, for McGraw's forces were still too disorganized to make any kind of serious attack on our supply lines. In addition, we were getting reinforcements, a regiment or two at a time, and these new troops served as train guards on the way down.

Six new regiments came in during the month, and were parceled out among Jonesy and Gavin and Billy Roth. Saint Chamans got three more batteries, and Dick Ross's third regiment was on its way and due almost any time. Counting Dick's regiment, the 12th Pennsylvania Cavalry, which came in on the first of November, the new troops brought the command up to full strength, and the morning report of the second of November gave us a total of sixteen thousand and forty-six, which was our high-water mark.

This brought us up to the size of a respectable army corps, and made a reorganization necessary. The reorganization was largely on paper. The brigades, which were already big and unwieldy in September, now became divisions, each with three small brigades. The new brigade commanders, serving at their previous rank of colonel, were all competent men, and some of them were outstanding. Nelson Keith, of the First Division, was probably the best of them. He was a stiff-backed, thirty-year-old West Pointer with cold eyes, an able, hard-driving professional who was expected by all of us to end the war as a major general.

Our military activities during the month consisted merely of routine patrols, scouting parties, and escorts for the topographical details and for the supply trains. Small brushes with the enemy occurred frequently in the course of these routine duties, but there was rarely more than a company engaged on either side, and our casualties were extremely light.

We had a party on Halloween. Both Dick and Gavin came in for dinner, bringing friends with them, and Robert brought over two of his new battery commanders. We had roast turkey and champagne, and sat at the table for a couple of hours after dinner was over. When Madame Lucy finally stood up, she apologized very sweetly for breaking up so pleasant a gathering, and after she had gone upstairs the general stayed on for another hour, talking to his nephews and the rest of us, in a very genial mood.

After the general had gone we decided it was much too early to go to bed, and that Halloween came but once a year and ought to be celebrated, so all of us moved on down to the Club.

This was on the second floor of a building across from the courthouse, and had formerly been a ballroom. Some of the men in Roth's division had started it, and originally it was meant to be an officers' club for the Second Division, but everybody started using it and the distinction was soon forgotten. There was nothing very elaborate about the place: the furniture had been picked up anywhere, and consisted mainly of plain deal tables and kitchen chairs, with an old piano on one side of the room and a makeshift bar on the other. It was a convenient place to stop in for a sociable drink, or to write letters, or to play cards. There was usually a group of devoted cardplayers there at almost any time of day, and in the late afternoon and evening the place was almost always crowded.

On Halloween, when we got there around ten o'clock, the place looked much as usual. There was a group around the piano singing "Swanee River," off pitch, of course, but at the usual barbershop level. There were five or six tables of cardplayers, some of them loud and cheerful and playing simply for fun, others playing with frowning concentration, including a captain in an Indiana regiment who was said to have won seven thousand dollars, and was beginning to be looked on with suspicion. There was a line up along the bar, with the two colored boys working as fast as they could, and the tables were filled with men who had come in for an evening of conversation and social drinking.

The atmosphere was a little strained for a few minutes after our arrival—a general, half a dozen full colonels, and most of General Pack's immediate staff—but the constraint wore off quickly. Most of us had friends there, and all of us had been there before; as soon as we broke up as a group we ceased to be formidable. Colin wandered over and joined the group around the piano with a glass of lemonade in his hand—he had a beautiful, big tenor voice, and loved to sing—and presently he was singing the tenor lead in "My Old Kentucky Home," supported by Ned Christie and another artillery captain, and Fred Lambert, of Billy Roth's staff. They were so good that everybody applauded at the end, and someone wanted them to sing "Nellie Gray," and someone else wanted "Flow Gently, Sweet Afton." They sang both of them, and a good many after that. The rest of us stopped listening after a while, and the singing was no more than a pleasant convivial sound in the background.

James and Saint Chamans and Dick Ross were sitting at a table with the colonel of the 11th Ohio, Jack Turquin, and a big, bearded lieutenant colonel from one of the Illinois regiments. The lieutenant colonel was telling a long, involved story about a colored preacher—a mighty exhorter and smiter of sin—and a particularly stubborn mule, telling it soberly, with a straight face, while the others at the table grew red-faced with laughter.

Jake and Gavin were still standing at the bar, arguing with the barman and with each other about a drink that called for champagne and brandy and something else, trying to decide what the something else was, and trying out various experimental mixtures. Hugo Bliss, with a modest glass of rum punch in his hand, went over to join the group at the piano, and when one of them dropped out, took his place with a fine baritone voice that none of us knew he had. Jack Maitland got himself tangled up with Billy Roth's inspector, who wanted more ammunition for training the new regiments; they got hold of Henry Winter, our chief of ordnance, and presently the three of them were sitting at a table in the corner, making out lists. Bob Kelso and I found a poker game going where we knew most of the players, and had ourselves dealt in.

The poker game broke up about an hour later. I had won seven dollars, and Bob had lost forty cents, which he claimed was a moral victory. The group around the piano broke up at about the same time, though none of us noticed that they had stopped: the place was as noisy as ever, and it was only the kind of noise that had changed. The crowd thinned out shortly afterwards, as the lighter drinkers and the men who were on duty the next day began to leave.

By twelve o'clock, with a five-mile ride ahead of them, most of the Roth contingent had left, except for the table of dedicated poker players, who continued to deal out their cards in silence and play them with frowning concentration. The Indiana captain was one of them, a clean-shaven, red-faced man of thirty-five, with a perpetual cigar in his mouth. Within the past couple of hours we had learned that his name was Wallace, that he was a lawyer in civil life, and that he had lost fourteen hundred dollars in the past three days. Everybody felt a little better about him.

The champagne and brandy and something else had been a potent mixture, and Gavin was feeling very mellow and expansive. He had decided that we were the best-officered command in the entire army: give us the Army of the Potomac and a hundred and twenty thousand men and there would be one more campaign; that would be all. There was a great deal of brandy and champagne in the statement, of course, but Gavin had served with or under nearly all the men who were commanding the armies on both sides, and knew their capacities well: his opinion was worth listening to and his praise worth having, drunk or sober. It was a highly popular opinion, at any rate.

The conversation at one point got around to Dick's cavalry

charge at the Willow Run battle. I had thought of this as a touchy subject, but, to my surprise, Dick was quite temperate in defending himself. He told James he knew it looked like damned foolishness, but that McGraw's attack looked so heavy and so menacing that he was afraid it might run over us by sheer momentum. What he was trying to do was simply to check it. He thought that if he could disorganize the attack, if he could bring it to a dead stop for just a minute or two, its momentum would be broken, and when McGraw got it started again it would no longer have the same weight. James accepted this. He thought maybe Dick was right.

I told Dick it was the most magnificent thing I had ever seen in my life, the way the beautiful straight line of cavalry came on at a walk, then a trot, then a full gallop, and smashed into the line of infantry.

For some reason this pleased Dick enormously. "Did it really look that good, Johnny?" he asked.

When I assured him that it did, he thought it over, then nodded his head with great satisfaction. "Yes, it must have been quite a sight."

The poker players were still there when we left, and both the colored boys were asleep behind the bar. Nothing in particular had happened during the course of the evening, but I remember it in detail and with affection. We spent the evening drinking together and all of us were somewhat drunk and some of us were disgracefully drunk—Gavin had Dick on one side of him and James on the other all the way home—but all of us were proven soldiers and gentlemen, and we were a band of brothers. It was around two-thirty in the morning, the morning of the first of November. The sky was dark, it was twenty degrees colder, and a drizzle of rain was falling.

Chapter 4

❦ ❦ ❦ ❦ ❦ ❦ ❦ ❦ ❦ ❦ ❦ ❦ ❦ ❦ ❦ ❦ ❦ ❦

One of the women we saw at the Robertsons' in the afternoon was a Mrs. Coleman, a young and handsome woman dressed completely in black, who always left as soon as one of us appeared. The first time I saw her, on my way out, I noticed her because she was an uncommonly good-looking young woman. The second time I noticed her because when I smiled at her, having seen her there before, she shrank away from me with a perfectly undisguised air of loathing, as though I were a particularly foul and venomous reptile. It was a new and highly unpleasant sensation, but it certainly served to fix her image in my mind. When I mentioned her to some of the others, I found that the basilisk glare wasn't meant for me specifically, but for all of us. She would have killed us all if she could.

What was behind this fiercely concentrated hatred was the fact that her entire family had been wiped out: she and her thirteen-year-old son, Cadmus Amyntas Coleman III, were the only survivors of a family which had been large and flourishing in April, 1861. Her father and two of her cousins were killed in obscure little fights in western Virginia at the very beginning of the war. Her only brother was killed at Bull Run. Her father-in-law, an uncle, and two of her cousins by marriage were killed in the fights preceding Shiloh—Mill Springs and Donelson, and others—and finally, her husband was killed at Shiloh, and his brother, who had become the last surviving adult male of the family, died of wounds a month later. Some of the women of the family had died earlier; others during this period. She had no female relations.

After this, her fanatical hatred for us was understandable. She must have been quite beautiful before the war. Now, in repose, the tragedy in her face was imposing: it seemed to call for silence and averted eyes, and I always backed away as quietly as possible.

A week before the Halloween party, on a bright Friday morning, I was coming back on foot from the west bridge, where our engineers were fortifying a bridgehead and supply depot, mainly for ordnance, on the far side of the river. It was about eleven o'clock, and very quiet and autumnal; the trees had turned and the leaves had begun to fall slowly, yellow leaves fluttering down one leaf at a time from the trees that lined the street. As I came abreast of the Robertson place, I looked in and saw the Judge, with a straw hat on his head and a cheroot in his mouth, puttering around among the zinnias at the far end of the garden.

At the same time I could hear cavalry, or rather a body of horsemen, probably a general and his escort, coming in from the east but hidden by the shallow rise of the hill. I remembered that Gavin was coming in for lunch, and felt mildly pleased with myself for having revised my estimate before I remembered who it was. Just after this, the quiet of the morning was broken by the sound of a rifle shot, followed by a moment of dead silence, then by the sound of loud angry voices and shouted commands, while the column came to a halt.

Obviously something was very much wrong up ahead, and I broke into a run. As I approached our headquarters, I saw that there were others ahead of me, running in the same direction. Jake Leslie and General Pack had come out and were standing on the porch, looking over to the left, beyond the courthouse. A little farther on I could see what they were looking at, the location, if not the cause of the disturbance.

Beyond the courthouse and a little way down the other side of the hill, the street was filled from side to side with men and horses, most of the men dismounted, the horses being held. One focus of attention was in the middle of the street, where I could make out the black coat and broad back of Dr. Ferguson, kneeling in the street, with a group of officers and men around him. The second focus of attention was in motion: soldiers coming out of a house on the right with a captive in their midst.

What had happened was plain enough: the captive had fired on the column and hit somebody, and the soldiers had gone in after him. But who had fired the shot? And who had been hit?

I reached the group around Dr. Ferguson first, and jostled my way into the center of it. The man lying in the street on a horse blanket with a saddle under his head, trying to smile and make light of his wound but obviously in great pain, was Gavin's chief of staff, Colonel Joe Marsh, a man we knew and liked, a personal friend of Gavin's, and a very popular man in the division.

The bullet had gone in between the neck and the shoulder blade, had barely missed the spinal column, and had come out in front on the other side. Dr. Ferguson had put a temporary bandage on the wound and checked the bleeding, and had called for a carriage, which was just being led up as I got there, to take him out to the hospital.

The doctor got in the carriage, and Gavin and a sergeant from the escort, a powerful young fellow, lifted Joe up as carefully and as gently as though he were a newborn child; the doctor put his arm around him and supported his head; Gavin got in on the other side so that the wounded man was supported between them, and they started for the hospital, about a mile away to the south.

In the meantime, I heard a woman's voice somewhere off to the right, wailing, "Oh, my God! It's little Minty Coleman! Oh, poor Clara! What will she do now?"

Looking over in that direction, I saw a dumpy little woman in black with her hand to her mouth, and I saw that she was looking at a blond, baby-faced adolescent of about thirteen who was being marched along without any unnecessary gentleness, but without any actual brutality, by a couple of very big men from the provost guard, accompanied by a dozen volunteers from the escort.

I stopped and talked to some of the men to find out what had happened, and reached the house just as James came in with a report from the hospital. The general was standing in the hallway by the entrance to the living room, talking to Jake. He turned around as James came in, and listened to his report.

"Dr. Ferguson says the wound is grave but not necessarily fatal, sir. No prognosis is possible at this time. None at all. All he can say is, that with luck he'll pull through, and without it he won't. He refused to say what he thought the odds were. He didn't know and refused to guess. I gathered that they were about even, one way or the other."

The general's face was grave. "This is a bad business, gentlemen. We can't have this kind of thing. Not for a minute. It's contagious. We'll have more of it if we let it go. What I will ask you to do now, James, is to get Judge Robertson for me. I want to see him at once, and if necessary you will make it clear to him that this is not a request but an order. I will be willing to send a file of soldiers for him if he feels that his dignity requires a show of force."

James' errand was unnecessary. The Judge had stopped only for the formality of a shave and fresh linen, and was already on his way to see the general. James met him as he was about to turn in at the sidewalk, and they came in together.

The Judge had cut himself in shaving, and had a strip of sticking plaster on his chin. In spite of this slightly disfiguring accident, he came into the house, his own house, with all the dignity in the world. There was no false cordiality in his manner, but there was no trace of awkwardness.

He bowed slightly. "I'm truly sorry to see you again under these circumstances, Arthur," he said. "That was a wretched business this morning. I suppose that is what you want to see me about."

General Pack inclined his head. "Yes. As you say, it's about as bad as possible. Come in, Judge, if you please."

He led the way back to the office, with James and Jake Leslie following, and the door closed behind them.

The conference was still going on fifteen or twenty minutes later, when Gavin came in, his normal, rather bristling good humor overlaid with grief and anger. I was on duty at the time, and was sitting at the desk in the hall, outside the office. I asked Gavin how Colonel Marsh was.

Gavin shook his head. "Bad, Johnny, bad. The doctor gives him a chance, and that's about all."

He knocked on the door of the office and went in. The conference was on the point of breaking up, and three of the four men in the room were already on their feet. Gavin stood just inside the room, with his hand on the doorknob.

The first words I heard were from the general, who was still seated at his desk.

"I thank you, Judge. That is most gratifying."

The Judge had undertaken, I gathered, to do all he could to prevent any repetition of this morning's occurrence and to discourage guerrilla operations of any kind.

He was unwilling to be thanked. "I see it as a matter of mutual advantage, sir," he said stiffly. Then, after a moment of hesitation, "What are you going to do with that wretched boy, General?"

"Do I have any choice?" the general asked dispassionately. "If the colonel recovers, we will simply hold him as a prisoner for the duration of the war. If the colonel dies, I will be grateful to you if you can tell me how I can get out of having the boy shot."

"Yes. Of course." The Judge's voice was lower. "I was thinking of his mother."

At this, Gavin straightened up with his mustache bristling. "As it happens, Joe Marsh has a mother, too, Judge. That probably wouldn't have occurred to you. He also has a wife and four children. His wife is a lovely woman, and she worships her husband. I hate to think of the letter I'll have to write her. I'll lie to her, of course, about the way Joe was killed, but you will excuse me, sir, if I don't have much sympathy left over."

James spoke up now, addressing Gavin across the room. "Joe isn't dead yet, Gavin. The chances are about even that you won't have to write that letter. It's about even either way." He turned to General Pack. "It occurs to me, sir, that we might take the line of treating the boy as totally irresponsible, and refuse to dignify him by treating him as a man and an enemy—"

"He was man enough to aim a gun and pull the trigger," Gavin interrupted angrily. "It was me he was aiming at, James."

James shook his head and twisted his face into a wry smile. "No, he wasn't. At least he didn't think he was. He thought he was aiming at the commanding general. It was practically a miracle of ineptitude. He tried to kill General Pack, aimed at General Ross, and hit Colonel Marsh. It was quite a performance."

Gavin was still irritated. "Maybe it was. It was as stupid and pointless as you like, but that doesn't help Joe." He turned to Judge Robertson again, with great earnestness. "Joe Marsh is a close personal friend of mine, Judge. He's also very popular with the men. They respect him and they like him, and what they felt this morning was grief as well as anger. They were perfectly wild. They were all for burning down the house and hacking the young fellow to pieces on the spot. It took all the authority I had to keep them in line. My men would feel that I had betrayed them, as well as Colonel Marsh, if I favored any leniency in this matter."

Gavin tried to smile, but found it difficult, as he added, "Suppose we pin our hopes on what our friend, Colonel Lake, just reminded us of. That Colonel Marsh isn't dead yet, and has about an even chance of recovering."

Judge Robertson bowed his head slightly in Gavin's direction, and said nothing at all. James withdrew from further argument, and, after a moment, General Pack delivered the opinion of the court. It was a very brief one.

He stood up and said, "I think all of us had better pray for Colonel Marsh's recovery. Good afternoon, Judge. I thank you for coming in. Good afternoon, gentlemen."

Joe Marsh's condition remained grave for three or four days. After that he began to improve at a steady, day-to-day, rate. By the end of the week he was able to lie in the sun on the long porch along the south side of the hospital, and a little later, to sit up in a reclining chair. Dr. Ferguson found his condition satisfactory, though he refused to say that he was out of danger, and refused to predict the date when he would be able to leave the hospital.

Actually, the good fortune of the command continued unbroken. The Coleman boy was universally condemned, though the townspeople were sorry for his mother. The general feeling was that if he wanted to kill Yankees that bad, he should have gone south and joined General McGraw. We were given a good deal of credit for our restraint in not shooting the boy on the spot. The officers were given credit for keeping their men in hand, the men for obeying their officers. We were given credit for not maltreating the boy in jail, and for allowing him to see visitors. If we had been compelled to shoot him, a majority of the townspeople would have accepted the act— reluctantly, perhaps—as one of exact justice.

The weather broke on the first of November. The misty drizzle that had been in the air when we left the club after the Halloween party, by morning had turned into a steady cold rain, driven by a gusty wind from the northwest.

I was aware of this change in the weather much sooner than I wanted to be, for I woke up in the middle of the night and heard the rain dashing against the roof and the windows; at the same time I realized that an orderly was standing by the bed with his hand on my shoulder, and that he was about to shake me again. I forestalled this by sitting up, and the orderly told me in a low voice that I was to report to the general at once.

I splashed some cold water on my face and got dressed, and

on my way downstairs I noticed that there was a dirty gray light outside the windows, which this late in the year meant that it was close to seven o'clock. The entire lower floor of the house was lighted, and a good part of the household was already up.

The general had a packet of dispatches for Jonesy, wrapped in oilcloth, which I was to deliver. He wanted Jonesy's opinion on the state of the river, and he wanted me to report to Jonesy on the state of the roads; he wanted me to point out any soft spots I might find to Jonesy, and to have him run a few guns and caissons and heavily loaded wagons over them, and to report on the results; and finally, I was to invite Jonesy to dinner, to meet the general's sister, Mrs. Morgan, who was expected sometime during the day.

By the time the general was through giving me my instructions, my orderly had brought down my so-called waterproofs, and my horse—or rather, one of James' horses, a big chestnut named Nostromo that hadn't been out for a week and needed exercise, a horse both of us liked—was at the door. Someone handed me a packet of sandwiches and a canteen full of hot coffee, and I went out into the rain.

The light was iron gray by this time; the rain was slanting down in long gray lines; the wet black limbs of the trees in front of the house and along both sides of the street were swinging in the wind, and the ground was covered with sodden brown and yellow leaves. As I turned into the street I had the wind and the rain in my face, and the not very comforting knowledge that I had fifteen miles to go to reach Jonesy's headquarters, and that I would be riding into the teeth of the wind all the way. And before I reached the edge of town, at the jog in the road leading to the bridge, I felt a trickle of cold water running down the back of my neck, and my waterproofs were proving to be about as dependable as I had expected them to be.

Somebody had put a sentry on the bridge for no reason that I could see. At least I brought some brightness into his life. I was crossing the bridge at a walk, slumped over in the saddle, and no doubt a perfect picture of dejection, when all of a sudden I found this young fellow in front of me with his rifle and his bayonet, and his, Halt! Who goes there? and an impish look of delight on his face.

I gave him a sour look and said, "You know damned well who goes there."

He stood aside and gave me an elaborate salute and an apology to go with it.

"Beg your pardon, Captain Lake. I would have recognized you, sir, only I didn't think staff officers went out on days like this."

I tried to think of a proper reprimand, then I saw that he was soaking wet, and had probably been feeling pretty miserable himself until I came along, so I merely gave him another sour look and said, "That's a nice idea of yours, soldier. Go up and tell General Pack about it, will you?"

I raised my hand as I went on, by way of returning his salute, and felt the water running down inside my sleeve. If he had known about that, he would probably have felt even better. A little farther on I remembered my bread and bacon and coffee, and afterwards felt more like a human being, though a very wet and miserable one.

The road was metaled only as far as the bridge; beyond that it went on as an ordinary country road. In dry weather it was not bad, but now, after a night's rain, it was cut up by wagon tracks and hoofprints, and crisscrossed with yellow-brown mud puddles, which filled all the depressions in the ground and ran together to form larger ones, sheets of muddy water pocked with rain, in some places covering half the road.

I acquired a great familiarity with this muddy, rutted surface: for a large part of the way that was all I saw, as I rode with my cap down over my eyes and my head bent over my horse's neck. Occasionally the rain would let up for a few minutes, and I would straighten up and look around, with only a spattering of rain in my face; then it would start coming down again, and I would bow my head to the storm and resume my contemplation of the road and Glamorgan County mud.

The sky was a sullen gray, with low clouds moving swiftly

past overhead. The countryside was familiar—I had been over the road innumerable times in the past month, and knew the turnings of the road and where the side roads went, and who owned the rare houses visible from the road—but I had seen it only in sunlight and under a blue sky, glowing with color, pleasant, and—so it seemed to me—quite friendly.

All this was changed. There were no glowing colors anywhere, and everything was darker: the silvery gray of the fence rails and tree trunks was almost black, the yellows and browns of the foliage were dark and sodden, and the green of the open fields was grayed with rain. Along with this physical darkening of the landscape went a corresponding feeling of estrangement. For the first time I felt that I was an alien and an enemy, and that I was riding through hostile country.

This was literally true, of course, but it had been equally true all month, and my sudden awareness was no more than a reflection of the fact that I was cold and wet and miserable. I had ham and eggs, and fresh bread and hot coffee at Jonesy's headquarters while my clothes were drying out. Afterwards I went around with Major Stewart and a couple of Jonesy's engineers to look over the roads and the works they were building along the river, and to have a look at the river itself, which was muddy and rising fast.

It was raining as hard as ever when I started back, but the wind was at my back now, and my waterproofs kept me at least fairly dry. It was the same road I was riding over and there had been no change in the landscape, but I had forgotten that it was hostile and that I was an enemy.

The principal event of the day and another turning point, along with the break in the weather, was the arrival of the general's sister, Judith Morgan, with her son, escorted in by Dick's missing cavalry regiment, the 12th Pennsylvania. This event had its ramifications.

The 12th Pennsylvania Cavalry had been promised us to replace a New York regiment that had gone to the Army of the Potomac in August. It had been promised originally for the middle of September. The two cavalry regiments already

134 ❧

on hand had lost heavily in the Willow Run battle, and had been badly overworked ever since.

Dick had complained frequently and angrily about the absence of his third regiment. General Pack had backed his complaints forcefully to General Crawford, to Halleck, and finally to the Secretary, and had been assured that the 12th Pennsylvania was on its way and should reach us in a few days. This was early in October. After that, the regiment simply dropped out of sight for nearly three weeks; neither Crawford nor Halleck knew what had become of it, and if the Secretary knew, he didn't tell us. The regiment finally came in on the first of November, and we learned what had caused the delay: it had been held up for nineteen days in order to serve as the personal escort of the wife of former Governor Morgan. Dick was furious, and the general was seriously annoyed.

The lady herself did nothing to help matters. When I got back from Jennings' Landing she had been in town for no more than a couple of hours, but in that brief time she had managed to infuriate everyone she met, from orderly to general. Everyone I ran into had some new story to tell, and Jake, ordinarily the most indulgent and even-tempered of men, already had a name for her: the Queen of the Night.

The first person she fell afoul of was the first person she met, the sentry on duty outside the door: he caught hell because he refused to leave his post to carry in her luggage. His commanding officer, Howel Jenkins, was her next target because he upheld his sentry. Howel got Bob Kelso, the next in line: Bob had her luggage brought in and her horses and carriage taken care of, but he didn't know that she was expected, nor where to put her luggage, which made him both stupid and insolent. And Jake, who happened to be the only senior officer there at the time—an added offense—came in for his share because he refused to have Jack Maitland's belongings moved out so her maid could have his room.

Others came under fire as they appeared: Colin for not meeting his aunt, or at least being on hand to greet her; the Countess because nothing, absolutely nothing, had been pre-

pared for her, and of course she would need the room next to
hers for her maid. She had a word for everybody until the
general came in. He listened for half a minute, then told her
that this was his headquarters, not a hotel, and she would
have to take what there was; that he was going to be busy for
the next hour, and would see her at dinner. I never did find
out where her maid slept.

Previous to this I hadn't given the general's younger sister
much thought. I merely expected her to be a big woman because everybody else in the family was on a large scale. Now,
after hearing about her arrival from a dozen different people, I
began to expect something on the order of the Witch of
Endor. I was wrong on both counts, and was quite unprepared
when the Countess introduced me to her in the living room
before dinner.

The woman whose not exactly triumphal entry I had been
hearing about turned out to be a slender, attractive woman
with beautiful violet eyes and long eyelashes, dressed in black
and gold with a pleasing amount of white neck and bosom
showing. She appeared to be about thirty and was actually
within a month of her fortieth birthday.

She looked up and gave me a most charming smile when the
Countess mentioned my name. "Captain Lake. I'm so happy
to meet you, Captain." Her low, warm voice gave meaning to
the empty formula; she sounded as though she really meant it.
"Lucy has been telling me all kinds of wonderful things about
you. I suppose you're related to the fascinating Colonel Lake?
But of course you are. You look very much alike."

This was highly flattering and just a little funny. I got out
my best manners and bowed. "Thank you, Mrs. Morgan. Yes,
ma'am, James is my uncle. If he's the fascinating Colonel
Lake. I never would have thought of the word, myself."

This seemed to entertain everybody, and was greeted with
laughter by the men around the sofa.

Judith Morgan scowled at me with mock severity and
sighed, "Oh, you men! You're so obtuse. Any woman would
know what I was talking about, wouldn't they, Lucy? Don't
you think the colonel is fascinating?"

There was a sudden awkward silence in the room, while the Countess gave her sister-in-law a startled look. She recovered herself quickly, frowned, and appeared to give the question her attention.

"I think I agree with Johnny," she said finally. "It's not the word I would use. James is a handsome man, of course, but so is Major Saint Chamans. I'll put you between them at dinner, and you can make up your mind."

There was an almost indistinguishable growl from somewhere by the fire. This was Jonesy, with his dried leathery face and bald head and drooping black mustache, incongruous in a new uniform buttoned to the neck and a high stiff collar, and annoyed by this contest in pulchritude. What he said, in a low exasperated growl, was, "Damn fine soldiers, both of them."

The general's sister looked at Jonesy with her most charming smile, and accepted the reproof. "I'm sure they are, General Jones," she said meekly. "I'm sure you would know."

As it happened, I ran into the two paladins almost immediately afterwards, and both of them were a little drunk. They were standing by the sideboard, drinking sherry on top of the Lord only knows what, and talking with great animation to a third man whom I had never seen before, a man as tall as they were but twenty pounds heavier, with a ruddy face and black hair, wearing eagles on his shoulder straps.

James broke off whatever it was he was saying to call me over, and as I came up he explained me rather than introduced me to the third man, who was obviously the commander of the new cavalry regiment.

"This is my nephew, Johnny Lake. If the war lasts long enough, and if Johnny lasts long enough—and he'll have to learn to duck at the right time; he wasn't so good at it in our last fight—why, he may turn out to be a credit to us. Otherwise, he'll go back home and take over his father's law practice, and be a pillar of the community, and a credit to the town of Lancaster and the Presbyterian church."

Saint Chamans looked at me, then at James. "Is that so dreadful? There are days when I can think of nothing more attractive than to live in a small town in the Auvergne and plead in the courts, and interest myself in the details of the things that people go to law about. To have a family and an office, and to leave promptly at nine o'clock every morning, and go to Mass on Sunday, and play whist with the prefect and his wife once a week. To be sedate and respectable, and a pillar of the community."

James laughed. "Maître Saint Chamans, eh? I can guess when this particular fancy strikes you. On particularly dirty gray Monday mornings. Or when you've been drinking too much champagne and talking too much. Talking to too many bright, intelligent, witty people, who cancel each other out."

James went on, and, while he was talking, the new colonel grinned at me and put out his hand.

"I'm glad to meet you, John," he said. "I'm Cam Heath, as James would probably have got around to telling you in another fifteen or twenty minutes. Your uncle and I were in college together, and since then we've made a habit of running into each other every two or three years. Usually in the damndest places you can imagine. The first time it was in a mining camp about forty miles out of Sacramento. James had a beard and a slouch hat over one eye, and a flannel shirt and a revolver slung around his waist. Just like everybody else. Only—you know James—he looked as though beards and slouch hats and navy revolvers were *de rigueur* that year, and the last word in elegance. You could tell him a mile away—"

James interrupted him at this moment with a laugh. "Here's a man who has been looking for you, Cam."

I turned my head and saw Dick Ross coming in our direction, his mustache bristling fiercely, his swagger very pronounced. He pounced on Cam Heath.

"By God, you finally got here, Colonel. I've been in a stew about you for three weeks. I swore I was going to tear you limb from limb. Now, by God, I find out that if I'm going to tear anybody apart I'll have to go to Washington to do it, and get my hands on the Secretary."

Heath had been waiting to see how this was going to turn out, his expression a little wary. Now there was a crooked smile on his face.

"You know, Colonel, that's a noble idea. If you go to Washington, I'd like to go along and help. Maybe I could hold a leg."

Dick stared at him for a moment, then gave a shout of laughter. "You sure as hell can. And while we're about it, we might as well have a word with old Fish-Eye." He chuckled over this, then said more soberly, "Anyway, I'm glad to see you, Heath, and glad to have your regiment. Only, I warn you, I'm going to work hell out of you and your men."

"That's what we're here for," Heath replied. "If you don't mind my saying so, Colonel, I've got a fine regiment for you. Good boys, the lot of them. All they need is a little experience."

"Don't let that worry you, Colonel." Dick's grin was a little wolfish. "We'll see they get it."

We had a full house at dinner that night. The big round table in the dining room was stretched out to an oval shape by means of boards in the middle, and the usual seating arrangement was altered slightly to put the guest of honor halfway down the table instead of next to the general. Here she had James on one side, and the blond Saint Chamans on the other. Colonel Heath had been annexed by the cavalry, but had been given a place of honor, next to Madame. The third newcomer, Lieutenant Derek Morgan, Judith's son, who had joined us as aide-de-camp to the general, was sitting three places away from me, but with Colin and Jack Maitland in between, I didn't see much of him until after dinner.

I seem to see this gathering at the dinner table with a double vision: from a later vantage point I find sinister overtones in the conversation, ambiguities, signs and portents of things to come. At the time, though, none of this was apparent to me. I was impressed by the general's sister, by the names she mentioned casually, and by the atmosphere of the great world she brought with her. We had two beautiful and distinguished women at the table, and it seemed to me that it was an unusually festive evening.

Judith was exerting herself to dispel the impression her arrival had created. She was pleasant to Bob Kelso and respectful to Jake, and charming to everybody. During a brief lull in the conversation, I heard her son, Derek, remark to Colin in a low voice that was both derisive and admiring, "My word! Mother is really laying it on tonight, isn't she?"

She was, of course. She had charm in great quantity, and could turn it on whenever she liked. Just now she had it on at full, with a warm smile for everybody, and a bright laugh that was delightful to hear. Much of this charm was simply thrown out at random, in all directions, like light from an open fire; but the greater part, greater and more intense, was directed at James and Saint Chamans.

For some reason James had taken it into his head to talk about Robert's family: in fact, he had introduced him as Count Robert de Saint Chamans, rather than Major Saint Chamans, to Robert's obvious annoyance. The general's sister was impressed, and Robert was bored and cynical, and possibly gratified in spite of himself. He corrected James on a couple of points regarding the family alliances, then laughed.

"You should talk to my great aunt," he said. "Tante Geneviève. She can go on like this all night without stopping."

"I have talked to her," James replied. "A couple of summers ago, if you remember. She talked steadily until bedtime, and the next day she gave me a book to read. I particularly liked the note on the fourth baron, Foulques le Barbu. It begins: 'Of this sacrilegious ruffian the less said the better.' Then it goes on for four or five pages. He was quite an ancestor."

Robert raised one eyebrow. "His mother was a witch. What would you expect? To be prosaic about it, he didn't like the monastery's eating up half his revenues. He didn't like monks, and the monks wrote the chronicles."

A few minutes later I heard Judith say, "You must be related to the Orleans boys." She laughed brightly. "Captain Perry and Captain Chatters. The Governor and I ran into them almost everywhere we went before General McClellan left Washington. I suppose you know them?"

Robert was pained but polite. "Not well, ma'am. The relationship is quite a distant one, and we were never exactly devoted to the Orleans family. My grandfather detested Philippe Égalité, and my father disliked his son." Robert's face brightened a little. "Of course, being a loyal subject of Abraham the First, myself, all this is none of my affair."

In the meantime, our new cavalry officer, Colonel Heath, was talking to Madame Lucy at the foot of the table. I caught an occasional phrase, and gathered that he was telling her about the Irish earl he and James had known in California, and about the earl's tumble-down castle and beautiful horses, and about James in a scarlet hunting coat and velvet cap. Madame Lucy listened graciously, and was delighted with the story. Colonel Heath, much gratified, went on to tell her more about his old friend and their regular encounters.

At the other end of the table, General Pack was talking to Jake and Hal Stewart. Major Harold Stewart, our chief engineer, was a sober, quiet man, and a devout Episcopalian, nearly bald at the age of thirty-one, with a few strands of dark hair combed over the top of his head. He and Jake had both been in Virginia the previous winter, and they were talking about the Virginia mud, and the fact that the rebels were able to move freely over terrain that we got hopelessly bogged down in. Jake thought it was an illusion: that the rebels knew when the roads were impassable, and didn't even try to use them at such times. Hal Stewart only half agreed with him. He thought that their familiarity with the local terrain enabled them to use byroads and country lanes, and to move cross-country, so that the main roads weren't overworked. Also, that as a general thing they traveled much lighter than we did.

General Pack remarked to the table at large that we hadn't seen much of Barney McGraw for the past few days, which pretty certainly meant that he was up to something. He wondered whether any of us had any ideas on the subject.

All our information, from sources that were quite reliable, indicated that McGraw had reorganized and re-equipped his command, but that it was still below its original strength, and not much over ten thousand strong. This disparity of forces, roughly fifteen to ten, limited the possibilities. Barney would avoid battle, and would try to chop us down to his own size with attacks on our supply lines and outlying positions, and with raids on the less-strongly-held portions of our lines.

Our problem was to meet these attacks without being swung from one end of the county to the other, wearing out men and horses in the process, and to make them so costly for Barney, in terms of at least equal casualties, that he couldn't afford them. This was a subject all of us had given much thought to, and it monopolized the conversation while fruit and sweets were being served, and lasted until the general and our two guests stood up, and dinner was over.

After dinner I spent most of the evening—the hour and a half I was able to stay awake, at any rate—with Colin and our new aide-de-camp, Derek Morgan. Earlier, in speaking of his cousin Derek, Colin had quoted someone's phrase, a silken young man, and had said I wouldn't like him. I could see where the word *silken* came in: he was slender and graceful, and except for a small mustache, had a complexion like a girl's. His manners were polished and he was almost painfully polite, but the curse was taken off this by his air of easy self-assurance. He had a good deal of his mother's charm and was an entertaining companion, and Colin's prediction was quite wrong: I liked him very much, and was pleased that he was going to be with us on the staff. He was assigned to quarters with the three of us—or four, if you counted Colin's dog—on the third floor.

Judith had made her choice by this time. She was clinging to James, looking up at him and blinking her lovely violet eyes. With the utmost tact, of course, and in the very best of taste, not slighting any of the men around her but making it clear, nevertheless, that James was the man of her choice.

Derek found this highly entertaining. "Oh, Lord! Look at my mother, will you?" He chuckled. "I should have warned you. Mother's an inveterate collector of scalps. Colonel Lake's your uncle, isn't he, Captain? I hope his hair is on good and tight."

"I think it is," I said. "James is pretty much attached to his scalp."

Derek was skeptical. "You don't know my mother. You don't know what a mighty hunter she is. I'll bet anything you like she has the colonel's scalp added to her collection before she leaves."

I was about to take his bet, when Bob Kelso came up, sandy-haired and jug-eared, his face glowing with excitement.

"You know what Jake just told me?" he demanded breathlessly, then went off at a tangent. "I thought the old man was looking pretty smug at dinner tonight. Like the cat that swallowed the cream. Jake says the message just came in a couple of hours ago. From General Crawford. You know, the general asked for Thompson's division, and if he couldn't get Thompson, he wanted Gerald Peale? Well, we're getting both of them. Thompson's coming in next week, and Peale right behind him."

This was good but not surprising news. The best part of it was that we were getting the men we asked for, good soldiers under good commanders, troops we could depend on almost the way we could depend on ourselves. Or perhaps the best part of it was that we were about to get under way again. Not that we had been wasting our time or stagnating: we had been reorganizing, securing our base, and preparing for our next move. But now that the move was at hand we were conscious, all at once, of the length of time we had been here, and were impatient to move on.

Derek was as excited as any of us—perhaps more so, since he had yet to prove himself—but he was more expert at concealing his feelings than we were. He had a mannerism, which I came to recognize later on, of responding to excitement or to anger with an exaggerated air of nonchalance, a languid drawl, and what we took to be a British accent.

Now he pulled on his small mustache, looked around at us with raised eyebrows, and remarked indifferently, "Well now, that should be interesting."

This served to remind the rest of us that we were seasoned veterans, who took such things as offensive movements and battles as a matter of course, and to make us feel a little sheepish about our previous excitement. All except Bob Kelso, who stared at Derek for a moment, then gave a hoot of derision.

"Interesting? Well, I guess you could call it that if you wanted to," he said in a dry voice. "You get some pretty interesting ideas about the morning of the fourth day when you haven't had any sleep for three days and nights. I suppose there is something interesting about a horse with both his front legs shot off. Or seeing a man hit in the belly by a cannon ball. It makes a soft sound. A kind of plop. It's a sound you'll remember. Then half of him goes one way and half the other, and the look on his face is quite remarkable. You'll remember that, too."

Colin interrupted him. "All right, Bob. Shut up," he said mildly. "You don't need to go through the whole catalogue. Derek knows it isn't going to be any picnic."

"I got the idea that maybe he thought it was," Bob said.

Derek looked at him with black anger in his eyes, then smiled blandly. "I've talked to soldiers before. I believe I've heard what Colin calls the whole catalogue."

That was all there was to it at the time. We went on to speculate about the command arrangements, and how the new divisions were going to be fitted in, and about the direction of the offensive. Whether we would break out to the east, through the mountain passes, and if so, whether we would cross to the south, near the river, or to the north, where the passes were lower. Or whether we would use our command of the river and the support the gunboats could give us to break out to the west. There were arguments in favor of each of these courses, but not enough specific information among us to carry the argument very far.

On Sunday Billy Roth gave a large and very elaborate luncheon party for Judith Morgan, and sent Horace Townsend in to escort her down to his headquarters. Horace was a friend of ours, a quiet man, stoop-shouldered and clean-shaven, formerly the publisher of a newspaper in Roth's Congressional district and now his adjutant. Colin and Derek and I went with him as part of the escort.

I noticed that Mrs. Morgan was no longer wasting any of her warmth and charm on me. When she spoke to me at all, her voice was peremptory and cold, and I began to see what the others had been talking about.

Derek noticed this change of manner, and was amused. "I see you're no longer in Mother's good graces, John. What have you been doing? Trying to steal her jewelry?"

I shrugged my shoulders. "Nothing that I know of. I went to bed early."

Derek laughed. "Something must have gone wrong with her head-hunting expedition. I suspect that the colonel got away with his scalp intact. That wouldn't please her at all. And you're the proverbial innocent bystander."

As a matter of fact, that was exactly what had happened, but in an aggravated form. Later in the day, Robert Saint Chamans told me that she had ended by offering James the key to her bedroom. He said that James had been conducting a marvelously skillful rear-guard action up to that time.

"But there isn't any graceful way out of that one," Robert went on. "Either you accept, or you make a mortal enemy. I don't know what James told her. That he was faithful to his dear wife and six children, that he was a Trappist monk on leave, or what. For that matter, I don't know what was wrong with him. She's an attractive woman. I would have jumped into bed with her like a shot. Anyway, whatever he came up with wasn't good enough, and she was a woman scorned. She looked like one of the Borgias. If she had had a dagger she would have stabbed him."

This had happened the night before after nearly everyone had left, or had gone to bed. I think I might have felt a little better if I had known this on Sunday afternoon. Judith was a woman with a strong personality, and she had a wonderful faculty for turning a man into a gaping fool with a single look, a raised eyebrow, a cold "Well?" She exercised this faculty on me two or three times while we were at Roth's headquarters, and each time it left me with a sheepish grin frozen on my face, a clumsy, half-witted country boy who had just knocked over the gravy bowl. When she had taken care of me, she turned on her charm again, and had Billy and most of the staff eating out of her hand.

The luncheon lasted until after four, and it was nearly dark when we started back. After we had delivered the lady to headquarters, I stayed long enough to find that there were no orders for me, and to get into some clean clothes, then got out of the house as fast as I could. I wanted to see as little of the general's sister as possible.

As it happened, I hadn't been in the Robertson house for some time. I had seen the Judge on the street and had heard Christina practicing nearly every day, and had passed by one afternoon when Blair Robertson was trying out his artificial leg on the walk at the side of the house. Instead of glowering at me, he called me over to show me how well he was getting on with the contraption, which pleased me. I assumed that the afternoon gatherings went on as usual in my absence, but I wasn't entirely sure. Hence my relief at hearing the sound of the piano as I approached the house, and at the sight of blue uniforms through the window.

Jake let me in. I was about to ask if he was another refugee from Judith Morgan's wrath, when he motioned me to be quiet. I stood where I was, by the door, and looked into the room. The light was shadowy, and came from a pair of candles on the piano, on either side of the music rack. The woman at the piano was not Christina, but the Countess, and there were only two other people in the room, Blair Robertson on the far side, and standing at the right of the piano with one hand on the casing, my uncle James, staring fixedly at the music in the rack, with an expression on his face I had never seen before, his face lean and grim and seemingly full of grief.

The Countess was singing, her voice richer and fuller than I remembered, floating over the deliberate figure of the accompaniment, rising as though lifted by the wind, and descending again in a slow curve over a few quiet modulations,

the song perfectly simple, only two pages long, and so beautiful it broke your heart. She came to the end with the two
quiet measures of the accompaniment, held the final chord
briefly, then dropped her hands into her lap and sat with her
head bowed.

There was a long silence. No one moved or even seemed to
breathe, and the room was still full of music. The spell was
still unbroken when young Robertson, visible only as a white
face and a pair of eyes in the shadows at the far end of the
room, said in a hushed voice, as though he were in church,
"That was very beautiful, ma'am."

The Countess raised her head, her hair coppery in the
candlelight, and replied in the same hushed voice, "It is
beautiful, isn't it? I love it."

The silence fell again, and was still in the room when Judge
Robertson came in. He was wearing a long cloak, very wet
around the shoulders, and a soft black hat which he took off as
he came into the room. He seemed to be greatly surprised at
finding us there, but recovered himself quickly and had a
courteous greeting for James and me, and a warm smile for
the Countess and for his friend Jake, and a smile and a nod
for his son, who had left off his artificial leg and came over on
crutches, with his trouser leg pinned up.

For a few minutes the conversation was general. It had
begun to rain. We were told this was normal for this time of
year. The roses were almost finished. They sometimes lasted
into December, but that was only in exceptional years. The
Judge remembered Mrs. Morgan very well. He remembered
her as an impressive woman, imperious and strong-minded.
The Governor, her husband, had been a man of considerable
ability at one time, but now he was old and burned out.
Burned out and very rich. Thanks to his wife, in large measure, for both.

It was nearly six o'clock, and time for us to be getting back.
We all started to leave at the same time, then Jake and the
Countess were called back, and James and I went on. The rain
had dwindled away to a mist, and a soft east wind was blowing in our faces.

As we started out, James was laughing at me and my troubles with the Queen of the Night, but as we went on he became thoughtful. Finally, just as we turned in, he said, "You know, Johnny, something is up. The Judge was worried when he came in. He covered it up very well, but he was worried. And Jake was bothered about something, too. I don't know that it was the same thing."

He was silent for a moment, then went on with apparent irrelevance, "Jake believes in second sight. Did you know that, Johnny?"

I was astonished. "Jake? An educated man like Jake? It's hard to believe."

"I know it is. Get him to tell you about it sometime."

Dinner was a family affair that night. There were only fourteen of us at the table, and the general's sister was the only guest. She had her charm well under control, and made herself agreeable to almost everybody, and was at least coolly civil to James and me. There was a great deal of family reminiscence in the conversation, which at times became a four-sided affair between Judith and the general, and Colin and Derek. At our end of the table I tried to steer the conversation onto the subject of visions and portents and the like. Jake remarked that he had a great-grandmother on the Isle of Skye who spoke nothing but Gaelic. That was as far as the subject got, for he went on to talk about the weather in the Hebrides, and to describe a certain quality of light that he had never seen anywhere else. The trouble that James had sensed earlier seemed to be completely forgotten. Then all at once our provost marshal, Major Lumley, was standing in the doorway, and there it was.

General Pack looked over at him with some surprise, and asked what he had on his mind. For some reason the major was unwilling to tell him in public. I suspect that he felt personally humiliated by the information he was bringing, and wanted to have as few witnesses as possible. At any rate, the general put his napkin on the table and excused himself, and went out to talk to him. A minute or two later he appeared in the doorway long enough to call for me, and when I joined them in the hallway he told me to go down to the hospital and get a report on Colonel Marsh, and come back with it as soon as possible.

In daylight I could have been down and back in ten minutes, but it was night by this time, and pitch-dark; it was raining, and there was no starlight, and no moon behind the clouds. Occasional dim rectangles of lamplight came from the houses along the street, but these were sparse and widely separated, and confusing rather than helpful in indicating the road. Under the circumstances my horse knew the road better than I did, and after I turned him into the south road I gave him his head and let him go at his own gait. There wasn't much else I could do. I couldn't have gone much faster, no matter how urgent my errand, and this one had no urgency at all. I knew what my report was going to be before I started, and before I was halfway to the hospital I knew why the general wanted it.

Joe Marsh was certainly dead. Dr. Ferguson had never given him better than an even chance, and with the change in the weather he had taken a turn for the worse. The wretched boy who shot him had escaped: that was what Major Lumley was so chagrined about. The Judge and Christina were involved in the escape. That was why Christina hadn't been at home, and why the Judge was worried when he came in.

Our hospital in the seminary was a model of comfort and cleanliness, as army hospitals went, but for all its excellence, the place gave me the horrors. The combined smell of gangrene, chloroform, and carbolic was repellent, and the sound of men in pain was always in the air.

Dr. Ferguson was making his rounds when I got there, and I talked to one of his assistants, Dr. Erdman, a young man with a reddish beard who had a cigar in his mouth and affected an air of callous toughness, but was obviously upset, both as man and physician, over the death of Joe Marsh.

"There didn't seem to be any change this morning," he told me. "His fever had gone down. His pulse was holding up. As a matter of fact, I thought he was better. Then about one

149

o'clock this afternoon, for no reason at all that anybody could see, all of a sudden he started going down. He wasn't trying any more. He just gave up. When they do that, Captain, there's nothing you can do about it. You might as well call out the burial detail and tell them to get the grave ready. He started going downhill, and he just kept on going. Down and out. He died about five o'clock."

I started back, riding perfectly blind in the darkness, simply letting my horse carry me. It was the right side of my face that was wet now, with a fine hissing rain slanting down on a soft east wind.

The atmosphere at headquarters was sober when I got back. Derek and his mother were playing a listless game of whist with Bob Kelso and the Countess, and Colin was looking on. There was no one else in sight.

The general was in the office. James and Jake Leslie and Major Lumley were with him, and Christina and Judge Robertson were sitting across the room, Christina in boy's clothes—gray trousers and jacket—pale, but surprisingly composed. She had evidently taken young Coleman's place while the boy, dressed in her clothes, walked out on the arm of the Judge.

General Pack looked up at me as I came in, and I could see that he was wearing the mask of expressionless calm that we had come to speak of as his great stone face.

"Well, John?" he asked.

"Colonel Marsh died at five o'clock, sir," I said.

"How long had he been in a dying condition?"

"Since about one o'clock, sir. I talked to Dr. Erdman. He said that Colonel Marsh began to fail about that time for no discernible reason. That he had been better this morning. The doctor said he simply gave up, and went straight downhill from then on. Down and out, was the way the doctor put it."

The general thought this over, then nodded by way of dismissal.

The session in the general's office lasted only a few minutes longer. Major Lumley came out first, followed shortly afterwards by Jake, with the Judge and his daughter.

My clothes were soaked again, from my ride down to the hospital, and I went up to the third floor to change. While I was pulling on a pair of dry boots I realized suddenly that there was considerable activity outside, with horses being brought around and voices calling back and forth, and cavalry forming in the street. I finished dressing and hurried down the stairs just in time to meet General Pack, coming from the office with a swish of rubber, in boots and long black waterproof. His face was no longer grim, and he greeted me cheerfully in passing.

"Your turn to get a night's sleep, John," he said as he went by.

He stopped off in the living room, bent over his wife's chair briefly, said something to his sister, and went out. Everyone else had left, and the two women were alone. The cavalcade in front moved off at a walk as soon as the general had joined it. In another five minutes they were out of hearing, and silence settled down again.

I went back to the office to ask Jake what was going on. Jake was at his desk, writing, and looked up at me with the pained expression of the busy man interrupted.

"Where's everybody going, Jake?" I asked.

"Over to the First Division. For the Jarvie attack."

I accepted this and let it go without further thought. There was something else on my mind. "How did the session go, Jake?" I asked. "I thought the general was looking pretty grim."

Jake leaned back and put down his pen. "Nothing much to it, Johnny," he said. "The only person in any kind of stew was our godly disciple of John Knox, Major Lumley. He wanted to hang somebody, or shoot somebody, or boil somebody in oil. He thought the eternal flames needed fuel. Of course he felt personally disgraced. Nobody paid much attention to him.

"James and I were relieved. As you say, Arthur was grim, but that was because someone else had taken the matter out of his hands. Arthur likes to make his own decisions. The Judge took full responsibility. The boy was a kinsman of his, and he was in honor bound to rescue him if he could. The girl—Christina—was marvelous. More courage and dignity than you can imagine. I thought she and the Judge looked better than we did. With Major Lumley on our side, anyway."

Jake let his voice fall. I waited for him to go on, then awkwardly approached the subject that had been bothering me.

"When I was down at the hospital tonight, the man I talked to—I think he's an assistant surgeon—Dr. Erdman. You know who he is?"

Jake looked at me impatiently. "Yes, I know him. Came out with an Illinois regiment. Ferguson liked him and got him transferred. What about him?"

"Well, he knew that Joe was going to die as early as one o'clock. A little later the whole hospital knew it. Anyone who went out there this afternoon knew it."

"All right. That's probably true. And then what?" Jake's voice was dry.

"The Countess was there this afternoon. On the way back she stopped at the Robertsons', and both Christina and the Judge were gone. She must have known that something was going on. In fact, all she had to do was put two and two together to know exactly what it was that was going on. Unless she knew all the time, because she was helping them."

Jake raised his eyebrows, and his voice was still drier. "Don't you approve?"

This stunned me, and left me floundering for words. "Oh, good God, Jake, no! I wasn't talking about approving of anything. I mean, if she does something, it's all right. I mean, that makes it all right. She wouldn't do it, if it wasn't."

I had more to say, still floundering, along the same general lines, but Jake interrupted me. "Thanks, Johnny. That's enough. Your general meaning is clear, though I thought for a moment it was going to be strangled at birth."

He twisted his leathery face into a scowl, then went on in a dry schoolmaster's voice that was about evenly divided between kindness and irony.

"You know, it amazes me how much you young fellows have to learn," he said. "For example, if Madame Lucy was aware of the situation at the hospital and that at the Robertson house, the two and two you mentioned, she was under no compulsion to put them together to make four. On the contrary, she would have been careful to avoid doing anything of the sort. An example I commend to you. It would have kept you from drawing unwarranted and unwelcome conclusions."

Jake paused, and gave me a speculative look. "You might remember that, Johnny," he said. "If you see two and two, you are not compelled to add them. If the answer is none of your business, or one you don't want to know, or if you're simply not interested, you can let your two and two lie where they are. You can leave them there, separate, and forget about them. It's only when the subject properly concerns you, and you definitely want to know the answer, that you have to add them: then they make four."

Jake smiled, and picked up his pen. "There you are, Johnny. Consider yourself instructed."

I started to leave, then suddenly remembered the answer to my original question, and turned back. "I thought the Jarvie attack was for later in the week. Why are they putting it on tonight?"

Jake was pained by my obtuseness, but bore with me. "You seem to have missed some of the implications of the affair this evening," he explained patiently. "In particular, its effect on the morale of the First Division. Joe Marsh was a popular man in the division. His death is going to be painful news to every man there. The fact that we let ourselves be tricked, and his murderer got away, isn't going to help. We look foolish. Our prestige is damaged, and our capacity for inspiring confidence in the troops is impaired. So we have to do something about it. We want them to hear about Joe, and about the Coleman boy, when they're feeling good about something, when they're feeling proud of themselves."

None of this had occurred to me, and I was impressed. Only one element seemed doubtful. "What about the attack, Jake? Isn't it pretty much a gamble?"

Jake's expression was sardonic. "Don't you approve of taking chances, John? All I can tell you is that it has been carefully prepared. James worked it out with Ross and with Keith, who is going to make the attack. Keith has taken his company commanders over the ground, at night as well as in the daytime, and every man in the regiment knows what he has to do. They've got Chapel and the 18th Wisconsin behind them, another good officer and another good regiment. The attack deserves to succeed and ought to succeed, but whether it will or not is more than I can tell you."

Jarvie Pass, which was to be the scene of the attack, was the shortest and most direct route to the fertile valleys east of the mountains, and carried the main road east from Tarsus to Camden, in the Loudun Valley. It was a broad, low pass, presenting no difficulties at any time of the year, even for artillery and heavy baggage trains. We held a fortified position at the mouth of the pass, and the heights on either side, but were unable to get so much as a cavalry patrol through because of the immensely strong position held by McGraw at the farther end. This was a position quite similar to the one at our end: a rocky, steep-sided island lying squarely in the mouth of the pass, heavily fortified, and commanding the exits completely.

The plan of attack was basically simple: the greater part of the regiment was to be passed all the way around to the rear of the position, under cover of darkness; two companies of picked men were to work their way up the steep face of the hill in front at the same time; both groups were to be in place by first light, when the attack was to be made. Detachments of the 18th Wisconsin were to be placed where they could give support to either group.

This was the way it was planned. How it was going to work out was something we would find out in another twelve to fourteen hours.

The Countess had already gone upstairs when I looked into

the living room about nine o'clock, and Jake was sitting on the sofa talking to Judith Morgan. She seemed less discontented than she had been earlier in the evening, and was listening intently to Jake, who was talking about painting. This had me puzzled for a moment: I found it hard to believe that she took that much pleasure in Jake's conversation. Then I realized that Jake was not talking about painting in general, but about portraits, and about drapery and materials and color, and that Judith was not spellbound by Jake's eloquence, though she was interested, but was holding a pose.

Someone said, "A little more to the left, please. The chin a little higher."

Judith altered her pose in immediate and unquestioning obedience.

I put my head in the room and saw that our topographical engineer, George Lovell, the former painter, had brought down his easel and his crayons and his drawing paper, and was making an elaborate sketch of the lady. I went over and stood behind him and watched him work for a few minutes, and listened to their discussion of silks and satins and velvets, and purple and ivory and gold, and of Judith's personal style of beauty and the materials most suited to it. Judith even had a welcoming smile for me. She was the center of attention again, and the world was as it should be.

Just before I went to bed I looked in again. Jake was still there, George Lovell was putting the finishing touches to his drawing, and Judith was still sitting on the sofa, though she had finished posing. This time, though, she was radiating charm; the air was crackling with charm, and she was full of animation. Robert Saint Chamans had come in and was looking over George's shoulder and carrying on a conversation with the lady at the same time. I went on up to bed.

The general and his suite got back about the middle of the afternoon, all except James, who had rather unnecessarily gone down in person for a couple of Billy Roth's regiments to take the place of the First Division regiments committed to Jarvie Pass. They were all red-eyed and drooping with fatigue when they came in, but smiling and in wonderful spirits. The operation had obviously been a success.

I found Jack Maitland in the kitchen, wolfing down a slab of bread and ham, with a look of great satisfaction on his bearded face. I got a mug of hot coffee from the stove, and went over and sat down with him.

Jack was enthusiastic. "Went like a breeze, Johnny," he said. "We got in there so fast that we were all over them before they even knew we were there. Keith had his Wisconsin boys trained down to the last inch. Not a single fumble anywhere. And as usual, when you've done a really good job in advance, you get a bit of luck to go with it. They had a supply train coming in this morning, and they held their fire for about half a minute because they thought we were the supply train. We were right in with them by the time they discovered their mistake. And when they began to pull themselves together and put up some kind of fight, our two companies came whooping in over the parapet and took them in reverse. That really finished them. Took all the heart out of them."

Jack got up and went over to the stove for more coffee, and diluted it with brandy and sugar. When he came back, he said thoughtfully, "You know that new fellow, Johnny, little Morgan? He's a little devil."

This could have been an admiring tribute. From Jack's tone of voice I gathered that it wasn't.

"Derek? What's he been doing?" I asked.

Jack wrinkled his forehead. "Well, he wanted to go along with the 17th, and the general let him go. He was supposed to watch, and see how they did it, and learn something that way. The general told him to stay out of trouble. He laughed about it, and told the boy his sister would have his head off if anything happened to him, but he meant it. Anyway, the little devil's idea of staying out of trouble was to go up with the two companies that were to make the escalade in front, and climb up the rocks like a goat, ahead of everybody else, and be the first man over, and shoot one gunner and bayonet another with a musket he picked up, and in general lead the attack all the way. He probably contributed to the success of the attack, but those sure as hell weren't his orders."

I was inclined to applaud Derek, and excuse his disobedience of orders on the grounds of inexperience.

"It shows he's got plenty of nerve," I said. "You can always learn the rules later on."

Jack shook his head. "The Wisconsin boys don't know what to make of him. I talked to Joe Green, the captain of one of the companies that made the attack. He says the man young Morgan bayoneted had his hands over his head and was trying to surrender. And why the bayonet, anyway? He had six shots in his revolver."

I didn't have any answer for this one, though I was still inclined to make excuses for Derek, and to attribute the incident to a combination of excitement and inexperience.

I talked to him after dinner. Derek was still full of charm and eager to please, and deprecatory about his part in the attack.

"I guess I was a damned fool," he admitted. "It was all pretty new and exciting to me. I forgot that I was supposed to sit it out, and I went right up with the rest of them, whooping and yelling my head off. After it was all over, I half expected the old man to pat me on the head and say, Well done, my boy! or something like that. My word, did I have the wrong idea! When he caught sight of me he scowled as though he were the Lord God Jehovah and I had just broken all ten of the commandments. I had disobeyed orders, which was at least seven or eight of them, and he was ready to skin me alive. By the time he got through, I felt as though he had."

I laughed. "That's commonly referred to around here as his two-ton voice. People are always a little surprised to find they're still alive after it has fallen on them."

"That was about the way I felt. Flayed, and flat as a pancake. I'm not anxious for any more of it, either. From now on I walk meekly in the sight of the Lord."

This was all quite disarming, and it conformed pretty well to what I had told Jack Maitland, but there was an elusive false note in it somewhere. Later in the evening I managed to place the false note. Derek was going on with his original role. He was still the modest young man, the beginner, eager to please and to learn, but he was no longer convincing in the part, which must have been an uncongenial one from the beginning. Behind the modesty and the deprecation was a new arrogance. He had been in battle. He had been blooded, and now he was a man of war.

Judith Morgan went to bed early, since she was to leave with the squadron of cavalry that was going up to Jellicoe Gap at three in the morning. Before she left, before she went to bed, she managed, characteristically, to fling a couple of effective Parthian arrows behind her.

She almost certainly had nothing to do with the first of these. She was a bird of ill omen and a bringer of bad tidings, and that was all. Not that she endeared herself to any of us by the obvious pleasure she took in the role.

She was talking to Dick Ross, who had stopped in to say good-bye to her before she left. Ostensibly she was talking to Dick, but there were six or eight of us standing near by, and another half-dozen within earshot. She was telling Dick how wrongheaded he had been in complaining about the late arrival of Heath's regiment. She had come to life again and was full of charm, her violet eyes and velvet eyelashes soulful, her voice sweet and a little poisonous.

"My dear boy," she was saying, "you were so very wrong about the whole thing. I did keep you waiting, I know, but if it hadn't been for me you never would have seen Colonel Heath's regiment. Absolutely everybody is clamoring for cavalry, and they're half out of their minds in Washington trying to find enough to go around. And of course everything, absolutely everything, is going to the Potomac."

She paused, and smiled sweetly. "I tried to tell my brother that, but of course Arthur knows all about everything, and wouldn't listen to me. But I do think you gentlemen ought to count on getting along with the troops you already have. Yes, I know. General Crawford thinks he has reinforcements for you. General Crawford is a sweet old gentleman, and I know he likes Arthur and wants to do everything he can for him. But everybody wants more troops, and most of them have more influence than General Crawford. If he can get as much as two regiments, let alone two divisions, out of the clutches of the Army of the Potomac, I certainly miss my guess."

At the time most of us were pretty skeptical. We knew Judith well enough by this time to be sure she was paying somebody off, probably her brother, for not having met her with a brass band.

The other shot was Judith's own, and the arrow was poisoned. This was a few minutes later. She was still addressing Dick, but the rest of us were still around and within hearing as she well knew, and this was obviously meant for general circulation.

She lowered her voice dramatically, and put her hand on Dick's shoulder and drew him closer. "Listen, dear boy," she said in a penetrating stage whisper. "I want you to look out for my sister. Arthur leaves her alone too much. I think he leaves her alone too much with the fascinating Colonel Lake. I know Lucy is a dear, sweet girl and a loving wife. I wouldn't say anything against her for the world. But you know what proximity does, and when people are left alone together—"

She left the sentence unfinished, with a pause full of meaning. After a moment, she abandoned the conspiratorial attitude, straightened up, and addressed all of us.

"Good night, gentlemen. I'll see some of you in the morning. Or later tonight. Whichever you choose to call it. To the rest of you, good night, and good-bye."

This was her exit line. She bowed gracefully to all of us, right and left, and went out. That was the last time I saw Judith Morgan. In the morning she was gone.

Chapter 5

❦ ❦ ❦ ❦ ❦ ❦ ❦ ❦ ❦ ❦ ❦ ❦ ❦ ❦ ❦ ❦ ❦ ❦

The Queen of the Night still had an arrow left in her quiver, as we learned late the next afternoon, when the remnants of a supply train and its savagely mauled escort dragged themselves into town just as it was getting dark. Out of a train of forty-two wagons, only seven had come through. Of the escort, Captain Gwin's squadron of the 4th Michigan had thirty casualties out of ninety-four men, with many of the survivors dismounted. In John Kay's 52nd Illinois the casualties were close to forty per cent. To make a bad matter still worse, the survivors came in quarreling bitterly among themselves.

Captain Gwin, who had served on the plains, thought that much of the train could have been saved if the escort had taken up a defensive position and sent for help, bunching the wagons as closely together as possible, and felling a few trees to strengthen the position. He claimed that relief could have reached them within two hours, and that the escort could have held out that long. The infantry denied all of this. The general opinion was that Gwin was right; that in any case, anything at all would have been better than the course actually taken, of continuing blindly ahead while both train and escort fell apart.

The quarrel over the wrecked supply train of November fourth had unfortunate repercussions. Gavin supported his regimental commander, Colonel Kay, as a matter of course. Harry Gwin was no particular friend of ours: he was red-faced and black-bearded, a braggart and a blowhard, and drunk a good deal of the time. For all that, he was a good squadron leader, took care of his horses and men, trained them well, and handled them well in a fight. He felt that Gavin had treated him badly, and came in to see James, and wanted him to do something about it. James listened to him, which was more than Gavin had done, and thought he had a case. When Gavin happened to come in, later in the morning, he spoke to him about it.

I was on duty that morning and was sitting at the desk outside the office, when I heard Gavin asking James if the general was in.

James said, "Harry Gwin was in this morning, Gavin. The man who got his squadron so badly cut up the other day."

"I know who he is. What about him?" Gavin's voice was cold. It was a tone of voice I had never heard him use before, to any of us, at any rate.

"I thought he made out a pretty good case for himself," James said. "I don't know the man personally, and don't particularly like him, but he's a professional, and he's competent, which is more than you can say for John Kay."

Gavin's voice had an edge to it. "Are you trying to tell me how to run my division, Colonel?"

James ignored him. "John Kay is a lawyer. A good one, for all I know. He's a lawyer and a politician and a friend of the governor's, but as a soldier he's an amateur, and not a very promising one either, as you know damned well. Now John Kay is blaming Gwin for his defeat the other day, and openly accusing him of cowardice. The accusation is false, and unjust to Gwin, and bad for the morale of the regiment. So, for God's sake, tell Kay to shut up, or send him back to his law practice, and say something to Gwin. We can get all the political colonels we want, but experienced cavalry officers are hard to come by."

Gavin had started to interrupt several times, but in the end he agreed with James, though not with any particular warmth.

"You're right about that," he admitted. "I'll look him up. A man shouldn't be called a coward unless you know damned well he is one. I don't think this fellow is. Kay got a bellyful of the war Tuesday. He'll be glad of an excuse to leave. Wing is the lieutenant colonel. He'll be an improvement."

There was a brief silence at this point, then Gavin resumed the cool and formal manner he had come in with. "I'm obliged to you, Colonel, for bringing up this matter. Will you have the kindness to tell the general I was here?"

James replied in the same manner, with a faint overtone of mockery added. "I thought it ought to be called to your attention, General. And I will be glad to tell General Pack you were here."

I found this exchange of formalities mysterious. It reminded me of a recent encounter which had seemed cryptic to me at the time. Two or three days earlier the Countess had gone out with the carriage in the afternoon. When she came back, James and Gavin were with her, Gavin sitting beside her in the back seat of the carriage, James accompanying them on horseback. There was nothing especially unusual about this: I had seen the three of them together often enough in the previous weeks. What was unusual, though, was the tense and angry silence that enveloped them. All three of them were looking straight ahead, the Countess remote, James expressionless, Gavin red-faced and angry. I had caught only a glimpse of them as they passed by, and had forgotten the incident until the cool formality of Gavin's manner this morning brought it to my mind.

I was about to go in and ask James what this was all about, and what kind of flea Gavin had in his ear, when people started coming in, first Jonesy and Brian Cooper, of the 17th Missouri, then Tony Bassett, then half a dozen others, all of them wanting to see James. Then General Pack came in with various things for me to do, and I was gone for the rest of the day. So I never did get around to asking James what was wrong.

If there was a coolness between James and Gavin, it wasn't the only such feeling that had developed in our midst. On the third floor, where the four of us—the general's four aides— slept together, we had a really vicious feud going. This was between Derek and Bob Kelso, while Colin and I tried to keep the peace. Bob and Derek had detested each other at sight, with the inborn animosity of cat and dog, Bob a shaggy, loud-barking, generally good-natured farm dog, Derek a pampered, silky-coated Persian, with a strain of leopard added.

With this natural animosity between them, it is impossible to say what the quarrel was about, or who began it. Derek's tactic was to treat Bob with lofty indifference, to stare at him with supercilious contempt while he was talking, then turn away without answering and address someone else. Bob, on his side, was perpetually baiting Derek. He affected the belief that Derek was about fourteen years old, referred to him as our mascot, and addressed him as Sonny. When Colin and Derek came back from Jenkins' Ferry on Tuesday, after escorting Judith Morgan that far, Bob greeted Derek with mock solicitude: "It's going to be mighty lonesome around here, Sonny, now that your mother's gone. I expect you're going to miss her." Derek's reply was unprintable.

The climax of this tiresome little feud came one night as we were all getting ready for bed. Bob was baiting Derek in his usual heavy-handed manner, this time about the rebel artilleryman he had bayoneted in the attack on Jarvie. Instead of retiring into a black silence, Derek replied in a smiling silken voice that I instinctively distrusted, and offered to demonstrate. He picked up a broom that our orderly had left in a corner, and still smiling, went through a few movements from the manual of arms with the broom as a musket, ending with a caricature of the standard position for a bayonet attack. Then, just as all of us were wondering what was coming next, he suddenly drove at Bob with a spring like a panther and a murderous lunge that would have driven the broomstick half-way through his body if Bob had not seen it coming, just in time, and thrown himself on his side. As it was, his shirt was nearly torn off his back, and there was a long bloody weal along his ribs.

Colin and I went into action immediately. I got my arm around Derek's neck and pulled him away with a strangle hold, which had the added merit of not letting him talk. And Colin, all six feet five of him, simply stood in front of Bob and pushed him back on the bed every time he tried to get up.

Bob moved out the same night, saying he was damned if he was going to wait to be murdered in his sleep. He gave up baiting Derek, and to that extent Derek had won his case. But he had made another mortal enemy among those of us who saw him every day, and had alienated a few more of his former friends.

Derek likewise found various ways to make himself unpopular with the troops, most of them springing from a native arrogance, which he took less and less trouble to conceal. I happened to witness an example of his methods, one November afternoon. It was an exasperating little episode, which had a drastic sequel later in the month.

Our headquarters guard at this time was made up of about twenty-five mounted men, taken from the two Michigan regiments, and sixty to seventy infantrymen from a dozen different regiments. It was an assignment that was greatly coveted. The men were all first-rate soldiers, and had been assigned for that reason, so that it was both an honor and a reward. The duties were light, and the living conditions, of course, were vastly better than those in the field. The men took considerable pride in their appearance and bearing, and were a fine-looking lot. They were devoted to the Countess, who knew them all by name and as individuals, and they were apt to consider themselves her private bodyguard.

On this particular afternoon everyone else was out, and Jake and I, with nothing better to do, were sitting in the living room, talking in a desultory way about one thing and another. Jake happened to glance out the window, then looked again, with a frown.

"Now what's that little hellion up to?" he muttered, and started for the door.

I looked out the window and saw that Derek was talking to the sentry. I would have turned away without further thought if Jake hadn't gone out in such angry haste. On looking again, I saw that Derek wasn't talking to the sentry but reprimanding him, and making him bring his musket to the formal salute position over and over again. The sentry was Bert Greene, the younger of two brothers in the guard from the Missouri regiment, and the expression on his face was mutinous.

I reached the door in time to hear Jake call out, in a sharper voice than he normally used, "All right, Lieutenant. I think the sentry has done enough saluting by this time. Would you mind telling me the reason for it?"

Derek stiffened with anger at the interruption. "Certainly, Colonel Leslie, since you choose to interfere. This man was insolent. I was trying to teach him some of the rudiments of military courtesy."

"We have instructors for that," Jake said in a dry voice. He gnawed on his lip for a moment, then went on: "We aren't very strong on formalities in this command, Lieutenant, as you would know if you had been here longer. One of the military courtesies we do observe, though, is that of not interfering with another man's command. If you think a soldier is insolent and needs instruction in the rudiments of military courtesy, go tell his commanding officer about it. The discipline of the troops under his command is his responsibility. If you still want to complain about young Bert, the man to complain to is Captain Jenkins. He must be around somewhere. Do you know where he is, Bert?"

"Yes, sir, I do. He's in his office over at the courthouse."

"There you are, Lieutenant. It's as easy as that. Now, if you care to come in the house with me, there are a few things I would like to talk to you about."

He put his hand on Derek's arm, inviting him to go first. Derek snatched his arm away. "As it happens, Colonel Leslie, I don't care to go in the house with you," he said in a voice full of cold rage.

Jake turned and looked at him with a wrinkled brow. "I seem to have put that the wrong way," he said mildly. "What I meant was that I want to talk to you, and I prefer to talk to you in the house. It was an order, not a request. Go ahead, sir."

For a moment Derek balked mulishly, then with very bad grace gave way, and went in ahead of Jake.

The sentry waited until they were out of sight, then burst out, "I swear to God, Captain Lake, if that fellow had kept it up for another minute I would have stuck this bayonet in him."

I could sympathize with him. "We've had some trouble with him, ourselves," I said. "Most of the time he's all right, but he's got a mean streak in him. You shouldn't have any more trouble, though. You heard what Jake told him."

I was wrong in thinking that Bert Greene wasn't going to have any more trouble with Derek. Within a week he was ordered back to his regiment, the 17th Missouri, which was in the most active part of the line at the time, and within four days of his return he was killed.

Afterwards this transfer seemed mysterious to me, and I asked Howel Jenkins about it. He said he was surprised himself when the order came through. Bert had a fine record, and there was no reason for sending him back to his regiment. He tried to see the general, to ask about the order and see if it couldn't be rescinded, but the general was gone for four days. Jake was with him, and James was up at Jenkins' Ferry, and there was nobody to ask. In the meantime, here was the order, with General Pack's signature, and he wasn't doing anything about it. So he finally sent the boy back to the Third Division, and sent over a note to Colonel Cooper explaining the circumstances. The fact that he was killed four days later was pure bad luck.

It was still mysterious. Derek couldn't have issued the order himself. There was no one he could have persuaded to issue it, General Pack least of all. The conclusion I finally came to was that Derek had written out the order and had forged the general's signature. That he had waited for an opportune time to deliver the order, and found it when the general was away and all the rest of us were busy.

The general was over with Gavin and the First Division because our brilliant coup at Jarvie Pass had been *contrecouped.* The forward positions we had taken ten days earlier had been strengthened at the expense of the positions in the rear, and McGraw had neatly duplicated our previous feat by a successful surprise attack on the natural fortress at our end of the pass. In fact, he had gone us one better, for he had not only taken the position at our end, but in addition he had cut off one of our new regiments, the 66th Indiana, and three companies of the 17th Wisconsin in the position at the far end.

These troops were in no immediate danger, given the formidable nature of the position, but we had no way of supplying them, and the provisions on hand would last for no more than a day or two. The only fortunate aspect of the situation was that, by pure chance, they had a first-class officer with them: Nelson Keith had been with the three companies of his old regiment when they were cut off.

General Pack had brought the three regiments of Roth's left brigade with him on the chance that our familiarity with the position might make an assault practicable. After looking over the position, and talking with Gavin, he decided against it: the attack would have been perfectly feasible, but the cost would have been too high. The only thing left was to make an attempt to extricate the garrison. This operation was planned for the following day, but it proved to be unnecessary.

Late in the evening we were startled by the sound of a heavy cannonade coming from the east and extending away to the south. The direction was that of our garrison, but the extension to the south was confusing. The firing in the south died away after fifteen or twenty minutes, but the uproar from the direction of the garrison kept up for nearly an hour.

We had patrols moving up the mountain on both sides of the pass as soon as we heard the racket, and a sporadic firing began which lasted all night over on the south side. In the first gray light of morning, the firing was suddenly taken up on the north side of the pass. Our men were immediately sent up towards the sound of the firing, which increased in volume for a time, then rather quickly died away. Within an hour the men of the 66th Indiana and the Wisconsin companies were streaming down the mountainside and into our lines. Colonel Keith, characteristically, was the last man down.

This was a dramatic little episode, and it raised our spirits enormously. On Colonel Keith's part it was a brilliant feat of arms: he had not only brought off his own command virtually intact, but had inflicted serious damage on the enemy, and left nothing of any value behind. He had fired off all the ammunition he could find a target for, and had blown up the guns with the remainder. As a final touch of impudence, the decoy company, which had broken off to the south with a couple of twelve-pounders under cover of the immense racket from the main position, showed up later in the morning over on the extreme right, bringing their two guns with them.

We went back to Tarsus in the afternoon and found that in our absence the rebel cavalry had made a foolish and ineffective raid on the town itself. They had lost heavily in the raid, and had been beaten off without difficulty, but the mere fact of the raid, no matter how harebrained, was ominous. By that time, too, we were beginning to have second thoughts about Keith's feat of arms. We were still full of admiration. It had been marvelously well done. But we began to see that it wasn't any kind of victory, but a salvage operation after a defeat. After you had admired the operation sufficiently, the fact remained that we had lost control of the pass at both ends, and that McGraw for the first time was calling the tune.

Late in the week we received another temporary setback when the first attempt to supply us by river failed. With the autumn rains the river had been rising steadily and had now been navigable for several days. The initial convoy consisted of three steamers loaded to the gunwales, escorted by one of the lightly armored river gunboats satirically known as tinclads. At a bend in the river the gunboat, which was leading, was fired on by a battery of rebel field guns; some damage was inflicted on the gunboat, and two or three men were wounded. The gunboat turned back without firing a shot, and the convoy with it, and we were informed the following day that it would be impossible to supply us by water because of the strong rebel fortifications.

Major Stewart was furious, and he and Jonesy went up to naval headquarters the same afternoon. The major, as chief engineer, had done all the planning for the water supply route, and Jonesy's command had done all the work. Both of them knew what they were talking about, and both of them went up with blood in their eye.

Major Stewart wanted to know what rebel fortifications they were talking about, and why the gunboat commander hadn't fired his guns, and why he hadn't gone over to the outer channel which was out of range of fieldpieces, and what so pusillanimous and incompetent an officer was doing in command of a gunboat, anyway? There was a good deal of bristling at this point, but the major had his charts with him, and pointed out the available channels and the very few possible gun emplacements on the rebel side. He wanted to know, finally, if they didn't have enough sense to reconnoiter the danger points themselves, or even to find out where they were, why in hell didn't they have sense enough to ask us to do it for them? We knew the river, and we knew both banks. And they hadn't so much as sent out a man in a rowboat.

There was more of it. The major was in fine form, and we won on all counts. They accepted our offer to reconnoiter the farther bank for them, and offered us a boat to ferry over our scouting parties and supporting troops. They agreed to get another convoy together for us, and to continue them regularly as long as we wanted them. Finally, as a testimony to the major's eloquence, they actually apologized for the lack of planning and the bungling that had resulted in the failure of the first attempt.

All this was fine, but as usual these days, there was a catch to it. It would be three weeks before the repairs to the damaged gunboat could be completed. They would try to get another from the river command, but the decision would be out of their hands, and they couldn't promise anything.

Another question left hanging in the air was that of our

reinforcements. Those promised us were overdue. We were repeatedly assured that there had been no change in their orders, and that any delay was strictly temporary, but still they didn't appear, and we could get no definite information from anyone. No one seemed to know in any specific way why the troops were delayed or when they would reach us.

Everything now was on a contingent basis; nothing was settled, nothing definite, and all our plans were subject to change without notice. The fact is, we had finally lost our forward momentum and had come to a grinding stop. The entire command, I think, was aware of the cessation of movement and of the loss of direction, and without having originated with any particular person or in any particular place, the question: What are we doing here? began to circulate through the camps.

❦ ii

At this time—about the middle of November—an ugly little incident took place that couldn't possibly have happened earlier. Colin's dog, the big, awkward, sad-eyed comedian he had acquired during the Willow Run battle, disappeared early in November, probably when Colin went up to Jenkins' Ferry with his aunt. He showed up two weeks later in the camp of one of the Second Division regiments, the 35th Indiana.

The 35th was one of our old regiments, not one of the most distinguished, but a good, steady, dependable body of men. It had its soft spots, however, and one of these was Company F, or rather the portion of the company headed by Lieutenant Epps. The particular bane of the lieutenant and his command was Sergeant Heinie Wilson, a squat, barrel-chested, two-hundred-pound ex-blacksmith, thirty-five years old, and a bully, a ruffian, and a thief. The lieutenant and the entire platoon were afraid of him, which explained his sergeant's stripes and the fact that he retained them through one offense after another.

The sergeant was a sporting man among other things. He had bought Colin's dog for a dollar from the man who had either found or stolen him, and had immediately matched the dog against the champion of the next regiment. The sergeant had no chance of winning, and placed his bets accordingly, but he knew the fraud must not be too obvious. Colin's dog, though young, was big and powerful, and the sergeant's training methods were thorough. When Colin finally saw the dog again, it was a vicious, snarling brute that he had difficulty in recognizing.

The dog was chained to a stake in front of the sergeant's tent. The sergeant sat on a billet of wood in the doorway with a cigar in his mouth and an axe handle in his hand. He had a jar of the local whiskey inside the doorway of the tent, and he acknowledged military regulations to the extent of leaning back into the tent every time he wanted a drink. He was a little drunk, and the native shrewdness, which ordinarily kept him from pushing a good thing too far, was dulled. He had thrown the dog a large bloody chunk of horse meat, and was using the axe handle to hit the dog with at the last moment, just as he was about to get his teeth into the meat.

Colin, who happened to be passing through the camp, sat on his horse and watched this for a minute or two, then dismounted and tossed his horse's reins over a post at the entrance of the company street. He walked up to the sergeant and said pleasantly,

"You know, Sergeant, I think that's my dog you've got there."

The sergeant raised his eyes. "Nothing doing, Cap. I paid five bucks for that dog. Got him off a fellow in the 25th Michigan."

"All right. I'll give you the five bucks," Colin said.

Between ill-use and hunger and the tempting chunk of meat, up to this time the dog had failed to recognize Colin. Now he began to whimper and wag his tail, and to tremble all over. As Colin turned and put out his hand to pet him, the sergeant reached out with the axe handle, swung viciously, and hit the dog across the face. This was too much, of course.

Colin swung around. "Don't hit my dog. Leave him alone," he said in a quiet voice. Sergeant Wilson, if he had been sober, would have recognized the voice as dangerous. Instead, he mistook it for a peaceful protest.

Heads were peering out of tents by this time, and a tentative semicircle of spectators was beginning to form. The sergeant was aware of his audience. He looked up and said, "That's my dog, Mister Staff Officer, and I'll hit him whenever I damn please."

Colin's face turned red. "All right, Sergeant. You're talking to an officer. Get up! And stand at attention, damn you! I don't know who gave you those sergeant's stripes, but that's all over. You aren't going to see them again."

The sergeant got up as slowly as possible, and grinned at Colin. "Yes, Mister Staff Officer, sir," he said insolently. "Oh, excuse me, sir. I beg your pardon, sir. I forgot something."

He bent over, and straightened up with a jar of pale corn whiskey in his hand—the second for the day, and no more than half full—and raised the jar to his mouth. This was a gesture of such shocking insolence that it was met with neither laughter nor applause by the men standing around, but only with a sharp intake of breath.

Colin knocked the jar away with a blow so sharp that it broke the jar and cut his hand as well as the sergeant's mouth. This was a mortal offense, and the sergeant looked dangerous —dangerous, but also wary, for now that he was on his feet he realized for the first time how big Colin actually was.

"Take it easy, Heinie," one of the bystanders said out of the corner of his mouth.

At the same time, a fat young man came towards them, a fat young man with a sweating red face, hastily buckling on a sword. This was Lieutenant Epps, and he was obviously on his second bottle too.

"What's all this, now? What's all this about?" he demanded, in the querulous voice of the peaceful man disturbed.

A dozen voices told him that he, the captain, this fellow, says Heinie's dog belongs to him.

Colin turned to the lieutenant and said. "That's my dog. I lost him two weeks ago. I don't know what this swine has been doing to him. He didn't look that way when I lost him. This fellow of yours, this former sergeant, says he paid five dollars for him. I know he's lying, but I'll give him the five dollars."

"Well now, that seems fair enough. You take the captain's five dollars and give him the dog. What do you say, Heinie?" The lieutenant had assumed the role of honest broker.

The sergeant had a wicked look in his eye. "Anything you say, Lieutenant. Only until I see his five bucks, this is my dog."

These last words ended in a grunt, for as he spoke he had bent over to retrieve his axe handle, and delivered a vicious blow along the side of the dog's muzzle.

At the sound of the blow and the dog's yelp of pain, Colin whirled around and snatched the axe handle out of the man's grasp, and flung it fifty yards away.

"I want this man in irons, Lieutenant," Colin said in a hard voice. "I want him delivered to the provost marshal in irons for outrageous and repeated insolence."

Lieutenant Epps began to splutter, with sweat streaming down his face. "Oh, come now, Captain. You can't do that. You can't come over here and interfere with the discipline in my company—"

"What discipline? I haven't seen any. Those shoulder straps aren't irremovable, you know. Any more than a sergeant's stripes—"

This time there was a gasp from the men standing around, and from the dog a howl of anguish followed by a long series of yelps. As Colin turned, he saw that the dog was on the ground, pulling itself frantically with its forepaws, dragging its inert and paralyzed hindquarters behind, and that its back was broken.

The sergeant straightened up and dropped the heavy billet of wood with which he had broken the dog's back. He looked over at Colin with an air of triumphant insolence, and grinned at him.

"All right, mister. I guess you can have your God damn dog." He laughed. "You can have him free. I'll give him to you. For nothing."

At this moment he began to see that something had gone wrong with his triumph, and the smile left his face, for Colin was coming towards him with a set jaw and a white face and the perfectly plain intention of killing him. The sergeant backed away and grasped at the nearest weapon in sight, a bayonet as it happened.

"Listen, Captain, I don't want to hurt you," the sergeant said carefully, as he continued to back away. "Only you lay a hand on me and I swear to Jesus I'll stick this knife in your guts. You started it, butting in when I was training my dog. Anything happens to you and it ain't my fault. It's what you get for butting in."

The sweating lieutenant hovered around them spluttering, "Gentlemen! Gentlemen, please! Remember, he's an officer, Heinie! You can't strike an officer! Captain, please! You have no business here!"

Colin moved a little faster, closing in on the warily retreating sergeant, then feinted suddenly with his right hand, as though to seize the bayonet. The sergeant jabbed at him. Colin caught his wrist with both hands as he jabbed, and with a single swift and flowing and immensely powerful movement pulled him forward and off balance, turned and bent forward to receive his weight on his back, then, as though wielding a gigantic flail, swung him over his head in a vertical arc and smashed him violently to the ground. As the sergeant staggered to his feet, Colin seized him by his blouse and broke his jaw with a tremendous blow that lifted him a foot off the ground, and left him lying in a crumpled and unconscious heap.

Colin stared down at him, his eyes full of hatred, until he was certain that the man was unconscious, then he deliberately opened the flap of the holster on his belt and drew out his revolver.

The lieutenant was hysterical. "Oh, no, Captain! You can't do that! You can't shoot an unconscious man!"

Colin looked at him with contempt. "I wasn't going to shoot him. You don't shoot things like that. You step on them."

He turned away and looked down at the crippled dog, still

chained, still whimpering, still dragging itself in aimless circles with its forepaws; then, with a white face but a steady hand, he killed the poor beast with an accurate shot through the head.

Half the regiment was on hand by this time, stirring about and trying to find out what was going on, and the revolver shot was all that was necessary to bring out the rest. Colin shouldered his way through the crowd, and stopped briefly to report to Colonel Franklin, then rode for home with a sick face, as though he had looked upon the devil—as in a sense he had.

He still had that look on his face when he came in the house, his eyes fixed straight ahead, seeing nothing. I was worried about him, though our relations lately had been rather cool, and followed him up the stairs. When I opened the door, he was on his knees by the side of the bed, praying with tears streaming down his face. I backed out hastily, greatly embarrassed by the sight, and left him alone.

The upshot of the matter, after Jack Maitland had gone over and talked to Colonel Franklin and some of his officers, was that Company F was dissolved and the men distributed among the under-strength companies in the regiment. The principal source of the rot in the company, Sergeant Heinie Wilson, would be in the hospital for at least a month, and could be dealt with when he got out. The company officers were allowed to resign, in view of their previous records. Even the fat Lieutenant Epps had shown up well on the way down, and at Willow Run. The regiment was reorganized, discipline was tightened, and more important than either, the men were given something to do. The regiment was detailed, with two others, to the support of the overworked cavalry, and from then on no further complaint was made of the 35th Indiana.

❧ *iii*

Actually, the Indiana regiment was not the only one that had disciplinary problems. This period of waiting and doing nothing, of indecision and uncertainty, loosened the morale of the entire command. We were still a good body of troops, still formidable, but we were no longer strung up to a high pitch, and no longer had the unanimity and the tense and responsive eagerness of October. In a sense, we had become a body of garrison troops, and all the characteristics of garrison life made their appearance. We drank heavily, and played for high stakes, and quarreled over the cards, and were bored.

Nearly all our pleasant October institutions were gone. The daily rides went with the change in the weather. The musical afternoons at the Robertsons' lapsed with an illness of Christina's early in the month. The Countess stopped in to see her every day, but there was no music and no gathering. Jake went down for a few more evenings to swap quotations from Homer and Lucretius with the Judge over brandy and cigars, then even these visits came to an end as the Judge took Christina, still not fully recovered, to stay with relatives farther south.

Our state dinners were a thing of the past. We still had company for dinner, sometimes in large numbers, but this was when the guests simply happened to be at headquarters at dinnertime. More common were the occasions when fewer than half of us were there; often there were only five or six of us sitting in a small group around the lower end of the table, on either side of the Countess.

The table was still set with silver and crystal on a fresh white tablecloth, and usually there were flowers, though they were harder to find now. We ate well, with Mrs. Mott in the kitchen, and were served in style by the houseman in a white jacket, with as many orderlies to assist him as necessary. We still made an effort to appear presentable ourselves at dinnertime. The Countess appeared in a different dress every night, her dark hair drawn smoothly back, and greeted us with a smile as friends and honored guests.

The dinner hour continued for some time to be the best part of the day, an hour removed from the war, a brief return to civilized ways and manners, but at some point this ceased to be true, or rather, it ceased to be invariably and dependably true.

The general's presence at the head of the table gave us stability, even though he was impassive and withdrawn, and spoke very little. When he was away, as he frequently was during this latter part of the month, the atmosphere was still comfortable and relaxed when Jake and Robert Saint Chamans were present; but when the general had taken Jake with him and Robert was off somewhere on duty it was sometimes difficult. It was apt to be particularly difficult when one of the Rosses came in with his train; Gavin with his new chief of staff, Benny Pace, who had adopted Gavin's quarrels and truculent attitudes along with his new duties; or Dick, who usually came swaggering in, a little drunk, with Tim Wales and a couple of his officers behind him.

Madame Lucy bore herself beautifully throughout this trying period. She spent most of her days at the hospital now, but it was no longer a matter of bringing flowers and spreading smiles and cheer among the wounded. With the increasing number of wounded and the influx of sick from the new regiments, they were shorthanded: there was work to be done, and she bore a large share, cheerfully and as a matter of course. Everyone at the hospital was devoted to her, doctors, attendants, and patients, everyone from Ned Ferguson to the latest farm boy with measles. They were her fiercely loyal partisans, and refused to hear a word spoken against her.

She came home from the hospital and reappeared an hour later, freshly gowned, beautiful and gracious, to greet us before dinner. At the time she seemed untouchable, as though she were surrounded by an invisible guarding force that nothing hostile could penetrate, a force coming from within, emanating from her own radiance, her own mind and character. Serenity is the quality that was most apparent. Not that she was incapable of anger, or laughter, or grief, but these were all passing emotions, and when they were over she was serene again.

Still, there were things that could hurt her. One of these, I knew, was the defection of Colin. She had always had a great fondness for the big young man, and he had returned this with a blind schoolboy's adoration. Now Colin had unwillingly sided with Derek and with his brothers in a quarrel that was still unclear to me. He avoided her as much as possible, and was red-faced and miserable in her presence.

The personal relations between the general and his wife was a subject I had never thought about. It was a region of thought so strictly forbidden that even its approaches were shut off; so far as I was concerned, their personal life ended at the stairway. In public their manner towards each other was pleasant rather than affectionate, unfailingly courteous, and rather formal. There was no change in it from beginning to end.

The one accidental glimpse I had of their personal relations came at about this time, on a Sunday afternoon just after the middle of November. I had been with Jonesy most of the day. In the afternoon he sent me back with a question of no great importance in itself, but one that only the commanding general could decide. I was told that the general was in the library.

This was the long room on the north side of the house with French doors opening on the pillared veranda. It was late afternoon, and the room was full of darkness. The distant wooded hillside and the meadows across the river were bathed in a hard red-gold light from the setting sun, and a dim reflection of this light came into the room through the closed French doors. At first I could see nothing at all, and thought the room was empty; then, as my eyes became accustomed to the dim light, I could make out two people, the general and his wife, sitting ten feet apart, each looking straight ahead, sitting in the dusk in a stone-cold silence.

The general noticed me after a moment, probably at the same time that I became aware of his presence, and asked if I had something for him from General Jones. He excused himself to his wife with his usual formal courtesy, and went over to the office with me, where I gave him Jonesy's message and got his answer.

All this dissension obviously centered around James and Madame Lucy, or rather, around Judith Morgan's sister-in-law and the fascinating Colonel Lake. I felt bitter about it, and went out of my way one afternoon to pick a quarrel with Derek.

He and Colin and I were alone in the living room. Madame had come in a few minutes before, and I had seen the hurt look in her eyes when Colin turned away to look out the window. She went out immediately, and when she had gone I turned on Derek.

"By God, it was a black day for this command when you and your mother showed up down here."

This seemed to entertain Derek. "Why, Lake? Now what have we done?"

"Your mother has laid a spell on us. We're under a curse. Since the two of you showed up, we can't do anything right. Look at Jarvie. Our losses are double what they were in October. Last month our reinforcements came in on schedule. The two of you appear and the reinforcements stop. You were the last reinforcements we got, and we could have gotten along fine without you."

Colin broke in now, in a tired, pained voice. "Oh, for heaven's sake, lay off it, John. Will you please?"

Derek wasn't having any interference. He was enjoying himself. "Lay off it yourself, Colin. I want to hear what Lake's got on his mind. Go on. What else have you got against us?"

"Plenty, by God. We were all friends until the two of you got here. Now we're at each other's throats. Half of us don't even speak to the other half. All because James wouldn't dance to your mother's tune. All because her vanity was hurt. The unforgivable sin, to be wiped out in blood. James' blood, and the blood of anybody who got in the way. The whole damned command, for all she cares."

"You've got part of it right," Derek said in a more serious voice. "You're right about the injured vanity. My mother's a handsome woman, as you could see for yourself. She's used to being the center of attention, with men flocking around her. She expected James to pay court to her, and her vanity was hurt when he didn't, especially since she'd laid herself out to be attractive. You can take my word for it, this was unheard of. She thought there must be something behind it, and she was right—"

I interrupted him sourly. "Certainly there was. James didn't like her."

Derek ignored the interruption. "He wasn't interested in my mother because he was in love with another woman. Her sister-in-law. The general's wife."

"That's a fine explanation," I said, with heavy sarcasm. "It certainly ought to have made your mother feel better. Only what of it? James is in love with her. So is Jake Leslie. So is Robert Saint Chamans. So is the one-legged rebel colonel down the street. So is half the command. And if you mean anything more than that, I'll tell you to your face, you lie."

Derek took this coolly. "I'm sorry to say I do mean more than that, and I'm not guessing. I found out. I know."

I clenched my fist and felt the blood pounding in my head, then caught myself with an effort, and glared at him.

"God damn you for a blackhearted liar," I said between my teeth. "That's a vicious lie. A wicked, slanderous lie."

I turned on Colin. "And what the hell is wrong with you? You let this miserable little French poodle stand there and slander your aunt, and you don't do anything about it. What's the matter? Has his mother put a spell on you, too?"

Colin looked at me mournfully. "Derek's mother is my aunt, too. Look, John. I'm not a liar. I think you know that—"

I broke in savagely. "No, I know you're not a liar. You're a dupe. A dupe and a fool, and a disloyal fool, at that. The hell with both of you!"

I turned away from them, bursting with rage, and went out.

🌿 *iv*

This quarrel, unfortunately, was nothing out of the ordinary. Two days later, on the eighteenth of November, the same factional quarrel flared up again, this time with drastic consequences.

I was off duty that afternoon, and because I had nothing to

do and it was a nice day, I went down to see an old schoolmate who had a company in one of the Ohio regiments. He was glad to see me, and we spent a sociable hour together. A month earlier he would have been eager for inside information, information straight from headquarters, and our entire conversation would have been about military affairs. Instead, since it was November, we talked about people we knew at home and laughed about remembered incidents from our school days, and forgot about the war for an hour. About three-thirty I started back.

It was a warm fall afternoon, with the scarlets and yellows of the foliage over the countryside mellowed and softened by a light haze in the air. It was a pleasure simply to be out and on a horse, and in no particular hurry to get anywhere. Madame Lucy would have loved it, and I wished that she were riding beside me. The image was a pleasant one, but it brought me back to the present, and the air seemed cooler and less peaceful.

This was not all metaphor, for in the distance, off to the north, the sound of firing had become audible. I stopped and listened: it was all small-arms fire, and came from a little east of north. I remembered that we had a wagon train coming in, an unusually large one, and that simply as a matter of course it would be under attack most of the way. At the same time, judging from the direction and the increasing volume of sound, the attack was remarkably close in and in greater force than usual. Just as I started forward again, a violent cannonade broke out.

I turned off the main road into a lane that led directly towards the sound of the firing. From a rise half a mile farther on, I caught a glimpse of the river ahead of me, bordered with trees on both banks, and some distance off to the right, the bridge and the road leading to the supply depot, the road filled with white-topped wagons moving at the sluggish mile-an-hour gait of all supply trains. The uproar to the north continued, but there was no confusion, no pile-up at the entrance to the bridge, and no sign of haste in the deliberate movements of the train.

This was contradictory, and it bothered me. I kept on for another ten minutes, following the windings of the lane with some impatience, in the general direction of the river. There was no letup in the fighting. In fact, the artillery fire seemed to have grown heavier, and at one place, through an opening in the trees, I could see smoke rising over the treetops across the river.

The next thing I saw multiplied the confusion in my mind: this was the sight of a cavalry column a quarter of a mile ahead of me, on the road south of the river, moving away from the battle.

This was Tim Wales' regiment, the 4th Michigan, with Dick Ross riding beside Tim at the head of the column. I pulled up where I was and watched the regiment go by. The men were bent over in their saddles, nodding with weariness, and the horses moved at a slow, shambling walk. They had been in motion for fourteen hours, and both men and horses were half-dead with fatigue. There was nothing very unusual about this; it was all part of the day's work in the cavalry.

What was unusual, though, was the air of defeat that hung over the regiment. I could feel it a quarter of a mile away, together with the sullen dejection of the men. To complete my feeling of mystification, there were no noticeable gaps in the ranks. As a matter of training, which had become instinctive by this time, I had estimated the number of horsemen in the column: five squadrons averaging ninety men apiece, with a full complement of officers. Their casualties, if any, had been light. Any number over ten or twelve, I would have noticed.

I waited until the column had cleared the road, then went down and turned right, and reached the bridge just as the last of the wagons jolted its way across. The cannon fire had stopped abruptly just before this; the small-arms fire kept up for a few minutes longer, then diminished in volume and drew farther away; after I crossed the bridge, a few scattering shots were fired in the distance, and that was all.

By this time it was about four-thirty, though the haze of smoke in the air made it seem later. From the bridge the road mounted slowly and crossed the North River Road at an oblique angle. The country here was mostly open meadow, crossed by windbreaks, and checkered with small clumps of woods. Before the war the Taylors had raised famous riding horses in this part of the county; these, of course, had long since disappeared. It was above the meeting with the North River Road that the fight had taken place.

Below the crossroads most of the men I passed had been teamsters and stragglers from the wagon train. Beyond the crossroads I ran into men from the 52nd Illinois, which had been attached to the cavalry and had formed the rear guard of the train. Farther on, Christie's six three-inch rifles were still in battery off to the right of the road, with a clear two-mile range in front of them. Out in front of the guns and halfway down the darkening field was another battery and a large body of troops.

I still didn't know what had happened, and I couldn't stay to find out because I was due back at headquarters. No one there knew any more than I did. Colin got up and left as soon as he saw me coming, which saved him the trouble of deciding whether or not to speak to me.

Five minutes later James came in with a grim face and spots of color in his cheeks, passed within a foot of me without even seeing me, pushed open the door to the general's office without knocking, and went in. This was unheard of, in view of James' usual punctiliousness in such matters, and he addressed the general without waiting to be asked and without the usual formal courtesies, in a voice full of bitter sarcasm.

"Well, General, I imagine it will interest you to learn that you no longer have a cavalry brigade. That precious nephew of yours has wrecked it so completely that there aren't even any pieces to pick up."

The general looked up at James, waited for the fraction of a moment, then said calmly, "It does interest me, James. When you have yourself under control again, I would like you to tell me what happened."

James took this without blinking. "Yes, sir. I think I should tell you that it was the 12th Pennsylvania that was wrecked, to explain my personal feeling in the matter. Colonel Heath has been a close friend of mine for many years. What happened is that Colonel Ross deliberately left a regiment under his command without support. He saw the regiment cut off and partly surrounded, made no move to assist it, and stated openly that he had no intention of doing so. What he said was, 'Heath got himself into this mess. Let him get himself out of it.' Some of the officers with him protested. They were shocked. So were the men. I reminded him that he would have been in pretty poor shape if we had acted on the same principle at Willow Run."

"Was Heath's position the result of disobedience of orders?"

"No, sir. It was the result of a strict and intelligent execution of orders, though there could be some question about the orders. The rear guard—Colonel Wing's regiment—was under attack, and had taken up a stationary defensive position. Heath's orders were to clear off this attacking force, and drive it far enough back so that Colonel Wing could move on and take his proper place, covering the rear of the train. Before he made his attack, Heath saw that his right would be in the air. He sent his aide, Lieutenant Breese, over to the 4th Michigan, asking them to look out for it. This was a normal request and compliance could be assumed in any normal command, so he made his attack without waiting for an answer. He drove the enemy beautifully. Colonel Wing was disengaged, and the train got in without further loss."

"You said there could be some question about the orders. What would the question be?"

"It would be about the phrasing of the order. Heath was to drive the enemy back far enough to disengage Colonel Wing. How far was that? How far was enough? Dick evidently expected Heath to break off before he did, but if that was what he wanted he should have said so. It certainly wasn't in the order. It wouldn't excuse his failure to support his other regiment, in any case. That is, unless he was fool enough to think that Heath could simply break off his fight and come trotting back unmolested. If so, the thinking, if you can call it that, would be about on a par with his sending off half the escort— the guns and the two First Division regiments—twenty minutes before he was attacked, without bothering to reconnoiter the road ahead. Without bothering to find out whether he was going to need them or not."

The general looked up at James with an almost imperceptible lifting of his eyebrows. "What were the losses in Colonel Heath's regiment?"

James was bitter. "Over forty per cent, sir. I can't give you the exact figure, but there were six hundred and fifty-four officers and men in the regiment this morning, and there are less than four hundred now. The loss was particularly heavy in officers. Nine-tenths of it took place in twenty minutes, in attacks on the unsupported right flank, while Colonel Ross and the 4th Michigan sat their horses and looked on. Nine-tenths of the loss was a direct consequence of the betrayal of the regiment by Colonel Ross. The regiment is completely wrecked, sir. The 4th Michigan, with about ten casualties, is wrecked. The men are ashamed. Half of them would desert tonight if they thought they could get away. By tonight, the 12th Michigan won't be in much better condition. No, sir. As I told you when I came in, you no longer have a cavalry brigade."

Dick Ross had come in, evidently by the side door, in time to hear James' account of the cavalry brigade. His reply was a bellow of anger.

"That's a damned lie, Lake. The brigade is in good shape. As good as ever. Maybe better. Maybe they've learned something. Sure the 12th Pennsylvania took some losses. Your friend Heath disobeyed his orders and got himself into a mess. Why should I lose a hundred men digging him out? Next time maybe he'll know enough to obey orders."

James stared at him. "I'd like to hear you ask that in front of Colonel Dove and Alfred Persant. The 43rd Ohio lost two hundred and four men, and the 34th Indiana lost a hundred and eighty-two, digging you out of a mess of your own making. I'll hunt them up for you, so you can tell them about it."

"And I'll tell you another thing," Dick went on belligerently. "You try anything again like you tried this afternoon and, by God, I'll put you under arrest."

"How?" James asked with open contempt. "After your performance this afternoon do you think you could find a sergeant and four men who would obey an order of yours? Any order?"

Dick swung around to face his uncle and said hotly, "These damned staff officers of yours are getting too big for their boots, General. They need to be put in their place. I'd like to know where Lake thinks he gets the authority to give orders to the cavalry brigade right in the face of its commander. For that matter, I'd like to know what kind of authority he has to give orders to the Second Division and the artillery."

The general looked over at James, inviting him to reply, and it was the general James addressed, rather than Dick.

"If you will remember, sir, Roth's two regiments were brought up north of the river to meet exactly this kind of situation. I will be glad to accept the responsibility for ordering them in. The guns were ordered in by the chief of artillery, who was with me. I believe he needs no authority other than his own, except in the presence of the commanding general. As to the cavalry brigade, if I had had any authority, I would have relieved the commander on the spot and sent him to the rear under arrest. Not having that authority, I merely told him that if his men weren't going to be used, they were in the way, and asked him to move them. Not very politely, perhaps. I was full of anger at the time, as I still am when I think of the circumstances."

Dick's response was a vehement and angry denial. "By God, Lake, you lie! Every time you open your mouth, you lie!" He swung around to face the general. "No, sir. When Lake showed up I was with the 4th Michigan. Heath was falling back and we were watching the situation develop, and waiting for a favorable opportunity to put the regiment in. Your blowhard staff officer comes up just then and starts hectoring me in front of my command, and ends by ordering me off the field. I see that he's brought up a whole brigade, with artillery, to fight off this little raiding party—"

"They seemed to be giving you a good deal of trouble.

About twelve hundred of them, according to the prisoners," James said, interrupting.

At this point I turned my head and saw Cam Heath coming down the hall. Cam was another one of the big men in the command, as tall as James and Dick Ross, but broader and heavier than either of them. Although he had come straight from the field, his smooth black hair was neatly parted, his mustache waxed and pointed. In addition, though, he had a black eye and a purplish contusion on the other cheekbone, and a long, deep scratch across the back of his hand; his clothes were dusty and torn; the top of his right boot was shot away, and he walked with a pronounced limp. He paused for a moment in the doorway leading to the office.

"Ah, the hero in person," he said. "Our gallant leader. The fearless commander of the cavalry brigade."

This theatrical flourish was uttered in a voice that was almost pleasant, and might for a moment have been mistaken for good-humored mockery. The illusion would not have lasted long, for a moment later, as he stood in front of the general, his voice was half strangled with grief and anger.

"Sir, I wish to bring formal charges against Colonel Ross. I charge him with incompetence, with personal cowardice, and with the deliberate betrayal of a part of his command. I will also ask that he be relieved of command until a court-martial can try him on these charges."

General Pack looked up at him and listened with the same impenetrable calm he had shown to James and his nephew.

"I've been hearing about your case, Colonel," he said quietly. "Colonel Lake has given me your side, and Colonel Ross has given me his own. I will want to talk to a few more of the responsible officers who were present, then we will see what has to be done."

Cam Heath said. "Yes, sir." He hesitated, then added, "I am obliged to tell you that I could not, in good conscience, transmit any order of Colonel Ross's to my regiment. To what is left of my regiment. If I did, not a man of them would obey the order."

The general was patient. "I don't think the cavalry brigade will require any orders tonight, Colonel. If any orders are required, I will give them myself. Tomorrow we will look into the matter further and come to a decision."

Dick thrust himself forward belligerently. "Does that mean that I'm relieved?"

"I think you heard me, Dick," the general said, still in the same patient voice. "The cavalry brigade is under my direct orders for the time being. If Wales or Bassett need orders, have them come in to see me."

Cam Heath had turned to face James. "Little Howie Brinkman's dead, James," he said in a somber voice. "Tommy Breese was killed. Art Hunter lost a leg. Harry Pyne was killed. Cas Edwards and Tom Morgan, both killed. Joe Haskins, Roy Keene, John Rollins, Ab Weatherford, all killed. The Miller twins, both dead."

Dick chose this moment to turn with a truculent air and address Cam Heath.

"See here, Heath. You can argue about your orders, and I don't give a damn. Maybe you thought you were right. But there is one thing you can't do. One thing I don't allow anybody to do, and that is to accuse me of personal cowardice."

Cam Heath stared at him. "But, Colonel, I did accuse you of personal cowardice. Formally. I still do."

Dick's voice rose. "Then, by God, I demand an explanation."

"I'll be glad to give you one, Colonel," Heath said. The note of almost pleasant mockery had come into his voice again, with the sinister undertone that I had missed at first.

"It was the only explanation I could think of for your not supporting me. I'll admit it was a big, wide open field, and there were a lot of rebels around, and they all had guns and a lot of them were shooting at us. I'll admit it was a little dangerous, and there was even a pretty fair chance of getting hurt, so it was thoughtless of me to ask. But I didn't really mean for you to come yourself. I just meant for you to send the regiment, or part of the regiment. Just enough to keep my right clear—"

Dick interrupted him with a scowl. "That's not what I meant, and you know damned well it isn't."

Cam Heath turned to James. "Oh, Christ!" he said with abysmal weariness. "Now the puppy wants me to apologize to him. He murders my sister's son and three of my closest friends and a dozen other wonderful fellows and half my regiment, and he wants an apology! The man's not only a coward, but a fool!"

He turned on Dick savagely. "You hear that, puppy? You're a coward, a sniveling coward, and a fool, and all the apology I've got for you is—this!"

He swung his arm and slapped Dick across the face with so heavy a hand that Dick was staggered.

Suddenly the general was on his feet, looking a foot taller than any of the three big men in front of him, and his voice filled the room.

"Enough, gentlemen! Stay where you are! Dick, stand back! James, will you kindly restrain your friend?"

The quarrel was suddenly extinguished, as a candle snuffer extinguishes the flame of a candle. Three violently angry men, two of them at least ready for bloodshed, were suddenly sobered and brought to their senses by the sheer weight of authority in the general's voice. It was impressive.

General Pack, still on his feet, waited for a moment to let the angry commotion subside, then he looked over at Cam Heath.

"Have you gone completely out of your mind, Colonel? You know what the regulations are. You know that in this command we enforce them."

Without rage to sustain him, Cam was suddenly haggard and beaten down with grief. He drew in a deep, shaky breath. "I beg your pardon, sir," he said in a low voice. "I think maybe I am a little out of my mind. This has been a sad day for me, and a disastrous day for my regiment."

"It has been a sad day for all of us, Colonel. You can have leave if you want it, of course."

Cam Heath came to life briefly. "Who would command the regiment, sir? My lieutenant colonel is dead. Major Hunter lost a leg. My four senior squadron leaders were killed, and the fifth wounded. The senior officer in the regiment, after me, is Captain Ralph Hubbard, who will be a good officer if he lives long enough, but he's only twenty-one years old, and was only promoted in August. I thank you, General, but I can't possibly take leave. Not at this time."

The general looked at him with a somber expression. "I suppose you still wish to prefer charges against Colonel Ross?"

Heath's answer was short, definite, and hard. "Yes, sir. I do."

This was the answer the general had expected. He thought for a moment, then addressed James. "I think Captain Bliss is still over at the courthouse, James. Will you have the kindness to take Colonel Heath over and have the captain draw up the specifications? He'll know what is wanted."

As soon as they had left, the general called me in and asked me to get Colonel Wing, of the 52nd Illinois, for him. To bring the colonel back with me, with as many of his officers as might have any pertinent information about the operations of the afternoon.

On my way out I noticed Robert Saint Chamans and Madame in the living room. Robert's nonchalance was a little less in evidence than usual. Madame had come down for dinner in a white lace dress that I had always admired, white, or rather cream-colored, with a slender line of gold running around the neckline, and a rose—tonight a deep red rose—pinned to the bosom.

When I first caught sight of her, coming from the savage quarrel in the office, I remembered the objection James had made at the very beginning, that a woman had no place in the harsh atmosphere of an active campaign. But as I looked at her, the impression I received was not one of defenseless fragility, but of fortitude and courage: it was only the lace dress, not Madame, that was out of place.

Nevertheless, that was what Robert was telling her, that the good days were over, and it was time for her to leave. He caught sight of me as I was on my way to the door, and beckoned me over.

"I have been telling Madame Lucy she ought to leave," he explained soberly. "Our luck is gone. The other side goes up, and we go down. The enemy gains strength and we grow weaker. Now we have begun to quarrel among ourselves, which is the worst sign of all. None of us knows how much longer even the town will be safe. So you must leave now, Madame. You must leave while you can." Here Robert paused, then his voice became dry. "And when you leave, I think it would be an excellent idea if you took the rest of us with you as a bodyguard."

"Robert, that's nonsense," Madame Lucy said.

"I fear it isn't," he replied, his voice sober again. "Johnny, what do you think?"

This was quite a large order. I tried to reply sensibly.

"Robert's right about the town, ma'am. The fighting gets closer in all the time. So you probably ought to go, though I hate to say it. The place will be empty without you. I don't know about the rest of it. I think Robert is wrong. I certainly hope he is. But I don't really know."

"Bravo!" Robert said. "You see, Madame? Johnny is an honest man. He agrees with me, even though he doesn't want to."

Madame Lucy smiled at us. "At least, Johnny is kind enough to say that he will miss me. But you're wrong, both of you. The time has not yet come."

With that she dismissed us. Later it occurred to me that it was an odd thing to say. There was nothing portentous in her voice—no change at all, in fact—but the statement itself was portentous, as though she were waiting with resigned patience for a portent, a sign from heaven, that would allow her to leave.

Chapter 6

General Pack went up to Jenkins' Ferry the next day with Robert and Jack Maitland, picking up Gavin on the way, and taking Cam Heath and the 12th Pennsylvania along as escort. This, I imagine, was to keep the regiment moving, and allow it no time to sit down and lick its wounds and contemplate its grievances.

The major grievance was still there, but the wounds, when an accurate count was made the next morning, proved to be less severe than had been thought. Three of Cam's officers, including his nephew, proved to be among the wounded rather than among the killed, and the total number of casualties was reduced from the two hundred and sixty estimated in the darkness and turmoil of the preceding night, to one hundred and ninety-eight. A heavy loss, still, but not so crushing as the earlier figure.

The general left about the middle of the morning. After he had gone, James and I went down to Roth's headquarters, where James was to meet Major Stewart and some of Roth's officers, and go over the ground to the south. They were particularly interested in the MacDougal Ridge, with the ten-mile view from the house and the unlimited field of fire, and there was some question of bringing in heavy guns and fortifying the ridge.

Their principal concern, however, was not with permanent fortifications, but with locating natural strong points that were mutually supporting, and could be made formidable in half an hour's time by an infantry regiment with axes and shovels. This was all quite routine and we had done a good deal of it farther out, but what it suggested now was that we were drawing in our perimeter and were preparing to stand on the defensive against superior forces. It was a prospect that called for the soldierly qualities of stubbornness and endurance, rather than those of boldness and enthusiasm. It wasn't a prospect to get excited about.

The day suited the errand and the prospect. The sky was a sullen gray; there was an occasional splatter of rain in the air, and, without being cold, it was raw and disagreeable. James was taciturn, which was unusual, and we hardly spoke to each other all the way down. At Roth's headquarters everyone was feeling gloomy about the open split in the cavalry brigade. Billy had a cold, and came out with a towel from an alcohol compress pinned around his neck, and went back to bed as soon as lunch was over. James and the others started on their tour of inspection after lunch, and I went back to Tarsus.

On reaching the house, I noticed a buggy and a led horse standing in the driveway, in charge of a gray-haired old Negro. A moment later I was absolutely astonished at meeting a rebel officer in the hallway, dressed in regulation gray, with a starred collar and swirls of gold braid on his sleeves. For a fraction of an instant I had the wild notion that the town had been captured in my absence, and that I was going to be called upon to surrender; then I realized that the officer was on crutches and that he looked familiar, and that, in fact, it was Blair Robertson. At the same time I remembered that he had been waiting to be exchanged, and that Jake and General Pack had arranged for him to pass through our lines into General McGraw's, without going through the tedious formalities of the exchange center. I noticed that he handled his crutches and his artificial leg quite expertly by this time, and that he was looking cheerful, which was an expression I had never before seen on his face.

"Afternoon, Colonel," I said. "You gave me quite a start in your uniform. For a moment I thought your fellows had taken the place, and I was trying to decide whether to run for it, or to make a dignified surrender."

This seemed to entertain him, and he laughed heartily. After a moment, still chuckling, he said, "We haven't taken it just yet, John. But if you want to be forehanded, I'll be glad to accept your surrender now."

I smiled and shook my head, and he let the joke go.

"I've just been in to see our friend, Colonel Leslie," he went on. "All the papers have come in, and Jake—the colonel—was kind enough to make out those that depended on the command here, and I'm on my way to Richmond for reassignment."

I said, "Colonel, you look as though you had just been let out of school."

He laughed. "I guess that's about the way I feel. I don't know what they'll have for me, with this damned wooden leg of mine, but it will be a relief to be doing anything at all, and a relief not to have to look at enemy troops in my home town and in my own house every day."

He pulled himself up short with an air of shocked disbelief at what he had just heard himself say.

"Oh, good Lord, John, I beg your pardon! No offense, please."

I wasn't offended. "Nobody likes strangers in his house, Colonel."

"You can see that. Of course. I should have known that you would." Here he made a little speech that I think he had composed beforehand. "Anyway, I hope you'll remember that in our other house you weren't strangers, but friends. Yourself, and your uncle James, whom I have admired ever since Shiloh, and my father's crony, Jake, and Robert Saint Chamans, and the Countess Lucy, whom all of us were in love with. I hadn't known what my father meant when he said there were gentlemen on the other side as well as on ours. I'm happy to tell you that now I do know what he meant."

We shook hands, wished each other the best of personal luck, and separated. If that had been all, and the parting had been final, it would have left a pleasant recollection behind it which would at least have sweetened the afternoon. Unfortunately it wasn't, for when young Robertson reached the door, he turned around and called to me. I turned and went back, a little curious as to what he wanted. He waited until I had almost reached him, then asked me in a low voice if Derek Morgan was a friend of mine. I told him with considerable emphasis that he wasn't.

Young Robertson hesitated, and looked a little uncomfortable. Finally he said, "I think James ought to know that Morgan has hired a man to spy on him. I think you had better tell him." He nodded in the direction of a soldier standing idly by one of the elms on the courthouse side of the driveway. "There he is now. That's Morgan's hired man."

I said I would tell James to look out for him, and thanked him for telling me. We had already shaken hands and wished each other well, so there was a moment of awkwardness; then young Robertson smiled and nodded, and swung himself over to the buggy on his crutches. I watched him get in, expertly and without any help. His coachman got in after him, and they started off down the driveway, with the led horse following. So that was the note we parted on: the noble sentiment overlaid by a feeling of rasping irritation.

I waited until the buggy was past the courthouse and out of sight, then I went up to the soldier, who was still loitering by the driveway, and addressed him in a bad-tempered drill-sergeant's bark.

"What are you doing here, soldier?"

I don't think he had expected either the question or the tone of voice. He looked at me and saw that I meant business, and replied meekly enough, "Why, nothing, sir. I was off duty today—"

"And you came in to see the sights. Naturally. What's your regiment?"

"Fiftieth Ohio, sir. Colonel Frazer."

This was one of Jonesy's October regiments. I knew that Jonesy worked his new regiments hard as a matter of principle, and that the 50th Ohio, in particular, was working on the fortifications at Jennings' Landing. I thought it highly unlikely that a private from that regiment would be taking time off to see the sights of Tarsus.

"In that case, you'll have a pass from Colonel Frazer. I think you had better go over and show it to Major Lumley."

I put two fingers in my mouth and whistled at the sentry. The sentry stared at me, then gestured in my direction to the corporal on duty, who came trotting around the corner of the house.

As the corporal approached us, the soldier said in a low voice, "I wouldn't do anything rash if I were you, Captain Lake. You might regret it."

That was all I needed. I didn't bother to answer him, but when the corporal came up I said, "This man claims to be from the 50th Ohio, Corporal. I know he's absent without leave, and I think he's either a deserter or a spy. Major Lumley will be able to find out which. And if Lieutenant Morgan shows up—our Derek, Corporal—send him in to see the major, too. And if any officer tries to interfere, tries to take charge and prevent you from seeing the major, I will want to know who the officer is. So will Major Lumley, and so will General Pack. Can you see to that? Or shall I go with you?"

"No, sir. I can handle it myself." The corporal seemed to be pleased with his assignment, probably because it had something to do with giving Derek one in the eye. "I can tell you who will try to stop me, sir. Lieutenant Groome. I'll tell him what my orders are. I think that will hold him, Captain. He's a little short on nerve."

The soldier from the 50th Ohio looked over at me and said, "You're going to regret this, Captain."

"So are you, soldier. So is Lieutenant Morgan."

I watched them start for the provost marshal's office in the courthouse, then went back to the house, and out of sheer boredom went up to my room on the third floor and went to sleep.

Before dinner, Derek came up to me in the hall with a scowl on his face and said, "By God, Lake, you take a lot on yourself."

I looked at him with astonishment, then gave him one of his own supercilious smiles. "You know, Derek, for pure, cast-iron impudence, that statement of yours would be pretty hard to beat. You always did have plenty of gall, but that one is a real masterpiece."

Derek bit his lip and turned away without another word.

The Countess came down for dinner dressed in somber black, relieved only by a fine gold chain around her neck, and, though she was gracious to all of us, she was obviously depressed. She had spent the day at the hospital, helping with the care of the hundred and fifty wounded of the 12th Pennsylvania, including a number of men Cam had brought in and introduced to her at various times. An unusually large number of men had received mortal wounds. A few of them were still unconscious and obviously dying; the others had worn through the initial anesthetic effect of shock during the night, and all of them were in pain.

When Jake was solicitous about her, she admitted she was tired, and added, "A military hospital the day after a battle is not a very soothing place. Excuse me, Colonel Leslie, I did not mean to say that. May we please talk about something else?"

Jake had spent the hour before dinner in drinking brandy with Judge Robertson, and had come back a little drunk and ready to talk about anything so long as he had a listener. Hugo Bliss brought up the subject of second sight again, and Jake told us more about his great-grandmother on the Isle of Skye, and about the banshee in his maternal grandmother's family. Then he told us about another old woman he had gone to see much later, when he was nearly thirty, in County Donegal—having an interest in such matters, as he explained. The old woman had told him, among other things, that at the age of fifty he would find himself a soldier again, though not for very long, only for a year and a half—

The Countess looked at him and asked soberly, "How long have you been a soldier, Colonel Leslie?"

Jake was startled. He looked as though he had just caught himself in time.

"About that long, ma'am. But I daresay it's all nonsense.

And if it isn't, I'm probably due for an attack of lumbago, or a kick from a mule, or something equally unheroic that will force me to resign, and take me off the scene in whatever is the opposite of a burst of glory. After that I'll hobble around, bent over a cane, and talk too much and complain about my liver until I'm carried off to the cemetery at the age of eighty-two."

All this was disingenuous. Jake was talking fast to cover up something he had said, or was on the point of saying. Madame was dissatisfied, and was about to ask Jake what he had started to say, when Hugo Bliss broke in.

"Do you really believe all that stuff, Jake?" he asked.

"Now that's an interesting question, young man." Jake was grateful for the interruption. "What makes it interesting is that I don't really know the answer. My inclination is about the same as yours, to be highly skeptical of all that stuff. But I find that every time I get myself comfortably settled in that frame of mind, something happens to jar me out of it, something that old Mary McSweeny described to me with perfectly fantastic exactitude fifteen or twenty years ago. Mind you, Hugo, this is of my own knowledge, not a story I heard somewhere that may have become garbled in the telling. So, I will ask you, how can I possibly disbelieve something that lies within my own experience, and that I know to be true?"

Hugo was still skeptical. "Do you mind if I suggest that what you heard was a lot of impressive gibberish that can be interpreted to mean anything you like?"

Jake smiled and shook his head. "Nothing like it, my friend. She was a dirty old woman, and she smoked a pipe. What she said was impressive, but there was nothing vague about it, and nothing to interpret."

Madame, still very sober, looked over at Jake again. "What was it you were going to say a few minutes ago, Colonel Leslie? When I interrupted you by asking how long you had been in the army?"

Thus pinned down, Jake was incapable of not answering, or of falsifying the answer. "It wasn't anything very definite, ma'am. The old woman had a liking for the spectacular, and in connection with the year and a half you were asking about, she said something about a sea of fire, and a great pillar of flame. What she meant by it I don't know. I thought it might be a guiding light, like the one the Israelites had in the desert, but she said that wasn't what it was, and that it was real, and not a symbol of anything. I imagine that it was simply a picture in her mind. She told me what she saw, and that was all. Does it mean anything to you, ma'am?"

"I'm afraid not." Madame Lucy appeared to be disappointed, and no longer much interested.

The early part of the evening dragged along slowly. Everyone was either busy or bored, and no comfort either way. Finally, about nine-thirty, I walked down to the Officers' Club.

It wasn't much better there, but there was some improvement: there were a few men I knew, and after a while we got a poker game started. For the first couple of hours my luck was abysmally bad. I held bad cards most of the time, and when I was finally dealt a good hand, the man across the table invariably held a better one. By twelve o'clock I had lost over two hundred dollars, which meant I would have to borrow money from James. Since James was inclined to be ironical about my abilities as a poker player, I wasn't looking forward to this with any pleasure. About that time, though, my luck changed, and by two o'clock, when the game broke up, I had won back nearly all the money I had lost.

Outside, in the courthouse square it was quiet—not dead still, for there was a faint intermittent breeze from the southwest that stirred the upper branches of the trees and sent the leaves rustling down, but very quiet after my friends from Roth's division had passed out of hearing and the sound of hoofbeats had died away. There were dim lights, largely hidden by the trees, in the lower windows of the courthouse, and more distant ones from our headquarters in the Robertson house a block away. These were the only lights that were visible, spots of yellow in the grayness of the night.

The sky was overcast and no stars were out, but behind the layer of clouds the moon was full and its light was diffused through the clouds, making the whole arch of the sky a luminous gray. This gave a misty, diffused light that cast no shadows; the branches of the trees were outlined in black against the gray sky, and the air was cool and damp. It was the early morning, two o'clock in the morning, of the twentieth of November.

I walked home through the gray night, neither pleased nor greatly displeased with myself and the world, and by this time very sleepy. There were lights burning in the hallway and in the living room, and an orderly was asleep on a sofa with his head fallen over to one side and his mouth open. I took the stairway off the kitchen as usual, instead of the main stairway, because it led directly to the third floor, and there was less chance of disturbing anyone late at night. On the second-floor landing I heard a vague sound from somewhere down the hall. Mildly curious, but almost too sleepy to care, I put my head around the corner to see where the sound came from.

I saw where it had come from, and was suddenly struck and riven to the very deepest part of my being, and stunned with pain. The sound I had heard came from the open door of the Countess's bedroom. My uncle James was standing in the doorway in a blue silk dressing gown. He was looking down, and a woman's arm, a naked white arm, was around his neck. His voice was a voice I had never heard before: everything characteristic was gone, the easy confidence, the boldness, the good humor. Now it was harried, the voice of a driven man, murmuring broken phrases: "Darling! How can I? How can I leave you? How can I bear it?"

And her voice answering him, low and passionate, and filled with anguish: "No, dearest! No! Don't go yet! Don't leave me! Oh, don't ever leave me!"

They drew back into the bedroom, and the door closed behind them.

I was able to draw back somehow and make my way up to the third floor, to the room that, fortunately, I had to myself that night. I threw myself on the bed fully dressed and tried to shut out the scene that kept repeating itself over and over again in my mind: the silk dressing gown, the naked white arm, the murmuring voices, the click of the latch as the door closed. I was shattered, as though I had been struck by a bolt of lightning, wondered that I had been able to survive the shock, and regretted bitterly that I had.

There was no thought involved in this, no activity of the mind, any more than there is in the cry of a man who has been badly hit, and begs for someone to put him out of his misery. I had seen men with such wounds, and the recollection finally led to the only comforting thought I had had in an hour or more: if I got up early and got on a horse, and avoided all the main roads until I reached the line of our outposts, with any kind of management I ought to be able to stir up a fight with the rebel outposts, and with any luck at all, get myself killed. The prospect was comforting, and while I was thinking about it I went to sleep.

In retrospect, the extreme violence, the suicidal violence, of my response to this love scene astonishes me, until I remember the nature and the power of the feelings that went into it. The atmosphere I was brought up in had lost most of the harsh puritanism of the early days. The frontier had passed by more than a generation earlier. We thought of ourselves as civilized, and had some pretensions to manners and culture. We took our churchgoing lightly and largely as a matter of public decorum—my father was a vestryman of the church, and read himself to sleep on Gibbon every night—and we smiled at the sour asceticism and hell-fire theology of the old-fashioned members of the community.

But with all the latitude we allowed ourselves in the matter of cards and wine, dancing and music and entertainment, where women were concerned our moral code was made of cast iron. There were no shadings in this moral code of ours, no grays, no gradations: it was all in black and white and perfectly simple, and the only question asked was: guilty or not guilty? There were only two kinds of women, the pure and the impure.

In common with my entire generation I was brought up on this ironbound code. It was in the air I breathed and was in a sense invisible, as a simple and obvious and universally accepted truth. It had never occurred to me to question it: it had never occured to me that it was questioned by anybody.

It was my belief in the enormity of the crime that had hidden it from me. I was certainly the last man, among those involved in any way, to believe in the existence of the affair between my uncle and the general's wife. The innuendoes of her sister-in-law and the defection of her nephews failed to move me, even that of Colin, her favorite nephew and my close friend. I knew better. I knew that she was good: therefore it was impossible for her to be guilty. It was as simple as that.

The same reasoning applied to James. While a vastly greater amount of latitude was allowed to men, still adultery was not a light matter by any means, and to seduce the wife of a friend was dishonorable. To continue on friendly terms with the injured husband, to greet him with a smile, added baseness to dishonor. I knew James well. I had known him all my life. I knew that he was the soul of honor, that there was no falseness of any kind in him. Therefore—as before—it was impossible for him to be guilty of anything base or dishonorable.

All this had been smashed in front of my eyes. I had been betrayed, mocked and dishonored by the two people I loved and honored most. The effect was shattering, like that of very great physical pain. Some ten days later, after I had received wounds thought to be mortal, and was lying on the frozen ground out near the extreme edge of pain, the sensation was not very different.

It persisted throughout the night, and sleep was only half an anodyne: I was aware of a hollow ache behind my eyes and of the reason for it even while I slept. Towards morning I got up and looked at my watch and disbelieved it when I saw that it was twenty minutes after six, and that I had slept for four hours. I hastened downstairs, anxious to be out of the house and on my way, and panic-stricken at the thought of being stopped. While I was still on the stairway, I suddenly knew that I was going to be stopped, and who was going to stop me. Still, I crossed the kitchen and the dining room safely, and had begun to think I might be mistaken because there was no sound in the house, when there it was! As I turned into the hallway, there was James coming towards me and only a few feet away.

What seemed strangest to me was that he looked just as usual. He had shaved and was wearing clean linen, and looked fresh and cheerful; there were no new and evil lines in his face, no marks of depravity, and he greeted me with a smile.

"Morning, Johnny. Or haven't you been to bed yet?"

As I tried to brush past him without speaking, he put out his hand and caught my arm in a powerful grasp. "What's the matter with you?"

I kept my head turned away, unable either to look at him or to speak, my mind locked and frozen into place. James answered his own question.

"Oh, Christ! I might have known it! It was bound to happen sooner or later."

He gave my arm a little shake and addressed me in a reasonable voice. "Look, Johnny. Nothing has changed. No one is any different. We're still the same—"

He seemed to feel that this was wrong, and broke off. When he spoke again, his voice held anger with an edge of contempt.

"Listen, boy. They didn't teach you everything there was to know in the Lancaster Sunday school. They didn't teach you everything there was to know about good and evil, and about human beings, and about men and women. They taught you nothing worth remembering about any of those things. Your ignorance of people and the world is absolute. I hope you know that. I hope you have sense enough to see that, and humility enough to accept it. If you can't take us as we are, I will ask you to suspend judgment. Ten years from now, if any of us live that long, I'll listen to you. If your judgment is adverse, I'll be sorry, but I'll accept it. At this time, by God, I will not have it! I will not have a raw youth, with all the presumption of ignorance, sit in judgment on us. You hear me, Johnny? I won't have it!"

James' voice rose in angry emphasis, then dropped suddenly, and ended on a note of entreaty. "Only, for the love of God, be kind to Lucy!"

With that, he released my arm, and turned away without waiting for any kind of answer.

The greater part of the day is entirely lost to my memory. The ruling idea, to begin with, was the one I had gone to sleep on, an unobtrusive suicide. The idea of suicide faded out sometime during the morning, but the momentum originally generated kept me moving towards our outposts along the back roads long after the purpose had been abandoned.

The sky was overcast, a pale uniform gray, and the day was unseasonably warm. I was operating on instinct rather than reason most of the day. To avoid any possibility of being followed, with elementary cunning I started out to the south and rode past the hospital, then crossed over to another road and doubled back to the north, and spent most of the day in the rough scrub-oak country to the northwest. Twice I got off the road and watched cavalry patrols go by, and thought sardonically that nothing could have been easier than to ambush them. Five minutes after the second of the patrols had gone by, I realized suddenly that it had been a rebel cavalry patrol, not one of ours.

At one time I turned off and rode into the brush for about a hundred yards, and turned my horse loose—my favorite horse, Persephone—and simply lay down and went to sleep. I think that I slept for a couple of hours, and that it was early in the afternoon when I went to sleep, but the shadowless day and the uniform overcast of the sky made it impossible even to guess at the time. From eight in the morning until nearly five in the afternoon, there was no change at all in the light, and no sign of the sun's location in the sky.

At any rate, it was close to four o'clock when I woke up. Persephone, with her head down and the bridle reins trailing, was contentedly browsing twenty feet away from me; the thin, undernourished oaks with leathery brown leaves were all around, and the same pewter-colored sky was overhead. I woke up at this time not only out of sleep, but out of the nightmare as well: the white arm I had seen around James' neck I remembered now as a woman's arm, not as an evil white tentacle or the boneless coil of a serpent; my mind was no longer locked hopelessly on dead center and unable to move.

There was great relief in this, but it was only partial, for as soon as I could think again the arguments began, stubborn on one side, loud and angry on the other: the love and admiration I felt for James and Madame Lucy on one side, the horrified repudiation that my entire upbringing demanded on the other. I found myself thinking in terms of the adulterer and his paramour, the harlot and her lover, the guilty couple, the sinful, lustful and wicked couple, then brought myself up short with the realization that the man I was cursing was my uncle James, for whom I had never felt anything but love and admiration since the summer he bought me a pony and taught me to ride; and that the fallen woman, the faithless wife, the harlot, was the gracious and beautiful Countess, the wise, kind, and loving Madame Lucy with whom I had fallen in love at first sight on the porch of the tavern at Jenkins' Ferry. After that it was the turn of what James called the Lancaster Sunday school, but was really the environment I had grown up in as a whole, until I was brought up short again, and so on, *da capo.*

By this time I was on Persephone's back again and riding downhill at a slow walk towards the main road between Tarsus and Jonesy's headquarters at Jennings' Landing. I reached the road about five miles out, and turned left as a matter of course, towards Tarsus and headquarters. This was entirely unconscious on my part: I had no awareness of reaching a crossroads or making a decision. Ten minutes later I realized that the turn, the choice of direction, had been a decision, the only possible one for me. With this realization, I felt a sense of ease flowing through my entire being, and presently, though my mind was still sore from the wrenching it had taken in the past fifteen hours, otherwise I felt wonderfully light.

It was now close to five o'clock. The sun was still invisible behind the even gray layer of cloud, but the light filtering through the clouds gradually diminished, and it was beginning to grow dark. Now that I had a home to go to again I was rather anxious to get there, so I pushed my horse up to a trot and fifteen minutes later crossed the bridge into town.

I found James sitting at his desk in the office with a pen in his hand and a pile of reports in front of him. He finished scribbling a note on the bottom of one of the reports, then looked up and gave me a cheerful offhand greeting.

"Hello, Johnny. How are you?"

"Sorry about this morning, James," I said, a little awkwardly. "I had to get out and clear my head."

"It was my fault. I should have said something to you. We were a little worried. I suppose you found what you were looking for?"

"I found out which side I belonged on. That was the main thing."

The question had been casual, hardly a question at all, and I had assumed that the mere fact of my presence here, in this room, had already supplied the answer. Consequently I was surprised at the relief and the depth of feeling in James' voice as he said, "I'm glad, Johnny. I would have hated it—otherwise."

He was about to add something further, then checked himself, looked up at me from across the desk, and smiled broadly. "You surely look terrible. You'll feel better with a shave and some clean clothes. I'll see you at dinner."

I went upstairs, and had our third-floor orderly bring up hot water, and had a bath and shaved, and put on fresh linen and a clean uniform. I glanced at myself in the mirror with approval before I went downstairs again. This was unusual, for vanity wasn't ordinarily one of my foibles. No doubt it was another aspect of the relief from pressure, and from the feeling of distaste for humanity, including myself, that I had felt in the past twenty-four hours.

There was no one in the living room but Derek, and I ignored him with great ease. The Countess came downstairs a few minutes later, dressed in green and gold rather than yesterday's somber black, a beautiful woman as always, but without her usual radiance, her expression calm and rather grave. I got up as soon as I saw her on the stairs, and went to meet her.

When she saw me coming, she hesitated for an almost imperceptible instant, with her hand on the banister, and seemed to shrink away. She recovered herself so quickly that an outsider, or an acquaintance, would have missed the moment of hesitation entirely, but I was not an outsider, and I was shocked and grieved.

She smiled at me. "Good evening, Johnny. Are you feeling better?"

By way of answer I made what I suppose was a rather absurd little speech, a boyish little puppy-dog speech, but I was shocked to find that she was afraid of what I was going to say—it seemed against right and against nature that she should be afraid—and I am rather glad I made the speech, absurdities and all.

"Yes, ma'am, I feel much better," I said. "I found out which side I was on. I'm on your side. If you will allow me to tell you so, ma'am, I've been in love with you ever since the first moment I saw you, on the porch when we came up to get you. And I have loved and admired my uncle ever since I was a little child. I think you are both wonderful people, and good and honorable. I think it would be possible for you to be wrong, but I don't think it could ever be possible for either of you to be base or dishonorable. If you were to be in the wrong, then I would be wrong too, because I would be with you and on your side, anyway."

Her expression changed as she listened. Her eyes, I noticed, were blue in this light, rather than gray, or green, as they were in bright sunlight. She reached out and put her hand on my arm while I was talking, and at the end she said quite simply,

"Thank you, Johnny. It was kind of you to tell me this. So very kind." She turned her head away, and added in a lower voice, "I hope—I do so hope—that you are right."

She gave me a quick little smile, then went on past me

towards the dining room and the kitchen, to look over the table setting and the preparations for dinner, and I went back to the living room.

Dinner was pleasant and rather festive that night. It was like a small family party, or a birthday party among friends. The Countess was relaxed and cheerful. Jake sat next to her, with our senior guest, Colonel Saunders, of Billy Roth's staff, on the other side. James sat two places away, as usual. Colin had discovered some necessary errand and had ridden off before dinner, so that Derek was the only member of the opposing faction at the table.

Robert Saint Chamans commented on this. He glanced across the table at Derek, then turned to me and remarked, "Young Morgan must be feeling rather solitary over there. He's the only one present on his side. What would you call it? The King's side?"

This remark was the first open recognition, to the best of my memory, of the fact that the command was now divided into two distinct and hostile factions. Robert's suggestion, that Derek was of the King's party, never came into any kind of general use. The general, in fact, stood above the fray. His position of authority, his pride, his sense of dignity would not allow him to admit the existence of a quarrel with one of his subordinates, nor to give any outward sign that he was aware of any reason for such a quarrel. The quarrel was taken up in his behalf by his nephews. There was no King's party, just as there was no Queen's party. The two factions were Ross and Lake.

The Ross party centered around Gavin, who was the most implacable of our enemies. The First Division followed its commander, and was solidly against us. Billy Roth was never able to make up his mind, first leaning to one side, then to the other, but James had commanded his troops in action, and the men in all the old regiments were entirely devoted to him. The men in the new regiments followed their lead, so the Second Division was as solidly on our side as the First Division was on the other.

In the Third Division the situation was different. Jonesy

was openly on our side, while many of his regimental commanders were against us. These were mostly older men, sober, responsible men, who had left an established place in the community from a strong sense of duty. There were good soldiers and fine men among them. They had been friends of ours, and it was distressing now to find them cold and hostile. It was as though we were not content with taking part in a major civil war, but insisted on reproducing the struggle within our own ranks.

This was the state of the command on November twentieth, when Robert's casual remark at dinner brought the subject into the open—formulated and put into words a situation that everyone was aware of, but no one said anything about.

We sat at the table for a couple of hours after dinner was over, and Madame told us something about her grandfather, who had served under the Archduke Charles, and had defeated Masséna at Aspern. Robert remembered presently that one of his great-uncles had a brigade under Saint Hilaire at the same battle. Afterwards we talked about other things, and were all cheerful and at ease, and it might almost have been October again.

I was glad later, that this dinner had been so pleasant, for it was the last time we had dinner together around the big table in the Robertson dining room. The following night, Friday night, I was down at Roth's headquarters at dinnertime. On Saturday night most of us were gone, and after Saturday there were no more dinners.

Chapter 7

ཌ ཌ ཌ ཌ ཌ ཌ ཌ ཌ ཌ ཌ ཌ ཌ ཌ ཌ ཌ ཌ ཌ ཌ ཌ

On Friday night, from about ten o'clock on, the rift in the command was actually visible to the eye. The occasion was a birthday party at the Officers' Club for Jack Maitland and Tim Wales, whose birthdays fell on the same day, November twenty-first. This minor coincidence had been noticed some weeks earlier under happier circumstances, at a time when any excuse for a party was welcomed, and a really sound excuse like the present one made a party a positive obligation. James and Gavin, who were the principal instigators of the affair, had each promised a case of champagne, and it was to be a party to remember—which it was, though not exactly as intended.

By this time everyone was ready to give the project up, including the two principals, not only because of the dissension in the command, but also because of the quite general feeling that this was no time for celebrations. Everyone except Gavin, who had ridden down from Jenkins' Ferry that morning with Jack Maitland. Gavin insisted obstinately and with some truculence on going on with the party.

"I promised you fellows a party, and, by God, you're going to have one," he told Jack. "I'll carry out my end of the bargain, and Lake can do as he likes."

This was one gift horse Jack was looking in the mouth. "All right, General," he said. "Have it your way. Only don't get any ideas about bringing over a lot of your fellows from the First Division and starting a row. If you do, I promise you that

I'll break every bottle of champagne in the place over your head."

Gavin laughed and let it go, and in the afternoon sent over two cases of champagne.

About five o'clock, James sent me down to Billy Roth with an order, or rather a suggestion—it amounted to the same thing—that he move one of his regiments out to the southeast to support the cavalry outposts in front of the southeast passes, and to move another regiment over where it would be in position to support the first. I was also to invite Billy to the party, along with anyone else who cared to come and could be spared.

I got there about dinnertime, and Billy had a place set for me at the table. He asked me why James was taking these precautions, and if he thought an attack was imminent. I told him he knew as much about it as we did. Barney was being reinforced, and, in particular, was getting a lot of cavalry. His new cavalry commander, young Taylor, Peter Taylor's son, was already known to us as a highly aggressive officer. He was certainly going to make an attack somewhere, or at least put in a big raid, but when—tonight, tomorrow, or next week— was anybody's guess. The only new information we had was a report from Tony Bassett, who was out to the northeast with the 12th Michigan, watching the upper passes. Tony reported that the enemy cavalry had been strongly reinforced in that area, and that his patrols had become extremely active. James was convinced that this was a feint, and that the attack would come through the lower passes, hence the precautions, and the strengthening of the line in that direction.

Horace Townsend asked me how James was bearing up under the weight of the command. The question had an odd sound at Billy Roth's table, since Billy himself, as senior brigadier general, was in nominal command.

I laughed and told Horace that I hadn't noticed any gray hair, but that I supposed he would be glad to see the general, even so. General Pack had applied for an increase in rank for James in August, and the War Department would probably get around to approving it in another eight or ten months, but in the meantime I doubted that the two Rosses would show much enthusiasm about taking orders from him.

Billy Roth bristled at this. "Who on earth do the Rosses think they are?" he demanded. "Authority doesn't change by being delegated. The authority I delegated to James is exactly the same authority I received. There isn't any argument about it. It's spelled out in so many words. James' orders have the same force as those of the major general himself. If Ross thinks he can disobey them, he had better have another look at the Articles of War."

An ironical aspect of the matter was that it was Gavin who had suggested the present arrangement, when the awkward fact of Billy's seniority first came to notice at the beginning of October. The chief of staff was associated with the senior brigadier general in the interim command, then a couple of subsidiary clauses were added, turning the actual exercise of command over to James. This solution of the problem satisfied everybody at the time. The normal order of succession was maintained. Billy Roth's seniority was acknowledged, which was all he wanted, and neither Gavin nor Jonesy had any objection to serving under James. This was before the storms of November, of course. In spite of the changed atmosphere, no change had been made in the order, and it was still in force at this time.

After dinner Billy had me ride out with him to see Colonel Miles Croyden, whose regiment was farthest out, and explain to him what James wanted, and why. We stayed there long enough to watch Colonel Croyden get his regiment under way, then we rode over to the camp of the 11th Ohio to see Jack Turquin, who was Croyden's commander, and was to support him if necessary.

Jack Turquin was one of our political colonels who had worked out, a red-faced forty-year-old politician with a piratical mustache, and a hearty manner acquired in fifteen years of handshaking at political rallies. Jack seemed to think it might very well be necessary to support Croyden.

"James has got the right idea," he told us cheerfully. "Barney's not going to let all those fine new cavalry regiments sit

212

around and eat up all his forage, and not do anything to earn their keep. And with the First Division all closed in tight around Jarvie, he's got a nice wide avenue to come up, with nothing to stop him but the 4th Michigan, and that won't be enough. Maybe the 4th and Miles together can stop him, but I think I had better be ready to pitch in with the 11th, anyway. Tomorrow—if you want my opinion, General—I think I ought to bring my whole brigade over to support the cavalry, and we ought to pry one of Ross's brigades loose from Jarvie and bring it over this way. And if Saint Chamans will send us a battery or two, the guns wouldn't do any harm, either."

"Your opinion is always wanted, Colonel," Billy replied. "John is going straight to headquarters from here, and will report as soon as he gets there. In the meantime, you are authorized to take any measures you think necessary."

Billy declined to come to the party, telling me quite frankly that he didn't think much of its chances as a social evening, and that he was doing his damndest to stay out of the row. He had no objection, though, if any of the staff wanted to go. Horace Townsend and young Fred Lambert rode back with me.

It was about nine when we started, and a full moon was just pushing up over the rim of the mountains in the southeast. The ride took us about an hour, and the courthouse square was bathed in moonlight as we approached the Club. We could hear the sounds of the party coming from the open upstairs windows: voices raised in loud and apparently amiable conversation, the clinking of glasses, the scraping of chairs, the tinny sound of the old piano, and the voices of a male quartet singing a doleful ballad. It sounded like a perfectly normal Friday night, any time these past two months.

Even though the Club had originally belonged to Roth's division, I felt that this was our party, and had Freddy and Major Townsend precede me up the stairs. The doorway was at the left of the landing at the top of the stairs, an open doorway with the light from the big room beyond pouring out onto the landing. We had gone up the stairs in single file, and, without giving the matter much thought, I noticed that both

Freddy and the major hesitated in the doorway, and looked both ways before they went in.

The curious part of it was that the place looked exactly as usual: a big, bare room furnished with deal tables and kitchen chairs, with a bar on one side and a ruinous old piano on the other, the air swirling with tobacco smoke and loud with talk, forty or fifty officers sitting at the tables or moving about. Even the thing that now struck my attention with considerable force had always been there, and I hadn't seen it before because it had been accidental and served no particular purpose. This was a lane, or aisle, running across the room from the piano to the bar, dividing the room into almost exactly equal halves. Tonight it was the dividing line between Lake and Ross, and the pause in the doorway was to see which side your friends were sitting on.

Actually, the first person I saw in the place was Jack Maitland, and he was on neither side, but in neutral territory. He was leaning back against the bar with his elbows behind him, bluff and bearded, casting a cynical eye over the party, looking more like the saloonkeeper than the guest of honor.

A glance at the right showed me that it was enemy territory. Gavin was sitting there and gave me a surly nod as I came in, in answer to my, "Good evening, General." He was sitting with Benny Pace, and with the commander of one of his new regiments, Colonel Hicks, a hard-bitten regular with an enormous waterfall of a mustache, and with a number of men I knew very slightly. Dick and Tim Wales were farther over, sitting at another table, and Colin, who had been one of the singers we had heard from outside, was moving away from the door towards the far side of the room.

Jack Maitland greeted the three of us as we came in. "Evening, Horace. Evening, Freddy," he said, then winked at me. *"Et ab haedis me sequestra,* eh, Johnny?"

The bar was neutral territory, and Jack's solitude was accidental and temporary. An enormous bowl of champagne punch stood on the bar, and a colored boy in a white jacket was stationed there with a ladle and an array of glasses to serve the guests. He ladled out a cup of punch for each of us,

214 🏵

and, while we were standing there with Jack, more customers came up from both sides, and with the usual line-up the bar looked more natural.

On our side were people I had never seen in the Club before. The most conspicuous of these was Dr. Ferguson, in civilian dress as usual, though he held the rank of major. With his graying beard, and his bulky figure dressed in black broadcloth, he looked like a country doctor who had wandered into the place by mistake. He had the red-bearded Dr. Erdman with him, and although Dr. Erdman was in uniform after a fashion, wearing a captain's shoulder straps, he carried on the great medical tradition by having them sewed onto an ordinary soldier's blouse, which he wore open, with a blue and white polka-dotted scarf tied around his neck.

The two of them were sitting at a table with Jonesy and Robert Saint Chamans, and two of Robert's battery commanders, Sam Brock and Ned Christie. They all had glasses in front of them and were talking with great animation, Dr. Ferguson with Robert and Jonesy, the younger doctor with the two gunners. These last three had discovered with common surprise that they came from towns within ten miles of each other along the Lake Erie shore, and were busy sharing the names of places and people. There was an entertaining contrast between Dr. Erdman's affectation of slippered ease and the martial elegance of the two artillery officers, which ran exactly parallel to the contrast between the two principals.

There were others I was surprised to see: the taciturn Colonel Horn—Maximilian Augustus Horn, Jonesy's chief of staff —who was sitting with Jake and Cam Heath. My surprise was not in finding that Colonel Horn was on our side but at finding him at the Club, in sociable surroundings. At the same table was a man I hadn't recognized until he turned his head and spoke to me, when I saw that it was Brian Cooper, Colonel of the 17th Missouri. I had thought of him as one of the Third Division elders, and was glad to see that he was on our side.

The one person conspicuously not in the room was James. I was looking for him, to report, and to tell him what Jack

Turquin had said. I stood at the bar and craned my neck from side to side, thinking he might be in some obscure corner of the room that I had overlooked. I was about to ask Jack Maitland where he was, when Horace Townsend, who had also been impressed by Turquin's opinion, asked the question for me.

"Where's the colonel, Jack?"

Jack looked over at him, then smiled broadly. "Why, there must be a couple of dozen of them here, if you count lieutenant colonels, Horace. Which one of them would you be interested in? Or is it James you're looking for?"

Horace laughed. "Don't be a damned fool, Jack. James, of course."

"He's out showing Marcus Pellam around. We've dug a few rifle pits and one thing or another since the last time he was here, and James thought he ought to know his way around. So did Marcus, for that matter. Very conscientious man. He's responsible for the town, which leaves you people free."

James came in about ten minutes later, and, by coming in with his usual air of easy assurance, as though this were any other Friday night, and all those present were his friends, he made an entrance. He gave the Ross party a wave of the hand and a cheerful, "Good evening, gentlemen," in passing, and went straight to the bar, where the colored boy handed him a glass of champagne punch.

James turned around with the glass in his hand, and—this was one of his talents—caught and held the eye of Tim Wales, raised his glass, and called out in so courteous and amiable a manner that it was impossible not to acknowledge the salutation, "Your good health, Tim. Many happy returns!" drained the glass, and put it down empty.

Tim's response, "Thank you, Colonel," was surprised, and oddly, rather grateful.

Jack Maitland looked at James with respect. James merely smiled at him and held out his hand for another glass of punch. He raised the glass with, "Your good health, Jack!" and drank it off. He put his hand on Jack's shoulder, then carried a third glass over to the table, and sat down between Jonesy and Dr. Ferguson.

This would be about ten-thirty. I had gone over to sit with Jake and Colonel Cooper, and some of Cooper's officers. Our topographical engineer, George Lovell, came over and sat with us for a while; Jack Maitland came unstuck from the bar and joined us for a few minutes; and, as I was about to get up myself, James came over to ask me what had been done down at Roth's division. I gave him my report, and told him what Colonel Turquin had said about the gap between the First and Second Divisions. James said he was going down that way in the morning and would talk to him then.

The aisle across the center of the room was pretty well obliterated during this period. There was usually a small group milling around the space in front of the bar, and a new male quartet, drawn from both sides, had begun again at the piano. In addition, there was a good deal of crossing of the now barely visible barrier by individuals going over to see individual friends on the other side, though the principals and the more prominent members of both factions kept largely to their own sides.

Some time before eleven, Dr. Ferguson got up and went over to talk to Hal Stewart. In view of the fighting that all of us knew was coming up—that had already begun, in fact, with McGraw's counter coup at Jarvie—he was anxious to clear his hospital of all cases that could possibly be moved, and he wanted Hal's opinion on the feasibility of moving them by water. Hal thought it would be possible, and that it would be both economical and humane, but that some agreement would be needed with the rebel command on the west bank; the boats would be undefended, and could easily be sunk by the rebel shore batteries. Hal came back with Dr. Ferguson to talk to James about the possibility of an agreement with McGraw. James didn't think McGraw's command extended that far to the west, but agreed to send out a flag of truce in the morning with a message that McGraw could either accept, or pass on to the proper commander. Dr. Ferguson and Hal Stewart left shortly afterwards, and a few others left with them.

Up to this time the party had been on the whole quite amiable. Unnaturally so, in fact, since by this time on a normal Friday night three or four angry rows would have flared up and died away. About eleven o'clock, though, we had the makings of what could have turned into a first-class brawl all by itself, and an intimation of trouble to come.

This started when a lieutenant came in, not to join the party, but looking for someone. I saw him when he came in, and for a moment couldn't place him, beyond the fact that I had seen him recently, but didn't know him very well. Then, just as I remembered his name and where I had seen him—he was Lieutenant Paul Jenkins, and he was Colonel Croyden's aide—someone answered his question, and pointed James out to him.

Lieutenant Jenkins came over to where James was sitting and saluted stiffly, by far the most military figure in the room. "Have I the honor of addressing Colonel Lake, sir?"

Jack Maitland turned to look at the young man with a mildly sardonic air, while James looked up and said easily, "You have, Lieutenant. Do you have something for me?"

"Yes, sir. A message from Colonel Croyden."

The lieutenant's formal bearing in these very informal surroundings had attracted a certain amount of attention. Jack Maitland, Robert, and Jonesy were listening, and there was a widening circle of silence around him as he delivered his message, which he appeared to have learned by heart.

"Colonel Croyden directs me to inform you, sir, that pursuant to orders received, he moved out with his regiment to take up positions on the Nine Mile and Hillman Roads, in support of the cavalry outposts presumed to be upon those roads. To inform you further, that finding no cavalry outposts on those roads, and no cavalry, he established infantry outposts. He now requests that you send a regiment of cavalry, and direct it to take up positions in support of these infantry outposts."

From the lieutenant's mechanical repetition of the message, it was impossible to say whether the tone was one of good-humored mockery, or of bitter sarcasm, but the facts stated were clear enough. The men at the table with James, who had begun by being amused at Lieutenant Jenkins' earnest formality, ended with grave faces, watching James rather than the lieutenant, waiting to see what he would do.

James heard the message through without interruption. As he listened, his face darkened, then became expressionless and wooden. At the end, he stood up.

"Do you know yourself, Lieutenant, that the facts are as stated? That the cavalry outposts have been withdrawn, and that there is no cavalry on either of those roads?"

Lieutenant Jenkins thought this over, then answered carefully, "Yes, sir. What I saw myself was that the cavalry outposts about half a mile forward from the Nine Mile Road, where they have been all week, were unoccupied. There was no sign of any cavalry forward of those posts. The colonel sent a few of us who were mounted along both roads to make sure. We went all the way to the foot of the passes without seeing anyone. There may have been cavalry behind us. I can't say. But I am certain there was no cavalry at all close to the Nine Mile Road, and I know there was none forward of that line."

The silence, which had begun by spreading out from our table, now engulfed the entire room as James, looking six inches taller than usual, crossed over to the other side and stood looking down at Dick Ross. James addressed him easily, in what appeared to be a normal tone of voice, except for the clear carrying power that anger or battle always gave his voice.

"Dick, I sent out an infantry regiment to support the 4th Michigan awhile ago, because our reports indicated that McGraw might be planning some trouble for us in that direction. He's been getting a lot of new cavalry, as you know, and we thought he might be planning to use it. Now the colonel of the 34th Indiana sends in an aide to tell me there isn't any cavalry to support. He's established infantry outposts, and wants a regiment of cavalry to back him up. Just where the hell is the 4th Michigan?"

Dick was leaning back in his chair with his tunic unbuttoned and a glass in his hand. He looked up at James with a pleased and insolent smile.

"Why, to tell the truth, James, we invited them all in to the birthday party."

James made no comment on this preposterous statement. He stared coldly at Dick, then said in a curt voice, "You can tell them the party is over. Have your men mounted and on their way back within five minutes."

There was a stir at the table as Tim Wales and two of his officers started to get up. Dick, no longer smiling, let his chair come forward and sat up straight.

"Wait a minute," he said belligerently. "I'm not taking any orders from you, Lake. Is that clear?"

James turned back and replied soberly, "I'll invite you to think that statement over before you put it officially on record. I'll remind you that General Order Number Twenty-seven is still in force, as you well know, and that in the absence of the major general, his authority and that of the senior brigadier are delegated to me. I'll point out to you that those are my orders too, whether I like them or not. And while you're thinking that over, I suggest that you go down and ask the orderly holding your horse, or the first drunken private you run into, what he thinks of the idea of leaving the roads unguarded that lead into the heart of our position, when we know the enemy has been reinforced and has turned aggressive. Ask him what he thinks of leaving our main supply depot unguarded, headquarters unguarded, the entire flank of the Second Division uncovered. Ask him what he thinks of the cavalry commander."

Tim Wales and the two captains of the 4th Michigan with him were on their feet by this time, looking greatly abashed.

Tim said to James, "Sorry, Colonel. I guess it was a damned poor idea." And to Dick, "He's right, Dick. We'd better be getting back, and not waste any more time arguing about it."

Dick looked up at him and said irritably, "I know he is, damn it. Orders or no orders. Go ahead."

James said, "Just a minute, Tim. You've got the 34th Indiana in front of you. You had better take the lieutenant along with you—Croyden's aide—and go on ahead with him, once you get the column started. And I think we had all better hope to God that our friend, Barney McGraw, will have the kindness to hold off until morning so we can get this mess straightened out."

The atmosphere had changed considerably by this time. For one thing, a good many bottles had been emptied. The champagne was long since gone, and the punch bowl had been refilled twice with whiskey punch. Hardly a man in the place was entirely sober. The careful and rather wary politeness of the early part of the evening was gone, and with it the feeling of constraint. The dividing line across the center had disappeared entirely, and members of both factions circulated freely about the room.

Not that all differences had been forgotten, nor that we had become a band of brothers again. On the contrary, there was a strong undercurrent of hostility beneath the outward harmony of the gathering, a current of hostility that kept rising to the surface and threatened to become the dominant mood of the party; then, just as it seemed as though a general brawl were on the point of breaking out, with men glaring at each other on all sides, a hearty laugh would come from somewhere, and everyone would relax and begin to smile again. At one moment I saw Dick Ross standing with James and Jack Maitland at the bar, all three of them convulsed with laughter over some remembered absurdity. Ten minutes later Dick was scowling at James, asking who the hell he thought he was, and informing him truculently that his trouble was that he was getting too big for his boots, by God!—and James was staring at him with cold distaste. This fluctuation of mood affected all of us, and I remember the latter part of the evening as a constant and bewildering alternation of the two moods, flickering back and forth from one to the other, comrades and good fellows one moment, enemies and damned scoundrels the next.

Quite late in the evening, after a good many had left, I was sitting with Jake and Cam Heath and Sam Brock and two or three others. Neither Jake nor Cam Heath was very good company at the moment. Cam was still deeply affected by the heavy losses his regiment had taken earlier in the week. He had been drinking steadily all evening, to no purpose—if anything, he was still more depressed—and with no noticeable effect on his speech or manner. Jake, on the contrary, was obviously drunk, disgracefully drunk for a man of his age and dignity, and if Cam was depressed, Jake was carrying enough gloom to fill a churchyard.

About this time Sam Brock nudged me with his elbow and said, *sotto voce,* "Batten down the hatches, Johnny. We're in for a squall."

I looked up and saw Dick Ross bearing down on us, his face set and determined, a drunken fixity of purpose in his eye. He made straight for Cam Heath, and I had time to wonder whether he was going to propose sabers or pistols, or whether he was going to start a fight with whatever happened to be handy, before he stopped in front of Cam and addressed him solemnly.

"Heath, I've been thinking about the other day, and the more I thought about it, the more I saw I was wrong. That's what I came over to tell you. To admit that you were right and I was wrong. In the presence of these gentlemen. They can bear witness. I want to make you the best apology I can, and ask you to shake hands to show there aren't any hard feelings."

Cam had gotten to his feet while Dick was talking. Once on his feet it was evident that the drink had taken effect after all, and that he was at least as drunk as Dick. He listened with frowning concentration while Dick made his apology, considered it earnestly, then made an equally solemn reply.

"Colonel, that speech does you honor. Not many men have the courage to admit it when they're wrong. It was a fine, manly thing to do, and I respect you for it. Only I can't shake hands with you, sir. There are too many friends of mine in fresh graves. There are too many dead men between us. I'm sorry, Colonel. I'm truly sorry, but I can't do it."

This left Dick in a foolish position, with his outstretched hand conspicuously ignored. I expected some sort of violent repercussion, but Dick merely let his hand fall, and said without anger, "Sorry you feel that way, Heath. I don't blame you. I know how it is. But I'm sorry, anyway."

He stood there awkwardly for a moment longer, then burst out with sudden bitterness, "A hell of a lot more of your friends, your friends and mine, too, are going to be in fresh graves if we don't get out of here pretty soon. We aren't doing any good here. Not any more."

As he turned away, Jake raised his head and said to Cam with drunken earnestness, "You shouldn't have said that, Colonel. You were wrong. Ought to have shaken hands with him and forgiven each other. May have been your last chance. No more peace and ease for us. Fighting from now on. God only knows how much time we have left, any of us. Only one thing sure, for some of us it isn't much."

Cam Heath shrugged his shoulders. "A lot of better men than I am are dead already. It's all right with me if there isn't much time left."

The gloom was getting out of hand, and it was contagious. I tried to do something about it. I looked over at Jake and laughed. "My God, you're cheerful this evening, Jake. What's the matter? Is your second sight bothering you again?"

Jake turned his head and stared at me owlishly. "You don't believe a word of it, do you, John? But since you ask, the answer is that it does. It does indeed. It depresses me immeasurably. I feel as though I had ghosts all around me. Some of them I can scarcely bear to look at. Whereas you are good, solid flesh and blood. Only you hurt. You hurt already."

I didn't believe a word of it, but my hair was standing on end. I interrupted him. "I don't believe you, Jake. As you say. But I'd rather not hear any more, even so."

"Sorry, John. I didn't mean to talk about it," Jake said humbly. He shook his head slowly from side to side. "Oh, Christ, I feel old! A drunken old man. A sad old man. Very drunk, very old, very sad. We had our day in the sun. We could have done anything. We sat down to rest in the sun, and when we got up we were no longer what we had been. Now the sun is down and darkness is coming on. All the ways are darkened. Well, well, thus it was willed. *Piu non dimandare.*"

He closed his eyes and let his head fall on his chest.

I was concerned about Jake. I had never seen him quite this drunk before. I leaned over and put my hand on his shoulder, and asked if he wanted to go home.

Jake opened his eyes. He smiled sweetly, a childlike smile astonishingly incongruous on his wrinkled, leathery face. "Thank you, John. I would like to go home, and I'm afraid I need a little help. It's very kind of you to offer."

The party was about over, anyway. We escorted Jake home in the bright moonlight, and got him to bed with his boots off and a blanket over him. It was a little after two in the morning.

Chapter 8

❀ ❀ ❀ ❀ ❀ ❀ ❀ ❀ ❀ ❀ ❀ ❀ ❀ ❀ ❀ ❀ ❀ ❀ ❀ ❀

Barney McGraw was not so kind as to hold off until morning. Shortly before midnight he began passing his cavalry over the two lower passes, and by three in the morning he had a strong cavalry brigade assembled, unmolested, on our side of the mountains. Here young Taylor, who was in command, rested horses and men for two hours while some of his troopers, young men like himself born and brought up in the neighborhood, went forward to look over the disposition of our forces. They found our outposts about where they expected them, though they must have been considerably surprised at finding our infantry out in front, with the cavalry in support. When the scouts were in with their reports, it was close to five o'clock in the morning. The moon was low in the southwest but still gave all the light that was needed as the rebels mounted quietly and began to move forward.

At this point the first of a series of lamentable incidents occurred, all of them characterized by sheer, and brutally bad, luck. Just ten minutes before the rebel attack hit us, Tim Wales, who had been uncomfortable in his rearward position for the past several hours, had sent word to the infantry that he was going to move out in front of them, and had mounted his men. The result of this decision of Tim's was complete chaos.

When the line of mounted rebels appeared in the dim light of the waning moon, the infantry assumed that it was the 4th Michigan and held their fire—an assumption that was all the more natural since the rebels in many places had filed through the gaps in the picket line and approached from the rear. Even after the firing began, they still hesitated and called out to the rebels to stop, they were firing on their own men. When this was met with a hoot of derision in rich Southern accents, they finally corrected their mistake, only to pile another on top of it. All cavalry was now enemy, and when Tim Wales appeared with the 4th Michigan and entered into the fight he was fired on by the men of the 34th Indiana, and a short battle followed between the two regiments. To add to the confusion, Colonel Croyden was killed in the opening minutes of the fight, and his second-in-command a few minutes later. At about the same time, Tim Wales was wounded and taken prisoner. Within twenty minutes, though their casualties were not remarkably heavy, both regiments were broken up and dispersed, and the way was open for the rebel column.

Not a sound of this reached us at headquarters. The principal focus of the fight was at the junction of the Granger and Nine Mile Roads, seven or eight miles away to the southeast. It was fought entirely with small arms, and a light southwest wind carried the sound away from us. The first sound I heard —the first any of us heard—was that of galloping horsemen coming in from Turquin and Billy Roth, and from Colonel Miller at the supply depot. Almost at the same time, from my eastward-facing window, I could hear the sound of distant firing from the direction of our big supply depot, three miles to the east. I pulled on my clothes in haste and started down the stairs, buttoning my blouse on the way.

I was somewhat shaken when I joined the rest of the staff. On the way down I had been delayed. As I made the turn on the second floor to go down to the first, I felt a hand on my arm, and saw with surprise the wrinkled-apple cheeks and black eyes of the Countess's maid, Gerda. I could make nothing of her German, but her grip on my arm was surprisingly firm and authoritative, and her meaning was clear: Madame Alexandra—I had forgotten that this was Madame Lucy's official name—wanted to see me.

Her door was open. For a moment I could see nothing, and the big room appeared to be filled with impenetrable darkness. As my eyes became accustomed to the darkness, I could see a dim, early dawn grayness through the big south window, and a faint rosy glow in the southeast bay.

The Countess was sitting in the window, with her hair in braids. She was more nearly distraught than I would have imagined possible. She wanted to know what was happening, how they had been able to penetrate our lines so deeply, why the cavalry hadn't stopped them.

I answered her questions as well as I could. When I told her about the cavalry, she insisted that it was no blunder, but a betrayal. Dick Ross had betrayed James. His brother would betray him later. They would betray us all. They would pull down the walls upon us if only they could bury James in the ruins.

I tried to reassure her, but without much success. The fact is, I needed reassurance myself. Now that the idea of a deliberate betrayal had been brought up, I found that I couldn't get it out of my head.

It was still with me when I reached the foot of the stairs and found the house brightly lighted and full of movement. Two reports had just come in. Bob Kelso, who had been out at the camp of the 25th Michigan in the fields north of town, had come in with one of them, a report from Colonel Fletcher.

Dan Fletcher was outraged. Why hadn't there been any warning? Where the hell was the cavalry? With ten minutes' warning he could have been at the bridge with his regiment and Lovell's battery, and with another five minutes he could have thrown his command into the depot. Now the rebels had a solid roadblock across the road five hundred yards this side of the depot, and they were felling trees and strengthening the barrier as fast as they could.

The other report was from Turquin, on the south side. He had run into a similar, though less formidable roadblock on the South River Road. He reported that the rebels were crossing everything over to the north side—prisoners, horses, mules, cattle, and wagons—and were preparing to burn the bridge. A long column of prisoners and booty was already streaming down the North River Road under escort, probably making for the Jenkins' Ferry Road and one of the northeast passes. Turquin wanted another regiment, guns to shell the rebel column from the south bank, and orders.

Tony Bassett was instructed to break off whatever fight he was engaged in, and join Cam Heath at the junction of the Jenkins' Ferry Road and the cutoff: both roads were to be blocked at that point. Colin was sent over to Gavin with a specific order—written, and in duplicate—to block the continuation of the River Road at Taylor's Run, and a general order to take appropriate action according to developments; he was warned that a demonstration could be expected out of Jarvie to cover the return of the raiders. I was sent down to Roth with orders for him to send Crego's brigade after Turquin's, and to watch the lower passes with his remaining regiments.

It was twenty minutes after six when I left the house. The moon was low in the southwest and the sun was still below the horizon. Mist was rising from the river and the low places, and the predawn grayness and the fading moonlight were diffused through the mist. The light grew stronger and the mist paler as I rode south, and the morning air was cool and damp on my face.

About half a mile past the hospital, where I had a clear view to the east for the first time, I could see that the fire had grown. Twenty minutes earlier I had seen it as a rosy glow, low in the eastern sky. The Countess, dimly seen, in a pale dressing gown, had been silhouetted against this glow as she sat in the southeast bay of the window. There had been a shocking moment when her self-control wavered and her voice became a lament.

"Oh, why did I ever come here? I brought you nothing but misfortune. That was my gift to James. To all of you. To all the fine young men you were so proud of. I have destroyed you. I have destroyed what I love most." Then, in an altered voice, a reasonable voice, with only an edge of distraction showing, as though she were asking a question she expected me to answer, "But how could I wish that I had never come here? That I had never seen James? That I had never known what it was to love and to be alive? How could I ever wish that?"

I closed my eyes tightly and shook my head at the recollection.

The fire was still growing. The rosy glow had brightened to an orange-red and now rose halfway to the zenith, as our accumulated supplies went up in smoke and flame. The sound of distant gunfire reached me from the north, where the rebels had crossed over and burned the bridge, and were retiring along the north bank. The sound of the firing increased in volume, with a heavy pounding undertone of artillery fire beneath, and the sound was in my ears all the rest of the way.

At division headquarters I learned that the losses of the 34th Indiana were not as heavy as had been feared: the men were coming in fast, and seemed to have recovered their spirits, now that they could see. The death of Colonel Croyden and his lieutenant colonel, and the wounding and capture of Tim Wales were confirmed. The 4th Michigan, like the 34th Indiana, had been dispersed rather than destroyed. I was less pleased to learn that it was Dick Ross who had collected and re-formed the regiment, and was frankly dismayed to learn that he had put it at the head of the column making for the Nine Mile bridge, and had assumed command of the entire column.

Billy Roth shrugged his shoulders. "Nothing much I could do about it, John," he said. "He ranked all three of my colonels. He ranked everybody on the field except me. The only way to stop him was to take over the command myself, and that was obviously out of the question. I'm needed here."

Horace Townsend went on from there. "We were talking about Dick a few minutes ago, Johnny. We decided that he's probably the right man, after all. Dick feels that this is all his fault, as it is. He's full of chagrin, and wants to redeem himself. He's furious about losing Tim Wales. And probably the most important thing, this is a job for cavalry, and Dick, when he wants to be, is a damned fine cavalry leader."

All I could say, a little sourly, was that I hoped to God he was right. I let it go at that.

It was full daylight when I left, though the sun was still below the rim of the mountains. The sound of the fighting, small arms and artillery, still reached me from the north and presently grew louder, until it filled the entire northeastern quarter. At first I thought this was an illusion, due to the wind and the terrain, but after stopping to listen I found that I could still hear the fighting along the River Road, and in addition the sound of a new battle farther to the east. This was pretty surely the attack out of Jarvie, to pin Gavin down, that we had expected.

I was on the Granger Road, five miles below and parallel to the river. Even this late in the year the country was green and fertile, woodland alternating with field and meadow. The land all the way up to the Severn belonged to the Robertsons. On thinking about it, I was impressed: it was—or had been—a magnificent barony. No troops had been quartered here, and the district was quite untouched by the war.

The war made itself visible beyond the first crossroads, six miles over. It was still Robertson land, but two of our Second Division regiments—well-behaved, orderly regiments—had been camped here for some time, and had left the usual area of bare, rutted earth behind them, littered with rusting metal and broken wood, torn cloth and loose paper. Here, in addition, I had a clear view to the north for the first time, and over the top of a distant fringe of woods I saw an immense pillar of smoke rising almost straight into the air from our burning supply depot. From here on, too, I began to run into an astonishing number of loose horses, mules, and horned cattle, wandering aimlessly or browsing by the side of the road.

The firing along the River Road dropped off about this time; the artillery fire, in particular, fell off rapidly, then stopped altogether. I assumed what was obvious enough, that the raiding column had turned up the cutoff to the Jenkins'

Ferry Road, and was no longer in range from the south bank. This was the road we expected them to take, and this was where we wanted to stop them: if they succeeded in reaching the main road first, there was nothing we could put ahead of them. They could turn off to the right, towards the northeast passes, on any one of half a dozen roads, and all that would be left for us would be a long and unprofitable stern chase.

About nine o'clock I reached the Nine Mile Road and turned north. The mist was still clinging to the ground and a lazy drift of air from the southwest, not strong enough even to be called a breeze, had carried over the smoke from the burning supply depot, together with the gunsmoke from the fighting, obscuring the view to the north. A few minutes later I came up with the end of the column, the last company of the 24th Ohio, swinging along at a fine pace, with the river and the bridge only a couple of hundred yards ahead. Dick Ross and Sam Crego, with a small group of aides, were at the side of the road, watching them pass.

As I came up, Crego was saying to Dick, "They march well. By God, they march well, Colonel. A damned fine regiment, though I do say it myself."

Dick acknowledged this with a nod, then turned his head and caught sight of me.

"Hello, Johnny. Where the hell did you come from?" he demanded. His face was flushed with excitement, and all his movements were full of restless energy. Without bothering to wait for an answer, he went on exuberantly, "You're just in time, Johnny. We've got them in a box. Oh, by God, we've got them in a box! And right now we're nailing the lid on. That lid is going to be nailed on so tight that not even a mule is going to get out. You tell James that when you see him."

The end of the column had passed us and was almost at the bridge. We followed at a walk. The fighting was ahead of us and to the left, heavier than before, and entirely small-arms fire. The cannonade in front of Jarvie, which was now on our right and behind us, had increased in volume.

"Sounds as though your brother might be having his hands full," Colonel Crego remarked to Dick.

Dick shook his head. "Nothing to it. Just a lot of noise," he replied contemptuously. "Gavin's too old a bird to be taken in that way. If McGraw meant business, we'd be hearing infantry fire."

We crossed the bridge at a walk and mounted the rise beyond in the wake of the marching infantry. Once on the level and with room at the side, Dick impatiently pulled his horse off the road and announced that he was going on ahead. After he had gone about fifty feet, he turned in his saddle and called back, "Push them along, Colonel. Push them along!"

The River Road was some distance back from the river at this point. Here I turned off to the left, while the column continued straight ahead. The River Road was lined with trees, like an avenue; on my right, on the other side of a stone fence, was the three-mile pasture where Cam Heath's cavalry fight had taken place earlier in the week. The haze of mingled smoke and mist was thick but patchy, so dense in places that it was barely possible to see ten feet ahead, thinning out in others to a mere smoky haze that only closed down after a quarter of a mile.

I was looking for an opening in the stone fence, in order to cut across the field and avoid the long acute angle I would have to make if I followed the road. While I was staring off to the right, I saw a horse that looked familiar, out near a clump of trees, a black horse with a white blaze on his forehead, still saddled, with a broken and dangling foreleg. It looked like Bob Kelso's horse, a vicious brute that had tried to bite me on more than one occasion. While I was trying to get a better look at the horse, the smoke thickened, and I went on.

Halfway down the length of the field, about level with the ditch and the double row of trees where Heath had dismounted his men, I finally found a break in the fence. I headed across the field at an open angle towards the cutoff, aiming at the point where it met the dense woods which formed the northern boundary of the long field and filled the upper half of the triangle formed by the three roads.

I found James sitting his horse in a little amphitheater

half a mile from the point where I struck the road, in the midst of a group of mounted officers from the two regiments detached to the north bank. All of them appeared to be cheerful and well pleased with the way things were going. As I came up, a captain from the Kentucky regiment, with a torn sleeve and a smoke-blackened face, was reporting to Colonel Powell.

"We're driving them nicely, sir," he said. "I think we've finally got them pried loose. We're all around them to the north, and they seem to be pulling out to the southeast." He laughed. "Much good may it do them!"

I found this incomprehensible, but just then James caught sight of me and called out, "Morning, Johnny. I was hoping you would show up. Which way did you come?"

"Nine Mile Road, James," I replied.

"Good!" James looked pleased. "I think we're about ready to close this thing out. We've got them pretty well flushed out of the woods—wait a minute. What are you shaking your head for? Who's at the crossroads? Nine Mile and River Roads?"

"Nobody," I said, "Nobody at all."

James turned his head and looked at something over the treetops, an immense distance away. When he turned back he was no longer smiling, and neither was anyone else.

"Listen, Johnny," he said carefully, "an hour and a quarter ago, as soon as we discovered their change of direction, I sent down clear and definite orders that the crossroads was to be blocked and strongly held. What happened?"

"Nobody got the order, James. Nobody had heard of it half an hour ago, when I caught up with the column just the other side of the bridge. They were pushing up the road as fast as they could to cut the rebels off from the Taylor Road. They were all feeling good because they were going to get there in time. They had the rebels in a box. That was the message Dick wanted me to give you. That they were nailing the lid down tight."

"I've no doubt," James said dryly. "Meanwhile leaving off the sides. You mean Dick Ross, I suppose. What was he doing there?"

"Pushing the column along. He'd got the 4th Michigan together and put it in the lead. Tim was captured—I suppose you heard."

James turned away with a scowl. A moment later he said to the men around him, "Why didn't they get my order? It was sent in plenty of time, by a responsible officer, and there wasn't a rebel within a mile of the route he was taking. Why didn't it get there?"

At this point I remembered something, and, before anyone could answer James' largely rhetorical question, I interrupted with an urgent question of my own.

"Listen, James. Was it Bob you sent down? Bob Kelso? Because if it was, I saw his horse about twenty minutes ago—if he was riding the Brute—with a broken leg. Out in the field, past the ditch and the trees. I didn't see Bob anywhere, but I didn't stop to look, and the smoke was pretty thick. I think that's what happened to your dispatch."

James was shocked. "You think his horse threw him? Oh, good God! Bob Kelso? The farm boy who was practically raised on a horse?"

"I don't know, James. All I know is that the horse had a broken leg. A foreleg."

James shook his head, the look of shocked disbelief still on his face.

We all sat and listened to the sporadic firing in front of us, and to the roar of artillery coming from the direction of Jarvie Pass, where it sounded as though a major battle were under way. This was an effect that was familiar to all of us: from certain directions any sound coming from Jarvie was greatly magnified, so that a single cannon shot sounded like an uneven salvo from a dozen guns. At this time there were probably thirty guns firing at most, but as the sound reverberated off the mountains walls it was multiplied by ten, and sounded like the opening of Wagram or Waterloo. While we were listening, more artillery joined in closer at hand, our own guns, on the other side of the wood.

At this James roused himself and said to Colonel Powell, "Well, Colonel, we still have a chance to round them up. If the bridge over Taylor's Run is blocked, we've got them. The ground is swampy on both sides of the road, and a regiment with a couple of guns could hold up an army corps. I sent young Colin over with the order to hold the bridge at six o'clock this morning. The order was positive, and the troops should be there. But I regret to say, Colonel, I'm not sanguine about it. Not the way things have been going. McGraw has provided Gavin with a pretext—a feeble one, but no doubt he'll find it good enough—for disobeying the order."

Colonel Powell was indignant. "By God, that's shaving it pretty close, James. Men have been cashiered for less. Hell, they've been shot!"

James had pulled himself together by this time, and had recovered his equanimity. "Maybe he'll think of that, Colonel. Let's hope he does. In the meantime we'll push them along as hard and as fast as we can. If Gavin is there, so much the better. But we won't count on it. I think we had better brace ourselves for a long, hard day."

That was exactly what it turned into. We found Bob Kelso's body half an hour later. We saw the horse first, the vicious black that Bob called Satin and the rest of us called the Brute, hobbling on three legs, the right foreleg dangling. The body was a few yards farther on, lying on its side: it looked at first as though Bob had simply curled up for a short nap. As we came closer we could see that the head was bent at an unnatural angle, and the face, though neither marred nor distorted, was the blank, empty face of a dead man.

This was fairly close to home, but I had no time just then to feel very strongly about it. I had a couple of soldiers help me go through his pockets, and had them carry the body over by the stone fence, with the vague idea of doing something about it on the way back. Afterwards I sent one of them back to shoot the poor Brute, and that seemed to be all I could do for my friend.

When I caught up with James, I handed him the dispatch Bob had failed to deliver. James looked at it, then put it in his pocket.

"What happened to him, Johnny?" he asked

"He broke his neck. His horse stepped into a rabbit hole—a hole of some kind—and threw him. Bob fell and broke his neck. He could have done that on his father's farm. He didn't have to go to war to do that."

James was still marveling at the event. "I was hoping you would tell me he'd been shot. Then it would have been an act of war. Now it's an accident. An act of God." He shook his head. "What are you to do about those?"

About this time the firing in front of us, which had died away for a time, began to pick up again, first on the right, then in front, then all along the line. It was picked up farther to the left, beyond our line, and presently our artillery joined in from the Jenkins' Ferry Road and from both sides we were up to the line the rebels had taken up, covering the crossroads. It was a strong line, with the old stone farmhouse in the angle of the road as its center, and low swampy ground on both flanks, and we were held up here for three-quarters of an hour. All this time we could see wagons, horses, and men streaming down the River Road without a check, and without any sound reaching us from ahead that would indicate any kind of attempt to stop them. The cannonade off to the right continued, but we were no longer in the path of the echo, and, reduced to its natural proportions, it was no longer very impressive.

Once we were past the crossroads, Dick Ross took the cavalry and some guns and went back up to the Taylor Road and crossed the valley there in the hope—the not very strong hope —of cutting the rebels off from the northeast passes. We sent back a couple of regiments and most of the guns, and the rest of us, the main column, pushed on after the rebels. The long, hard day James had told us to expect was under way.

It was long and hard, and full of frustration as well: a long, fatiguing, unprofitable stern chase that lasted until after dark. The rebels still clung to their booty, which slowed them down, and we were continually on the point of catching up with them. But long before that we would have heard the ringing of axes and the crash of falling trees, and just as we were about to overtake them, we would come to a turn in the road, or a defile, or a narrowing of the road, and find a breastwork of felled trees across the road with a line of sharpshooters behind it, supported by a pair, or an entire battery, of twelve-pounders—our own guns, a part of the booty from the depot.

There was nothing for it but to stop and deploy, and work a company or two around one flank or the other, and force them to pull out. This was not difficult, but it took time, and while we were prying out the rear guard, the main body would have gained another mile and a half. We did them some damage, picked up a few prisoners and forced them to disgorge a part of their booty, including about a third of the prisoners they had taken from the 63rd Ohio, but these were meager results, disappointing, poor compensation for the amount of effort put forth.

Full darkness had set in when we finally broke off the pursuit and encamped for the night. Early in the evening a nervous patrol from the 12th Michigan blundered into one of our outposts and started firing, without bothering to find out who they were firing at. It was a brief flurry, but one of our sentries and the lieutenant in command of the patrol were killed, and three or four men were wounded before it was over. Shortly afterwards it began to rain, a gentle shower at first, then a steady, drenching, cold rain that lasted all night.

We spent a wet and miserable night, huddled under whatever shelter we could find, and started back at six in the morning. We stumbled forward—we hoped it was forward—in pitch-darkness for nearly an hour before a dim, watery daylight began to appear. We slogged along through deep mud all morning, with frequent halts to pull guns and wagons out of nearly bottomless mudholes.

The rain stopped towards noon and the sun came out, and, as we moved out of the shadow of the mountains, the surface of the road improved, and we were able to move along steadily. By this time we were too tired to care, and there was no sense of accomplishment to lighten our fatigue. We had been outmaneuvered by the enemy, and let down by our friends.

We were defeated, and tired, and surly, and we had no use at all for the First Division.

This last was a feeling that was intensified when we came to the bridge over Taylor's Run, about three in the afternoon. This was the bridge, a mile and a half east of the crossroads, that Gavin had been ordered to block. I am certain that every individual soldier, from colonel to private, in our three-quarter-mile-long column saw two things as he approached the bridge. First, that the swampy little stream was impassable except by the bridge and the fifty-yard causeway leading up to it—a company of sharpshooters in the woods on the far side could have held the position for hours, and a regiment with a couple of guns could have held it forever. Second, that the tents of Gavin's nearest First Division regiment were visible from the bridge, and less than a mile away.

Under the circumstances it was unfortunate that one of Gavin's new Regular Army officers, a Colonel Strawn, tried to push his way with a mounted retinue into Turquin's column, into the short interval between companies.

Colonel Strawn was wearing polished boots and yellow gauntlets and a new campaign hat, and the aides, friends, and brother officers riding with him were all freshly turned out and presentable, in marked contrast to the muddy, dirty-faced, weary column of infantry that was coming up to the bridge at the same time.

"Stand back and let us pass," the colonel called out in a pleasant enough voice, but with authority.

The answer he got must have surprised him. "Like hell we will! Nobody passes ahead of us." This was from Captain Horatio Latimer, at the head of the column, one of the line captains I happened to know.

"You're addressing a superior officer, sir." The Regular Army was outraged. "Stand back, damn you!"

Latimer didn't even bother to answer this, but turned his back on the colonel and beckoned his men forward.

This was too much for Colonel Strawn, and he called out angrily, "Damn it, Captain, for the last time I'm ordering you to stand back and get your men out of the way, unless you want them to get trampled on." He turned his head. "Come along, gentlemen. We'll push on ahead. We can't allow these scarecrows to hold us up."

Latimer looked around as the troop of horsemen began to move forward, and, absolutely beside himself with weariness and rage, called out in a loud voice, "Company! Fix bayonets!"

The company, which had been slogging along half-dead, and stupid with fatigue, and had scarcely bothered to listen to the argument the captain was putting up because they knew they were going to lose this one too, suddenly came to life, and the bayonets clicked briskly onto the musket barrels.

The horsemen stopped short. Colonel Strawn, apoplectic with fury, sputtered, "God damn you, sir, this is mutiny! Do you know what the penalty for mutiny is? Do you know what happens to mutinous officers? They get shot. By God, sir, they get shot."

Latimer, now feeling much better, looked up at him and said, "No, sir. Not mutiny. You can pass as soon as we get by. This regiment, and the regiment behind us, and the guns, and the caissons and the wagons, and the last mule in the column, and the yellow dog following the last mule. After that you'll be perfectly free to cross, sir. That is, if Colonel Lake doesn't decide to burn the bridge."

While this was going on, everyone was converging on the place. Jack Turquin was making his way back across the bridge, his big mustache bristling, his face red and belligerent, the men gladly making way for his big chestnut.

As he came up, he called out, "What's going on here, Latimer? What's holding up the column?"

Latimer, positively cheerful by this time, replied, "The First Division, here, was in a hurry, Colonel. They wanted to cross ahead of us. When I declined to let them break into the column, they tried to ride us down."

Colonel Strawn was making indignant demands. "By God, Turquin, I want this man put under arrest. He's mutinous, and he's insolent. What kind of discipline do you have in your regiment, anyway?"

Jack Turquin stared at him. "Where were you yesterday, when we needed you, Colonel? You're a day late, sir. You're about thirty hours late. If you can afford to wait that long, it won't do you any harm to wait for another couple of hours. I certainly won't allow you to break into my column."

By this time, Gavin had pushed his way to the front, bristling with anger. "All right, Turquin. I've had about enough of this nonsense. Tell your men to put their bayonets away and let us through."

"I'll be God damned if I will. My men are tired, and they know who they have to thank for it. And if you're giving me an order, by God, I can disobey orders, too."

James came up while Gavin was still glaring at Jack Turquin. James seemed to get some entertainment out of the situation. He said,

"You'll probably save time, Gavin, if you go back and take the other road. This bridge can be held, as you see. It looks to me as though it were going to be held for quite a long time. Did you enjoy your waltz with Barney McGraw yesterday?"

Gavin jerked his head around as though he had been stung. "Waltz, hell!" he said fiercely. "We fought a serious engagment yesterday."

James' voice was brisk and hard. "What were your casualties?"

"None of your damned business."

"You can add a hundred and twenty to your half-dozen or so. The rebels got away with a hundred and twenty men from the 63rd Ohio. They marched them across this bridge under guard, in plain view of your camp. Your Ohio regiments must have found it quite a sight."

Gavin scowled. "My men were fully occupied yesterday. And in case you don't know it, Lake, you're no longer in command of anything. The general got back this morning. You're relieved."

"I'll let the general tell me what my duties are when I see

him," James said evenly. "This morning was when we expected him."

There was an uneasy silence. Finally Gavin said impatiently, "Well, damn it, are you going to get your men out of the way and let us go through?"

James' reply was short and clear. "No," he said.

Gavin swung his horse around, muttering under his breath. He raised his voice, "Come on, gentlemen. Since they lack the courtesy to let us through, we'll take the other road."

Turquin waited until Gavin and his entourage were under way, then looked down at Latimer with a broad smile. "You saved the day for us, Captain. I think your men can put away their toad stabbers now."

As Latimer turned and gave the order, the men protested. This little incident had been as good as a night's sleep to them, and they didn't want to spoil it. "Sure they've gone far enough, Captain? Sure they won't be back?"

Latimer grinned at them. "Put them away, boys. If they come back, we'll put them on again in a hurry."

Colonel Turquin turned to James. "By God, that did my heart good."

James laughed. "Mine, too. We ought to pin a medal on Latimer and promote him on the spot. The citation might be a little hard to explain, though. If Ross tries to give you any trouble, let us know, and we'll take care of it."

The column got under way again, with Colonel Turquin pushing on ahead to catch up with his leading company. James and I, with a couple of couriers behind us, turned off on a lane that ran north, with the marshy little run on our left. The lane led up to a diagonal cross-road which ran up to meet the Taylor Road, coming straight across from the east.

Captain Latimer's defiance of the First Division had provided us with a short interlude of good humor, but it faded out, and presently we were again plodding along on spent horses, bent over in the saddle, and stupid with fatigue and loss of sleep.

The floor of the valley between the Jenkins' Ferry Road and

the mountains is uneven. In addition to its general downward inclination from north to south, it is divided by a low, irregular ridge down its center. The road we were on crosses this ridge at a point about a quarter of a mile from the Jenkins' Ferry Road, which first becomes visible here. The hillside beyond the road is covered by a dense plantation of firs, a shadowy dark-green background that runs on in unbroken gloom for more than a mile.

At the time we reached the top of the rise, the wood was in the shadow of the hill; the sun was low and red in the southwest, on our left front. As we halted here for a moment, a carriage came into view from the left, a black and silver traveling carriage drawn by two matched bays, going north at a brisk trot, with outriders in front and behind. There were two women in the carriage, one of them small and muffled in black, the other a beautiful woman even at this distance, with bronze hair and a long white scarf wound around her neck. She turned her head and looked in our direction, then leaned forward and spoke to the soldier on the coachman's box. The officer riding in front glanced back, then looked over at us and said something to the coachman. The coachman brandished his whip, and the horses increased their pace.

James caught sight of the carriage at the same time. He gave a sudden shocked cry of grief and anger, and dug his spurs into his horse. The weary animal bounded forward for a few paces, then fell back into its former plodding gait. James dug his spurs in again savagely. The horse gave another bound, but was obviously near the end of its strength, and fell back immediately into a walk.

"Don't, James!" I called out in distress. "You'll kill the poor beast."

James kept his eyes on the carriage, and gave no sign that he had heard me, but he stopped spurring the exhausted animal, and pulled up a moment later.

There was a signal from the carriage now, as the Countess unwound the long white scarf from around her neck and waved it in farewell. James swept off his hat, holding it up and out, at arm's length, in reply, and sat frozen in that position, bareheaded, with arm outstretched, like an equestrian statue, while the carriage with its hurrying outriders moved rapidly along the road, the white scarf fluttering against the dark and melancholy background of the evergreens, until a wood intervened and they passed out of sight.

III

Chapter 1

The final week in November—our last week in Tarsus—
was interminable, an entire leaden winter in itself, each day
hundreds of hours long, the morning distant and half-
forgotten by the time we went to bed. We were idle and bored
and short-tempered during the early part of the week, with
both sides inactive. When military operations were resumed in
the latter part of the week—by McGraw, at any rate; we sat
still and did nothing—the days were even longer, and we were
still bored and sullen, but in addition we felt an anxiety, a
mounting tension that grew stronger day by day, and expressed itself a hundred times a day in such questions as,
What is the old man keeping us here for? Why don't we get
out while we still can? For God's sake, why don't we do something? Towards the end we sometimes had the dreamlike
sensation of being in the path of something falling, an avalanche, a tree, a tower, the wall of a burning building, and
running for our lives with agonizing, leaden-footed slowness,
and no certainty that we were not too late.

The weather was sullen, like ourselves. The sky was dark
and overcast throughout the week, except for a few hours of
watery sunlight on Sunday afternoon, and it rained every day.
The early part of the week was stormy, with high winds and
heavy rain, and the temperature hovered around forty degrees.
On Thursday the weather began to moderate, and the wind
shifted from west to southwest, then to south, the temperature
rising with each shift of wind. By Saturday afternoon it was

unseasonably warm, a false and precarious return of summer, with showers dropping apparently of their own weight from an atmosphere surcharged with moisture. The south wind fell away to a light breeze, then died entirely, and for the last two days the air was heavy and oppressive and perfectly still.

The atmosphere at headquarters, even the Robertson house itself, changed out of all recognition. It was no longer a small enclave of civilization, a citadel we could return to at night. The light and warmth went out of it with the departure of the Countess, and all cleanliness and order with the departure of the servants. Now the house was merged into the barren landscape of the war.

The rain was beating against the windows when I woke up on Monday morning, and when I went downstairs I found the house nearly deserted. The new dispensation was already beginning to show, and breakfast was served on the soiled tablecloth left over from Saturday night. There were three of us at the table, the others, like myself, left without orders. None of us had anything to say. We ate in a morose silence, and avoided each other after we left the table.

James came in about eleven, wet and splattered with mud. He had a folder under his arm, and as soon as he had thrown off his waterproofs he asked me to come back to the office with him. The folder contained Roth's, or rather, Horace Townsend's report on the five days of the general's absence. It was scribbled over with corrections and interleaved with sheets containing notes in James' handwriting. James wanted me to make a fair copy of the report.

I sat down at Jake's desk and began copying, while James went up to put on some dry clothes. When he came back he looked over my shoulder to see how I was coming, then went over and stood by the window, staring out at the courthouse, the bare trees, and the rain. We were alone in the room, and he had put off the mask he wore in public: I could see the lines of grief, anger, and fatigue in his face. This loosening of control which he briefly permitted himself carried over into his manner as well: he was irritable, and when I looked up from time to time to ask about an undecipherable word or phrase, his answers were impatient, occasionally sarcastic, then as he caught himself, excessively apologetic.

General Pack came in while I was copying the report, and the room was suddenly filled with tension, crackling in the air like electricity yet wholly invisible, felt rather than seen: I could feel the current running through me, but I could see nothing at all. The general looked entirely as usual, big and calm, and full of accustomed and easily borne authority. His manner too, though cool and distant, was courteous, and he returned James' civil, "Good morning, General," with an equally civil, "Good morning, James." His voice was that of a major general addressing his chief of staff.

He sat down in his usual place behind the Judge's desk, unbuckled his sword, and put his buckskin gloves on the desk.

"Is that your report the captain is copying, James? I will be interested in seeing it," he said.

James had his mask on by this time, as perfectly opaque and impenetrable as the general's.

"Not exactly, sir," he replied easily. "We went by the book, and officially this is Major Townsend's report for General Roth. Actually I spent most of the morning down there, looking over Horace's report and adding things here and there—seen and approved by Billy, of course—and what Johnny is copying is the result. Officially it's still General Roth's report, but it's one that I concur in fully and can sign. If you like, we can have Johnny add a note to that effect at the bottom, and Horace and I can both sign the report."

"That might be a good idea," the general said. "I think we will do it that way."

One of the general's long impassive silences followed. These silences could be disconcerting, could grow heavier and more oppressive with each tick of the clock, but James was accustomed to them, and merely waited without impatience for the general to speak.

The silence was finally broken. In a deceptively mild voice the general said, "The condition of the command isn't quite what it was when I left, James."

This quiet and apparently innocuous remark implied much more than it said. It was an accusation and a rebuke: the command had been mismanaged, and had suffered as a result. An accounting was demanded.

"No, sir, it isn't," James replied evenly. "The affair on Saturday hurt us in more ways than one. I will have to accept the entire responsibility. I knew what to do and didn't do it. I hoped it wouldn't be necessary, and I was wrong."

The general gave no sign that he was even listening. James supplied his own question, and answered it.

"The day you left, sir, I debated seriously whether or not to advise General Roth to relieve the two Rosses for the entire duration of your absence. It would have been a drastic step and would have stretched our authority considerably, but we could have done it. With Keith in command of the First Division, and the cavalry under either Wales or Bassett—men amenable to military common sense, however they felt about the temporary authority of General Roth and myself—McGraw couldn't have done us much harm Saturday. Our measures would have been perfectly adequate if our orders had been carried out."

General Pack wasn't giving James anything. "It is your contention, then, that those two officers should bear the entire blame for your defeat on Saturday?"

James answered this one carefully. "The ultimate responsibility is mine, sir, as I said before. It was my business to see that my orders were obeyed. Otherwise your statement is correct. Our losses on Saturday were due solely to the insubordination and the totally irresponsible conduct of the officers in question."

The general thought this over. Finally he said, "Well, James, what do you propose to do about it?"

"The matter is out of my hands, sir. General Roth will be forced to bring charges whether he wants to or not, and of course I will associate myself with him. The feeling in the

Second Division is very strong. The troops—officers and men —are bitter. They feel that Colonel Ross ought to be cashiered and that General Ross ought to be shot."

The general opened his eyes a little wider. "As bad as all that?" He looked around for confirmation, and addressed me, as the nearest available source. "John, have you heard anything of the sort?"

I looked up from my desk. "Yes, sir, I have. Shot, or strung up. And a lot of the men are saying they would rather fight the First Division than the rebels, any day."

James said, "General Roth and I will file our charges this afternoon, or tomorrow. Both of us realize, of course, that an immediate court-martial is out of the question. General Roth will suggest, and I will concur in the suggestion, that both officers be removed from command pending the court-martial."

The general acknowledged this—that he had heard what James was saying—with a barely perceptible nod. A long and oppressive silence filled the room. Finally the general buckled on his sword and stood up.

"I think we had better go down and talk to General Roth and some of his officers, James," he said. "To some of the officers of both divisions. I will ask you to come with me."

I went back to my copying, and finished the report about an hour later. Nothing came of it. The Rosses were not relieved of command, and the date of the court-martial was set for some time after the New Year, a vague date in a future that none of us really believed in.

A message from General Crawford had been waiting for us Sunday night, on our return: the two divisions assigned to us had now gone to the Army of the Potomac, in direct contravention of assurances repeatedly given him by the War Department. No other reinforcements were in sight until spring, at the earliest. He deeply regretted this interruption of an operation which he regarded as most promising. Under the circumstances he could only suggest that we fall back to our former position on the Blackwater and wait for better news, or more sense in Washington.

This suggestion, which could be considered an order, was strongly supported by James and Jack Maitland, and by Jonesy, who came in on Monday to see what was holding us up. The general returned the same answer to all three of them. He listened gravely, then politely closed the door in their faces.

"Thank you, Colonel. Thank you, General. I am always glad to have the opinion of my officers. Good day, sir."

We did not get under way on Monday, nor on Tuesday, and no orders preparing for a withdrawal were issued. In fact, during this early part of the week, very few orders of any kind were issued, and all of them were concerned with ordinary, routine matters. Taken as a whole, they indicated that the general expected nothing out of the ordinary in the foreseeable future. Here we were, and here we stayed.

I found this inexplicable, and contrary to all reason. It bothered me, so I went in to see Jake one afternoon. I wanted to see if he had any kind of answer to the question all of us were asking: What are we doing here?

Jake was sitting at his desk in the office with his spectacles on, reading Thucydides. A bottle of Judge Robertson's twenty-year-old cognac was at his elbow, with another bottle on the floor in reserve. Jake was already a little drunk. By dinnertime he would be disgracefully drunk, sunk in gloom, and muttering in the tongues. After dinner he would make a miraculous recovery, and stay up long enough to read another three or four chapters and finish the second bottle of brandy.

I mentioned one of the theories circulating around the camps: The old man can't make up his mind, and here we sit. By God, he better hurry up, or pretty soon old Barney Mc-Graw's going to make up his mind for him.

Jake was contemptuous. "You ought to know better than that, Johnny. When did Arthur ever have any trouble making up his mind? If he had meant to withdraw at all, we would have started on Sunday afternoon, while you and James were still out chasing young Taylor." He took off his spectacles and put them on the desk. "How is James these days, anyway?"

The change of subject surprised me. "All right, I guess. So

far as I know, anyway. I've hardly seen him all week. Why?"

"I haven't seen him either. I wondered how he was getting along." Jake paused, then added thoughtfully, "It must be a considerable strain, to go on day after day, expecting an order at any time that you can't in honor refuse to obey, and can't expect to survive."

This was a new and shocking idea. "Oh, good God, Jake, no! He couldn't do that!" I was appalled.

Jake was pained by my obtuseness. "What on earth makes you think he couldn't? Whether he would—or will—is another question. I don't know the answer. But such orders are issued every day, in every campaign. To assault an impregnable position, to hold an untenable one—in effect, to go out and get yourself killed. Most of the time such orders are necessary. An inescapable sacrifice. But sometimes they aren't."

While I was still shaken by this, Jake went back to my original question.

"Now, as to why we're still here, I should think that would be obvious enough. We're here to fight. Arthur wants a battle, and since he is the commanding general, we are going to have one. If we win, all the risks will have been justified. It will be a triumph for the general. We can withdraw at our convenience, or if we like we can stay on. And don't make the mistake of underestimating the general, John. He might just —almost—do it."

I was dismayed, and full of objections. "This is no time to fight a battle. No time and no place. What if we slug away all day and nobody wins? What if it's a drawn battle? Even if we win, we'll lose a lot of men and material. How do we replace them? Artillery horses, for example? And who said we were going to win anyway, the way things are going? What happens if we lose? How do we get out of here, with McGraw's cavalry bushwhacking us every foot of the way?"

Jake was pained again. "All good questions, Johnny, and all perfectly irrelevant. You didn't ask me what I thought we ought to do. You asked me why we're still here, and I told you. Such is Arthur's pleasure. The anger he has been keeping in all month has begun to show through. Now he wants to smash things. Even at the risk of getting smashed himself. He wants to fight a battle, and in the process he expects to settle his quarrel with James."

Jake held up his hand to check the vehement protest I was about to make. "No, Johnny, I don't think so. James is a valuable officer. Now that Arthur has his battle, he will do everything he can to win it. He needs James. He can't afford to throw him away in some hopeless and unnecessary attack. No, my opinion, if you want it, is that Arthur thinks of this as a trial by battle. To be more exact, a trial by the ordeal of battle. The battle is to decide his quarrel with James. Heaven is to judge between them, and may God defend the right!"

I found this incredible. "Do you really believe that, Jake?"

"I do indeed," he replied gravely. "I won't say that it's the whole answer, but it certainly is a large part of it. Your trouble, John, is that you don't know Arthur. You underestimate him. You don't seem to comprehend his staggering, his truly majestic arrogance. Arthur appeals to heaven because no lesser judge than God Almighty will do. Heaven is to render its verdict in the midst of battle. Arthur won't spare himself. He never has. And he won't spare James. Both of them will be under fire as much as necessary, which will be most of the time. Arthur's conviction, I am certain, is that only one of them will come off the field alive."

About the middle of the week an incident occurred which revealed the decline in our morale and the low estate we had reached. I had spent the morning down at the Second Division. McGraw had been demonstrating in front of the lower passes, but there was no weight behind his attacks, and they had been repelled rather easily. On the way back I ran into Hugo Bliss near the hospital, and we rode up the hill and into town together. It was still raw and disagreeable, with an occasional splatter of rain in the air, and we could hear the heavy booming of artillery fire from the direction of Jarvie Pass.

As we rode past the hospital, Hugo remarked that there had been a little excitement while I was gone, and asked if I remembered two brothers named Greene in the headquarters company.

I said I remembered them very well. "Bert and Abner Greene. That was when the company was the Countess's bodyguard. And our Derek had Bert saluting him for ten minutes one day, until Jake went out and stopped him."

"That's right. Bert Greene. Derek got even by getting him transferrred, and he was killed a couple of days later. The brother was bitter about it."

"I know he was. I talked to him."

"Well, that was taken care of this morning."

Some demon of perversity had gotten into Derek earlier in the morning. He hadn't liked the expression on Abner Greene's face. The man was surly. The man was insolent. So he proceeded to discipline him as he had disciplined his brother some weeks previously, and to teach him the rudiments of military courtesy. Abner submitted patiently until Derek was through, then he went to his quarters and loaded his rifle, and went out looking for him. He found Derek crossing the street just beyond the courthouse, and shot him dead in the middle of the street. Then he took a horse from the rack and simply rode off. Nobody interfered with him. When Major Lumley tried to start a pursuit, he couldn't even find anyone who remembered which way Abner had gone. Hugo was pretty sure that he got safely away.

I thought about this while we plodded the rest of the way up the hill. Finally I shook my head as though flies were bothering me, and said, "I don't like it, Hugo. I hope the rebels catch him."

Hugo looked at me. "Derek a friend of yours?"

"You know he wasn't. The Greene boys were friendly young fellows and good soldiers. I liked both of them, and I don't doubt that Abner had all the provocation in the world. But I still don't like it. It's all wrong. The walls are crumbling. Everything is falling apart."

Hugo nodded gloomily. "I know what you mean. I can see it, too."

As we rode into town we could see that the language I had used in a figurative sense was literally true of much of Tarsus. Everywhere there were broken windows, sagging porches, broken-down fences, yards overgrown with weeds and filled with debris, and the town as a whole was shabby, deserted, and ruinous. This was Tarsus at the end of November, under a gray sky, with the rumble of artillery in the distance. It was hard to remember that it had ever looked otherwise.

The bombardment in front of Jarvie was a feint, like the cavalry raid out of the south passes which had been so easily handled by the Second Division. With the First Division pinned down in front of Jarvie, with the Second Division bemused by the cavalry demonstrations in front of the lower passes, and with the Third Division entirely out of the field of action, McGraw was confronted in the northeast by one regiment of infantry and two worn-down regiments of cavalry. There was no fight: McGraw simply pushed them aside with his two cavalry brigades. By four o'clock in the afternoon McGraw had his entire force across the mountains and encamped in the fields north of the Taylor Road.

This made nonsense of Gavin's position in front of Jarvie, and of Roth's position covering the lower passes. In fact, it made nonsense of our dispositions as a whole, which had been made with the expectation of large reinforcements and the use of the river as a supply line. Obviously our dispositions had to be changed, and, half an hour before dark, orders were issued for a concentration in front of Tarsus, in accordance with a schedule worked out in October to meet the laughably remote contingency of our going on the defensive. The orders went out before dark, but it was close to midnight before they reached some of the outlying commands; consequently, all night long we heard the sound of men and horses moving along the roads, and it was after daylight before all of them were in.

We had now lost our freedom of movement, and the shut-in feeling began in earnest. This feeling—of being hemmed in within narrow boundaries, of being wound about, of surrounding peril—grew more oppressive on Friday, when Hal Stewart and George Lovell, friends and daily associates, and an infantry colonel who had come in on regimental business, disappeared in the course of routine errands, simply vanished without a trace.

On the following day, it was Jake who disappeared, not kicked by a mule as he had predicted, but after he had been thrown by his horse.

I had spent most of the morning talking to him. We had begun by talking about the Countess, and Jake got out the Judge's *Almanach de Gotha* to look up one point or another in connection with the family. Afterwards we talked about the Judge. Jake told me he had been one of the principal opponents of secession, and had worked against it to the end: this was why he had been left to rusticate in Tarsus, and had no part in the present government. We talked about young Robertson and Christina, and about the family alliances in the county, Robertson and Taylor, MacDougal and McGraw; about the state of the county before the war, and about our present difficulties.

We were in the office and Jake was sitting at his desk, leaning back with his hands clasped behind his head. There was a pile of reports on his desk, routine paper work, which he glanced at with distaste from time to time. I had to leave, finally, to be at Second Division headquarters by noon. As I stood up and went over to the door, Jake put on his spectacles, made a wry face, and picked up a report from the top of the pile. That was my last sight of Jake in this incarnation, so to speak: the last time I saw him as a soldier, as Jacob Leslie, Colonel and AAG.

Early in the afternoon he went out with Major Nichols, of Jonesy's staff, who had some business at the ordnance depot, across the river and west of town. Afterwards they continued along the River Road until Jake's horse was suddenly frightened, and reared up, then bolted with him. Jake was thrown and badly hurt; the major thought he had broken a leg. He galloped into town for an ambulance and returned immediately, leaving the ambulance to follow. In spite of all his haste, he was too late. Jake had disappeared.

We searched until dark, all to no purpose. We could find no trace of Jake, nor of his horse, nor even any vestiges of the rebel force that must have captured him. The house took on a deeper air of gloom that night.

Sunday began like the preceding days with an overcast sky and the wind in the south. The light wind slackened during the course of the morning and died away entirely about noon, leaving the air stagnant and heavy. There was a quality of excess in the weather: it was too still, too humid, and—for the last day of November—too warm. It was abnormal and precarious, and couldn't possibly last.

I had come in earlier, and happened to be in the living room about eleven o'clock. The copy of Thucydides Jake had been reading lay on the table, face down, open at Jake's place. I picked up the book, suddenly depressed, and read a few lines. I still had the book in my hand when I realized that somebody very big, who half filled the doorway, had come in. I raised my eyes, and saw that it was Colin.

Both of us were elaborately casual. Colin said, "Hello, Johnny," then looked around the room with an expression of distaste. "What on earth happened to the house? I haven't seen it for a week. It looks like a pigsty."

I glanced around and saw what he was talking about. Muddy boots had left trails of dried mud on the carpet; spurs had torn the upholstery and gouged the furniture; cigars had burned holes in the curtains and scarred the woodwork. Formerly these small accidents had been repaired as they occurred: a week's accumulation of them had been astonishingly destructive. In addition, there were empty bottles, dirty glasses, and cigar butts on the tables and window sills, and over everything was a layer of dust.

"It certainly didn't look like this when she was here," Colin said. He turned away and looked out through a dirty window. A moment later, still staring out the window, he added in a low voice, "When you see Aunt Lucy, give her my love."

Before I had time even to guess at the implications of this request, Colin turned around with a somber face and said, "I just heard about Jake a little while ago, Johnny. That's what I came to see you about. First there was Bob, then Hal Stewart and George Lovell, and now Jake. Derek, too, even though neither of us cared much for him. We've got a lot of heavy work in front of us, the way we're penned in here. Nobody can tell who will be next. I don't believe in presentiments. Everybody thinks he's going to be killed, and some of them are. That's all there is to that. I just came over—I just wanted to tell you that I'll be a lot happier going into our next fight if I don't feel that I'm quarreling with my friends."

I suddenly felt cold. Colin's disavowal of any belief in presentiments was simply not true. He had made that statement out of his usual thoughtfulness and courtesy—as I realized with a stab of compunction—in order to spare my feelings. He was perfectly certain that he was going to be killed in the battle that was a few days, or a few hours, ahead of us, and I knew it, too. I was appalled, and at the same time deeply moved.

"We should have stayed out of it, Colin," I said. "The only good thing you can say is that we never went in very far. We never really thought we were enemies. But we should have stayed out of it entirely. We could have been loyal to our friends and kinsmen without quarreling with each other. I wish to God we had thought of it before, but anyway we know it now."

Colin's face lighted up. "I hoped you'd say that, Johnny. I'm glad you feel that way."

He turned his head and stood looking over at the grimy window. I think he was trying, as I was, to find something appropriate to say in parting, to find the right thing to say, something warm and affectionate, but easy and offhand, and not slopping over. Neither of us succeeded.

In the end, Colin turned around and said awkwardly, "Well, I guess I had better be getting back."

"Oh?" I said. "Well, I'll probably see you tomorrow."

These were our parting words. They were probably about as good as any.

In the afternoon the sun came out and it was warm, and all the doors and windows were open. The sound of distant fighting came sporadically from all directions, even from the north, where Jonesy had pushed a regiment up the hill road to see what was there. Judging from the sound, the light, intermittent crackle of rifle fire, there wasn't much; but judging from the fact that it remained stationary for half an hour at a time, and moved on very slowly, whatever was there was strong enough, and strongly posted enough, to hold up Jonesy's regiment while it fell back to the next position and called for reinforcements.

On Sunday evening the interminable week of waiting finally came to an end. Just after dinner, with most of us gathered in the living room, a lieutenant from Heath's regiment came in with a dispatch for the general. He took the dispatch, glanced over it, then called James over and asked him to read it aloud.

The dispatch was from Dick, and said that a large enemy force, estimated at six thousand men of all arms, was reported on the Davis Road, twelve miles out, and was moving north towards Davis bridge and the River Road. It was probable, though not yet confirmed, that it was Taylor's division, with cavalry and guns attached. Confirmation was expected from further reports which were now coming in. These reports would be sent along within the hour.

As James finished reading, General Pack glanced around at us. "Well, gentlemen, it seems to be our move," he announced in a genial voice. "We will wait for confirmation from Colonel Ross, of course. As soon as that comes, we can go to work."

The waiting was over, and all of us had suddenly come to life again. There was still some grimness in the air—we had a battle in front of us, and no one thought it would be easy—but the principal feeling was one of vast relief. We were finally going to act, we were going to do something about the situation we were in. We had also regained our confidence.

McGraw had made a mistake, and we were going to make the most of it.

The crucial question was that of time. How many hours would we have tomorrow for our attack on McGraw's weakened main body? The answer seemed to be that we would have five hours at the very least: it would take Taylor that long simply to march back from the Davis Road. If we put a strong enough force in front of him to compel him to march deployed, or to stop frequently to deploy, we would have all the time in the world. The size of this containing force was a fine point: it had to be large enough to be effective, but not so large as to impair our main effort.

The general sat in an armchair by the fire and listened for the most part, and smoked a cigar while the rest of us talked. There was no change in his appearance or manner that could be singled out and given a name, but the change was there, and was felt by everyone present. This was shown in small ways, in the sudden silence that fell on the conversation when the general spoke, in the deference with which his opinion was listened to. There was nothing strange about this; in fact, there was something very familiar about it, but it took me some time to realize what it was: this was the way the general had looked in September. General Pack was himself again.

Dick's second report came in half an hour after the first, and confirmed it in all respects. The force on the Davis Road was positively identified as Taylor's division of infantry, with just over five thousand men; Horton's small cavalry brigade, of about eight hundred men; and Watson's and McCardle's batteries, of four twelve-pounders each.

With the arrival of Dick's second report, we went back to the office and started work. Hugo Bliss and I were drafted as secretaries, and wrote as fast as we could to the dictation of James and the general, and Jonesy and Robert and a dozen others who were in and out of the crowded office. In the intervals we made copies, or three or four copies, of the orders we had written. Everything was urgent and nothing could wait. Afterwards, after writing until my hand was numb and my mind was as numb as my hand, I spent the rest of the evening and most of the night in delivering the orders I had written.

Now that the command was drawn in around Tarsus, there were no long distances to cover and all the roads were perfectly familiar. This was just as well, for the night was abysmally dark, with no moon in the sky and the stars hidden by a dense layer of cloud. In spite of the darkness, the night was full of sound and movement. On my way down to Second Division headquarters, I was held up for fifteen minutes while the 12th Michigan went past, on its way out to join Dick on the West River Road. Two hours later, about one o'clock, I had to get off the road while two batteries and an infantry regiment were brought down from the meadows north of town to join the main force. And on my last errand, when I was sent down to the Second Division again with orders to remain there, at three in the morning, there were still horsemen on the roads.

Chapter 2

☙ ☙ ☙ ☙ ☙ ☙ ☙ ☙ ☙ ☙ ☙ ☙ ☙ ☙ ☙ ☙ ☙ ☙ ☙ ☙

I awakened from a melancholy dream in which John Boys,
who had been killed in August, three weeks before we opened
the Tarsus campaign, was trying to tell me something that I
knew was of vast and far-reaching importance. I strained my
ears to hear what he was saying, but there was little time and
his voice was growing fainter. Then the time was up and I still
hadn't understood what he was trying to tell me, and with a
sinking heart I saw a black and silver carriage, with outriders
in front and behind, come around the corner of the hill at the
left and pass rapidly across my view and out of sight, with a
white scarf fluttering against the gloomy evergreens and the
twilight of the forest.

Still half asleep, I could hear men and horses moving all
around me. Close by, I could hear men's voices, greetings and
snatches of talk, the pawing and snorting of tethered horses;
farther out, bodies of troops moving past quietly, in broken
step, orders given in low voices or passed down the line, then
the sound of straining horses and creaking leather as a battery
was led behind the infantry. All movement seemed to be
slowed down, and the sounds were muffled and indistinct.

This strangeness merged with the fading dream and for a
brief moment left me totally disoriented, as I threw off my
blanket and sat up. I was in a tent, a closed tent, for I could
see nothing but the dim light of the interior; a tent at Second
Division headquarters where my last errand of the night had
taken me, but why was the tent closed? On looking again,

startled and now fully awake, my heart sank: the flaps of the tent were open, and what I was looking at was a dense wall of fog that had closed in on us during the early hours of the morning. This was disastrous. We had to beat McGraw in a strictly limited number of hours. How many of them were left? How long had I slept? I pulled on my boots and groped my way over to the headquarters tent to find out.

I found Billy Roth drinking coffee with some of his officers at a long table that had been set up in the open, outside the headquarters tent. Billy's cold was still with him. His nose was red, and he had a gray knitted scarf wound around his neck with the ends falling forward over his shoulders. His big campaign hat, usually propped up by his ears, was on the back of his head; he had a half-smoked cigar in one hand and a damp handkerchief in the other, and he looked thoroughly miserable.

He peered at me through the fog as I came up, and greeted me with, "Well, John, you had a good night's sleep." He turned to Colonel Dove, who commanded his second brigade. "Andrew, what do you think of a young man who sleeps until eight o'clock the morning of a battle?"

Colonel Dove, gray-haired Old Man Dove, replied with his usual ponderous dignity, "General, the young man is to be envied. I wish I had slept as well myself."

Billy nodded with a wry face, then added morosely, "Not that he couldn't have slept until noon, the way things look now. A damned poor way to start the day, if you want my opinion, Andrew. A damned inauspicious beginning. Pack tells us we have no time to lose. Every minute is precious, he says. And here we sit, two hours late already, and perfectly helpless until this miserable fog lifts."

"Nothing much we can do about it, Wilfred," Colonel Dove said with resignation.

Billy was increasingly depressed. "Taylor knows this country like the back of his hand. What if he gets around Ross in this fog, and comes in on our right?"

Old Man Dove tried to reassure him. "Colonel Ross is an

experienced and vigilant officer, Wilfred. I don't think Taylor
will be able to get around him."

Billy Roth shook his head.

Troops were moving steadily down the road, not far away,
but outside the range of our vision. I asked who they were,
and was told that it was the First Division, probably Fiske's
brigade, moving into position. Billy's inspector, Colonel
Saunders, confirmed this when he came in a few minutes
later, and added that Gavin was pushing his men all the way
down to the road that McGraw was holding with his picket
line. Other members of Billy's staff came in, one by one, and
for a time there was a disjointed, much broken discussion of
our prospects for the day. All of us were disheartened by the
delay, and the fog made us uneasy.

After half an hour of this, the fog appeared to be as thick as
ever, as though it were going to last all day, but on looking
across the table and over towards the road, I found that where
there had been nothing but impenetrable pearl-gray fog when
I sat down, and later a vague looming mass of some kind,
there now stood, clearly visible, a large spreading oak tree, its
gnarled branches black with moisture, its withered brown foliage perfectly motionless.

There had been firing along the picket line, desultory single
shots, occasional brief exchanges, sometimes distant, sometimes
fairly close, for an hour or more. The rate of fire had gradually increased: it was still individual fire, picket-line fire, but
now the exchanges were frequent, and went on for two or
three minutes at a time. Mingled with the firing, sounds of life
and movement began to reach us from behind the enemy
lines, three-quarters of a mile away: the distant note of a
bugle, the faintly heard ring of axes, the distant crash of falling trees. And at about this time, prematurely, with the fog
still thick, the deep reverberant boom of a single cannon shot
came from somewhere over on the left.

James rode up while the air was still vibrating. The fact
that I could see who was coming and could distinguish his
features even before he dismounted was another measure of

the thinning of the fog. I noticed that he was wearing a fresh, beautifully tailored uniform, gleaming English boots and silver spurs, and a new pair of yellow gauntlets; his kepi was canted at a more rakish angle than usual, and a cheerful ebullience of manner was added to his usual air of easy assurance. Both costume and manner announced a day of battle.

He dismounted and came over to the table. "Good morning, gentlemen," he said, smiling. "Someone over on Barney's side of the fence seems to be a little nervous."

Billy Roth looked up. "Morning, James," he said irritably. "Who wouldn't be nervous in this damned fog?"

"It's clearing up, Billy," James said. "In another fifteen or twenty minutes we'll be able to see where we're going." He glanced across the table at me. "Morning, Johnny. Get some sleep?"

Billy answered for me, as though this were still another grievance laid upon his shoulders. "Slept like a baby. We had to wake him up. Some of you young fellows seem to think a battle is a Fourth of July picnic. Lots of fireworks and fun for everybody."

We could hear the sound of a large group of horsemen approaching, and presently, while they were some distance away, we saw the general and his entourage emerge from the mist. General Pack was breathing his native air again, and he looked bigger than life-size and vastly impressive. We got to our feet as he approached, and there was as much of natural deference in the act as there was of military etiquette. At the same time I think we forgot a large part of our worries: we handed them over to the general.

"Good morning, Wilfred. Good morning, gentlemen," he said easily. "Keep your seats, please. We have too much to do this morning to be ceremonious."

He came over to the table and called for coffee, then turned to Billy with the mug in his hand. "Well, Wilfred, we'll be starting off in a few minutes. I trust everything is perfectly clear to you."

"I think so, General. The entire division in reserve. No change in the original orders." Billy's voice was still querulous. "Only what about this miserable fog? Isn't that going to make any difference?"

General Pack smiled tolerantly. "None whatever. I think we can assume it has been as thick on the other side as on our own. We have been able to push our attacking force well forward without alarming General McGraw's pickets. On the whole, it may have given us some advantage. You are in touch with the other divisions, of course?"

Billy nodded. "Yes, sir. Of course."

"Good. We don't want any unnecessary casualties, you understand, Wilfred. Don't expose your men needlessly. On the other hand, we want them kept close enough so they can go in at once when the time comes. I will leave you to reconcile those two conditions."

My horse had been brought up in the meantime, and I went over to join the column in the road. I drew up beside Hugo Bliss, who was serving today as a volunteer aide. The general remained in conversation with Billy Roth and his staff a little longer, then turned away with a pleasant nod, came over to the road pulling on his gloves, and swung himself into the saddle.

There were now more than a dozen of us with the general, between the staff, and officers from each of the three divisions, and, with Howel Jenkins and the twenty-five mounted men of the headquarters company, we made a respectable small body of cavalry as we started forward.

The fog was now little more than a haze, but our vision was still limited. The line of battle was three-quarters of a mile away; we could make out, though dimly, the outline of a small wood on rising ground another three-quarters of a mile farther on. This mile and a half was the extreme limit of our vision, a limit that remained unchanged all day. The air was perfectly still, and as the fog disappeared, the smoke of battle rose in its place.

McGraw's line, a constantly renewed line of gunsmoke, was behind a tree-bordered farm road which ran crookedly across the field, all the way from the turnpike on the right, to the millpond on the left. The entire field was undulating, nowhere quite level, low wooded hills alternating with field and meadow. The woods were black and brown and wintry, the fields pale with withered grass, the meadows still green.

A swell of ground, coming in from the left across the wagon track we were following, hid the left of the line from us as we started out, but we had a clear view of Jonesy's line on the right, all the way to the abrupt wooded hillside beyond the turnpike which closed in the field of action on that side. The firing had increased greatly in the past few minutes; it was now continuous, though not yet heavy.

The long lines of the First Division came into view as we rode over the crest of the rise. Just at this moment, as those of us in the middle of the column passed over the crest, there was a loud, ugly rushing sound overhead, and a fluffy white ball of smoke appeared against the slope of the hillside three-quarters of a mile to the south; the resonant boom of the distant cannon reached our ears, and at the same instant we heard the crash of a shell exploding close at hand, and the vicious hissing of the shell fragments. We got off the road automatically and at once, but not before a second bloom of smoke appeared on the hillside, and a second shell burst somewhere in the rear.

Someone near me grunted with surprise and pain, and a riderless horse dashed by on the other side of the road. Before I had time to look around, we were shaken by a thunderous triple roar from behind us as three of our batteries opened fire simultaneously on the enemy guns. An instant later the entire face of the distant hillside was covered by shellbursts.

By this time I could see Colonel Horn out in the field by himself, dismounted, clinging to the saddle to hold himself up. Two men of the escort were stretched out on the ground, and at least one other had been hit. Hugo Bliss was still in the middle of the road. His horse was shivering, and Hugo was clutching his left shoulder with his right hand, a look of great surprise on his face.

Although I was badly shaken at the moment, I suddenly remembered Hugo's plain, sensible little wife, and the shining look that came into her eyes when he appeared, and I was wrung with grief. I went back to the road and asked Hugo how badly he was hurt. Blood was running over his fingers and down the front of his uniform.

"I don't know, John," he replied in a low voice. "Chest or shoulder. I don't know which. It feels pretty bad."

Howel Jenkins came riding up at the same time. "Go on, Johnny," he called out as he approached. "We'll take care of Hugo and Colonel Horn. That's one of the things we're here for."

I turned away reluctantly and went on. Two minutes later I had forgotten about Hugo and his wife.

The general and his following had halted by a small clump of trees in back of the road when I caught up with them. The fighting, which was already fairly stiff, was mainly in the two hills, low wooded turtlebacks, across the road. The one on the left, rising directly from the swampy borders of the millstream, was close to the road; the other, straight in front of us, was two or three hundred yards farther back. A country road, usually called the mill road, ambled away to the south between the two hills; through the notch between them a third hill was partly visible, higher, steeper, and more formidable than the others. At this moment all three of them were gradually fading from view as the smoke thickened.

Gavin and Benny Pace had come up and were talking earnestly to the general and the group of officers around him, Gavin on a big white horse, bareheaded, his sleeves rolled up, his big mustache bristling, and as always in battle, his face flushed with anger. It was Keith's brigade out in front. So far the opposition, though stubborn, had not been as heavy as expected, and there were some indications that the two hills were merely being held as outposts, with a stronger force behind them, possibly the greater part of McGraw's three divisions.

General Pack sent me over to Jonesy to give him this information and to watch the development of his attack, then come back with a report. As I moved away from Keith's attack on the two hills, I could hear the sound of Jonesy's battle in front of me: Harper's twelve-pounders firing rapidly and the crash of musketry in what was evidently a local attack, and beyond that, from the extreme right, the guns of Brock's three-inch battery firing deliberately, in pairs, at some distant target.

I had no difficulty in finding Jonesy. Jonesy believed in being comfortable when he went into battle, and today he was wearing his usual battle costume: leather-patched trousers tucked into his oldest pair of boots, a black and white checked shirt with a star pinned to the shoulder somehow to indicate his rank, a navy revolver slung around his waist, and a disreputable slouch hat over one eye that must have dated from his days on the plains.

Jonesy greeted me impatiently. "All right, boy. What's Arthur got on his mind? Not making enough noise to suit him?"

I shook my head. "Nothing like it. He's over with the First Division. Keith's going after those two little hills out in front. He thinks McGraw may have a big force behind them. That's just a hunch. They don't know yet. The general wants to know what you've got in front of you, and what kind of opposition they're putting up. That, and anything else you want me to tell him."

Jonesy scowled at me fiercely, then relaxed. "Barney's got more men somewhere. Maybe they're on Ross's side. Maybe they're over here. We'll find out. Right now he's got about a brigade in front of me. Five or six regiments. Not much artillery. Four-gun battery, two or three guns with the infantry. Sammy Brock and young Harper took care of them. Not one of them still firing. Opposition?" Jonesy pushed his hat onto the back of his head. "Hell! I don't know, Johnny. Spotty, so far. Some of them hard to move, some pretty easy. Tell you better in a few minutes. We already got Carlstrom in, and Bobby Duke's just putting in the rest of the 14th. See how it goes, then you can tell Arthur about it."

In front of us I could see Colonel Duke's bristling cropped beard and spare figure in a group of men close to the road. He was talking to two of his line captains and from time to time he was pointing. A hundred yards away to the left, Gareth

Harper, his elegance still untarnished, was directing the fire of a pair of his guns.

All of us stood peering into the smoke. The rebel line, marked by a barricade of rails and the smoke from the firing, ran along the edge of a wood beyond an open field overgrown with weeds. The return fire still seemed to be fairly heavy, but, in the occasional half glimpses possible through the smoke, we could see that our men were nearly across the field and approaching the wood, and very few of them seemed to be down. The smoke thinned out as they reached the edge of the wood and passed beyond; the sound of the firing receded and diminished in volume.

Colonel Duke watched his third company enter the wood, then turned to Jonesy with a smile that expressed both relief and satisfaction. "Well, General, there's a parcel of land I guess you can have."

We went for our horses and moved to the higher ground in back of the lines. From here we could see that the two penetrations made by the 14th Iowa had coalesced into a single wide and deep salient whose still expanding boundaries were marked by a line of smoke rising over the treetops. Farther to the left the 24th Illinois had pushed in another deep salient, with its outer flank protected by a ravine and a brook. The enemy force left between these two penetrations in a counter-salient of its own was slowly but visibly crumbling.

Half an hour later it had disappeared and we occupied in its entirety the small wooded plateau that had formed the center of the enemy line on this side of the field. Jonesy ordered Pellam to push forward with this entire brigade, and swung Vickers in against the flank of the rebel position in the center. As soon as these movements were well started, he sent me back to report to the general.

It was ten minutes of eleven. Since I had been with him, Jonesy had neatly dismantled the right half of McGraw's line. His own casualties had been light, while those of the enemy had been disproportionately heavy. What impressed me was the sheer professional competence of the operation. Jonesy was given a job to do. He went about it in a workmanlike manner, without any flourishes, and got it done. I told Jonesy just that, before I started over to the left. He was pleased, but inclined to deprecate the compliment.

"Those fellows could have given us a lot more trouble than they did, Johnny," he said. "They just sat still and waited for us. If they'd moved around some, and put something more than a few scouts up the hill on the right, they could have made it a lot harder. Fact is, I don't think Barney really expected us. He thought we'd just sit still and wait until he got everything ready."

He stopped short and held up his hand. The sound of the battle on the left had been audible occasionally, even while the fighting was still in progress on this side of the field. Now that the guns had ceased firing and the battle line had moved farther away, it was loud and clear, and seemed to come principally from the hills on the left, a mile and a half away. It had grown louder while Jonesy was talking, and as we listened it became tremendous.

"Quite a row they're making over there," Jonesy remarked mildly. "Must be seventy-five or eighty guns firing." He listened for a moment longer, then turned back and said, "Tell Arthur we're doing all right on this side, Johnny. We got that damn' rock pile up ahead. Farmhouse. Billy Roth's old headquarters. Four-foot stone walls. Barney's ditched it and thrown up a lot of earth. Pellam thinks he might have trouble with it, but we can take it, all right. Ask Arthur how far he wants me to go."

The uproar on the left was still growing in violence as I started off. The air was heavy and oppressive, and the clouds had thickened overhead; a column of black smoke was rising from a barn that had been set on fire behind the hills, and the air was filled with the smoke of battle. The low clouds and the smoke had darkened the air to such an extent that the flash from the gun muzzles was red and glowing, instead of the barely visible stab of orange seen in ordinary daytime firing. This effect was particularly noticeable on the higher hill, where McGraw had collected a great mass of guns, drawn up in a double row: a truly infernal effect, as the red glare of the gun flashes lighted up the column of smoke and the dark lowering clouds.

The firing was disagreeably accurate. Shells were bursting just ahead and just behind, and on one side and the other, two or three in the air at a time, all of them much too close. This was while I was approaching a pair of our batteries on a shelf of high ground on the left of the road. Just as I was passing them, a caisson blew up in back of me with a tremendous roar, and a shell fragment ripped through my sleeve. My horse stumbled, seemed to catch herself and went on for a few paces, then gave a strange and wholly unexpected bound, and fell, stone dead.

I got to my feet, jarred by the fall and full of aimless rage —at the loss of a good horse and the humiliation of being on foot, at the pain in the ankle I had twisted, at the deafening noise and the bursting shells, at the general and Barney Mc-Graw and the whole damned war—and limped along wrathfully for five minutes, until someone saw me and sent one of Howel Jenkins' men out to meet me with a led horse.

General Pack and his entourage were over to the left, on rising ground some distance behind the lines, in front of a grove of oak trees. The general was a little in advance of the others, talking to an officer whose face was hidden from me, on a very big gray horse. I thought I recognized the horse, and as the rider turned away and started over to the left, I could see that it was Colin. As he rode off, another officer came up to talk to the general, Robert Saint Chamans, red-striped, elegant, and wholly at ease.

As I rode up he was saying, "If I bring Brock over, General, I can cross the fire of forty-two guns on the position. General McGraw couldn't keep a gun or a regiment there. He couldn't even keep a platoon of sharpshooters in action."

General Pack glanced over at me, acknowledging my presence, before he replied:

"No, I think not, Major. I'm sure you can make the position wholly untenable, as you say, but I'm not at all sure we want that. General McGraw is reinforcing here. Drawing in his reserves. On the whole, this seems to me a fine place for them. As far away from General Taylor as possible. I don't think we want to drive General McGraw away from here. We want to keep him here, but make it very expensive for him to stay. In the meantime we can push down on the other side, then roll him up from below. And he has the millpond and a swamp in back of him. Doesn't that seem to you our best method of procedure?"

Robert bowed respectfully. "General, I am a foolish child."

General Pack corrected him mildly. "Nothing of the sort, Robert. You simply weren't looking at the field as a whole."

While I was waiting, I noticed the three regiments of Gavin's third brigade over by the mill road, the road which came up from the south between the hills we were fighting over. Gavin and Benny Pace, Gavin on his big white horse, were in front of the leading regiment, talking to the brigade commander, Colonel Driscoll.

General Pack finally turned to me. "Well, John, I see you have a new horse."

"Yes, sir. Very poor climate for horses around here."

He smiled. "How are things going over on the right?"

I gave him my report, together with Jonesy's message. While I was talking, James appeared over on the extreme left, coming down the side of the hill to our left front, jumping a ditch and a fence, then trotting easily up the mill road. He stopped briefly to talk to Gavin and Colonel Driscoll, then came slanting up the hill at a fast trot. He gave me a wave of the hand and a greeting over the general's head, then addressed him urgently.

"Keith doesn't think the 66th is going to hold, sir. He says he can hang on all day on the left, but he's going to need help on the right. McGraw is bringing up more troops. Two more regiments. That makes either six, or seven. Keith wants to bring the 66th out of the woods entirely and bend it back along the mill road, but Gavin hates to give up ground. If the 66th can hang on a little longer, he's going to send Maxwell in to support them."

"He won't have time," the general remarked. He had kept

274 ❖

his eyes steadily to the front while James was talking, fixed on the line of smoke showing over the treetops of the low hill five hundred yards in front of us.

The general was right. The first indication of the break was the appearance of a very big gray horse, riderless, galloping up the road in terror. There was a sudden startled movement in the group of officers around Gavin, then Benny Pace, with an expression of absolute fury on his face, jerked his horse around, dug in his spurs, and started down the road.

He was killed before we even saw the cause of his rage, toppled from his horse by a bullet through the head. Half a minute later we saw the first demoralized fugitives come tumbling out of the woods into the mill road.

A company officer, who had kept his head in the midst of the general panic, was with them. He took his stand in the middle of the road with his sword drawn, and gestured the men over to the left of the road, where a ditch offered shelter to the panic-stricken, and a defensible position to those who still wanted to fight.

Three of our guns, the remnants of Cummings' battery, came into view, retiring down the mill road, just in time to be overrun by the yelling swarm of slouch-hatted rebels emerging from the woods. The artillerymen barely had time to swing their guns around and fire a round or two apiece before they were overrun, but these few rounds of canister at close range were highly destructive, and the impetus of the rebels was checked. In the meantime, two companies of the 17th Wisconsin had been bent around to connect with the line that was forming along the edge of the road, and when I looked again in that direction a line had been firmly established, and the rebels were falling back across the mill road.

I missed much of the latter part of this action on the left because my attention—everyone's attention—was distracted by the break on the right, which was sudden, spectacular, and disgraceful. The men came bursting out of the woods and simply ran, without a backward look, without even the semblance of an attempt at making a stand. Colonel Blanchard, who was proud of his regiment, was nearly weeping with rage and shame. He would stop with his sword in his hand, and hold out his arms and try to check the flight, sometimes by himself, sometimes with one or two of his officers. The men were too far gone in panic, and simply avoided him. After each failure, he turned and ran a few paces with his men, then tried again. Finally he gave up, and came plodding back with his head bowed and his sword trailing in his hand.

Actually there were a good many extenuating circumstances, but all we saw at the time was a regiment in disgraceful flight, with one line after another of yelling rebels emerging from the woods in pursuit. The spectacle was an alarming one, and there was a moment of wild surmise at first when I was certain the general had never counted on anything like this, that something had gone wrong and he had lost control of the battle. A moment later I heard his voice and forgot the surmise.

"Well, here they come, James," he remarked in a tone of mild interest, as though he and James had a small bet, a two-dollar bet, on the outcome of the race across the open field. "I think we had better have some support over on the right. Get Colonel Maxwell, will you please, James?"

The race now became three-cornered, as James and Colonel Maxwell led the 54th Illinois over to the right at a run. The situation at the moment was critical, with the rebel first line in close pursuit of the demoralized 66th, and strong forces coming on behind.

Fortunately this precarious state of affairs lasted only a short time. As the 54th came into position to receive the men of the 66th, and braced itself to meet the pursuing rebels, the deafening uproar along the front line was suddenly deepened by the jarring concussion of artillery fire, and multiplied by a row of shellbursts in front of the rebel second line, not much more than two hundred yards out—an astonishingly even row of shellbursts that seemed to remain in place like a curtain, or like the jet of water from a fountain, as the guns kept up their fire.

Within half an hour McGraw's counterattack was definitely broken. The second line had been badly hurt by our artillery fire, but continued its advance until the first line began to fall back, after taking extremely heavy losses. The two lines fell back together and were received by the third line, which had halted fifty yards out from the edge of the wood. Shortly afterwards the entire force withdrew.

This was what the general was waiting for.

"Well, gentlemen, General Ross seems to have matters pretty well in hand on this side of the field," he announced. "I think we might as well go over and see what General Jones and his men have been doing."

The atmosphere was less murky than it had been earlier; the clouds had thinned out to the usual high overcast, and the air was fairly clear to the right and left, though still thick in front. Jonesy, with some help from Fiske, had driven the rebels out of the wood in the center, and our line no longer ran straight across the field but slanted downwards, towards the southwest. The gunners had raised their sights to follow the enemy retreat and were now shelling the woods in intricate crossing patterns, and Gavin was gathering his troops together for a counterattack.

As the others started over to the right for a look at Jonesy and his works, I started for the Second Division with orders for Billy Roth to bring the division forward. From there I was sent back to the First Division to get Abel Hasbrouck, since Friday our chief of engineers, with a report on the defensive strength of the positions held by the First Division.

Gavin's counterattack had been under way for some time, as I approached. The fighting was still severe, judging by the sound, and appeared to be centered on the low hill, almost invisible in the smoke, from which Colonel Blanchard and the 66th Indiana had been driven earlier.

After I reached the road, I began to meet large numbers of walking wounded coming out of the battle. Stretcher-bearers were bringing off the more seriously wounded, and rows of white-topped ambulances were lined up along the road and around the corner, down the mill road.

Out on the field I noticed an orderly leading a big white horse down out of the woods. With my attention attracted by the horse, I saw that it was being led behind a group of men, one of them an officer, carrying a wounded man out on a stretcher, with one of the regimental surgeons walking along by his side.

It occurred to me rather idly that it must be someone of importance to be getting that much attention. Then, with a sudden shocked awareness I remembered the horse, looked again at the man on the stretcher, and saw that it was Gavin. Suddenly I was full of distress: I forgot the month that he had been our enemy, and remembered the year that he had been our close friend. I swung my horse out into the field and cut across the corner to the mill road, where an ambulance was waiting with an assistant surgeon and a couple of medical attendants beside it. They had almost reached the ambulance when I met them.

Gavin had a blanket over him. His booted left foot emerged from beneath the blanket, turned inwards at an exaggerated and shockingly wrong angle. He had been given a pint or more of brandy since he had been hit, and he was smoking a cigar. His face was red and dripping with perspiration, and he was obviously in great pain.

I dismounted and went over to the stretcher. "God, I'm sorry you're hurt, Gavin," I said with deep concern.

He turned his head. "Hello, Johnny. All in the day's work, I guess." He made a grimace. "Rather not work, some days. How's James?"

I put my hand out and knocked on the wooden frame of the ambulance. "So far he's all right," I said. "Only it's too early in the day to ask how anybody is."

"That's right. Shouldn't have asked." Gavin closed his eyes, then opened them again with considerable effort. "Johnny? Something I want you to tell him."

Between brandy and shock he was having difficulty in keeping his mind in focus.

"Wrong about him. Good man, no matter what. Man of honor. Don't understand it. I was wrong. Johnny? Tell him that. Tell him I'm sorry."

He closed his eyes again. As the attendants lifted him carefully into the ambulance, I asked the regimental surgeon how badly he had been hit.

"He'll lose his leg," he replied. "Hit squarely in the knee-cap. Smashed all to hell. Minié ball. They'll amputate just above the knee. A couple of other wounds. Minor, neither of them serious. He ought to be all right. You never can tell, though. Wait and see is about all the prognosis I can give you."

I asked about the circumstances. The surgeon shook his head, indicating either his ignorance or his haste, and started after the ambulance. The officer who had helped carry Gavin down—Major Craig, Gavin's adjutant; I simply hadn't recognized him—answered for him.

Craig was distraught. "It was that damned white horse, John," he said. "Everybody aims at a man on a white horse. The general knew it as well as anybody, but you know the Rosses. As long as we kept them moving, it was all right. They were stubborn, and it was hard work, but we were moving them. Then we got to the top of the hill, and McGraw threw his counterattack at us. Fresh troops. You never saw such a slugging match in your life. Nobody giving an inch. Maxwell killed right at the beginning, Maxwell and a dozen others. And there was the general all up and down the line, right in the line, on his damned white horse. Officers with him killed right and left, all around him. Nearly killed himself a dozen times before he was finally hit. Not that he had any business being there. Only he had just seen Benny and young Colin killed within the space of about two minutes—"

"I saw Colin's horse running loose," I said, interrupting. "I was pretty sure he had been killed, but I didn't know."

The major looked at me curiously. "That's right. Friend of yours, wasn't he? If it will make you feel any better, he never knew what hit him. Clean shot through the head. Killed instantly."

Craig's voice became bitter. "Not all of them got off that easy. George Wharton had his arm shot off at the elbow and bled to death. Young Russel got a bullet through the lungs, and Ramsay got one in the intestines. Both dead before they could be carried off the field. All three of them friends of mine. So was Humphrey Maxwell. So were Benny and Ned Chapel. Corny Driscoll's hurt. So is Blanchard. I don't know how many men we've lost, but it must be over fifty per cent. The First Division is wrecked. There isn't much left of it. And all these good men and good soldiers killed and the division smashed on account of a quarrel over a woman. All because your uncle was sleeping with the general's wife."

This was totally unexpected. For a moment I was stunned and unable to say a word. I thought of James protesting when the general announced that he had sent for his wife, and of the general's displeasure. I thought of my first sight of the Countess on the long, shaded porch of the tavern, and of the glittering tin dipper they drank from on the way back. I thought of Jake, and of the general's unbending arrogance, and of his appeal to heaven and the trial by battle. I thought of Madame Lucy with her hair down her back, sitting in the window, framed against the red glow of the burning supply depot, lamenting that she had brought us nothing but misfortune, yet not quite able to wish that she had never come.

All these images were crowding into my head, but it was too difficult, too long, too complex to try to explain to Major Craig, and what I said finally—the only thing I could think of—was:

"Fighting a battle here wasn't James' idea, Major. When he was up at Jenkins' Ferry on the thirteenth, he told General Crawford that we would begin our withdrawal on the twentieth unless our reinforcements were within a day's march. Unless they amounted to a full division and were within a day's march on November twentieth. General Pack wouldn't back him up."

"I didn't know that," Major Craig said. "Does it make any difference?"

His bitterness had left him, and he was conciliatory but depressed. "I'm not trying to blame anyone, John. I've always had the greatest admiration for James. All of us did before this thing came up. I'm not saying it's his fault. I'm not saying it's hers, either. I always thought she was a woman of fine character. It just happened that she was brought up differently, that she's a foreigner and a countess. A lovely woman. A beautiful and charming woman. But I wish to God we had never set eyes on her."

I started to tell him that she had said nearly the same thing, then remembered that in the end she hadn't, and while I was trying to put this together in my mind I realized that no answer was called for. Major Craig wasn't waiting to hear what I had to say, but was listening to the sound of the firing over the hill: it was steady, and moving slowly away from us.

"Have them out of there in another fifteen minutes," Major Craig said. He had recovered himself, and there was satisfaction in his voice. "Old Barney hasn't been having any picnic either. What does the general want us to do now, John? Do you know?"

"I know what he wants you to do, but I haven't any orders," I said. "He wants you to keep Barney here. To look aggressive, and threaten him, and to prepare a strong defensive position in case he calls your bluff. Jonesy is moving down on the right. As soon as he has the MacDougal Ridge, Roth will swing in, and he and Jonesy will move back up the field together. McGraw will be in a sack, with no way out."

"Except over us. Those defensive works had better be good and strong!" Major Craig shook his head. "By God, you can't say there's anything timid about our leadership. Or anything modest about our aims. Who the hell does Pack think he is? Hannibal? A common ordinary victory isn't good enough for us. Nothing short of encirclement and annihilation will do."

The major's orderly had brought up his horse, and both of us mounted. "Keith will be in command, I suppose," the major remarked. "The old Iron Man. I'd better look him up and report."

He nodded to me and started back towards the sound of the fighting on the hill, and I went to look for Abel Hasbrouck.

There was a notable change of atmosphere in the group around the general when I rode up with Captain Hasbrouck, an air of cheerful, even exuberant, confidence. Ten minutes earlier my friend, Smitty—Captain Darius Elwood Smith, of the 4th Michigan—had come in with a hastily scribbled note from Dick Ross:

"Noon. Minges Road. Taylor still back of this road, seven miles west. Has tried both ends, Thorne Road and Fletcher Road. Got a bloody nose both times. Now trying to get us to stand still so he can hit us. Not a chance. Taylor will arrive about midnight at present rate. Losses moderate. Taylor's heavier. Short of rations. All other supplies adequate. Request rations sent out Fletcher Road."

This cleared the air. With Taylor seven miles out and McGraw's right badly hurt, and contained by the First Division, we had only the force in front of Jonesy to think about. The artillery was methodically pounding in the walls of the Bascom farmstead—Jonesy's damn' rock pile—and Pellam had sent the entire 10th Iowa up the steep side of the hill across the turnpike. The general and most of the men around him had their field glasses trained in that direction, and were watching the regiment move into position on the flank of McGraw's improvised fortress. It was not yet two o'clock, and we had time enough in front of us. Even the day had brightened, and traces of blue sky were visible through the high thin layer of cloud.

The general sent me back with Smitty to see about the rations. Smitty's eyes were bloodshot and he looked as though he hadn't slept for a week, but he was full of enthusiasm.

"You should have been with us this morning, Johnny," he said, as we started back. "I know the way you and James feel about Dick, but if you had seen him this morning you would have forgotten all about it. You would have loved him. He had old Peter Taylor running around in circles before the morning was half over. Every time he tried to move, there we were in front of him. Every time he shifted over and tried to move in a different direction, there we were again. I swear to God, Dick must have been reading his mind."

The sun came out and shone brightly for five minutes as we were approaching the commissary depot. The depot was off the road at the left; the hospital was farther along on the other side of the road; and straight ahead of us, half a mile away, was Tarsus on its hill. The distance was great enough to conceal the ruinous condition of the town, and it looked neat and rather pretty. The trees still retained much of their autumnal foliage which was suddenly bright in the unexpected sunlight, and gave the streets a festive air, as though they were decked with flags. At the same time an accident of light and perspective exaggerated the steepness of the approach, giving the place for the moment the look of a fortified hill town: a hill town *en jour de fête,* bathed in sunlight, against a background of menacing black and purple clouds.

The effect was brief. When I looked again, on the way back, the opening in the clouds had closed over. The sun was hidden, and the town was drab and sullen on its low hill.

Smitty turned off to the right to go back to his command, with two loaded wagons behind him, and I kept straight on down the turnpike. Ahead of me the guns were still firing steadily, but elsewhere the battle had entered a lull, with nothing more than a bickering exchange of small-arms fire along the entire line. Halfway back, I had to turn out into the fields to ride around Brian Cooper's two big regiments, in column on the turnpike with Lovell's battery behind them. After I turned out, I could see the imposing heights of the MacDougal Ridge ahead of me, half a mile to the south, the roof and upper story of the house I had once admired appearing over the crest of the ridge.

Jonesy was with the general when I got back. He was about to open his attack, and at the moment was talking earnestly to James and the general. Billy Roth had come down from the Second Division, and officers from all three divisions were with them. Everybody was watching Harper's guns move down and swing into position to batter the unprotected inner wall of the Bascom place.

We were suddenly enveloped and half stunned by a jarring crash of sound, as Harper's twelve-pounders opened fire. A billow of smoke rose up and obscured the view, but through occasional rifts in the smoke we could see the Iowa troops coming down the precipitous hillside beyond the turnpike, their progress marked by the line of smoke from their volleys, each one lower than the one before. The artillery fire continued and increased in volume until Harper's cross fire seemed about to plow into our men coming down the hill, then it stopped abruptly, as though cut off with a knife. In this sudden silence the sound of the bugles was clear and bright, and the 18th Michigan rose up in front and went over the ruined walls with a cheer. The impossibility of any further defense was as clear to the rebel commander as it was to us, and as our men came in over the front the garrison went out at the back.

With the collapse of this stronghold, McGraw's entire line was uprooted and forced to fall back, all the way from the turnpike to the line of hills coming in on the left, where McGraw's battered main body still faced our equally battered First Division. The enemy troops on Jonesy's left drifted farther in that direction as they retired, and finally reached the position of the main body in front of the hills. Those on the right, including the defenders of the fortress, had a more difficult time, with the strong Iowa regiment on their flank pressing them inwards. About a hundred of them were cut off and forced to surrender. The remainder, after losing heavily, gave up the fight and streamed backwards up the slope of the ridge and into the temporary safety of the works along the crest.

All of us were now looking up at the MacDougal Ridge. At the opening of the battle, this formidable position had been behind McGraw's center, and a mile and a half to the rear. As a result of Jonesy's advance down the field, it was now on McGraw's extreme left, the guardian of his flank, and the key to the entire battlefield.

For more than two months it had been merely a hill, and the site of the MacDougal house, a perfectly ordinary part of the landscape, ridden past or seen from a distance nearly every day. You could walk up the hill in less than five minutes; you could ride a horse up the hill, though you might have some trouble with the steeper places. Now both its character and its appearance had changed: in enemy hands, with the raw earth and freshly cut logs of a line of field works along the crest, it loomed up like a mountain.

Nevertheless the ridge was vulnerable. Formidable indeed from the front, it was open to a flanking attack, and we had Cooper's brigade in column, with a battery of rifled guns in support, only waiting for the turnpike to be cleared to move up through the woods to the flank and rear of the position on the ridge. With a strong brigade coming in on his flank, McGraw would be unable even to man the entire line of the crest, and we had two brigades to go up the hill in front. McGraw could meet one attack or the other, but certainly not both.

A man I had never seen before, a line captain from an Ohio regiment, turned to me and said, "You know, by God, sir, I think we've got McGraw. Unbelievable as it sounds."

"I was just thinking the same thing," I replied. "And wondering what I had left out. It sounds too good to be true."

"I agree with you, sir. I can hardly believe it either. But once we've got the MacDougal Ridge, we've got McGraw. It's as simple as that. And we can take the ridge. There isn't any question about it."

Everyone around us, I think, had reached the same conclusion. There was still work to be done, but quite soberly we knew we could do it. The way was clear and the end was in sight. All we needed was a little time.

It was this that failed us: we had run out of time. Our advance down the turnpike had cleared the opening of the small country road that followed the base of the hill around to the right, then ran approximately straight west through the woods. We generally referred to it as the Woods Road: it was the first road below Tarsus and the river coming in from the west. The turnpike was now clear, and we could see Jonesy, in his checked shirt, motioning to Cooper to bring his men forward.

Just after this there was some commotion at the mouth of the Woods Road, but the low clouds and the stagnant smoke made it difficult to see what it was. A number of mounted men seemed to have come in, and Jonesy was riding back at a gallop. Cooper halted his men short of the Woods Road and went forward to meet him. We could see both of them in earnest conversation with one of the cavalrymen—no one any of us recognized—who had come in from the right.

The conference between Jonesy and Colonel Cooper and the cavalry officer was brief, then Cooper signaled his men forward and turned them off to the right, down the Woods Road. At the same time a messenger was sent galloping across the fields in our direction.

Beside me the Ohio captain uttered a single word of abysmal bitterness: "Taylor!"

The captain was right. The messenger—Lieutenant Harry Byrne, of the 12th Michigan—had been sent to tell us that Dick Ross's covering force had been destroyed, and that Taylor's entire division was coming in on our right flank. The lieutenant's report gave us some of the details.

The essential cause of the defeat was simple attrition. With a force of eighteen hundred men, Dick was able to impede Taylor's six thousand, and slow them down to a crawling advance of three miles in four hours. The difficulty was that in the process Dick was necessarily exchanging casualties with Taylor at a substantially equal rate. By two o'clock Dick was facing Taylor's five thousand men with a force of less than nine hundred. With this disparity of numbers, Taylor was able to hold Dick in place with his main column, while he sent nearly a third of his force around to Dick's rear. Once this had been accomplished, the fight was over.

Dick was killed while he was trying to hold his shattered force together by sheer furious will power. Tony Bassett was missing. Cam Heath had been captured an hour before while covering a withdrawal. Fairbanks' guns had been lost one by one, and Eugene Fairbanks himself had been killed half an hour earlier by a sharpshooter. The commanders of both infantry regiments had disappeared at some stage of the fighting, and the two regiments, now little more than a single company, were under the command of a captain.

should add that, in a wild, unearthly way, the feeling was one of intense pleasure.

They were all over us almost as soon as we saw them, and we were in the midst of an utterly confused melee of straining horses and shouting men, all full of murderous rage. They were all around us and between us, and each of us was engaged in his own separate fight, dodging and parrying blows from all sides, attacking with thrust and slash, using even a rearing horse as a weapon. I had my revolver out and was firing at them left-handed—something I could do at the time —and the more men I hit, the more there were of them. Two of our men were beside me, then one of them was down, then I went down myself as my horse was killed, and was knocked down again as I tried to get up, and horses were all around me and over me, passing back and forth. When they finally moved off and I started to get up, two ragged infantrymen had their muskets leveled at me, and I was furious because my revolver was empty. And when, unaccountably, they lowered their muskets, then dropped them and raised their hands, I was more surprised than relieved, and not particularly grateful to Colonel Cooper and the company of the 17th Missouri that had rescued me. About three minutes had elapsed in all.

As the rage drained out of me and I began to see with normal eyes, I was aware of Brian Cooper, who was a friend of ours, bending over me, solicitous, and asking, "How are you, Johnny? Are you hurt?"

I looked up at him. "I don't think so."

He gave me a hand, and I pulled myself to my feet, and realized how wrong I was. I made a grimace that was meant for a smile, and said, "Oh, hell, Colonel, I've been sabered, shot, trampled on, and kicked, and I hurt all over, but I'm pretty sure there's nothing serious."

He smiled. "Glad to hear it, Johnny. I must say you look pretty awful. Here, let's see if we can't get you cleaned up a little."

The regimental surgeon was busy with two of our men who were down and badly hurt. One of his assistants came over and swabbed off my face and found that what had appeared to be a frightful gash, from ear to chin, was nothing more than a long scratch. An orderly brushed off my clothes, and another brought me one of the captured horses—a nice-looking, smallish chestnut mare—and by the time I was mounted again I was fairly presentable.

Jonesy had come up in the meantime. He looked over the ground, and remarked, "Quite a little fight you and your fellows put up, Johnny."

As a matter of fact, we had put up quite a fight, but we had not gotten off lightly. We had lost three men, two severely wounded, one killed; and the two survivors, the sergeant and I, were considerably battered.

Cooper's two regiments were holding the line of Allen's Creek, a small and formerly insignificant tributary of the Severn, but now, after the rains of the past month, a respectable obstacle. The only good crossing, at the bridge, was solidly blocked by breastworks and by Lovell's guns. The two regiments were thrown out on either side of the bridge, with a strong company drawn back from each to serve as a fire brigade. The line seemed precariously thin to me, but as Colonel Cooper said, this was the kind of fighting his boys were good at.

According to our prisoners, Taylor had mostly cavalry in our front, with the infantry only partly up and coming in slowly, the men much fatigued after a long day of fighting, and of marching and countermarching over heavy roads. Nevertheless, most of them would be in before dark, and Taylor would then have between four and five thousand men on our flank.

Jonesy accepted the odds without hesitation. The message he gave me for the general was a flat statement, without qualifications of any kind: he would hold the position until dark; a quarter of an hour after full darkness had set in, he would begin his withdrawal.

I asked if James had made his assault yet. Jonesy glowered at me, then shook his head unhappily.

"Just putting them together, last I saw. Two damn' fine

brigades he's got. The very best. And I don't mind telling you, a damn' fine soldier to take them in. If he's lucky, if they're all lucky, they'll make it. Only it's a hell of a way to do it. Well, we got a job to do here. We'll do it. You tell Arthur that, Johnny. We'll hold his right for him. He can forget about it."

The sergeant and I started back along the narrow Woods Road in silence. The three men we had lost were the sergeant's close friends, and, now that the action and the excitement were over, he was full of grief. My silence was one of brooding anger, intensified by pain, and by my concern for James and for Jonesy's two damn' fine brigades and all the men I knew in them.

The Woods Road entered the turnpike a short distance below the battered ruins of Billy Roth's old headquarters. At this point the turnpike makes a great bend to the east to avoid the MacDougal Ridge, a long slow curve that never quite flattens out, but continues until the road is running nearly east and west, then begins its return curve to the south around the base of the ridge. Beyond the half mile of nearly straight road was a broad strip of meadow, where the MacDougals had kept their riding horses in better days; beyond the meadow the ground rises in a steep, irregular slope to the crest of the ridge.

As we approached the turnpike, and the woods opened out on either side, we could see that the assault was under way. The artillery fire, which had been thunderous and incessant as Robert pounded the works along the ridge, fell away as the gunners shifted to targets on the flanks, and to carefully aimed single shots over the head of the advancing troops. They had crossed the turnpike and the meadow and were just coming to the foot of the ridge, the line somewhat uneven, since James had taken the regiments as he found them and pushed them forward at once, but straightening out as they advanced. James and Marcus Pellam and Colonel Vickers were still mounted, and as they rode back and forth along the lines they looked like anxious sheep dogs, herding their charges forward.

The firing from the works along the crest was light and sporadic, and though men were being hit here and there, there were no noticeable gaps in the line. As they reached the slope, just before the advance became a charge, Pellam and Vickers sent their horses back and went up with their men on foot. James waited a little longer, with a mounted orderly behind him ready to take his horse, waited to see the advance well under way before dismounting.

It was going well. The lines were remarkably even now, from one end of the line to the other. They were already more than a third of the way up, and the men were cheering. I was admiring the advance of the 10th Iowa on the extreme right, the men keeping their alignment and moving as steadily as though they were on a level parade ground.

Suddenly from beside me I heard a choked cry, a grunt of pain—the sound of a fist in the stomach—and the sergeant's shocked voice, "Oh, Christ! Look, Captain! Over on the left!" His hand shook as he pointed.

I turned my head, and was appalled: our entire left flank appeared to be dissolving. The two Illinois regiments which I had seen marching forward in orderly double ranks, one behind the other, no more than a minute before, had lurched forward and to one side, and had run together and coalesced into a single disorderly mass of confused men, moving slowly forward up the hill and pressing inwards against the center regiments.

Over beyond them a light cloud of gunsmoke was rising over the position from which this unexpected attack had come, a position hitherto concealed by the terrain. The rebels had held their fire until our lines had gone past them, then had opened a heavy and brutally effective fire into their flank and rear. The entire left side of both regiments had been chewed away, and all the field officers were down, either killed or disabled. Shells were now bursting in the smoke, and a roar of swelling violence came from our artillery, as battery after battery went into action.

James had been in the center, on the point of dismounting, when this disaster overtook his exposed flank. No sign of it was visible from the center, but he must have felt, or sensed, that his left had become sluggish and heavy, and was not moving well, and that something was amiss on that part of the line. He waved the orderly away and raced over to the left, the anxious shepherd again, and as soon as he was clear of the Ohio regiment in second line, he could see that something was indeed amiss on the left.

James was riding his favorite horse, Cinderella, a beautiful, light-footed bay mare coveted by half the command, and was conspicuous now as the only mounted man on the field. He passed rapidly along the rear of the two broken regiments, calling out to men he knew, encouraging them and pointing up the hill, and at one time—evidently to a man who had warned him against going farther—pointing over to the left, where the enemy position was completely smothered by shell-bursts from our artillery. He passed around the outer flank at a fast trot, and put the mare to a gallop as he turned the corner and rode to the front. At the center of the line he drew her up to a rearing stop, and swung around to face the men.

He called out to them in his battlefield voice, inspiriting, exhilarating, and piercing as the blast of trumpets: I had heard it a dozen times, I almost thought I could hear it now, over the sound of battle and two-thirds of a mile away. What it was he called out to them no one could remember. Pretty certainly it wasn't, God for Harry! England and Saint George! but the effect was the same. With that, he drew his sword, swung it around his head with a flourish and pointed upwards, then, without bothering to look back, he turned and started up the hill at a fast walk.

There was no need for him to look behind. The men gave a shout, and ran to catch up with him as he started forward, and after the first few yards he was riding in the midst of them, and they were all going up together.

They were going up together all along the line, the two Iowa regiments, the 18th Michigan, now intermingled with the 50th Ohio, and the two Illinois regiments with James, the line approximately even from end to end. The fire from above was now severe and they were taking heavy losses, but the crest

295

of the ridge was less than fifty yards away; they were still moving steadily, still formidable in spite of their losses.

They continued to advance while we watched and held our breath and tried to push them up the last few yards and over the crest by sheer force of willing it, until finally on the extreme right, with the help of the sharpshooters who had come up through the woods, a portion of the 10th Iowa broke over the crest and into the enemy works. At the same time, however, with the left also approaching the crest, a marked sag began to develop in the center. The fire was heaviest there, as usual, and the center regiments had suffered severely in the advance. Just under the top of the ridge, fifteen or twenty yards short of the crest, a long horizontal depression in the slope gave a considerable degree of protection from the enemy fire, and here the center stuck fast.

Complete success on the right and stalemate in the center were balanced by complete disaster on the left. With success almost in their grasp, with no more than a few steps to go, the two Illinois regiments broke and ran as James went down. James had picked them up and carried them this far: already hard hit by the flank attack, they had taken still heavier losses on the way up without flinching, and they would have gone on to the last man so long as James was with them. Without him, leaderless, with no one to look to, they broke. Only the small handful of men nearest to him stood their ground briefly, not as a part of the attacking force but out of personal concern, to see how badly the colonel had been hit, and to see what they could do for him.

Actually the colonel had not been hit, and there was nothing much they could do for him but help him to his feet. It was his horse, the beautiful bay mare he had been riding, that had been killed. James had been thrown heavily and briefly stunned, and had twisted his ankle: except for the damage to his pride, that was the extent of his injuries.

The damage to his pride, however, was extensive: I could see it, I could almost feel it, two-thirds of a mile away. He stalked down the hill after the Illinois men, limping slightly, full of rage and damning the bullets, carrying his sword in its scabbard with the sword belt wrapped around it, carrying it grasped in the middle as though it were an umbrella. The fact that he was not hit was due partly to pure miracle, and partly, I think, because many of the rebel marksmen deliberately withheld their fire out of admiration for a brave man. I have seen our own men do the same thing.

The Illinois regiments had drifted to the right while the attack was in progress, and continued their drift in that direction when they broke, carrying part of the center regiments with them. This oblique course, downhill and to the right, brought them to a point where the deep woods on the right of the field offered the nearest shelter, and they altered their course still further, making directly for the woods.

James, stalking wrathfully after them, saw that there was merit in this choice of direction, and shepherded the remnants of the center regiments out of the hollow they had taken refuge in, and sent them the same way. The Iowa regiments, with the rest of the line gone, fell back likewise, and the entire command disappeared into the shelter of the woods—the entire command except for the several hundred dead and wounded men who littered the slopes.

I watched James' attack and its repulse from a swell of higher ground on the left of the turnpike. The sky was dark, and growing darker, and there were a few drops of rain in the air. The woods were gloomy, and the hillside and the fields in front of it were obscured by a thickening haze of smoke.

The general was at his most Olympian when I reported. He listened impassively, asked no questions, and dismissed me with a civil but remote, "Thank you very much, Captain."

Preparations for a second assault had begun while the first was in progress. Guns were brought down, battery by battery, and put into new positions closer to the ridge, and the Second Division was pushed down across the turnpike, with two brigades in line and the third behind the interval in the center. Crego and Turquin had both dismounted and sent their horses away, and were standing in front of their outside regiments, waiting for the order to advance.

A brief message from James came down at this time, to the effect that Vickers' brigade was too badly shaken to be of any further use on the present battlefield. That Pellam's brigade was in good condition in spite of its losses, Colonel Pellam being among the wounded. The brigade, now under Colonel Duke, was pushing up through the woods to take up a position on the enemy's flank, and would endeavor to reach it in time to attack in concert with General Roth.

We had crossed over behind the division, General Pack and what was left of his staff: we had just learned that Jack Maitland had been severely wounded in the fighting on the left, and Robert Saint Chamans had been carried off the field ten minutes earlier, bleeding from a severed artery in the leg.

Billy Roth was still with us. He was sitting his horse on the general's left, nervous and unhappy, a shabby and slightly comic figure beside the general's magnificence. His cold was still with him; his nose was red, and he had a flannel compress wound around his neck and fastened with a safety pin. As usual when he was on horseback, all his clothes seemed too big for him: his sleeves were too long, and his big hat rested on his ears and threatened to fall over his eyes. His nervousness had infected his horse, a handsome gray, ordinarily a tractable animal but now in constant uneasy motion.

General Pack turned his head and looked at Billy thoughtfully, then said to him with grave courtesy, "You will of course wish to lead your men, General."

Billy gave him a stricken look, but the general had turned away and was looking out over the field. Billy swallowed hard, then, with a white face, touched his horse with his heel and moved away from us. He turned the corner and trotted past Crego's two front-line regiments, riding with his usual martial grace, lumping up and down with his elbows flapping, and drew up at the center of the line.

It was just four o'clock, and very dark. The rain that had begun a few minutes earlier had stopped, but clouds were piling up ominously in the south, and the air was absolutely motionless. The guns had been shelling the ridge steadily, and the entire field was heavy with smoke.

The lines went forward across the open field in beautifully even ranks without having a shot fired at them. There was no return fire from the ridge even after the lines had come well within range, at three hundred yards, and it began to seem possible—we began to hope—that the artillery fire had shattered the defense.

The hope even had a little time to grow. At the foot of the ridge Billy Roth raised his sword, the buglers sounded the urgent repeated notes of the charge, and the men started up the hill. The guns fell silent, and in this sudden silence—disagreeable, somehow, as though it had disarmed us—for the first time we could hear the sound of Jonesy's battle over on the right: Lovell's rifled guns, and Taylor's twelve-pounders in reply, and the sound of small-arms fire, the battle a satisfactory mile and a half away.

The silence was not a long one. When our men were a third of the way up the hill, an irregular spattering of rifle fire began, which dropped men here and there without slowing the advance. Except for this, the enemy troops held their fire until we were halfway to the top, then a streak of orange-red fire ran along the crest, and a volley was delivered that staggered the entire line. At the same time a battery that had been hastily brought up fired successive rounds of double canister that tore great holes in the center.

For a moment the attack wavered unsteadily. Billy Roth stood up in his stirrups and turned to survey his men. He still had his sword in his hand, his hat had been shot off, and he had finally forgotten to be afraid. He shouted at his men and pointed upwards with his sword: the men closed their ranks and pushed up the slope behind him.

We were watching the progress of the assault with a tense concentration, a single-minded anxiety that was almost physical pain. As we watched we kept inching forward little by little, until we were nearly at the foot of the hill, and spent musket balls were falling around us.

The enemy was keeping up a heavy fire, and the gun flashes flickered incessantly along the crest. Billy got within a hundred yards of the top. At that point we saw him turn in his saddle and lean over as though to speak to Horace Townsend, who was beside him on foot; he kept on leaning farther and farther, very slowly, then fell into Horace's arms, shot through the head.

By this time the center had been badly hurt. With Billy's death it began to fall behind the rest of the line, creating a sag in the middle like the one that had developed in the previous attack. This was dangerous. If McGraw were allowed to ignore his center and concentrate on his flanks, the entire attack would be in jeopardy, and if the attack were to fail all our labor would have been in vain, all our toils and pain, our wounds and the blood of our friends, all gone for nothing, all wasted.

To three of us, at least, the situation was unbearable. Those men had to be moved. They had to be pushed forward with the rest of the line, up the hill and over into the enemy works. We started off with a common impulse, one of Keith's men and I, and a third man who disappeared before I had a chance to see who it was. Keith's man was on a faster horse then mine, and he drew ahead of me. Although we had only three hundred yards to cover, he was several lengths ahead of me when he reached the stalled line of the center regiments, bareheaded, swinging his sword around his head, and shouting at the top of his lungs.

The men were relieved. All the field officers and all the best of the company officers were gone, killed or disabled. Here was a man on horseback, a man from the general, with orders. They no longer had to think, to make up their minds, in the midst of this hellish bedlam. Now they had orders. Up the hill! All the way up! The men gave a shout just as I reached them, and all of us started up the hill.

All this was in a state of pure delirium, of rage, of berserker fury. We were oblivious to everything but the furious necessity of getting up these last hundred yards, these last forty yards, these last few feet, getting up and over the works and killing the enemy, damn him, before he killed us. It had grown very dark and the smoke was thick. Something was happening over on the right, a swelling of the battle. This was expected, but

I had forgotten why, and it was too dark and murky to see the cause. They were still firing heavily at us from above, the course of the bullets a swarming sound in our ears, the muzzle flashes streaks of fire in the darkness, men still dropping on all sides.

At one point I found myself slipping backwards out of the saddle and was wholly astonished, until I realized that we had come to a part of the slope that was simply too steep for my horse to climb. I slid off, threw the reins to a soldier coming up behind me, and went up on foot. Then some damned fool was firing in the wrong direction, and I was about to blast him when I saw that a lot of others had the same idea, and they were all wearing the wrong kind of uniform. I reached for my revolver, and checked myself just in time when I saw that the man I was aiming at was one of our men. Then everybody I saw was in blue and there was no one to fire at, so I put my revolver back in its holster and put away my sword. A soldier I had never seen before came up leading a horse, and said respectfully, "Here's your horse, Captain Lake." I mounted the horse he offered me, and unbelievably, there we were! I looked around, wholly incredulous at first, then I saw the MacDougal house on my left, quite close by, and a little farther along a group of rebels surrounded by one of Turquin's regiments, sullenly piling their arms in the center. Keith's man was nowhere in sight: I never found out what happened to him, or who he was.

We had now attained our objective. The MacDougal Ridge was in our hands, and from the ridge we commanded the cramped exit from McGraw's position, and his supply line as well: we commanded the causeway and the bridge over the millstream, and we commanded the lower hills to the northeast which were still held by McGraw. In the only position left to him, we could attack him simultaneously in front and on both flanks. He was in a narrow oblong box, backed up against a swamp, with supplies and ammunition running low, and no way to replenish them. His losses had been heavy, fully as heavy as ours, and his artillery had been simply beaten out of existence. We had McGraw in a trap. All we had to do was shut the door.

It was still half an hour before sunset, and in spite of the clouds there would be half an hour or more of usable twilight after the sun had gone down. With all our losses we still had a decisive preponderance of numbers; we could bring thirty guns into action; and we had all the advantages of the position we had won. We had time enough, and men and guns enough, to complete the task, but now, at the very end, our strength failed.

We were fought out, exhausted, emotionally spent. The spring was broken: the driving force was gone. We had lost more than half of our officers, and two-fifths of our men. Robert had gone off the field with a severed artery and a boot full of blood. Jack Maitland had a shattered collarbone and a broken arm. Gavin had lost a leg. Jake Leslie had disappeared, and Dick Ross was dead. Poor little Billy Roth was dead. Jonesy was off the field and had his hands full where he was. There was no one to order the batteries to be brought around to the left of the ridge and to open fire, no one to reduce the disorder of the troops, and compel them into ordered ranks and send them forward. Only the general could have done this, and it would have taken all his energy and all the great weight of his authority. In September he could have done it, but this was the first of December. Like the rest of us he was exhausted, and for the moment, stunned. The last cogent order of the battle was given by James, when he had Sam Crego send the five hundred disarmed prisoners down the hill under guard of the 63rd Ohio.

It began to rain while we were rounding up the prisoners, a warm rain, coming down in big splattering drops. There was a preliminary flash of lightning somewhere off to the south, followed half a minute later by a soft roll of thunder. With that much warning, we were suddenly enveloped in a blinding glare of light and were simultaneously swallowed up in a vast splitting crash of sound, as lightning struck and shattered the great oak at the left of the MacDougal house. Immediately

302

afterwards, as though shaken out of the atmosphere by the concussion, the rain came pouring down.

The downpour lasted for fifteen minutes, long enough to soak us all to the skin, then dwindled away as the storm passed over. In the east we could see it breaking over the mountains, with an incessant flickering of lightning and a continuous low rumble of thunder. Overhead the clouds grew thinner, and for a time the light grew stronger, gray still, but with a yellow cast. An uneasy, gusty wind came up, veering from point to point, and the temperature began to fall.

More than three thousand men of the two divisions were on the ridge at this time, out of ranks, and in complete disorder, but not milling about—on the contrary, moving very little— and not talking very much. For some reason, perhaps a superstitious fear of being confused with the dead, nearly all of them were on their feet. They stood together, not looking at each other, nor at anything in particular, in a stunned silence. Those who were talking kept their voices low. All of them were waiting. Possibly they were waiting for orders, but I think not: I think they were simply waiting for night to fall.

During this half-hour of failing light, while the wind shifted from south to southwest to west, and the temperature dropped another ten degrees, we watched McGraw's troops file down and march across the narrow bottleneck leading to the south. They were as exhausted as we were, and plodded across the front of our position in loose, ragged columns, with the stragglers outnumbering the men in the ranks: we had only to put out our hand to gather them in. Conversely though, to gather them in we had to put out our hand: we had to bring up a few guns and start firing, we had to put enough men in line to give us the semblance of a line of battle, and even that small effort was beyond us. So we sat apathetically on our hill and watched the enemy escape from the strong coils we had wound about him. That was the way the battle ended.

General Pack issued no orders at all during this half-hour. The last order I heard him give was his courteous invitation to Billy Roth to put himself at the head of his men. I saw him as he moved about among the men; at times I could hear what he was saying, but I made no effort to join him. This was not from any feeling of hostility—even that was gone—but purely from lassitude. I had begun to feel the mauling I had taken over on the Woods Road and I hurt in every muscle, from head to foot. I was mortally weary, and heavy as lead.

Presently I rode over to the southern edge of the MacDougal grounds, dismounted, and stood looking out over the ten miles of open country sloping away to the south. The clouds were coming straight from the west now, and there was a cold, gusty west wind, accompanied by a fine mist of rain.

After a minute or two I became aware of two officers standing near me, dismounted like myself. The one on the outside, standing by his horse's head, I recognized at once as James. The other officer, a big, bearded man, was standing bareheaded by the side of his horse, with his forearm resting along the saddle and his head resting on his arm, as though overborne by fatigue and grief. It was only when he raised his head and spoke that I recognized the general.

"This is my fault, James," he said in a voice full of quiet lamentation. "I had a personal quarrel with you. These young men, all these fine young men, had nothing to do with it. They had nothing to do with our private quarrel."

James' voice held the same note of mourning. "I will have to share the blame with you, sir."

"No, sir. You do not. You cannot. This was my command, and this was my responsibility." The general's voice softened. "God! It was a fine command, wasn't it, James? Officers and men. I was proud of them. Any man would have been proud of them. We could have gone anywhere. We could have done anything. Before we quarreled. Not after. God knows I forgive you. Both of you."

"God forgive us all," James replied humbly. Then, after a moment, "May I say this? There was never any dishonor in our hearts. We met a force that was beyond our strength. Too strong to be resisted. An inevitable force. There was nothing we could do."

"I believe you, James," the general said after a pause. He

sighed. "Yes, as my poor friend, Jacob Leslie, used to say, 'Thus it was willed; ask no further.' Thus it was willed, thus it had to be, thus it is."

With these last words his voice gathered strength, as though he were putting on his armor, and when he spoke next, after a long silence, his voice was that of the major general, fully armed.

"I think the men are about ready to be moved, James. We had better get them into some kind of order, and see that they get some food. After that, we'll see what is to be done."

Both men mounted, the general and his chief of staff, and, as they started back, the chief of staff said, "There might be some advantage in using one of the back roads. We couldn't carry a heavy baggage train over any of them, but we aren't going to be encumbered with much in the way of baggage."

"Which road did you have in mind, James?" The general asked, as they passed out of hearing.

The retreat got under way three hours after dark, with a rising wind, and the temperature close to freezing. The main body, about six thousand men and twenty guns, moved out with Keith and the First Division in the lead, followed by the other two divisions, and by the wreckage of Dick Ross's covering force, three or four hundred men who had come in from the right with Jonesy after dark. By nine o'clock the entire force had passed up the turnpike to the north, leaving their camp-fires to burn brightly for a time in the strong wind then die away.

James was left behind on the MacDougal Ridge with two regiments and three of Harper's guns, to hold the ridge until midnight, then follow as rear guard.

The wind rose and shifted to the northwest. The rain changed to sleet, then to stinging pellets of snow, and by midnight the temperature had dropped another fifteen degrees and a full gale was blowing. At exactly twelve o'clock we marched down off the ridge, leaving the MacDougal house lighted from cellar to attic, and filled and overflowing with wounded.

We marched down in the teeth of the gale, and in a darkness that was almost total. We were sheltered from the wind during the first half of the march by the range of hills on the left, but as these fell away we were exposed to its full force. It struck us from the left quarter, on the left cheek as we marched north, a violent, malignant wind, driving horizontal streaks of snow in its front, bringing with it a numbing cold. It was two-thirty in the morning when we marched up the hill and into Tarsus.

Here we made a two-hour halt. The Robertson house was no longer ours: it was strange and hostile, and bitterly cold. We stayed in the kitchen, and sat around the stove for warmth. At four-thirty James looked at his watch, propped up on the kitchen table, then stood up and announced that it was time for us to move on.

The wind was roaring in the treetops when we left, and Judge Robertson's thermometer had gone down to eight degrees above zero. Overhead there were occasional rifts in the swiftly moving clouds, and for a moment, before the rift closed again, we had a glimpse of a black sky set with cold, remote, and glittering stars.

The bridges were blown as soon as we had crossed over to the north bank of the river. The ammunition depot was to have been fired at the same time, but in view of the direction and the violence of the wind, James had countermanded the order. Nevertheless there was someone in the magazines, deserters, undoubtedly, in search of guns or loot. From the meadows north of town we could see small, intermittent glimmerings of light moving around inside the works.

These fitful glimmerings suddenly turned into an enormous red glare which lighted up the hillside and the town, then rose straight up into the air and kept on rising to an unbelievable height, first as a solid column of pure flame, then as a column sparkling with innumerable lesser brightnesses as the fixed ammunition exploded. While the column was still rising, a massive concussion, a blow in the chest rather than sound, reached us, followed by the crepitation of the exploding shells. The column rose straight into the air, then slowly began to bend as it was caught by the wind, a great plume of fire bending over the town on the hill, then an arch of fire, falling deliberately, and finally a rain of destruction.

The town caught fire from end to end, in a hundred places at once, while the northwest gale, acting as a gigantic bellows, blew the flames up to a heat so fierce that even the trees were burning like torches. The separate fires ran together swiftly into a single great fire enveloping the entire town, with an immense ragged banner of flame rising into the black sky until it was caught by the gale and bent over, flapping wildly, to the east and the south. Through this sheet of flame, reflected in the black flowing surface of the river, the familiar landmarks were visible, the church, the courthouse and its belfry, the white pillars of the Robertson house, and the familiar shape of the hill.

We turned away reluctantly from this grandiose and appalling spectacle, and went on. The bridge over the North Branch was a mile and a half ahead of us, and the full force of the winter gale was in our faces as we approached the crossing. Once across the bridge and on the westward road, we were largely protected by the rising ground on our right, though we could always hear the wind howling in the treetops. On our left there was a red glow in the sky that lasted until full daylight.

The sun rose at six forty-nine, according to the almanac, but none of us knew it. As we plodded along the narrow road, leading our horses and stumbling over the frozen ruts, the sensation was that of having finally become accustomed to the dark, of the vision having finally adjusted itself, so that it was possible to make out dimly the shapes of the men and horses ahead, and to stop when they did instead of running into them. It was only when I happened to look upwards, and saw that the sky was gray, that I realized it was morning. The morning of the second of December. The morning, as it happened, of my twenty-second birthday.

It was full daylight when we reached the crossroads and the bridge over the North Branch where Gavin had defeated Martin Helper the morning of September twentieth. We went on for another half mile, and halted along a stretch of road where we were well protected from the wind. It was during this halt that the enemy pursuit caught up with us.

The pressure on us from then on was continuous and fairly hard, especially during the first few hours. We met it with a series of roadblocks which compelled the enemy to halt until they could get a flanking force out and in position to attack. We hung on until they had their attacking force in place, then pulled out ahead of them at the last possible moment. In the meantime our second regiment had moved on and set up another roadblock half a mile to the rear of the first. We kept up this system, of keeping out a rear guard to the rear guard, all morning and part of the afternoon.

From daylight on we had been picking up stragglers from the main body, perhaps a hundred or a hundred and fifty of them in all. We got very little good out of them; they marched with us for an hour or two, then dropped off again. Occasionally there was a dead horse by the side of the road, and abandoned equipment was common, muskets and knapsacks and cartridge boxes. At one point, one of our guns had been abandoned; the iron gun barrel lay beside the road, and off to one side was a charred place on the ground where the carriage had been burned. Twice we passed a place where a halt had been made, marked by the blackened circles left by campfires and by abandoned cooking vessels. From time to time we passed men huddled over small fires with blankets over their heads, too weak to go on, and too exhausted to care.

Late in the morning the big wind died down. Part of the time we had been sheltered from it by the hillside, and at other times we had been pushing ourselves forward against it, but always up to this time we had been conscious of the roaring of the wind. The air was still and cold after the wind had died away; the ground was frozen hard, and about noon a pale and cheerless sun appeared through the thin cirrus clouds.

We were all stumbling along, half dead with cold and fatigue by this time, the men with blankets over their heads, the officers dismounted and leading their horses. Nevertheless we were still a functioning and effective rear guard. Our three guns were posted in advantageous positions with our two regiments alternating in support. As the enemy caught up with us, there was a brief flurry of activity, a spattering of rifle fire, the booming of cannon for a minute or two, then the guns were hastily limbered up, the men were withdrawn, and we moved on to the next position.

From two o'clock on we heard the sound of cannon ahead of us in the direction of the river. After an hour the firing had become stationary and was growing louder. Presently the sound of musketry was mingled with that of artillery fire, and some time after that we began to hear the hoarse shouting of our men, the whinnying of horses, and the shrill yipping cry of a rebel charge a mile away. Twenty minutes later we came to the edge of the woods, and came up with the main body of the command, standing at bay in an amphitheater on the hillside.

We had come to the edge of the woods, and had on the left and to the front an open field sloping gently down towards the river, the slope entirely open except for a small clump of oak trees off to the left. The sun, low and red, was just to the right of the clump of trees. The withered grass, the frozen ground, the black leafless trees, the low red winter sun, were all intensely familiar. This was a place I had seen before. This was a place I knew well. This was defeat. This was disaster. This was the end.

Standing at bay behind a hasty breastwork of felled trees, a sadly reduced main body was keeping up an incessant fire over the breastworks. The blackened gunners in the intervals were moving tirelessly, sponging out the gun barrels, loading, ramming home the charges, firing, and then around the circle again, sponging, loading, ramming, firing, again and again without pause. At the moment the rebels were falling back in the face of this furious activity, giving ground sullenly, taking cover wherever they could find it, behind a fallen log, a dead horse, in a shallow depression, and from behind this cover they were returning a heavy and damaging sharpshooters' fire.

The only field officer in sight was a major from Cooper's brigade. He was bareheaded and on foot, gaunt and hollow-eyed and sagging with fatigue, and he was watching still another enemy attack forming off to the right.

When I went forward to report, our two regiments were only a short distance behind, and while I was making my way over to the major they came into view, James riding at the head with Colonel Powell. Just as they appeared, in the intervals of our now more deliberate artillery fire, I caught the sound of firing to the rear, as the enemy pursuit caught up once again with the rear guard. James wheeled his horse around and started back at a fast trot, while Colonel Powell halted his leading companies and sent one of them up the hillside to protect the flank. Firing broke out immediately, then seemed to spread and to come from everywhere at once. It rose to a high pitch of intensity, then fell away, and quite suddenly stopped altogether.

At this moment I caught a last glimpse of James. He had evidently come galloping back up the road, only to find it blocked in this direction too, by a line of rebel cavalry. James had pulled up his horse, accepting the situation, and when I caught sight of him he was approaching the leader of the enemy cavalry at a walk. The enemy commander was a big, black-bearded young man with an ostrich plume in his hat, young Taylor, as I learned afterwards. James was holding both his sword and the reins in his right hand; his left arm was hanging at his side, useless below the elbow, the buckskin glove blood-soaked and dripping. He tossed up his sword, caught it by the blade with his gloved hand, and offered it to young Taylor with a wry smile and a courteous bow. Taylor accepted the sword with a few courteous words and an even lower bow, and they moved out of sight.

The major had seen the new threat to his flank and was grimly improvising a sketchy line of defense to meet it, when the sound of heavy firing broke out in another direction, ahead and to the right. Before we had time to locate and assess the weight of this new attack, the line of rebel skirmishers out in front rose up and came on with a yell, with a line of battle charging in behind them, and a second, still heavier line, coming in behind the first.

On looking back to see where our reserves were—knowing we had none, but looking anyway—I caught sight of General Pack for the first time. Fifty yards behind us, elevated by the slope of the ground above the fury and confusion lapping over the breastworks, he sat his horse and surveyed the scene with imperturbable calm. At the moment he was completely alone, horse and rider perfectly still, the general bearded, gauntleted, still maintaining his majestic air of command, still appearing to hold the scales, to control events, to rule and order the battle, even though a line of yelling rebels had come perilously close to breaking over the breastworks, and another one was following close behind. His appearance was deceptive then—or was it? Perhaps this was what he had willed—*sic volo, sic iubeo*—this was the order he had given the battle.

The second line of rebels was thrown back in front, but on the extreme right they were over the breastworks, and the line began to crumble. The break expanded swiftly towards the center; some of our men began to run, others threw down their arms and surrendered. At this moment the general was hit four successive times in the chest: for one incredible moment he seemed to absorb the blows and to be impervious to the bullets, then slowly he began to lean forward over the neck of his horse, and to slip over to one side.

With the death of the general my vision was suddenly cut off. I saw him killed, but I did not see him fall. Before that I had been hit myself, and my eyes were covered with darkness. For me, as well as for the general, the battle was ended and the war was over.

IV

❀ ❀ ❀ ❀ ❀ ❀ ❀ ❀ ❀ ❀ ❀ ❀ ❀ ❀ ❀ ❀ ❀

These events, which I have remembered and tried to relate, are shut off from the present by a great bank of fog, a long period of delirium and pain which lasted, with some remissions, for more than two years. I had been shot through the neck, through the lungs, and through the small intestine. Both these latter wounds were considered mortal at the time. I have the very dimmest of recollections of lying on the frozen ground and being passed over as hopeless time after time, until finally a voice asked, "Who is he?" and another voice replied, "Young Lake. The colonel's brother, or nephew, or something. We might as well get him in out of the cold, anyway."

I was brought in out of the cold, and spent the next eighteen months in Southern hospitals, surviving and gaining strength, to everyone's astonishment, until a yellow-fever epidemic struck the hospital I was in. I was able to survive that, but only by a thin margin, with patients, doctors, and attendants dying all around me. In the spring I was sent home to die. Having survived yellow fever and two mortal wounds, it seemed wrong to die then, so I got well instead, though it took me another year.

The complete destruction of the command in a military sense did not mean, of course, a general slaughter of the survivors. Several thousand of us survived wounds and imprisonment long enough to be exchanged. Many of those who were exchanged served under different commanders in new fields, and fought in the later battles of the war. Many of our close friends survived the war and were the friends of our latter years, though all of us were sadly diminished.

James was exchanged shortly after he left the hospital, where his left arm was amputated at the elbow. He resigned his commission as soon as the exchange was completed. He and Madame Lucy were married a month later, and went abroad to live.

I saw them again for the first time in England, a year or two after the close of the war. They were changed, as all of us were. The bright colors, the ebullience and laughter were gone: they smiled, and were calm, and talked in quiet voices. The Countess was still a beautiful woman, but the radiance that had dazzled my eyes at Tarsus had become something different, softer, not bright but warming, a soft pearl-like glow.

They had no children, and lived quietly from the beginning. In their later years they turned more and more to religion, became increasingly devout, and eventually went to live in Rome. Our mutual affection remained unchanged, but religion lay in a direction in which I was unable to follow them: our affection remained, but it now came across a great distance.

The wearing of sackcloth was an aspect of Christian humility James could never quite accept, and though his clothes were in somber blacks and grays, they came from the best tailors, and the cloth was always of the finest weave. In spite of his white mustache and pinned-up sleeve, and the grave, almost Spanish dignity of his later manner, he was never able to bring himself to put a hat on quite straight, and in the slightly rakish tilt of his hat I saw the last faint trace of the James I had known before the disaster of December second.

As for myself, if I may be allowed, I joined my father's law firm, prospered, married, raised a family, and was a pillar of the community for thirty years. Now that the thirty years have gone by, I find it hard to remember just what was in them: they seem to have been evanescent, empty, a long anticlimax. Certainly they weigh less in the total balance than the thirty-one days of October in Tarsus.

While General Pack was still questioning Lieutenant Byrne, Jonesy rode up. The general dismissed Lieutenant Byrne with a courteous, "Thank you, Lieutenant," and turned to meet him.

Jonesy wasted no time. "Sorry to hear about Dick, Arthur, I got Cooper out on the right with Lovell's battery. Good position half a mile out. Deep stream, with steep banks. Have to make a ten-mile detour to get guns or wagons across. Cooper's men all good woods fighters. Only thing is, I think I ought to go myself. Coop's a good man, but I'm a better bushwhacker than he is."

General Pack agreed. "Yes, I think you had better go, General. And I will ask Colonel Lake to take in your other two brigades."

Jonesy nodded, "That ought to be all right," he said with satisfaction. "They'll go with Jamie. He can take them as far as anybody. Only he'll need another brigade. Pellam's taking Cooper's place. Sam Crego's nearest. Good brigade. About time the Second Division did some of the work, anyway."

"Colonel Crego isn't in position, General."

"Neither is Pellam. No sense in starting until he is."

"Colonel Pellam will take part in the assault."

Jonesy looked at the general with disbelief. "For God's sake, who's going to be on the flank, then? Nobody?"

General Pack's voice stiffened. "We haven't time for embellishments, General. If the attack is made at once and resolutely pushed, there will be no need for any distraction on the flank."

Jonesy took off his battered old campaign hat and slammed it against his knee, while spots of color appeared on his cheeks.

"Oh, no! God damn it, no! Assault that God damn' ridge with six regiments and nothing behind them? McGraw sitting there with damn' near that many men, and nothing to bother him? Nothing on his flank, nothing to spoil his aim? And what about the Second Division, anyway? If they aren't in position to assault, they aren't in position to support, either. And where's the First? What's Vickers going to have on his flank? Oh, Jesus Christ, no! We haven't got time? Hell, I'll get you time. Only for God's sake, do it right!"

General Pack had retired to some remote Olympian height and was looking out over Jonesy's head no longer even listening.

James addressed him now in a flat, impersonal voice. "I am in complete agreement with General Jones, sir. In my opinion the flanking attack is absolutely essential. I think the assault should be made by Vickers and Crego, with the rest of the Second Division immediately behind them. I think it should be held up until the First Division is in line, and able to protect the flank of the attacking force."

Horace Townsend braved the lightning and said urgently, "The Second Division is ready, sir. We can be up, and ready to go in with Vickers and the others in less than a quarter of an hour."

The general looked at him. "Thank you, Major," he said gravely. He turned to James again.

"Colonel, I want the assault made at once while there is still a good possibility of going up the hill and into the works with McGraw's men. That is a direct and positive order, sir. With any more delay the opportunity will be gone."

There was a moment of breathless silence as James turned his head and looked out over the field. He turned back and said in a frozen voice,

"Yes, sir. Under a direct order, I will make the attack. Your attack, sir. Not mine."

I moved up to go in with James as a matter of course. He would need an aide, and I was the natural choice: he knew me, knew the exact measure of my capabilities, and could depend on my loyalty. The general caught sight of me as I pressed forward, saw my obvious intention, and checked me with a gesture, a gesture that caused me to pull up short even while it filled me with mutinous anger.

Now that the decision had been made, James' manner changed. He turned to Jonesy and said rapidly, "Tell Marcus to work his two companies of sharpshooters around to the right. If they can pick off some of the gunners, it will help. And tell him to take Campbell in with him. I'll push Worth and Frazer along right behind them. And have Brock and Harper plaster the crest with everything they've got." Then, to the general again, "Vickers' left will be entirely in the air, of course. Will you have Saint Chamans cover it as well as he can with artillery fire? And push Keith along in the meantime?"

"We'll do everything we can for you, James," the general said evenly. "Good luck!"

James gave us all an easy wave of the hand, then wheeled his horse around and started forward at top speed.

There was a pause, a moment of dead silence, after he had gone, then with a steady, unhurried series of orders, the general dispersed the group of officers around him. Jonesy started back to the right, still muttering angrily, taking Lieutenant Bryne with him.

My mission, the one the general had kept me back for, was to find Colonel Cooper and send back an immediate report. Sergeant Hughie Walters and three of his men from the headquarters company were assigned to me as couriers. This errand took me over to the right while James was gathering up the scattered regiments of the two Third Division brigades and forming them for the assault.

The sky had darkened again, and heavy storm clouds were piling up in the south. The sound of firing began to reach us from the right as we approached the Woods Road, a small fight, so far, but slowly growing. The dark day became darker as we entered the road. The black branches of the trees met overhead, the dense undergrowth walled us in on both sides, and a bend in the road shut off our view thirty yards ahead. It was an uncomfortable place to be in, and an uncomfortable place to have behind you.

What was ahead of us was mostly confusion, for the sounds were muffled and distorted by the terrain: the fighting appeared to shift back and forth between left and right, and the sharp crack of Lovell's guns seemed to come from both sides at once. The stream and the good position Jonesy had mentioned were about a third of a mile in front. Taylor's artillery seemed to be that far away—we assumed that it was held up at the bridge—but the infantry firing was closer.

A little farther on, the road grew wider and the woods opened up; the trees were bigger, with open spaces between them, and we could see for some distance into the wood. Climbing plants with bright red berries grew over the fences, and on the far side shadowy purple flowers grew in the underbrush. At one point we came to a glade where all the foliage was bright yellow, giving a momentary impression of sunlight; at the same time an erratic breath of wind cleared away the prevailing smell of gunsmoke and for a brief moment I had the fresh autumnal smell of wet leaves and wet earth in my face.

We were still unable to locate any definite line of battle. The only fixed point we had was Taylor's artillery at the bridge. Lovell had evidently divided his guns, and was firing from at least two positions. There was no infantry firing at all ahead of us: it was all either to the right or to the left, and intermittently was fairly heavy. We had slowed our horses down to a careful walk, and were keeping a wary eye out for any kind of movement at the sides.

Some distance ahead of us we caught a glimpse of two of Cooper's men as they changed their position, running at a crouch, trailing their rifles. Just after this there was a vicious outburst of firing on our right, just ahead, and another a moment later on the left. The firing grew in volume and moved in on both sides. Suddenly a wild uproar broke out dead ahead of us, and out of absolutely nowhere a yelling horde of rebel cavalry came bearing down on us, shaggy ferocious men, yelling open-mouthed, eyes and teeth gleaming with hate, not rebel soldiers, not even human beings, but the incarnate enemy.

The four men with me were all veterans and picked men. They knew as well as I did that there was no place to run to, and nothing we could do but fight, and what we all felt, with the blood pounding in our ears, was an answering rage, an answering fury and excitement. They wanted to kill us, did they? God damn them, we'd see who got killed! Perhaps I